The Mad Game
William's Story

Chris Cherry

Love and War Series
Book 1

ISBN: 1493510851
ISBN-13: 978-1493510856

DEDICATION

This book is dedicated to the men and women, from all nations,
caught up in the tragedy that was
The Great War

Also by the Author
Love and War Series

The Mad Game - Odile's War
(coming Spring 2014)
The Mad Game - The Third Light
(due out Armistice Day 2014)

CREDITS

Cover Graphic Design – Mark Bowers at The Devil's Crayon
Cover Photography – Bernadette at Bernadette Delaney
Photography
Copy Editing – Helen Steadman at The Critique Boutique
French Language Consultant – Sandrina Parry-Bargiacci

PRAISE FOR THE MAD GAME

★★★★★ A Great Read
A thrilling account, well written and I could not put it down.
Moved to the point that I will be visiting the Somme.
Chris T

★★★★★ Captivating
Beautifully written, telling the story of ordinary human
aspirations in desperate times, the book evokes a deep sense of
gratitude for the sacrifices made. Of course, it's impossible not
to fall in love with William!
Amanda J

★★★★★ Gripping and vivid
The Mad Game is a wonderfully written account of life in the
trenches. Graphic, descriptive, evocative and an emotional
journey for the reader. The account of the battle is incredibly
vivid, putting the reader in the centre of the battles. I did not
know the War was like that, and I am all the more thankful for
the sacrifice. I would not just recommend this book, I would
urge everyone to read it. The characters are beautifully
conceived, clearly researched and I fell a little bit in love with
William. A book for men and women. Thank you for the story.
Brenda

★★★★★ A Must Read!
Once I began to read this exciting tale it was impossible to put
down. I highly recommend buying such a gripping novel that
elicits such a deep emotional response. You can clearly tell the
author has put in such amazingly hard work into crafting this
masterpiece. This book deserves at least 7 stars.
Georgia

★★★★★ Gripping
A story of travel, love, loss and hope; The Mad Game is gripping.
Historically well researched the story sets the scene of a peaceful
setting with war drums in the distance. I particularly enjoyed the
pace of this story.
Sean

★★★★★ Gripping
This book had me gripped from start to finish. It was a journey
through the horrors of war through the eyes of a brave young
man whose love for a young French girl carried him through
many dark days. This book took me on an emotional roller
coaster as I was able to vividly imagine each chapter - this was
entirely due to the skilful writing of the author who clearly has
put a lot of thought, research and planning into this
Gillian

★★★★★ I really enjoyed the story
As you progress through the story you will be absorbed by the
main character's emotions and inner most feelings along with his
will to survive the horrific conflict. This book is extremely well
researched and written, it will hold your attention from the first
page walking you through a story that can be visualised. It is also
written with great sensitivity and an understanding of human
emotions. Next !!!
Paul

★★★★★ Beautifully written tale of broken hearts and souls
A beautifully crafted tale of difficult times, true love and paying
the ultimate price for freedom. Gripping from the start with
excellent detail and description which makes it easy to imagine
the horror these men endured and the worry those left behind
must have felt. I would think it impossible not to be moved by
this story. There is a simple line that any parent will crumble at
reading, "I am proud of you son". Every girl dreams of a man
who will fight for her love.
Little Red

ACKNOWLEDGMENTS

I would like to thank the following for their kindness, support, dedication to the cause and general all-around belief in me and this work of respect. To the citizens of northern France, who gave their time, shared their experiences and who were also kind enough to share their family stories and memories. Especially important are the citizens of La Boisselle, Bazentin-Le-Petit, Montauban and Longueval. They did not mind the sounds of motorbikes, nor the imposition of a nosy camera poked into almost every yard and field of their beautiful countryside. To the Belgians in Ypres, Wijtschate and Messines, and especially Roger and Muriel at Cavell's. We will be coming back to stay soon!

My friend, Mark Fletcher, for cups of coffee and comradeship, enroute to the battlefields. I am especially happy that writing this book helped me find him again. Fellow Blood Biker, Mark Bowers for delivering a fabulous cover that tells the story in pictures and fellow Manchester 500 advanced bikers, whose encouragement and friendship was a source of motivation and inspiration. To Bob Oates, for test reading the early manuscript, thanks Bob. Thanks to Helen Steadman, from the Critique Boutique, who turned words on a page into this story. Whilst I am at it, I would also like to thank the whole volunteer team at the North West Blood Bikes Manchester. We are all volunteers and their encouragement and massive support kept me going.

To my son Calum McDonald, the face of William Collins. When his mother and I saw him put on the uniform of a Tommy to go out to the photo-shoot, we both had the same sudden sombre reaction. Unexpectedly and deeply moving, I felt at once a connection, down the ages, with those parents. For them it was to wave goodbye. Chloe Wallace, as Odile. Her patience and generosity of spirit in the photo-shoot was appreciated.

There are three people who deserve special mention. Paul Rogers, a fellow Blood Biker and Manchester 500 rider, who accompanied me on my last research trip to Picardie, as well as reading the novel at an early stage.

Sandrina Parry-Bargiacci, a close friend and (luckily) a native French speaker. It is, hopefully obvious, how she contributed to this novel, providing the voice of Odile.

Lastly, my darling wife, Caroline and our two fantastic sons. It is difficult to say in words exactly what she means to me and how she has contributed to this story. So, I will simply say thank you, I love you. Boys, well turned out.

CHRIS CHERRY

INTRODUCTION AND FOREWORD

The Great War was a defining moment in world history. There is little doubt that its catastrophic impact on humanity was significant then and indeed, is significant now. Apart from the population demographics, cultural and social inheritance, the emotion and feeling of the Great War is very evident, even to this day. Modern history reflects on the war as being a desperate, attritional and ultimately futile endeavour, fought by imperialists' worker subjects in order to define map lines and satisfy the inflated ego of nationalist fervour. That in itself is not unique to that war. The uniqueness is the timing in history of the outbreak, coming at the dawn of a truly mechanised age. Ten years before was the age of the redcoat, or the bluecoat, with rifle and cannon then being the pinnacle of mechanisation. The ultimate deterrent still being the cavalry charge, a weapon of terror, it was usually decisive.

The Great War saw the immediate deployment of the machine gun. Operated by a trained team of men, it could lay down fire that savagely and mercilessly took the lives of the enemy. Coupled with the refinement of larger artillery, the bodies of soldiers stood little chance in fields of flying metal. Indeed, the odd transition from old to new can be seen in the photography of the time. Gun limbers charging headlong around Hellfire corner in Ypres, artillery still drawn by horses. Mules dragging artillery from the Flanders mud and the tank accompanied by mounted troops as the cavalry evolved into the tank regiments.

The generals have often been vilified for their wasteful, profligate conduct in the war. Historians, politicians and the mothers and fathers of lost men at the time, did not necessarily hold this view. The war was all-consuming and simply too great for a simple, common sense solution. The failures of the politicians and the willingness of the imperial classes to continue the war, were equally culpable. Indeed, the returning generals were oft feted and held in the highest regard. It is quite clear that they were aware of the losses, felt them deeply, but the tools to hand were cruder and clumsier than today. Trenches were safe, but for any chance of victory, men had to leave them to attack and this meant losses. The generals were perhaps being realistic, rather than careless. Far from being remote, billeted in beautiful chateaux, over seventy British and Commonwealth generals were killed in the lines, from brigadiers leading a trench attack, to generals blown from their cars or hit by shrapnel near the front.

For every soldier killed in modern wars, a news item accompanies the loss, amplifying the effect, rightly, in the minds of the population. At the peak of hostilities in the Great War, the British and Commonwealth were suffering in excess of 40,000 casualties a week. The scale is almost inconceivable from the viewpoint of modern sensitivity. Indeed, this sensitivity can shield other realities of the Great War.

There is, of course, much evidence of pride being taken in having served. The treatment of legitimate conscientious objectors in some communities, understandably, but not necessarily correctly, was harsh and brutal. This may have amplified the positive impact of service and army service had many perks to offset the probability of injury or death. It is always interesting to compare the experiences of Great War soldiers with those of the Second World War and of modern veterans. The positive impact of service is possibly linked to the legitimacy of the conflict in some regards, as well as the fighting conditions. The horrors of the trenches were very real and words alone, in any modern context, cannot convey the experience and certainly not from one hundred years hence, with the survivors no longer with us.

The tactics of the war evolved, albeit desperately slowly, from lines of riflemen behind a barricade, to the dug-in positions of the trench system with the cavalry charge, to the creeping box barrage with tank, aeroplane and observer communications perfected, after stuttering starts on the Somme. The desperate push to advance precipitating a poorly planned premature deployment. When walking the battlefields, it is still unbelievable to see the shallowness of the advances on the Somme after almost five months of fighting. The tactics of the first day of that battle have become the symbolic paraphrase of the entire war. The Great War conjures up images of soldiers going over the top, walking very slowly (fifty yards per minute, with five yard separation) and straight into a merciless wall of bullets. Perhaps some Flanders mud added, but that is the image of the war on the Western Front. Tactics changed rapidly after the first day of July 1916, and the Somme thus continued as a series of smaller engagements, focusing on each line of defence in turn. Perhaps the hesitancy of launching large battles was borne from the residual shock of the unimaginable losses, due to the opening day underestimation of the strength of enemy defences and overconfidence in the success of the artillery barrage.

The tactics, however conceived, were still rooted in Victorian values. Officers holding an authority often disproportionate to their skill, training and experience. Junior officers are regarded sympathetically, as being leaders of men into actions over which they had little discretion or control. The more senior generals viewed as preferring to field men in numbers, to offset any weakness of planning. The use of poison gas, mines and flamethrowers were all greeted with outrage at the time. Men were also vaporised by shrapnel, cleaved in two by trench-maces and traumatically disfigured, but these were more readily accepted as consequences of war. Even today, some struggle with the concept of a war with rules, as surely anything goes? It is total war isn't it?

The involvement of civilians as non-combatants first became an issue in the Great War. Zeppelin raids, initially on coastal towns, took the war to the home front. This marked a significant departure for the families at home limited to reading official accounts of battles in Southern Africa, or the sub-continent, over breakfast. The politics of the prosecution of war and the rules of belligerent nations were tested in the extreme during this part of our history.

The concept of Special Forces operations formally emerged during the Second World War. Of course, ancient history is littered with good examples of underhanded and sneaky tactics, from the Trojan Horse, to the use of biological weapons (firing plague victims over the walls of castles with a trebuchet). In the Great War, behind the lines was considered out of bounds for operations. Spying was one thing, but fighting that way was an alien concept. Apart from the communications, equipment and training required, the probability of success was deemed too low. The rules of war also created an appetite for frontal fighting as being the preferred strategy.

In researching this book in particular, rather than for general professional interest, I have visited the battlefields twice, riding my motorcycle to the most inaccessible military cemeteries to say thank you, to capture the geography and the scale of the conflict. I wanted to work out the finer details of the true events, to make the book plausible in every detail, even though the story is fictional. But in doing so, I never imagined some of the outcomes, nor expected the impact of the war on me, one hundred years later. Visiting Caterpillar Valley cemetery, I felt myself in conversation with the rows of gravestones, showing off my bike and asking forgiveness that I have intruded on their rest, as they garrison the valley forever. The fact that there were so many stones caused a deeper impression on me, as in fact these stones represented the soldiers who were actually recovered from the field. There ought to be more, but the churn of the battles took away the dignity of burial from many thousands more - who would otherwise be here. The monument at Thiepval, being their battlefield commemoration.

I walked the path of the 34th Division from La Boisselle towards the higher ground that they took on 1 July 1916. Around me were farm vehicles and the sounds of a busy farming community. Always accommodating and incredibly respectful, the farmers told me that every day, literally every day, something is uncovered from the war. From a bullet casing, to clothing and unexploded ordnance. In fact, to prove the point, I kicked around in a field at Bazentin-Le-Petit and uncovered a dud shrapnel shell and a mills bomb, with the fuse pulled. I photographed them and left them, as we must. At my most recent visit in October 2013, I discovered the distal end of a human tibia (shin bone), exposed after ploughing, in Caterpillar Valley. I buried it out of sight from the surface, with care.

However we view the Great War, it was a war fought by young men. Nations put at risk their future generations, their greatest assets, with terrible and lasting consequences, echoing through the ages even to this day. These young men aspired to marriage, fatherhood and a life of productive work at home. The richness of literature, letters and pictures laying eternal testament to men who thought of home, of sweethearts, mothers and a future when the war was over. These men, though, had their destiny cast as soldiers. Men needed to be capable of unspeakable brutality through necessity, with millions never returning to their homelands.

We can never know the true feelings of men going to fight, or the true nature of the battlefield at that time. Standing in High Wood today is eerie, but peaceful and quiet, very quiet. Hill 60 is surrounded on three sides by new housing developments and playing fields. It is impossible, even with informed imagination, to rewind to the days of the war, but it is imperative that the memory is passed to later generations, if only to ensure that humanity is retained, even if the will is weak.

CHAPTER ONE - NOVEMBER 1915

I arrived at the school gates as the first bell sounded. It was the start of the last day of the autumn term. School was ending a week early, because two of the teachers were due to leave for army service right after the last bell that day. The war had now been raging across much of the world for over a year and those early hopes of a quick end, with the Germans retreating back across the borders, were now long gone. We were now set for a second Christmas in the trenches. The newspapers were printing stories that were different from the realities of the Front, but for me, the Front was a definite and certain reality. I had come home on leave, without any real desire to do so and without feeling a real connection with my family. This had surprised me and made me feel sad and ashamed. Here I was at my old school, after accepting a chance invitation from my old schoolmaster keen for stories of adventure. Certainly not tales of that definite reality in Belgium and France.

The boys were breathless from running but still keen to hear a story or two from the Front. In truth, I had no such comfort for them. Being honest, I really did not want to say anything to them about the real war. All they really knew was what was left after the army reports were censored. Those reports were filtered to the newspapers and retold by fathers keen for their sons to embrace the war being fought by other people's sons. Tales of heroism from *The London Gazette*, medal citations and all that. Most of the stories were true enough I suppose, inspiring patriotism and a thread of keenness in the young men running now before me. Their fathers, outwardly boisterous still, but in truth hoping that it would be over before their own sons come of age or their nephews get killed under the rattle of machine gun fire in a distant battle. It was different for fathers of boys already trudging through France and Belgium. Their words carried a heavier, worry-weary note that everyone recognised, politely and sympathetically nodding along in time to the words.

I knew a different story. I knew the real Front and the terrible and horrific daily sights of death and destruction, a world away from this splendid calm. Even writing it down here cannot describe the intensity, the imminent, circling peril and the human disbelief that someone who looked like me would kill me if I let him. But, write it I must, even if only to keep a record of the time spent away from my family and my love. By 1915, we had long ago seen the end of the chivalrous, glittering cavalry charges, such as those that are loved and recalled by the generals. Cut down under the ceaseless clattering of the dreadful invention, the machine gun. Horses and men labouring resolutely in miles of mud. The generals really aren't so stupid; I suppose they are just realistic. They know all too well the story of the war, even if not the detail of terrain and bloodstain. The war won't be won in a hole in the ground. To win, we must leave the safety of the trenches and take on the enemy headlong. But for the foot soldier, there is nothing like an impenetrable wall of bullets and shrapnel raining from above to put a stop to horse charging. There is, as yet, nothing in man's invention that has found a way to still the devilish beating heart of the gun. So now, inevitably, there are lines of trenches, a halted southward sweep, the Schlieffen Plan, and no fruit of the imagination to end this weary table game.

A deep breath, still trying to find the words to begin my big speech to my old school. What the bloody hell was I going to tell them? Not the truth. They would not believe me and that would be the end of it. I could not tell them about hanging my cap on an unattached leg (in German boots) that was dangling over the top of the fire step, or of the sentry shot through the eye as he looked over the parapet, a lapse in a moment of extreme fatigue. No telling of the German cleaved in half by a trenching tool because his dying body was causing a dangerous obstruction in the filthy trench. I certainly wasn't going to tell them of the German soldier leaping down from the parapet onto the upthrust bayonet, which impaled him to the stock. How could I save them from finding that out for themselves? The war would inevitably find them. The sinewy finger of conscription, in deep shadow of ashamed resignation, pitied no one and sought out youth in avaricious pleasure. The war was just too big. Perhaps I could get them to think about the war differently. If only one of them was saved the agony of this conscripted death, if only one of them was to...

'Welcome gentlemen please, an old boy of the Friary; a boy who only a few years ago was a cheery fellow like all of you! Come in please William, there we are, say hello to these young men. Welcome my fine chap and look at your uniform! How you have grown. All of your time in France has been well spent, eh? Learned a lot living in France as well, I expect. Come on, tell us everything from over the sea!'

His words fell into one long ribbon of meaningless fog and I just thought to smile and nod and speak when the ribbon reached an end. And end it did.

'Hello boys. I'm pleased to see my old school again. It has been such a long time, well not really, but it feels like it. As you can see, I have been in the army for over a year now, mostly training to be a soldier. Not doing much actual fighting. Just hanging about, a lot of marching and shouting and polishing buttons and all that, ha ha.'

The lie at that moment, the thin deception to save an innocent, pressed heavily upon me. My stomach, a lead weight, dropped to the floor. Images of terrified faces in fetid trenches, faces not much older than these boys. Afraid to move and afraid, not of death, but of being dead and missing a life of fun and love and anything but this war. The faces of the young, who would overcome their terror, the uncontrollable shaking and the involuntary shouts as waves of fear gripped them while shells flew over their heads, before jumping off.

Unable to carry on with this stupid thing, I felt anger rise and subside, the need to tell all came and went and left me feeling empty and sick.

'Sorry sir,' almost to myself, 'I just can't do this properly. I shouldn't really have come here today.'

My old teacher looked pale. He half raised an arm to console me, but lowered it as I lifted my head again, finding the need to speak just once more.

'Look boys, you all play cricket, right? I know the war isn't a game, but here, see it like this. When you go out to bat, you survive ball by ball. You knock some away and some whizz past your ear if you don't duck. The fielders are watching every move and will pounce on you with every sinew of their being if you make a mistake. You can bat for ages, all day thinking it's alright and nothing can touch you, over after over, deep breath and a sigh of relief as each ball passes, one nearer the end of the game. But remember, the bowler only has to get through once and it's all over.'

It was a weak and silly thing to say, but anything else would have made it all come forward, all of it, in a tide of condemnation and no doubt followed by contradiction and disbelief. I coughed and walked out, not daring to look back. I could see curled-up lips and nudging, and I could hear quizzical whispers and boyish giggles. The last thing I heard was the creaking closure of the door that I had heard so many times before. A familiar, solid and safe noise imprinted in my brain. Today though, it was anything but safe, it was more like the boom of a howitzer blasting overhead, bringing destruction to some poor bugger who didn't yet know how to recognise the sounds and watch for the change of note. Ashamed and feeling oddly dirty like the trench, stained like the corpses that haunted my days, I was sick on the entrance floor, splashing the benches.

I wiped my face and left. Perhaps my stomach was weak, or perhaps it was the devil himself, angry with me for trying to deny him his battle harvest of innocent souls.

I was sorry to leave that way, but what was to be expected? Countless of my soldier brothers must have done the same thing, going to their old schools and showing off their uniforms. To me, this wasn't a game. It was bloody real and bloody dangerous. The silly rubbish in the papers about the 'race to the sea' and that we would all be home for Christmas in 1914 was idiotic and impossible. In France feelings were the same, the difference being that the war was being fought on their doorsteps and in their fields.

By this point in 1915, a new army of young recruits, Kitchener's Army, was being formed from boys just like those in my old school. If we experienced soldiers couldn't survive the putrid trenches, how would they? The madness of such clean countryside for miles around, without a whiff of the war, then right in the middle of paradise, a strip of horror, like Hades' own lava flow, chewing up machines and men. Day and night, blind to uniform and politics. These boys don't know this, their fool teachers don't and as sure as mutton is mutton, the people I pass in the street don't.

There is much gossip at home, in the taverns, fields, in the street and behind closed curtains. They hear it is all to get much worse, with a big push soon. Big push? Those German fellows are bloody good soldiers and they *wanted* to be there it seemed, well at least it did to me. They are digging in and making a fine display of their trenches. I've seen them close to. We still live in temporary dugouts, because we are supposed to be advancing and sending these chaps back to Germany with their tails between their legs. We are all told the same, over and again, perhaps a delusion and perhaps that's right. But it's our lads hanging in bits on the old barbed wire.

Head down, I continued walking away from the big door, thinking back to France. Coming upon the old Head's bench, I decided to sit for a while. In fact, it had been a long time since my last safe sit down. My wounded back ached, as a reminder that there was still a war on and me a part of it. I still looked around for danger before sitting. As I relaxed and sank down, a wave of memory washed over me. A silly-boy daydream, except this silly boy had grown up bloody quickly and had been sent out in cattle-truck train journeys from an English coast to France and Belgium. France, a country I had actually come to know quite well as it happened. I let my daydream wash over me and tried to forget the bombs and the noises and the smells, even if only for a few minutes. I thought of my comrades and those who had died alongside me. Their faces came into my dream then faded away; for a fleeting moment, my mind was my own again, without the constant percussion, screams, shouts and orders heralding the appearance of death.

This War to end all war,
Take a life to save a life,
A stone cut ready to bear your name,
Testament that you played out
in this, The Mad Game.

CHAPTER TWO APRIL 1912 - AN ADVENTURE!

My father was an engineer by trade. He was good at fixing up vehicles that had stopped working, and inventing devices to replace and mend broken parts. He often bought odd machines and made them more appealing, with better quality levers and handles, wheels and seats. We lived in the country, where new machines were just becoming part of the farming life cycle and so his business was profitable. His reputation extended overseas to farming communities in France. I loved working with him and found a talent for machines and engineering, for being someone who could fix problems fast and for being a quick thinker. Often, I was asked to help out which, despite being a diligent pupil, I preferred to school. Near to the end of my schooling, I was thinking about an apprenticeship, or perhaps studying engineering. A proper gentleman with a spanner, Mother! I was going to make something of myself and live a comfortable life in the country. Staying on in school was an option, but there was nothing left to teach my naïve younger self. Get out and make a start, that was it for me. Besides, the money would be good for me and my family. An adventure beckoned in northern France. Perhaps it would be good to see a bit of the world.

I pleaded with my father to let me go to France with him to buy and improve some farm equipment. It seemed a great adventure and this was the life of a true gentleman's apprentice. He had done some business a couple of years ago with a farmer from Bazentin-le-Petit, a little village on the road out of Albert, in northern France. Father had been there for a short trip, only intending to visit Amiens. For me, it was a chance of freedom as I had never been away from home before and never so far! As a fast-growing boy in my teens, it would be an amazing journey to where the people did not speak my language.

My father agreed, he welcomed the company anyway, and we set off on the boat train with two large cases of equipment and tools. The only problem would be the last part of the journey, as it was a distance away from the railway and we did not have a cart arranged in France. We would find a way, my father always did.

A loving man, he always had his arm around me as a boy, always showing off about my engineering talents. He loved nothing better than for both of us to be elbow deep in oil and spanners, calling out details of what we had found. He taught me the imperial measurement system and I could count fractions very easily as a result.

The day came to leave. Mother fussed as usual, more so because she did not want me to get my clothes dirty and show us all up. She was strong and calm in every respect. With me, she was caring and loving. I could not have wished for a better send-off, with enough to feed ourselves and everyone we met. As we set off, the news came of the sinking of the new steamship, *The Titanic*. Imagine the loss of so many lives all at once. I could not imagine at the time anything so terrible ever happening again. How many people is a thousand? I could not imagine that at all and never wanted to see death on that scale. As I boarded, I felt sick to my stomach with fear and worried about the sea-worthiness of our vessel.

On the journey, my father talked a little about where we were going. It was the very north of France, near to the border with Belgium. The train might take us through Lille and Bethune on the way, but he was not too sure. All he knew is that we would have to find our own transport from Amiens and neither of us spoke much French. Smile and speak slowly, my mother had advised.

Finally, we reached our destination after nearly four days of travelling, such a long journey, it felt like we were on the other side of the world. At Amiens, we found a cart going towards Albert and for a few coins, the farmer allowed us to ride with him. Such slow progress, but such a huge and beautiful country. We took lodgings in Albert, which was a small town surrounded by small and quiet villages in rolling countryside on the border of the Pas-de-Calais and the Picardie regions, according to the map. I was studying the map while we waited for my father's contact.

We first met the Lefebvre family in a café in Albert to discuss farm equipment (that's all I knew) and to see it moving. After arriving, we sat down and ordered coffee, which we came to know as soup, as it was so strong and aromatic. I was bored with this meeting as it was lots of slow talking, constant misunderstandings and hand gestures. About an hour into the meeting, an oil-smeared girl propped a wobbly old bicycle outside, then came in and sat between me and Monsieur Lefebvre. This girl, who was later introduced to me as his daughter, immediately joined in a heated discussion about an odd-looking motor car, set at the side of the road.

Straight off with the conversation, neither invitation nor introduction. How was that, if you please?

Odile was beautiful and not at all shy, which for me was a powerful attraction. I liked her immediately, perhaps just because she was French and because it would be different to know a girl from another country. She had an open outlook to life and we found ways to communicate with our own misunderstandings and hand gestures. What came with it, alas, was her persistent desire to punch me hard in the arm while calling me 'imbecile'.

'My name is William. That is, William Collins. I am from England. I like your country very much.'

This was said slowly and loudly as if she could neither comprehend words generally, nor ones spoken more than ten inches from her face. I enjoyed looking into her eyes.

'Oui, yes, I know you are from England. William. Is a strong name, yes? Like, William the Conqueror, who was from France, no?'

'No. Er, yes. Ha ha. I have travelled with my father to see your father. Do you go to school here?'

'Yes, they have schools in France. They teaching English to us better than French to you boys, oui?'

Odile was teasing me, but not cruelly. I really liked this girl, a lot, and would have to learn French to catch up with her. I was not sure how to do this, but the solution was given to me.

'One, day, William-not-the-Conqueror, you come to France again and you learn French. You can show us how to build machines. Is a fair trade, you think?'

'Yes,' I laughed, 'is a fair trade.'

'Imbecile.' I felt the familiar punch in the arm.

'Thank you. Merci, mademoiselle.'

'Your French is very bad, William. I will have my work to help you learn French.'

I would certainly be a willing volunteer.

My father managed to conclude this part of the meeting and the two men shared more coffee. It seemed that business was concluded and that meant we would be parting for the day. I wanted to spend more time with Odile and hoped she thought the same about me. So I suggested she show me the countryside (using hand gestures, I am ashamed to say), around where she lived. Our fathers agreed that this would be acceptable, as long as we told them where we would be going and when we would be back. To them, we were still children, but I felt every bit the grown man, with a girl as my guide. We set off on a small cart out of Albert and up the road towards a town called Bapaume.

'So, William, tell me about your country. Is not beautiful like France, yes? That is why you want our kings to be your kings of course, eh?'

'Yes, well, perhaps. England is very beautiful. You have a lot of land in France and not so many people. It is quiet.'

'It is very quiet here. Not so much happens. A boy from England is something a bit different.'

'Where will you take me?'

'Aha, I have some surprises for a walk, King William-not-the-Conqueror.'

Odile suggested a walk on the road up the hill from her home towards another village. I walked with her, glancing over the sweeping ridge to a large wood on top of the hill. She told me it was beautifully cool in the summer because the trees provided dense shade. We agreed that we would walk there tomorrow if permitted. As we continued our walk, I began to look at Odile with different eyes. I felt strange feelings of nervousness and recall sweating at her every touch. Perhaps this was what love felt like, but at the time I just wanted not to make a fool of myself and trip, or fall over, or spill food onto my shirt.

'You like my village, William? It is small and farming, but it is beautiful and has lots of forest over here.'

'Oui, Odile, it est very belle.'

'Oh, William, imbecile. Your French is horrible.'

She looked away, put her hand to her face and laughed. Odile was definitely teasing me. I was lost and every word turned to fog in my brain. My hand on her arm felt rough and my fingernails were dirty with oil. Her arm was pale with tiny freckles and even with closed eyes, I could remember every one.

The next day, our fathers spent the hot morning taking pieces off the odd car and examining them. Both were now up to their elbows in grease and enjoying every moment. My father was making pencil drawings and Monsieur (I had learned some French) Lefebvre was explaining the working with grand gestures and engine noises. Comical perhaps, but both men were talented engineers and whatever they came up with would be exceptional. I stayed with them until Odile finished her chores, when we would go for a picnic. Odile's mother seemed less sure of our intentions, but my earnest pleading to see the countryside won her over.

This time, we set off on the road to Longueval, turned left up along a narrow sunken track, past a windmill and up to the edge of the wood. It was not a steep slope, but from the wood you could look over the ridge down to the villages. Over the hill was a small village called Montauban and it was lit brightly by the sun that morning. We stepped into the wood and clambered over the undergrowth, which was dense and wild, as cool as Odile had said. We found a clear spot and sat down overlooking the countryside. The ground was damp, summer not yet in the soil itself.

Odile smiled at me, which was probably because we did not understand each other very well.

'Odile,' I proudly announced, still in English, 'I am pleased to be here in France with you. I did not know when I came, that your father had a daughter.'

The curled lip and narrowing eyes showed that I was not doing very well at explaining myself.

'Er, when I came to France, I did not know that your father had a family, or I would have brought a present from England for you. Do you understand?'

'Yes, William, I do. You did not bring me a present from England, thank you.'

'Well, yes, I suppose so.' Resigned to being teased, I did not care.

Odile smiled and laughed. She picked up some grass and chewed it as we ate our picnic. The bread was fresh and the cheese, although it smelled terribly, tasted very good and I wanted to eat it all.

'You think William, that French girls are jolie?'

'Quite jolly, and very pretty as well.' It was my turn to tease and this time on a more pleasant subject.

'You think I am pretty?'

'Oui, Odile. Je prends tres jolie.'

'Je pense, imbecile!'

We both laughed. But the question set my pulse racing. She would not have asked the question unless she wanted the answer from me. At once exhilarated and nervous, I could see my hands trembling.

'Er, je pense tres jolie, Odile.'

'It is good enough, William, stupid boy from over the sea. You are handsome man too, I think.'

Leaning back on the tree, I was, although I did not know it at the time, falling in love for the first time.

'Odile, I like your village very much. I will have to go home. Will you let me write to you from England?'

'Can you write William? I think if you do, you do it in English. Otherwise, I will never know what you are saying, eh?'

'I will try to learn some French, even if it is only to stop your teasing me.'

'Oh William, the face you make when I tease you is why I try. You are so funny.'

The next day we had to begin our journey back home. My father had concluded his business and as I held Odile's hands and gazed into her oil-smeared face, I knew that I must return.

'Next time, I will return, if only to fix that stupid bicycle.'

'Ah, why thank you, Monsieur Engineer. If you return, I will try to teach you my language, so you are not such a stupid—'

'I know, imbecile!'

She punched me in the arm and the ribs and both hurt for some time afterwards but I did not want the pain to go away as it reminded me of her.

I loved the country here and imprinted every bit of it in my mind, promising myself to return when I was old enough. It might well be just a silly dream, but it was enough to keep me going. Odile may forget me soon enough, the novelty English boy from over the sea. But almost before we had returned to England, I was thinking of coming back to France.

My father was at first reluctant, but since I made it quite clear I wanted to see France again so soon after coming back he must have known that I wanted to see 'the girl', as he called her, and stay there to work. He agreed finally and wanted to arrange passage and payment for the trip as a reward for helping him so often. He booked me onto the boat train and, once again in France, I would find my way to the train that would take me to either Amiens or Albert. I am sure he expected me to be only a few weeks in France, visiting, exploring and checking the odd-looking motor car for him, while he arranged for it to be brought back to England. For that reason, I was allowed to travel to France again.

CHAPTER THREE - NEITHER HERE NOR THERE – SEPTEMBER 1912

Bazentin-le-Petit was just as I had remembered it, nestled in rolling countryside. Villages, whose names are now all too familiar to the British Army, lay all around. Flers, Courcelette, Longueval, Contalmaison. At the time, the little villages were bathed in sunlight and so peaceful. Only the occasional clip-clop of hooves or the rare rumble of a motor car broke the silence. I ought to have written first of course, but I also thought the surprise would be more fun.

Content on my long walk towards Bazentin, I noticed the countryside rise and fall around me, watching the ridges fall away to forest and hills rise gently in the distance. This was no mountain region, the highest spot was little more than a man could jump. Having underestimated the walking distance, I had to sleep in the open on my first night in France. I felt unable to beg for a lift as my French had reverted to appalling in the weeks since I was last here. However, I finally found my way to Albert and then up to Bazentin, remembering to turn right upon seeing the old church spire, and continued until the very front door of the Lefebvre house. Odile would most likely not recognise me as she was not expecting me and I worried in case she had promised herself to another boy. To a boy who spoke her language, expressing his love in ways to melt her heart forever, which I could not do as yet, but wanted to try. At her garden wall, my nerve failed me a little, so I foolishly lurked in the bushes to see if she still lived there. Of course she did and yes, her father and the odd-looking motor car were still there, right on the corner, right opposite the church.

Odile appeared in the early summer evening and my heart nearly jumped out of my mouth. I would go to her now and wave my arms to show my love for her. I burst through the flowering bushes, startling everyone, and her father first looked angry and gestured dangerously towards me.

Luckily, Odile recognised me alright and smiled at me. It made me so happy. Her father also now recognised me, instantly bursting into laughter and slapping me on the back. He kept saying 'idiot' a lot and punching me on the arm. Like father, like daughter.

I must have looked a sight as Odile walked me to the hand pump and made me wash my face and hands. Her gentle touch made me shiver, but the water was cold and that was that.

'William, you smell very bad I think. You have come to France again, for why?'

'To see you, to stay here for a time. It is beautiful and I want so much to speak French, so that you can know my feelings. I have come to France to find you again. Do you understand?'

'Oh, my William. Yes. I will see if you can stay here for a time. I am surprised to see you, but my heart is pleased that you come back to France. It makes me happy to see you, English.'

'Here, I have some money to pay for my stay, but the coins won't work here, I think.'

Odile looked at the coins which, of course, would be of no use in France. She agreed with her father that I could work around the yard for a few coins and the honour of spending some polite time with Odile. I don't suppose many boys from over the sea got to spend time with French girls in those days, but I was one and loved every moment.

Monsieur Lefebvre cleared the outbuilding of equipment and found a small mattress and spring bed. The first evening was spent in the outbuilding as there were no rooms inside and where my presence, anyway, was not to be encouraged. It was not too cold as summer was still in the air, and there were bread and potatoes to eat, which were most welcome.

Odile tried to speak to me again in French and I began to understand a few words. Some French words are not so different to English and these made a good starting point. She was really and truly surprised and pleased to see me, but perhaps not as surprised as I had expected. I noticed she blushed often when we spoke and I hoped that meant she had feelings for me. After all, my trip from England was to see her.

'So, er, Odile. I have come back to France so that you can teach me some French words. Will you do that?'

'Oh William, it will take much time to teach you French and for you to get it right, I think!'

'I am willing to try. Let's see. Here is a table? That is right? And here is a, er... Oh dear.'

'Oh William, are you going to be a difficult student? I will try, but I might not be able to help you, imbecile.' Again, I felt the pain of a dig in the arm.

In a short time my put-together room in the outbuilding became quite homely. Odile and I spent more and more time together and I felt that we had become closer, which pleased me, but it may just have been a fondness increased by memory. Even then, I liked to think that we might be together, even if she was from another country. We walked for hours through the fields and woods near her home. The fields were agricultural and we enjoyed walking between the crops, often out of sight, where at last I was able to steal a polite kiss.

'My love, Odile, would it be so difficult to be with a boy from England, do you think?'

'William, we have a life in France. I would want to stay in here with my family. Oui, I would like to see England and your home, but I would want to be in here for to live, you understand?'

'Yes, and I would be happy to live here, if I could learn the language. I have no trade, and although good with machines, I am not an engineer yet.'

'I understand, but it is something to look forward to isn't it?'

I had to agree. To really, honestly, have a life with Odile, I would either have to go home and finish a trade, or learn French properly and work in France. If that was even allowed.

We were able to spend more and more time without a chaperone and more and more time thinking about how we could be together in France. I had resolved not to convince Odile to move to England, but still wanted her to visit. We would walk through the woods and picnic near the road, talking of these things. The French do like their bread and cheese and I was happy to oblige in the sampling.

To practise my French, I tried to get to know others in the village and to earn some extra money, I used to run errands for the older people in the surrounding villages, which they appreciated as winter drew in. Soon, I knew the roads, the tracks and the shortcuts over the fields, where all the houses were and how long it would take to reach each one. I would walk frequently from Bazentin to Albert, picking up vegetables and bread from Pozieres, on the main road to and from Albert.

Occasionally, I was able to borrow a bicycle, a rather awful and uncomfortable French one with hard wheels and a mind of its own. Odile and I would cycle towards Contalmaison and the small chateau nearby. The weather always seemed to be perfect, even late in the year. It wasn't, it just felt like it. I was beginning to feel at home in France and could now manage simple conversations without Odile to help with translation. I could not write in French and, silly as it sounds, I did not read it well and had difficulty recognising the words, with punctuation everywhere on the pages it seemed.

Monsieur Lefebvre spent a lot of time inventing clever devices for the home, to make extra money. It was how he came to know my father I suppose, as he had travelled to England and Scotland to sell his devices.

He made machines that could spin clothing to dry them or to wash food. He even invented a way to plant seeds in neat rows without touching them, using a small steam motor.

Odile was also very practically minded. She loved nothing more than getting greasy, even with her delicate arms and fading freckles. The motor grease looked beautiful on her face. She was able to put together and take apart the machines that her father had made. I was now in love and never wanted those times to pass away. I wanted my French to improve to impress Odile and to stop the bruising on my arm. I would not miss that!

One darkening afternoon, out on our bicycles, we came upon an old shed owned by a family Odile knew quite well. We stopped to see if we could put some more air into the bicycle tyres. Inside was a broken motor bicycle. It smelled of petrol and rusty metal, but it wasn't an old machine.

'Do you think we could ask to take this home and repair it, Odile? Is that allowed?'

'I know the owner, we can ask. Maybe he will let us use it if we can make it start, yes?'

'Maybe. I can try and free the motor and see if we can make it start.'

'Here, let me try to turn the engine. Look, the oil is coming out, so it will move.'

We fell upon it and tried to make it work but it was seized solid. With the owner's permission, we got the vehicle onto the back of his cart and took it to Odile's father. He loosened it up and got it to turn over a bit more, but not to start. Never mind, it was a wonderful machine and although it did not belong to me, it became my evening project to get it to work and then use it for my deliveries, providing I had permission.

I had not counted upon Odile. She too wanted to take up the project of the motor bicycle and we realised it would provide a perfect opportunity to spend time together, with permission from her father, in an unsupervised labour of love. For every turn of a spanner, I stole a kiss or a gentle caress of an arm. We spend many evenings like this and even managed to get some spares to help the motor bicycle come to life. Odile liked to brush her finger lightly on the back of my hand, to tease me, but I did not mind. It became a sign between us and it made me happy to feel her touch.

'Shall we go and ask if we can have the machine to have fun with, William, perhaps as a present from Père Noel?'

'Yes. Let's take the bicycles and go and ask.'

Odile knocked on the owner's door and asked in very fast French whether we could use the motor bicycle. The owner of the motor bicycle just shrugged, so we took that to mean he did not want it. If he knew that we had got it to work, he might have thought differently.

'He says it is a piece of rubbish now. It is only four years old, but has never worked properly. I think it is because he is so fat!'

'I hope you did not tell him that? Or that we have nearly got it working?'

'No, imbecile. I said you wanted to use it as a bicycle to get fit and to make me laugh.'

After almost a month of cold evenings spent fiddling and adjusting, we were able to start the bicycle properly. It was a frightening clanking roar, especially as the tank for the petrol ran along the bars near your body. As I stepped onto the cycle and admired the design, I felt a surge of excitement. I rode off and learned how it worked as I went, trying to work out which lever put power to the chain and which one made it go faster. Squeeze the levers and pull the pistons seemed the right way to go (while trying not to fall off in front of Odile). Off I went on the frosty road. Part cycling and part motor cycling, it was fun to ride and would certainly reduce my errand time. It was slow up the hill but faster down. My education with machines felt more complete and my love for Odile felt without end. Her father seemed to like me and perhaps even saw me as a candidate to marry his daughter. I did not know if that would be allowed or if it would be seen as a dishonour, but no matter. I grinned every yard of that ride on the motor bicycle.

As spring came in, my errand runs now grew in length and complexity as my riding and French improved together. I could speak the language quite well, but was still not very good when it was written down. Soon, it got round the village that I could get to and from the markets in double quick time. It was even easier after learning some shortcuts through the woods and across the fields. In fact, I used to try and time myself by counting down the seconds. I'm not sure that it worked out too well, but it passed the time. Odile would sometimes help me load and unload and it was a great way for the villagers to get to know me and to trust someone from over the sea. I would sometimes ride right up the hill towards Thiepval. The landscape was much different on this side of the road, with lots of valleys and newly green woods to hide in.

Before long, I made some frames for the motor bicycle to carry more goods, which doubled as a seat for Odile. Not very safe admittedly, but on short trips it made for some fun and laughter, except when she fell off, which was often. The motor was not really powerful enough to do much more than reduce the need to pedal, but it was a smoky freedom that left us smelling of petrol and oil. We were allowed out to travel around in the lengthening evenings and to sit and watch the sun set over the ridges. It was here that we first talked of serious and grown up plans for the future. I rode Odile to the edge of the wood, looking down towards the sunset and we stopped to sit down and let the vibrations in our body subside.

'Odile, would it be very strange for us to marry and live in France?'

'Yes William, it would be strange. Everyone in the village is expecting to marry someone from another village, or this village or that. Perhaps you could start, a, how you say, some business over here. You are English and that would be interesting to our people perhaps? I do not know. But I would like to think that we could try. My father knows most people you know.'

'Is that enough Odile? Is that enough for you?'

She smiled at me and stroked the back of my hand with one finger. I was unsure if that was a yes or a no.

Perhaps we would have a repair shop as a hobby and Odile would keep a garden, or I would train to be an engineer. I had no idea if I could work in France or even manage to live the language, but I was more than willing to try. Throughout that summer, we spent more time arm-in-arm in the open and no one seemed to mind. We were even allowed to hold hands when her parents were around. I usually forgot to write home because I was spending time with my French love. Odile's mother had enquired regularly about my writing home and gently shamed me into ensuring that two or three actually went home for birthdays and Christmas at the very least.

We would often ride down the main street and coast down the surrounding hills. Sometimes, we would turn left to Longueval and sometimes right to Contalmaison. If we went uphill from the village we could visit the churchyard and spire of Martinpuich. Often, we would stop under a farm wall that shielded us from the wind and talk about nothing in particular. This farm had some outbuildings and a small shed, which we often raided for tools (always putting them back) because we did not always want to carry tools to keep the motor bicycle running. That tool shed became an important place for us, because in there, we were truly alone and it was where I learned most of the French that I can speak today. And it became a secret post box where we would each leave little notes for the other – silly things that made us laugh, or sometimes things we were too shy to say in person

Odile would make a point of teaching me some words and phrases and made sure that I replied properly and not with a silly English accent. She tried to have more rapid conversations and to make my French more real and not like I was reading from a children's book.

'William, if you are going to be an engineer in France, you have to know the language well. From now, I am only going to speak in French and you are only going to reply in French, however hard it might be.'

'Yes Odile. I am now only gone to speak in France. Is that true?'

'Ha ha, nearly, mon chéri, nearly. More practising for you, I think!'

I would complete my errands, collect my small wages and wait by the wall with my little book of words and sentences. In time, it became easier to use different ways of saying what I wanted, needed and felt and I could answer most questions.

Sometimes, if it was warm, Odile would ride her bicycle and meet me at the tool shed, or I would ride with her and we would stop in the sunshine. If there ever was a special meeting place, it was in that little shed, a space just for us. It was where I told Odile for the first time that I truly loved her, in a proper way, in French to make sure. Every time I said it to her afterwards, I thought of the first time in that little shed.

'Darling William, my father and mother like you very much and can see how hard you work and how hard you are trying to learn our French. My mother is worried that you have not spent time with your own family, even if it is only for a short while. You might have to return to England anyway for legal reasons, but my father is not sure about that. It would be good for you to see your family again and tell them all of your plans. Do you think that?'

'I wish every moment of every day to be with you, my love. But I should visit home and see my mother and father again, if only for a while. I have not written for some time and they might be worried.'

Often, I would often sit quietly and think about what was happening in my life. Here I was in France, with no real right to be, if truth be told, part of a wonderful village and feeling every bit the local from over the sea. Not many of my age and background ever got to do this and I felt very privileged. On occasion, I would think about home and the way of life over there, especially since Odile had mentioned it to me. While it was often hard here, it seemed to rain less for some reason. I'm not sure whether that was true, but it felt like it at the time. Odile was the difference of course, she would look into my eyes often and made me realise that this was where I wanted to be. I was learning the language fast and was becoming better at solving problems and using my common sense to figure out how things worked.

So, in the spring of 1914, I planned on returning home for a short while to see my family. I was encouraged in this by Odile's parents who thought my mother and father should like to see me again. My savings meant a trip home without having to walk and sleep in the open country, but I did all the same, as I wanted to save for my future, whatever that would be. In fact, it was all too clear to me, if only I knew how to make it all happen.

When I finally got back to England in the freezing cold, everyone who was dear to me, with one exception, was there to greet me. I had come from France as a grown man perhaps and thought that every time I returned, it would be joyous like this.

My father smiled and nodded knowingly. He must have realised my extended absence was because of the girl. He mentioned that he was pleased because I had managed to send some money home this made me a man providing for his family. That seemed to make him proud of me in his way, even if I was sacrificing some time at school or in learning a trade.

'You would do well at school William. You should learn a profession, properly. If you must go to France again, then it should be with a trade in your pocket at least, otherwise they may not let you stay. What would Odile's father think then, eh?'

'I know Father. But I can learn a trade in France and my French may be good enough soon to take the tests and to work with engineers. I have a motor bicycle now that I use for work. We have managed to make it run very well.'

He roared with laughter at the absurdity of a bicycle that you didn't need to pedal. We discussed the odd-looking car as well and he told me that he was intending to use it for his business, as it would be a novelty and uncommon.

I had intended to stay for just one full month, but had a fall, which hurt my arm and shoulder. It was nothing really and healed quickly, but I was not able to travel back to France for a couple of months. So, I spent some time working with my father, who was trying to convert the odd-looking car into something more useful, to carry goods. In fact, he had removed the rear seats and converted the storage compartment to be open to the air to carry more boxes and bundles. Quite the neat job really.

Odile was constantly on my mind whilst back in England and I wrote to her often, without knowing if she got any of my letters. Mainly, I wrote in English but tried some written French, which was, of course, not very good. I never received any letters from her, save for a strange telegram that must have become confused in translation. It may have been an invitation to return to France, but the words did not come out right at all. The telegraph office was not able to help as they were not exactly sure where the message had come from. In any event, it kept me going through my period of healing, as I wanted to assume it was Odile wishing me back to France.

My arm felt good enough to travel by the end of July and I had intended to plan a way back to France before the harvest was over in September. The motor car was now working passably. My mother and father had now realised that Odile was a real prospect and not a boyhood daydream. I had been serious about learning French and had been serious in planning a life in the village with my beautiful love.

Then, at the end of June, the Archduke of Austria-Hungary was shot.

At the time, I did not realise that Odile had received my letters. It was only later that I would discover that she had. In the time since I left France, she had diligently tried to find out whether a boy from England could live and work in France and marry a French girl. From what she was told, it seemed we would not be able to build a life together. The rules were quite strict and even if I was allowed to stay, what would my work be? What prospects did I have to the eyes of French bureaucracy? There were so many ways that I could fail in my dream of a life in France.

Perhaps these hurdles helped to cool Odile's feelings for me and the life we had planned. Perhaps just the time and distance did enough. I did not receive any letters from her and it made me sad. There may well have been a war coming, and at the time, it looked more likely than not. Whatever happened, I hoped it would not take us away from each other.

Odile did not write to me, and I decided it was because she knew I would want to know how her research was progressing. To write down such bad news was upsetting and so she chose not to write. No news would literally mean no news.

Word of the assassination broke at the same time there as here, although no one anywhere could imagine the horror to be unleashed from that one event. Odile was apart from me and I was apart from her. That was that. As if the storybook of our courtship, open to the sunny page with the words dancing in the air, was slammed shut.

CHRIS CHERRY

CHAPTER FOUR - THE MAD GAME BEGINS JUNE 1914

It wasn't the main headline in the local paper, but everyone knew it was not going to end well. For some months, our politicians had been engaging in some pretty strong fencing with the Germans and the Austrians – although it had all seemed very cordial with the Austrians when I was in France. There was now much to destabilise the continent, to further heat up the lands of Hungary and the Balkans – wherever they were – to fervent fury. It was commonly thought that Europe was itching for a fight, whether it was a big family feud at the top, or jostling for more land for people to live in. Either way, it was not going to go away without the bullies having a scrap over the lines on a map and the traded insults of the political war wolves. This was going to be a terrible and destructive war. But it would be all right, France would have it out with Germany by looking eastwards. Maybe the Russians would want a part of it, but that would be it. Odile and her family would be safe and well and nothing much would happen over here, as we weren't bothered with most of them. That was the way I had figured it.

The talk in the street was of peace and resolution. After all, we had some mighty battleships and a professional army used to having it out with the enemy. Who had they ever had a fight with? No, they wouldn't do it if it really came down to it, would they?

Never, in all my quiet moments, had I thought that any harm would come to Odile or her family. Yes, they were in northern France, realistically quite close to the borders, but any fighting would be brief and surely to the east? The Germans would be foolish to look to France. They didn't want the land or the kingdoms did they? No, it would be nonsensical.

But the powder keg of Europe was dry and the tinderbox was lit in a fury. Belgium was invaded and the wheel of the German Army fell full tilt on the lowlands of Flanders and, to my horror, on into my northern France, close to my all-time love and her family. My dearest was, most frighteningly, directly in the firing line. No letters or telegrams came out of France and nothing seemed to go in. Certainly, there was nothing from Odile and my father heard nothing either, so that was that on the communication front. Most definitely ending any notion of marriage and romance. Maybe coming back home wasn't the right thing to do after all.

The war was going to change everything. We did not know it at the time, but our whole world, our experiences and our futures, if there were to be any, were no longer in our control. The failure of men to communicate was now leading us headlong to destruction – from farm carts to armoured vehicles and from the rattling sabre charge to the murderous rattle of the machine gun.

So, I decided to join up and not wait a moment longer. It wasn't about a patriotic gesture or a need to serve King and Country. I did not want to wait and be told to enlist, which everyone thought was coming, once the early skirmishes failed to force the Germans back into Germany. I wanted to choose my destiny and my best move was to join a regiment where it was possible to build things and solve engineering problems. Joining the Engineers would be the best thing. I wanted it finished, the new enemy out of France, to get to Odile by any means, even if that meant working outside of orders. I wanted this war over in a damned hurry.

So I joined the army, which seemed easy enough as I was recruited one night going to the theatre on a miserable November evening. Recruiting had just really got into its swing and I was one of the first from our area. The recruiting officer promised me sights and experiences that would make a man of me. I really wasn't full of the romantic patriotic zeal of the other young men around me, just full of romantic zeal for Odile.

The medical took place the next day, although my parents did not know about my enlisting. I needed my birth certificate. What a man I was! I knew where the documents were kept, in a special father-only drawer at home. As I sneaked in to get it, my father appeared, saw me rummaging and I thought for an instant he would be angry. But he just came and placed that familiar arm around my shoulder. His warm hand comforted me and his voice was soft.

'Here, William, let me find it for you. Yes, here it is, the thing you are looking for. My fine young man. I won't stop you going, for I would have done the same. Your mother will be fine. There will be tears, of course. You know, we know and that is all that matters. Go and get some sleep and see what the morning brings.'

In the morning, my mother's instinct led her to rise early. Although bustling and cheery as always, something was different. The same difference in thousands of homes across the whole of Britain and the Empire, I expect. Everything was spotless and not an item was out of place. Her face was pink, perhaps she had been crying, and perhaps she had not slept.

'I have made you some breakfast before you go, Will. Do you come home again afterwards, or is that it? They take you straight away? I do not know.'

'Mother, I need to do this – joining the Engineers to build bridges and dig positions and things like that. I won't be a soldier in the usual way.'

'Still going to France or Belgium or wherever, though. Funny, I was pleased for you going back to France. I don't suppose your girl will be waiting for you now?'

This realisation had not truly dawned upon me until that moment and I looked down.

'Sorry William, I did not mean to upset you. Not today of all days. Your father will go with you to that place. You will do well. You are a fine strong boy, they are bound to take you and that is that.'

'Mother, I need to do this,' the same words again, I could think of nothing to offer my mother. 'I cannot bear to think of Odile under the heel of an enemy that does not love her, or care for her. They will tear down her home and it seems they have already destroyed the prospect of our life together.'

'Eat up before it goes cold.' She bustled out of the kitchen and her sobbing came through the closed door, followed by some murmured words from my father.

The medical was detailed and invasive, much more so than for the later members of the New Army. The interview was easy and the recruiter was impressed by my knowledge of France, the language and engineering. He made some marginal notes on my forms and at the time, I thought no more about it.

First, I was enlisted as a private, the lowest rank of all, as my formal education was incomplete and lacking in some areas. It was disappointing, but good behaviour and hard work might change that in time. Much of my adolescent education was outdoors in France, after all. My ability to speak French seemed to impress, at least. My mind was already riding on the road to Longueval and not on the road to Catterick Garrison or some bloody middle-of-nowhere freeze hole in Wiltshire.

After a couple of weeks as a sapper in the Engineers spent marching around and keeping everything tidy, I got my hands on a weapon after being issued with the army standard Lee Enfield rifle, which I loved for its technical detail. I took it apart often, including in the dark as we were instructed, taking out all the pins and locking bolts and giving them names to remember the sequence.

We were taught to shoot rapid fire, emptying our ten-round magazines and a spare five-round charger, in less than a minute.

We heard tales of the heroism at Mons and the miracle of the Marne. We were immersed in fieldcraft and open country fighting. Our training was about moving in the open and using cover, hand-to-hand work with a bayonet and the taking and holding of isolated positions. Training was like this, because at that time, the horrors of prolonged trench warfare were still for the future. The race to the sea and the establishment of the static trench line was only just moving from the minds of the planners to the open fields.

For some time, we moved around a lot from place to place and our routine was exercise, shooting and drilling, eating and cleaning. Day after damnable day. March, run, eat, shoot, drill, eat, sleep, clean, parade. The lads though, made it bearable. They came from all around – Wales, Ireland, Scotland, England – lads from all over. There were some units forming around that time that were all recruited from the same towns, I think they called them 'pals battalions'. These men joined together on the promise of serving together. It was a stroke of genius on the part of Kitchener. He created a sense of pressure and expectation, that you could not watch your schoolmate go to war and stay at home safe. The women of the towns were expected to encourage men to join and fight. It began to get a bit out of hand if I'm honest. No one saw the drawback until much later when the telegrams arrived, one after another, working their way down the street, shrouding each house in a black curtain for the rest of the war.

I became much fitter and also more determined than ever and began to think analytically about the tactics the army were using. We were being trained for open country frontal attacks, straight at the enemy and all that. The assumption being that the enemy would have been softened up by preliminary artillery barrages. But that did not make any sense to me. Straight at them pell-mell. *Hmm*, I thought, *we could do better*. I wasn't yet sure how exactly, but it seemed to me to be too blunt a tool, lacking a bit of imagination. For me, weight of numbers and last man standing wasn't the way to fight a battle. Why was no one thinking of other ways to attack the enemy? I thought of the marsh ticks on the backs of cattle. Constantly scratching at a wound bled them to death from a tiny mark that infected, festered and poisoned. I would think more on that in the time to come.

Soon, I was assigned to a new unit specialising in mining and engineering. I had shown some talent for machinery and in particular working out what needed fixing. I liked this enormously. We had been told quite early on that we would be moving to France in early 1915, perhaps even as early as March, when the weather improved on what was now known as the Western Front. Now sporting corporal stripes because I showed some talent at leading men, I was trained to look after ten or so soldiers at any one time. This meant being immediately moved out of basic infantry training, which was no problem to me, as I hated the mundane, numbing boredom of drill. Now properly in the Corps of Engineers, I was asked to think about ways to assemble and disassemble light railway tracks and the small pumping engines that went with them, normally under enemy fire. It was impossible to imagine being under fire and the extra stresses and pressures this put on a thinking engineer. I spent my spare time poring over the plans for the engines and samples of the rail and track and looking at ways of improving techniques for carrying kit into the front line. The engines needed to be assembled and broken down quickly, in the dark and in the face of enemy activity. The best place to practise was on the football pitch, which had been ploughed over and modified to simulate a section of trench and mine tunnel system.

The use of mines dug under enemy positions was a fascinating idea to me, exactly the kind of thing we should be doing instead of slugging it out at the point of a bayonet. Yes, it would kill soldiers horribly, but immersed in the theory of this war, it seemed that it was simply kill or be killed. They were not backing down in this fight at all, so nor should we. I was not about to quit my desire to free Odile and the French and selfishly return to a normal life in northern France. I resolved to be a soldier, whatever it took and wherever the war took me.

Our unit orders came through to move out to Belgium at the end of February 1915. By then, I was an almost-trained infantry soldier and an almost-trained sapper. Not much of a Tommy just yet. I had no time to write to my family and of course, did not write to Odile, assuming that nothing would get through to the French on what was increasingly looking like the wrong side of the line. If only she had lived in the south of France!

Belgium was closer to Odile and better than staying in an English camp. I began to make plans to find her again, if the chance ever arose. So, I would once again be going over the sea, but this time, in much different circumstances.

February 1915

Our train arrived at the docks in Folkestone. The place was now turned over entirely to the military. There seemed to be no sense of a rapid conclusion to this war by the looks of things here. New railheads, a rebuilt dock and quayside and soldiers in uniform absolutely shoulder-to-shoulder. Polite channels for embarkation had given way to swaying mobs of caps and good-natured swearing. This was to be a long campaign.

There were about four hours until I was due to embark. As it turned out, it was to be fifty hours – given the chaotic planning and poor weather hampering troopships and loading units. With an unexpected six-hour leave to remain in Folkestone, I went in search of something to eat and drink and walked off to the slope, the route down the hill to the dockside. The units marching down were ordered to 'step short' to avoid slipping down the slope and taking their mates with them. The embarkation officer allowed me down the slope and onto the dockside.

I had not yet made any close friends in my unit, but that was more because of spending my spare time figuring out new ways to get at the Germans, rather than socialising. My ideas were good, but I was fearful that my companions would think them ridiculous. I did not wish to look a coward or worse, a deserter. Anyone reading my ideas on paper would most certainly think me that, or worse still, a traitor.

I walked about the quayside, aimlessly at first, taking it all in. Then the troopship began disembarking and I went over to see some real soldiers and get some news from the front. The ship had been diverted from Southampton because of the weather and the threat of being torpedoed in the Channel. I pushed my way to the front of a crowd, all doing the same as me, watching the scene of return. I was instantly horrified at the sight that met me. It turned my blood cold and numbed me. *My God, what was happening to us?*

CHAPTER FIVE - DEPARTURE FROM FOLKESTONE

The orderlies were bringing out stretcher cases when I first arrived on the scene. There were around sixty lined up along the quayside, enlisted men just like those of us standing there. Most were amputees – single and double. Arm or leg, or both. Many had parts of their bodies shot away, lumps of flesh and bone simply missing as if bitten off by some terrible mythical creature. One poor chap had lost his lower jaw completely. He was in a bad way. A handsome young man once, seemingly cut to pieces from the blast fragments of a shell. Some waved in our direction vaguely, but none of the lads so eager for news moved forwards. They stood petrified, in motionless horror, numbed and shocked to the soul, like me.

Over to the left of the dock were some men who at least were able to walk and shuffle. Many had blindfolds on. At the time I did not know why they were blindfolded. They had on our uniform so they were not wounded enemy. I asked a soldier near me if he knew.

'Gas cases, you thick fucking idiot.'

I reeled at the venom and acidity in his voice but nodded in my new wisdom while my stomach churned. The Germans had used gas in January on a small part of the Front. It seems they were testing a new weapon. Apparently over a hundred had been killed outright and here were another hundred damaged by the gas. Some of the walking wounded were also missing parts of their bodies, but these wounds were less serious. Perhaps they had 'copped a Blighty one' and would see their service over.

Disembarking from deep within the ship continued the limping, endless line of wounded. These fellows seemed much less damaged than those on crutches and stretchers. Some men had bandages and slings, but had no wound at all, save for an empty and faraway expression. Two or three seemed very unsteady on their feet and wobbled almost comically.

Some of the lads here laughed nervously, assuming that they were fooling around, but the orderlies were not laughing. One or two were roughly manhandled onto the waiting lorries, but most were shepherded towards the transport lines. Once more stunned, I felt as if nothing more could shock me, but I was wrong. *Oh my God, was this the war I was going to? Nobody had told us about all of this suffering.*

None of the wounded wanted to talk about anything much. One or two pressed a palm to the ground when they disembarked, touching home soil again. One soldier called across to us. It made me snap back to life again. What he said must have surely been a joke.

'Hey you lucky bastards, all of you. This is all that's left of the Fourths. The others are propping up the wire in Wipers. Hurry up! Get over there to mop up the stragglers, ha ha.'

Surely, he could not have meant that? Every man gone? Every one of his battalion dead all at once? We were told things were quiet and settled and that our attacks were pinning the Germans back, moving them ever closer to their borders again. It must have been a terrible joke.

I had seen enough for now. I had seen what a bomb, a bullet and this new weapon of gas could do. No uniform or protection was adequate for this war and men were being ground down to wet dust by the terrible machines of metal. I doubted we would see a cavalry charge again.

Wherever I turned there were wounded. The field ambulances, carrying officers with injuries every bit as bad as the other men, lined the dock side. War seemed blind to rank. The most senior wounded officer I saw was a major. According to one of the returning men nearby, he had been shot while strangling a German in a trench. He had simply taken too long and become a target and had been hit over the head with a spade and shot, almost at the same time. The German he had strangled was already dead. The major had almost crushed the bones in his neck with the force and fear of the attack.

It turned out that not all the wounded and hospitalised were there because of enemy weapons. Apart from the odd man who had injured himself deliberately to avoid the battle (who would be arrested and shot no doubt), most were struck down by disease and illness. Cholera and typhus had appeared sporadically on all sides, because of the unsanitary conditions of the battlefield. This was new to the military planners and had not been expected. No one had factored in rotting corpses and decaying faeces in shell holes used for drinking water. Field latrines were being bombed, even targeted, spraying foul water into the faces of the infantry cowering nearby. They had not considered trench warfare and if they had, it was temporary shallow trenches without any fresh water cisterns and well-built latrines.

Other diseases and infected wounds were all over the place on the quayside. Even slight wounds could be lethal. One chap had been cut badly digging in. The wound had not been treated and now he was likely to develop lockjaw and die if his arm wasn't amputated. But it was little more than a scratch on the grand scale of the wounds this war inflicted.

So much then for patriotic zeal. I bet none of the nice ladies encouraging other women's sons to join up and fight had been to this place. If they had, they might not be so fervently encouraging enlistment. To be fair, it was not their fault really. It does seem all right to go and fight for freedom, even someone else's. But if these chaps on the quayside were anything to go by, war wasn't the way to solve the problems of a continent.

I turned away and made my way to the assembly area, my hunger now irrelevant. Back up the slope were some ladies offering free comforting tea, from a kiosk. A brigadier in a smart new uniform was taking tea with two other officers in amongst the men. The cakes were most welcome and the brigadier nodded in my direction as I asked to pass by. He looked every bit as scared as the rest of the troops I saw.

Never a smoker in my youth, I learned how to smoke on that quayside in the gentle rain and cold breeze, waiting to embark. Tobacco was a currency, a distraction, a disinfectant and a comfort. I learned the concept of the third light and all manner of other silly superstitions and customs. Third light to me seemed sensible, but some of the others less so. My own superstitions were based on common sense – getting dressed in the same order. That way, nothing ever got forgotten or missed out. If anything was missing, it would break the chain and make me start again from the beginning, even in cold weather in my underthings.

In the early hours of the next day, I was able to take some breakfast. Hot tea was welcome and some decent bread with almost-ripe cheese. That was fair enough, given the volume of chaos and madness on the docks. My unit checked in and we learned that the overnight weather in France and the Channel had been bad and our ship to Belgium was delayed on the other side. It would be a full day before it arrived and then it would have to take its turn at the breakwater before docking alongside the quay. This provided another day to idle away, thinking seriously about the waging of this war.

What if we did not send over a thousand men in full view of the enemy? Or, if we did, what if this did not represent the main attack? What about if we sent over just a few sneaky buggers to create some confusion in the trenches and behind the lines? Ha ha, they would be thinking our assault would look just like all the others, but this time someone had messed about with their kit beforehand. My reckoning went like this. When I had to have a fight, it was better to prepare the ground first. Maybe a bit of good-humoured chatter before, just getting a point across, followed by a few softening-up tactics or the threat of an even bigger chum to come along and help. As a last resort, tie the bugger's laces together.

That would stop him chasing you.

Imagine a battle where the enemy all had their laces tied together. That must be it. Yes, we shell and bomb the supply lines and we send out raiding parties, but these don't get right at the heart of it, right where it hurts. If we could only find a way of doing it, without them finding out.

My notes were made in code for fear of discovery. After all, I had written things like, *leave the trenches and sneak away*, which sounded very cowardly and was liable to get me into trouble. That wasn't what I meant. I spent the boring, wet and bloody cold day refining my thoughts and thinking of a way to get this to the military planners. Surely they must have thought of this idea already? They most likely had and thought it was impossible or fanciful.

Eventually, the time came to embark, two days after arriving in Folkestone. The crossing was vile and the weather appalling. We were all standing in great big pens, crushed to a man, with vomit and any other manner of awfulness sloshing around our putteed legs. The zigzag crossing took hours, but we did finally arrive in port, where we were quickly disembarked to form up in our unit groups on the dockside. The destroyers in the distance were ever watchful for submarines, but we never saw any that day. Perhaps the weather was just too bad.

My unit was always a little less formal than the regular army units. Most of the men in the Engineers by this time were miners, or tradesmen used to the discipline of regular work. The army seemed to encourage this business above the needs of drill and marching. They turned a blind eye to the informality, coarse language and dangling fags of the lads. Salutes were occasionally remembered, although they were usually fumbling and slack efforts.

We were reasonably quickly onto the railway, heading into Belgium, I knew not where exactly. We arrived after about two more days of travelling, even though it could only have been eighty miles or so. An interminable time, full of stops and starts, either because of clogged lines, damage or the need to accommodate the never-ending stream of lorries and trains carrying the wounded. It seemed the best way to win a war wasn't to kill the enemy, but to wound him seriously. The cost in time, lives and resources in managing injuries seemed infinite. It was unbearable to think of the contents of the carriages, but they were imprinted on my mind. Stretcher cases – men with no jaws, testicles, arms or legs – soldiers with damaged limbs, organs and minds.

We were transferred to a small camp of engineers, outside a small town in the Ypres sector, near the safe area of Poperinghe. My first taste of the Western Front was to be Belgium, not France. Although no nearer to Odile here than in Folkestone, I liked to believe that I was. Now that we had arrived, I felt so small and helpless amongst this enormous military machine. Perhaps my ideas were naïve and fanciful after all. Here, in this place, they seemed pointless and impossible, doomed to drown in the mud of the battlefield without seeing the light of day.

March 1915

In Poperinghe, we were let off completely from any notion of army routine. Our sole task was clear. We were to practise mining and excavating techniques and perfect the use of trench galleries and countermining. Countermining was the search for enemy mines and miners doing the same things we were, but in the opposite direction. We practised digging straight and deep with others trying hard to discover us, drilling and practising in the safety of a training ground. Clay-kicking, spade-slicing, dead-hammers – all of it. Very occasionally, a German aeroplane flew overhead and we were allowed on one occasion to take potshots at it. This was normally strictly against the rules, probably in case we shot each other by mistake. We were miners after all, not snipers.

There, I gained a whole new kind of education. All about how to spend money, talk to women, proper mining, cards, drinking, hard work and loyalty to the team and the objectives.

Teams were assigned to excavating, which was done lying on your belly on a flatbed train-truck about three feet square. Others were detailed with the assembly of light narrow-gauge railway tracks, which ran up to the front lines and secretly, beyond and under No Man's Land towards the enemy positions. These tunnels for explosives would work best with the enemy on higher ground. No trudging up under murderous fire, being spied on from above, without every move reported to the gunners. The higher ground meant more earth would have to be moved in the blast, but more damage caused to the enemy. Not every mine would have the luxury of a light railway and many mines were regularly at risk of flooding, so other teams worked on more traditional clay-kicking and picking techniques.

Some teams were detailed with tools and acted as mechanics. They had experience in peacetime of driving trains as engineers on the footplate, not that the mine galleries were that big, of course. They were able to look after the steam pumps and prevent them from over pressuring or running dry, causing explosions in the wrong places. That would be the last thing a soldier wanted. Many were worried about shrapnel shell hits, or shell fragments puncturing the engines at the wrong moment, so some of us designed deflector shields. If only we could have designed some for the troops as well.

My role, accepted with great eagerness, was to be a mobile problem solver. My little team came up with ideas to solve real problems whenever the military identified them. We worked on ways of reducing the noise of excavation; if the enemy heard us, through observation or in their own mining tunnels, it would give our position and intentions away, including the likely timing of any action. Occasionally, it was said, miners met in the middle, causing a frightful fracas and deaths to many, all at once in a tiny confined space. I had not realised that in some excavations, nearly a thousand miners would be working underground on a single dig at the same time.

One problem I was asked to solve was the positioning of charges to maximise damage, but still keeping the battlefield clear enough to fight over. Conventional practice was to load the empty gallery with boxes and boxes of high explosive. This worked well in training in England, but the explosion was brutal, with the outcome uncertain. In any event, it just caused the most enormous crater with steep slopes either side. It was hard to occupy and hard to defend, even with the bewilderment and obliteration of the enemy. I began work on a different approach which, if successful, would take about six months to plan and execute. This would be just in time for any summer offensive action, which was normally expected.

At this time, I accepted a promotion to sergeant, because it meant getting more done as a result of my greater authority. Occasionally, I did spot my unit officers discussing my work in huddles. Usually, after one or two raised eyebrows and more than one or two twitching moustaches, they would nod wisely and move on. Perhaps my ideas were not as stupid as some of them might have looked.

In late March, as the weather slowly relented, we heard the terrible news of a gas attack in the south of our sector, south-east of Ypres. It was clearly another enemy test and caused only a few casualties, but gas was always a spiteful, hateful weapon. One of our team had been working on simple ways to combat gas. We knew that the gas was chlorine and that it worked by turning your lungs into fire as it reacted with water to make hydrochloric acid. We also knew that it was bright green, very visible and heavier than the surrounding air so it sank into holes and trenches. The solution seized upon at that time used the knowledge of one of our team, who was a proper chemist outside of the army. The simple solution was to use a wet handkerchief, one that had been soaked in soldiers' piss. Was that the best he could come up with? We laughed at him all evening. *Do you piss on your own hankie or do you use someone else's? What if you can't manage a piss, do you use someone else's piss? Ha ha!*

But by using piss to soak up the gas, it protected soldiers from the worst of a surprise attack, even if not for very long. He was right and we certainly didn't laugh at him after that.

We moved around quite a bit in those days, in the usual fashion of the army. We were moved slightly north, away from the weakening front line, to prevent our work from being discovered, or us being in range of any shelling. Work had already begun on several exploratory mines locally, to better understand the geology. Various low-lying ridges and hills were chosen as potential targets, the thinking being that we would be advancing and would need to take them soon. We were still thinking movement and not consolidation. I understood that, but it made so many more of our chaps die through inadequate cover and respite. Constant aggression in small chunks was only going to end in more stretcher cases in the Folkestone rain.

We arrived near Langemarck in mid-April 1915. Our task here was to support the consolidation of trench systems for the French colonial troops being stationed there. The soldiers wore French uniforms but they were from a faraway place called Martinique. Their dark skin was fascinating and their French a bit odd to my ear. I was asked to lead the party, as my French was fluent enough and communication was so important. We installed, in about two days, a light railway that brought supplies and ammunition and allowed the troops some extra rations, which was welcomed and certainly needed. It also provided them with some security that they could be relieved and moved without the ever-present gaze of the Germans. They went about reversing the trench they had just taken and were in a happy mood, chatting about cricket and at having troubled the scorers in this war, at last.

On the morning of 22nd April, we were finishing off the rebuilding of the French colonial troops' bombed support trenches and the installation of some new lighter weight water pumps, in the second and third trench lines. For this work, I carried a weapon and hand bombs, just in case of attack. We were finished by about 1630 and chose to rest a little way back from the lines, in a relatively sheltered low ridge. I was pretty much at the front line, which was both exciting and terrifying in equal measure, but when I was there, it was thankfully quiet. The land around was so low-lying and everything we did could be seen and overlooked by the enemy. It was as if they were toying with us and that at the very point of safety, we would be cut down in an act of cynical pleasure. Our boys would do the same in a similar position, most likely. We had heard sporadic gunfire and caught sight of occasional German soldiers through binoculars, which was fascinating. Here I was, William Collins, actually at the very front line. We could go no further, except through the enemy.

Later that day, we heard that the Germans were transporting some strange devices to the front. Our team had been asked, as we were already there, to establish what the equipment was. We all agreed that it was likely to be some corrugated metalwork to reinforce the trenches. We had no idea of the horror that was about to be untethered.

At just after 1730, a cloud of green and grey mist began moving towards our lines from the German side, on the pleasant easterly breeze.

We found out later that the enemy had released over a hundred tons of gas on the poor fellows from Martinique. These men had not heard of the handkerchief-in-piss technique and they broke ranks and fled when the burning gas disabled their comrades so completely. They ran past us in great numbers, shouting, wailing and in total terror. The whole line was now empty and deserted and terror struck me too. I could do nothing alone; the enemy was surely following behind the gas clouds. Certainly, we few could not defend this amount of ground and so we all chose to run as well. The powers-that-be could call for a counter attack from further back. For an hour, the gas hung like a deathly pall over the line at Langemarck, totally undefended. However, the Germans appeared equally afraid of the gas and did not follow it in any great number. The French rallied quickly to shared relief and reoccupied the areas in small groups. A few Canadians were alongside them with me acting as a translator for the few Canadians who didn't speak French.

It was here that I killed my first enemy soldier, having no other choice at the time. When I think of that moment, it is with some shame and, in truth, some relief. He was most certainly intent on killing me, although he did not know me and my life, nor I his.

Running between two positions with my handkerchief-in-piss held to my face, a bald head popped out of a small hole. I shouted a greeting and he replied with a wave and *Hallo!* As I went towards him, he raised the muzzle of an unmistakably German rifle. Terrified, I jumped on him and caught him fully in the face with my knee, somewhat unintentionally. His broken nose was pushed into his brain and he died immediately. I felt the crunch and to my shame, I vomited over the dead man's body in a wave of nausea that I could not help. His left leg shook for a few seconds before I turned away and ran. I had now become a front-line soldier. He was going to kill me, so I could not feel bad for too long, to do so would be corrosive and render me useless to my comrades. It was quick, sudden and necessary. No one around me cared and no one behaved any differently. The regular soldiers just shrugged, told me to *get the fuck on with it*, not even wanting to know. *So you've killed someone, just fuck off, there are a million more you know!* But I had killed someone, a person. My life would be different now. I had taken a father, or a brother, certainly a son. But he had a gun and was going to shoot me, wasn't he? Was he trying to surrender? Would he be feeling this way, if he had killed me?

By nightfall, the line was at least no worse than in the morning. The French and Canadians had made a splendid effort, in small groups, of retaking the abandoned trenches when the gas dissipated. It was only at dusk when the line had settled down that I saw why the French troops had fled. I entered their lines, intending to make notes on the effects of the gas and saw sights that turned me to ice. This was worse than Folkestone – much worse. The dead were in grotesque poses, clearly taken by surprise and many were flopped over the parapet and parados with gaunt and yellow faces contorted into the agonies of a criminal death. *My God! I had not realised that men did not die with their eyes closed.* They stared openly into the distance, the life force gone to a glassy film that would never clear. They had looked up to get a view of the clouds that enveloped them. The gas caused these men's deaths through painful suffocation and very painful irritation to the eyes, throat and lungs. These poor buggers had died of suffocation in minutes – not seconds – agonising, disabling and traumatic for those left unharmed. I can see why they ran. At that moment, I felt no more sorrow for the German I had killed, no sorrow for the death of any German I saw. He had been given a quick and painless death, but here, the death was anything but painless and not all of these poor men were dead. Many were still alive but blinded, choking, clinging on to the light and forever damaged. I remembered the lines of gas cases in Folkestone and supposed that if these poor men lived, they would be part of some sorry homecoming in their country, in Martinique, wherever that was.

Corporal Adams banged me on the arm.

'Fuck me, Sarge. No fucker told me that this went on in Belgium. What kind of bastard soldiering is this? It is no way for a bugger to die. Do we tell their mothers and wives they choked their life out and spat their lungs onto the ground?'

'That's enough, Corp. It is horrible. I have to admit, I've never seen this before. None of us have. Just let's see what we can do if there is a next time. But you are right, I had never imagined anything as horrible as this.'

'At least if you are shot or hit by shrapnel, it is a soldier's death. This, well this, it is a bloody insult.'

I patted Adams gently on the shoulder, and took out my notebook to capture what I could of this terrible scene. In my mind, a man with a bald head popped up with a gun and shot me. I was dead. My mind was reasoning my actions, I could see that. My knee ached where I had caught the enemy soldier in the face. I rubbed my knee until it felt better. It didn't really.

We had to get back to our own positions and left the scene under cover at about 0100. Some sporadic fighting over the unoccupied land took place in the night, but I worked the countryside well and found my way back without engagement. I had little equipment and an empty notebook that I had intended filling with details of the gas attack. The mental images seared on my brain would be quite sufficient and perhaps tomorrow I could write this down, but not tonight. No one was around to hear our story at that time of night, but everyone heard about it afterwards, even if they did so with a slightly bored look. The news of the gas had caused a sensation up and down the Front, mostly about its ability to cause such a rapid break in the line. The Germans were acting illegally according to many on our side. But surely, though, everything was fair game – right? Why would poison gas specifically break the law when beheading with a spade was accepted? No, that seemed slightly nonsensical to me, even after witnessing the contorted death pose of the Martinique warriors.

The battles here gradually increased in intensity, right up and down our lines. We were used more and again in forward positions building, repairing, reversing trenches and out in the saps, excavating and observing. More than once I had to become an infantryman and defend a position – more often than not, taking charge of a position until a regular soldier came alongside who knew the men and had the authority to command them. The faces of the gas-dead kept me focused and unsympathetic now to the enemy.

Then, in early May, we were working on supply lines for the defences at Hill 60. The hill was in the middle of the bulge out of Ypres. Not much of a hill really, more of a big bump in the ground, created from spoil when constructing the railway line. There were plans to mine it properly and to dig suitable preparatory galleries to allow this to happen. We had also alerted every soldier we came across, whenever we could, on ways to behave when gas was around. *Don't run, it makes you breathe harder and makes the gas work faster and deeper in the lungs. Use the piss-handkerchief device, don't laugh, it bloody works so shut up and listen. Stay out of the holes and trench bottoms and remember it dissolves in water, so stay near water, there is always plenty around. Don't drink the water that gas has been in, even if you boil it, don't forget. Get your wounded up and away quickly, stretcher cases moved on, off the ground.*

We set about making simple pad respirators and taught some local nurses and some Belgian citizens how to make them. We used muslin, gauze, bits of flannel and even some cut up uniforms from the wounded – there was plenty around. We used string ties to attach them and told everyone to drink plenty of water to allow enough piss to flow for the respirators. When we explained, using the words of our chemist, no one laughed anymore. We got the pads issued with the ration parties and we were now quite well prepared for the assault, which intelligence from captured enemy soldiers told us was coming. And we stopped the issue of the useless respirators from England. They were ineffective when dry and suffocating when wet – air would not pass through them as they waterlogged. So, we redoubled efforts to come up with a design, however odd, to help us survive a frontal gas attack. We knew a better full-head flannel mask was coming, but it would not be here in time for the German attack. That attack came on 5th May.

Odile,

I look into your eyes and realize this is where I want to be. There will be nothing in the future, I am sure, that can take us away from each other, nothing that can break our bonds of love. This is my hope. I do hope that you feel the same about me, or this may be a wasted heart, walking the halls of life empty, cold and shrouded in a great darkened cloak.

23 December 1913

CHAPTER SIX - AN ATTACK

I wasn't present when the attack started. We had finished our ground works on Hill 60 and had retreated towards Poperinghe for some temporary rest, which we had collectively earned. We had a reputation now as a mobile support, advice and problem-solving unit. Our numbers had grown steadily greater, as had our expertise. We were due to complete some earthworks at Hill 60 when the terrible gas canisters were opened again. The gas attack here was brutal and sudden. Nearly a hundred British were gassed to death, before they could take any action. There were over two-hundred other gas casualties as well. Those that made it to the dressing stations were in a bad way and there was not much that could be done. Almost half of those eventually, and mercifully, died.

The German attack was partly successful, but they too were held back by the gas pooling and lingering, a major drawback of this dreadful weapon of outrage. Without our help, there may have been more killed and hopefully we saved some lives that day. We returned the following day to look at the effects of gas, but I could not stay long. I had seen these faces before. Even with the pad respirators, casualties came quickly and with such destruction to the human body.

For me, the rest of May was spent working up and down the Ypres area, supporting mining operations and fixing machinery that was broken. I was occasionally able to return to the problem of massive mines and talked with my team about a way of doing less digging and more accurate targeting. I think that they were impressed.

We all sat down with strong army tea. One thing in our war that had to be good was the tea. The army tolerated many lapses in discipline, protocol and etiquette from us, but also knew that hot food and good tea meant we worked better and thought faster on our feet.

'Paddy' Paddock was a miner before the war. In fact, he was a mine supervisor in the North East. Coal in his blood and dust in his lungs.

Hugely fit, despite his coal dust cough and twenty-a-day. He wore small, circular spectacles that weren't made for him and squinted at everything. 'Fixer' Cowling was a gentleman railwayman. He had built railways and cuttings throughout Europe and had been to Canada. His speciality was blasting – he was a problem solver like me. 'Digger' Butler was a miner as well. He was a foot slogger, digging and blasting and liked nothing more than chipping away underground where he felt safe and at home. My pitch was prepared and the conversation started hopefully.

'How about if we dig a gallery straight at the enemy, but when we are about halfway, we create a hub and dig off to various key points in the line. At each terminus we place a smaller charge and then track the charge along the trench, so we only blow the trenches and dugouts, and don't create a bloody great crater. We time this for when the artillery barrage ceases, give the enemy time to emerge – which they do – then we set off the mine. At the same time, our chaps jump off and get to the trenches as the dust settles. What do you think?'

'Fuck off,' said Paddy. 'We would be digging all those silly side shoots to a main gallery not just up to, but along the fucking trench. They will most definitely hear us and reverse towards us. No, it's mad. I like the concept of a clean blast, you know that, but it's just too bloody risky.'

Fixer thought for a moment, drew his pipe out of his mouth and held forth.

'Now hang on Pad. The hub galleries would be smaller and they won't be listening under their feet in the trench, there is always plenty of noise right in there. It seems to me the first gallery is the most dangerous because they will be listening for the direct routes at the hill or whatever we select as the decoy objective.'

I liked that thought and nodded in agreement. Digger poked the ground with a stick, smiled and added his contribution.

'Sorry, Paddy, I'm with these two fools. It is an excellent idea and will be a surprise to them. They won't be thinking about a gallery along their lines. There will already be a lot of noise and stuff going on. We just need to be careful of any dugouts they've made. We can normally feel where they have dug and we can listen ourselves. We should give it a try.'

Fixer looked at me and slowly drew himself up on his elbows.

'You come up with this idea yourself Will?'

'Well I just wondered how much easier it would be to only blow up what we needed to, not create a massive hole we can't defend.'

'Well it's a neat idea Will. Better than anything these two Herberts have managed to come up with.'

We all chuckled at Fixer. Paddy poked Digger with a stick to focus his attention.

'Digger, how wide would a gallery have to be right under a trench to be able to blow it up, quite shallow, full width?'

'Well, if you were as bloody mad as Collins there, you would only need to be as wide as spread elbows, enough to kick or pick and wide enough to drop explosive boxes along the length. It probably won't make that much noise.'

Paddy thought again. 'Alright you fools, I'm convinced it is worth a try. What we have to do now is get the infantry to work with us properly. Not take the piss and muck about with our equipment. A proper tunnelling operation.'

Paddy was right. The problem we really faced was with the army themselves. They were bold and brave in using soldiers' lives in familiar fashions, but cautious and suspicious with engineering. They knew clever tactics and new ways of doing things were right, but getting a plan agreed could be torture. Our captain was great at the politics of planning and – given that we were viewed as an unusual bunch – communication with the army brass was never according to convention and protocol.

But, later in May, our plan was grudgingly approved and work begun. The digging of the main gallery was technically easy and quick, but the trick was keeping quiet and out of sight of the Germans, who saw everything. We disguised our engines and the machinery used to dig and remove the spoil. The tunnel made progress and we soon reached the point of moving off into eleven separate hubs. This presented more of a challenge, keeping eleven smaller hubs running at the same time, but using hubs possibly reduced the risk of discovery and would help us to plant very precise charges into the terminus for blasting. It was good to work with Paddy, calculating the amount of charge and the timing of the blasts. I kept up the pressure on the artillery to shell the gallery positions from above to prevent any possibility of discovery through listening posts. Shelling can deafen a listening sapper and would allow enough confusion to miss the telltale rhythmical sounds of mining, the scraping, the occasional echo of voices and the noise of any mishaps or collapses, which sometimes happened.

Over the coming weeks, the work progressed very well. I was on site regularly and in other areas working on trench reinforcement. Occasionally, I got caught up in the trench raids, but was lucky enough to escape unscathed.

Fixer and I seemed to work on the same things at the same time. Paddy and Digger came and went, where the need arose. It was a familiar position of changing faces and short relationships, but Fixer was always there when I turned around.

'Will?'

'Yes, Fixer. Now what do you want me to sort out for you, you useless bastard?'

'Ha. Nothing. It's you I'm talking about. You were there for that bloody gas attack, with those French boys, right? I know it got to you, I can see it in your face and see it in your work. You are like a ticking clock, the mechanism is working smoothly, but there isn't the drama that goes with it. It's the same old routine. Do you follow?'

'Suppose so. It's just I didn't get the chance to work it out and truly realise that we are here to kill. An enemy popped up on me. I killed him, but not in a way you would recognise, just falling on him and smashing his nose into his brain, by accident. The crunch went right through my body. I carry his soul on my shoulder and did not ask for it.'

'Will, if you had not reacted, you would be dead.'

'Yes, I know. Every shell is shot at me in anger. I would kill willingly now, if only to protect my comrades. It's just that no one prepares you for that. Somewhere in Bavaria or Prussia or in the country, is a widow or mother, who has no idea that her husband or son is dead and I did that.'

'Will, twenty-thousand a week is the casualty rate. Do you think it makes one bit of difference?'

'Well it fucking does to me. I want to think of my girl and my home, not of this stinking fucking foulness. I will do whatever is asked of me to get back to a normal life.'

'Hang on to the thoughts of your girl. French isn't she, how did you manage that you lucky bastard?'

I smiled but did not answer, not being really that sure myself. Odile was probably in a camp somewhere – not at all happy. At least in England, everyone was at home.

'Look Will. Let this bloody German go. He is dead, that is it. If you survive, you will have to kill again. Imagine if he was one of the soldiers who opened the gas canisters on those poor French lads. How does that make you feel?'

I picked up a small stone and threw it idly at the wall, 'No better Fixer, no better at all.'

'Mind you, I will be glad to get through this without killing anyone, you know, one-on-one. Killing with the mines is different, it is quick on the enemy, isn't it?'

'Perhaps we should ask them, Fixer.'

June 1915

June brought a welcome warm spell, even if it rained a bit. I was ordered once again into a forward position, checking some calculations on the mining operations and setting up a countermining listening post. The enemy launched a lightning raid on our positions, which they often did, so it was not unexpected. I was armed since even miners were targets for enemy bayonets as we were seen as particularly vicious killers. I was cut off in a section of trench, as the enemy overran the position for about two days. Our infantry were well equipped and confident that a counter attack would take back the occupied line. I with some Scottish soldiers, called the 'devils in skirts' by the Germans. These Highlanders were tough talking and hard drinking, but fearless and professional, with good officers who were courageous, brave and not wasteful with their soldiers' lives. I had arrived in their position and ended up helping out with their trench repairs under fire. They had occupied what were originally German positions, but everything was, of course, back to front. They had made a pretty good effort on reversing sandbags, but the dugouts were lethal, because grenades and minnies could land and go straight inside now they faced the enemy. Also, the positions were designed for defence and so it was difficult to observe and move in and out of the trenches without causing a commotion, especially rapidly during the planned attack they wanted to make. However, our hand was forced when the Germans attempted a counter attack. The bags provided some cover, but not nearly enough to properly defend a position.

About 2100, as the light began to weaken before dusk, the Scots stood-to as usual, especially alert in a newly captured position watching for the enemy, as dusk and dawn are the best times to attack. The traditional grumbling and setting of soldiers in place took just a minute to complete in this precarious position. They were up on the trench reverse wall watching for German movement. The Germans in this part of the trench preferred little or no preliminary bombardment, they quite liked surprise, especially as the trenches here were only about one-hundred-and-twenty yards apart at the narrowest point and had been theirs until very recently. The Scots knew 'Auld Fritz' wanted the position back and could be upon you in less than a minute.

The Germans attacked at just after half past the hour. About four-hundred Feldgrau uniforms descended upon the trench carrying stick bombs, trench spades and bayonets, which these soldiers held in their hands. They didn't carry rifles as they were expecting hand-to-hand fighting and a rifle was just a stick with little force once the chamber was empty of its single shot. It was terrifying to see them launch from above, despite rapid fire from the Scots guns felling tens of them in the dash across the gap. Unprepared for this type of fighting, I arrived in the forward trench as three Germans landed over the parapet. I shot the first one full in the face with a revolver and he fell. Unfortunately, this blocked the way past for any soldier and provided an obstacle that took time and attention to negotiate. One of the Scots saw this, brought a spade down on the dying man, cut his arm off and cleaved the torso so that it fell away in two pieces to the bottom of the trench. The second horrified German, no doubt a comrade of the first, stood motionless and received a blow to the face from the barrel of my pistol. He fell forwards, unconscious, and was bayoneted to make sure he would not get up. The third received a fearsome country haymaker from a bayonet-wielding Scot that broke his jaw. The German fell forwards, now unconscious, but in doing so plunged his own bayonet into his assailant's chest. It went deep into the lungs and the Scot died, pinned to the parapet wall by the bayonet. In less than fifteen seconds the episode was over. The German with the broken jaw most likely drowned in the water at the bottom of the trench, kept there in summer in case of gas. I did not have time to check or linger as there were other German voices around the corner and I had to move on. I had to force myself to move, or the paralysis of thought would have taken me over and left me as a static target. At any point, a death blow could come to me unseen, perhaps from above. I had to do my best for the sake of my comrades all around. We had to depend completely upon each other. I expected a German to emerge from every turn of the trench and was ready to strike, the tension was so high and my sinews stretched to the limit. I needed to keep thinking and not get confused and lost when the trenches branched. After all, I was in a captured German trench and the support trenches would lead back to German lines, not British. There were signs saying 'Berlin this way' to help, but in the battle, bombs dislodged the signs and it was easy to become lethally confused.

'You, ye bloody English engineer. Not that fecking way.'

'Shit, where?'

'There, left. Follow me and keep your stupid head down.'

We made three full turns before coming upon other enemy soldiers. I moved over two dead Scots, both of whom were entwined with two dead Germans. In both cases, blades had been plunged into hearts at almost the same time. Further on were three dead Germans. One had obviously slipped and broken his neck and two had tried to help him and been shot cleanly at point blank range. I passed a severed, but still bleeding, arm and a pile of spilled guts and organs, still pulsating gently and glistening in the wetness of amateur traumatic surgery. At the next corner I saw a German edging backwards. My reloaded pistol was brought to shoulder height and I fired at his body, hit his right arm and he spun around. To my horror, he had a stolen British service revolver. Luckily, he could not fire it properly. He squeezed the trigger and it bucked violently from his grasp. A sound of tearing newspaper in my ear meant the bullet had passed close but missed. I fired again straight at him. He was now probably unarmed but this was no time for compassion. As I fired, there was a sharp pain in my lower back, but I could still move. Nothing serious, probably a fragment of something whizzing in the air. Some blood, but it could be managed and I would be able to carry on. The enemy were dead. Was I supposed to keep count? Was it three? What would be the right number for my duty?

'This way, fella. Mind your head on the plank there!'

'Right, I see it. I will go left and you stay right. You will get round the corner first and I will cover you with the pistol.'

By staying left, I hoped to cover my comrade's movements.

I rounded the next corner past other dead soldiers from both sides and two wounded Scots. I could not stop to help right now but remembered where they were and planned to come back for them. At the next turn, fighting was still going on in a mad tangle of bloody limbs and debris. The Germans had poured in here in great numbers. I was in the middle of it now. About a dozen bodies were engaged in hand-to-hand scuffling. Punches being thrown – a battle of muscle not metal. Grunting and struggling for life, to live and not be the one to be killed. There was a strong smell of sour sweat and it was into this that I plunged. I wasn't necessarily large, but had lugged my fair share of engine parts and was quite strong. I shot a German in the back and semi-bayoneted another with a rifle I picked up from the trench, the injury causing him to break off his attack and instinctively grab his wound. He was killed by another bayonet through his chest. I received a heavy blow from behind that was doubly painful as my new wound was located in the same area. As I ducked in pain, a Scot reached over me and shot the German who had landed behind me. Alarmingly, a German bomb dropped right in front of me and I expected nothing but death in a bright flash, but then noticed it was not live, it had simply fallen off a German's equipment belt. A splatter of bloody tissue landed full in my face, causing me to recoil backwards as I leaned down to use the bomb on the enemy. The air was warm and sticky and smelled of sweet treacle for an instant and an abattoir the next. It was from a Scot, killed by a German spade attack. The spade was rammed into his face and pulled out with a twisting motion. It seemed the Germans here preferred a spade to rifle or bayonet as an effective close-combat weapon. Two Scots, thinking I was wounded but alive, grabbed me by the arm and dragged me roughly around the corner I had just come from. The stretcher bearer and medic immediately gave me the highest priority. They assumed my protests were shock and they told me that flesh and brains were hanging off me. I needed to go to the dressing station, yes – but I was not the priority they thought.

'Shut up. The shock is making you panic. Stay calm, you are done fighting.'

'Look, I'm fine. It isn't my blood. See, it wipes away.'

The initial attack had now been repelled and the Scots had dug in according to my instructions, but it was tense. The remaining living Germans had escaped with two Scottish prisoners and some equipment as a souvenir. At the dressing station, I was finally able to confirm the brain and lung splatters on my face were not mine and the deep cut to my back was dealt with quickly. It was not too disabling and the dressing could be attended to at my own unit. I spent the night with the Scots in the forward trench, as there was nowhere else to go and it was impossible to move quickly with a fresh wound. To leave now would be suicidal, as all of the trench positions were still being consolidated and no one was sure if any section was held by friendly or enemy forces. We assumed we were cut off for now and would have to wait until a relief was possible. During the sleepless night, it was difficult to rest on my wound so I took out the tiny picture of my love and thought of Odile and her family, and guessed in which direction they would be from here. Slightly south and east, most likely. I did not know if they had been evacuated, captured, killed in crossfire or if they had been able to stay.

In the morning, very early, the Germans came again. My back had stiffened and the human tissue soaked into my clothes had dried and caked on my skin. It made me feel awful and sick, but I had to go to it again. Fight or die, simple as that. And I was not ready to die whilst Odile was in danger.

The first German appeared over the parapet a little before five. He was young and ruddy faced, breathless from the sprint over the short distance. He had received a light wound from a bullet fragment in his leg and it was bothering him, which proved to be a fatal distraction. I shot him and hit him in the throat. He was dead as he hit the trench. There was no longer any feeling of remorse as they were intent on killing, there was no doubt at all. This was active brutality on a massive scale, across the whole of the line.

The next appeared terrifyingly close. A Scot on my right bayoneted him as he fell into the trench. Unfortunately, the bayonet went through him along with half the barrel up to the stock. He had to leave the rifle impaled and fight with a spade dropped in the trench by a dead German. During the previous night of consolidation, the Scots had put the German dead over the parapet to deter another attack and to provide a grisly, morale-sapping obstacle to another assault. This successfully hampered the attack and many were killed and wounded just short of the trench itself. There had not been time to install all of the wire, as the trench was newly captured and of course the wrong way round. That was why they could get to us so quickly. The air was filled with groans in German from the wounded and dying. Despite waiting expectantly for more Germans to appear over the top, no more came. I was wound up like a spinning top, anyone could come for me now. Feeling like a wild animal inside, I would kick and spit and defend my life with all my strength. They would not take my life. But still none came and my tension subsided slowly. That was the most frightening part, the constant and expectant waiting.

Along the trench, some Germans had made it across, but too few to take back the ground successfully. Around a hundred Germans had attacked a section of trench held by three-hundred. The soldiers that made it into the trench took many lives, but none this time were allowed to return. There were Germans with bayonets through the skull and one fully decapitated. The head, minus the helmet, was thrown back towards the Germans as it was a ghastly medieval sight to look at in the trench. Still, for now, I was isolated in this position, unable to get back to the road because the enemy were still probing the lines on either side. I would be an infantry soldier and had better get used to it.

Then, joyfully, there was shouting in English from behind and Scots voices responding. We were going to be relieved, if not rescued. A path back to the road was finally secured around 1500 by the Engineers and some of the brave, fearless Scots. I made my way back to my unit unhampered, apart from a still sore and slightly bleeding back.

That evening after my dressing had been changed, I thought again about how we could wage this war more intelligently. I had seen up close, again, the stupidity of charging at trenches, time after time – the enemy tactics differing very little from our own. We could do this differently and better, if only the army could be made to listen. What I needed was the opportunity to test this out for real.

By the end of July, the shallow mine gallery was almost complete. We had all calculated the charges that would demolish the trenches, but not create an enormous crater that would be undefendable. We had the opportunity to test out a very small-scale trench in mid-July in our secret location in Poperinghe. The mine charges, small but well-placed, went off in sequence. Each caused the trench to collapse, but none created the traditional massive crater that marked the explosive detonation point.

Fixer was very pleased with the result.

'Blown it up, brilliant isn't it?'

'Yes Fixer. A very professional and targeted detonation.'

'I reckon we could blow up the Houses of Parliament, and not a single block would fall in the Thames, ha ha!'

'That has been tried before, although admittedly it would have been a big explosion.'

'You know, William old boy, we have got it. This is the way to do it. We can press on with the hubs now. Can Adams there get a photograph for the brass?'

'Yes, just give me a minute.'

'A nice big one we can shove right up their bloody noses!'

We received very reluctant authority – even with the photographic evidence – to complete the mine works and to prepare, but not detonate, the larger full-test rig. We had also received warm, if not enthusiastic, permission to detonate the real thing to coincide with a push at the end of

August, if this test proved successful. That would be perfect, if the weather held. The infantry officers were ready for it, but the more senior staff were apparently unsure that it would do enough damage to the trench works. We knew we had done our arithmetic and we had it right.

Paddy and I went to conduct the bigger test and we thought we needed about an ounce of explosive for every hundredweight of earth to be moved. We only had to disturb the earth to cause confusion – as long as it all went up at once. The difference with our technique over mines was that one big explosion obliterates and destroys. Our method should kill all the living creatures above, but the earth would settle in such a way as to allow the navigation of our troops over less disturbed and more level terrain.

Fixer had mapped out the whole area, down to the finest detail. He explained how he calculated distances underground to link up with the surface. He was uncannily accurate. It was about estimating speed and taking measurements accurately with the occasional plumb line. Anyway, he reckoned he had the galleries right at the trench line. All we now had to do was to link them up and extend the digging along the forward enemy trenches. We had authority for three-thousand yards of destruction, but we settled on one mile, as we felt the troops could take and defend this break in the line. The site we chose in May was just south-east of Ypres, where we had spent most of our time. We were looking at straightening out the line a bit. Now it was nearly complete, we were confident that we could pull this off.

'Paddy, Fixer. We have this right. We can take out a mile of line and allow the infantry to push through. Perhaps if not level enough for the cavalry, level enough for occupation – quick and clever.'

'Yes, with you there Will, we'll make a fine mess of them.'

'We must make sure,' Paddy's voiced noticeably quietened, 'that we have the trenches full of enemy for this to work. We won't be in a position to destroy all deep digging with this type of mine. We will get them if they are unprotected.'

Fixer held up a calming hand, 'That's one for the infantry to sort. We've fixed our side of the bargain. Is there any tea?'

Fixer went off to ensure the infantry knew their job, Paddy was taken off the mining work in the final week to make sure the explosives were correctly laid. Some lads from the new mining corps proper were with us, Aussies, Kiwis and Canadians along with the British, as they had taken an interest in our methods. We were now doing the same type of work, only a bit more secretly. They were good honest chaps, but were more diggers than planners and so Paddy had to make sure they understood the idea of smaller placed charges. Together, we made a dangerous team. They could quickly dig big galleries – we saw them do it. They were hard men, they wanted a big bang and they would soon enough get one.

We worked day and night, as long as we could keep the opening of the mine covered, we were alright. The small trains and tracks were visible to the enemy, but since the trains were running day and night anyway and were regularly shelled and repaired, it did not seem to make too much of a noticeable difference. Certainly, we did not see any extra attention given to our work. The little trains pulled and pushed all the time and the smoke was no more than a normal trench under some shellfire.

We were visited by Major Norton-Griffiths at the end of July. He had successfully laid and set off the big mines on Hill 60 earlier in April. Despite my initial misgivings that he might be a bit put out by our work because the plans had not gone through him, he was impressed with Digger and Paddy. He was less enthusiastic about our mechanised pumps, considering them dangerous as they could blow up in your face or else attract unwanted shelling through smoke and fumes. However, I showed him the little device, which Paddy said was a dispersal plate that broke up the smoke so it looked no different to the other smoky fumes around an active front line. He seemed to like the cleverness and our inventive style of mining. I wondered what he would think about our shallow mine attack.

Fixer spent the final afternoon in the tunnel with Paddy, supervising the removal of the tracks and sleepers. It would have been easier to leave them and bury them, but it was useful to have them and meant we did not have to transport everything at once, or get fresh supplies of this narrow gauge. I took one last look at the terminus line and thought in all honesty it did not look enough to cause the destruction we wanted. The explosive we used was ammonal, a standard army mine explosive, but I had mixed it with some boiled horse fat to make it stack a little easier and be shaped to blow upwards in a fan shape, rather than straight up in a mushroom or dome. Some of the stacking work was done by a couple of brilliant, funny Welsh miners, who did not behave at all like soldiers and had no interest in military matters. They worked hard and then moved on to the next action, grumbling, cursing and drinking all the rum.

'Well, Fixer. This is it. Shit or bust as my father would say.'

'It will be shit, but not for us. Come on let's get out of this fucking trench. I'm not up for a knife fight tonight.'

The mine was set and ready early in the August of 1915. We had planned the explosion with the artillery gunners and the infantry officers together. They knew what we needed of them and they knew what kind of mine we had dug. I did not have the authority of rank to take part in these meetings and that annoyed me, because these were my ideas and I bloody hoped they knew what we had proposed. Perhaps it was necessary to move up in the army to get some of these ideas put into practice. I know though, that our officers came back with big smiles, and what seemed a new way of fighting trench battles was now going to happen for real. This was excellent news. Fixer and I shared some tea and we thought once more of where we had come from.

'Fixer, we have built a mine that is going to kill a few hundred soldiers all at once. I know it means our boys will be safer, but it's getting to me a bit.'

'Well it would. It is your idea and a bloody good one. Good ideas in this war are hard to come by and good ones mean more dead for the enemy to look at. Might make the buggers want to go home for good, curse them.'

'Maybe, but I can't help it. It is making me uneasy.'

'It isn't your nature to kill, clearly. But nor is it in the nature of everyone else here. All these lads came here to do this unspeakable thing and they feel like you. Come on Collins, get on with it. You are a soldier now and they won't hesitate to kill you, remember that. Better be a killer and live, than be a thinker and have all eternity to ponder your inaction. Don't bloody forget, this is a fucking war. Death is what we have to do and be damned for it.'

'No Fixer, I could not possibly forget.'

Ordinarily, for an attack, we would send over a massive bombardment right into the front-line trenches. The idea was to soften up the enemy sentries and soldiers, force them into their dugouts and cut the wire in front of the trenches. Raiding parties and wire-cutting parties went out into No Man's Land to clear paths for infantry and to check the wire. It seemed to me these paths just forced large numbers of soldiers together, making shooting and bombing them easier. When the Germans had attacked me before, they came from all directions, making it quite hard to defend yourself.

The bombardment would stop and soldiers would climb out and run across. It was hoped that positions would be destroyed and that we could get across before the Germans could set up the machine guns. It sometimes worked, but mostly it did not and many casualties were suffered. This plan was better.

The big mine at Hill 60 created a massively deep crater, as well as other holes which took the top off the hill. It made a soft and earthy sloppy mound to attack, which was then difficult to defend. It utterly shocked the Germans, but they were able to counter attack as well, once they could regroup and recover.

Our plan was quite different. Although it was, in the bigger scheme of things, quite a small enterprise, it would show off some new ways of taking a trench. We would not have a bombardment at all and that worried the infantry – we wanted the enemy up in their trenches for this to work properly. Sounds odd, but we were going to blow just the trench line. It would be risky if mines did not go off, or if we had not set enough explosive, but it was still going to be better than ordinary trench assaults.

We would get the infantry to cause a commotion on our side, making it look like an attack was imminent, or at least a bit of action worthy of observation and standing-to. The artillery would throw over a few shells to make it look like an ordinary attack was coming and create a bit more confusion. But then the mine would go off under their feet, our boys would wait for the initial blast to settle for just a few seconds and then go. If all went to plan, the mines would have destroyed surface trench lines that were manned, and taken out support trenches – if our digging calculations were correct. The artillery would then take out the second and third positions, keeping them pinned down until our men had properly taken the position. Some tunnels had extended to these positions further back, but our maps of those enemy trenches were not accurate enough to dig a gallery forwards and set mine traps – although that was an idea for another time.

Once we had taken the position, it could be quickly turned into a British defensive position and held. We did not think it would be a decisive battle, because the scale was so small, but it would prove that this way of rapid mine advance could work. Maybe on a larger scale the works would be too visible and too noisy and take too long, but I wanted to see if this could at least be tried successfully.

The date for the action was set for 15th August and the mines would go off at 0515. The odd time might add to the surprise, especially if we could encourage more soldiers into the line from the dugouts, with amateurish preparations and as Fixer put it, 'Sloppy hullabaloo'.

Paddy and Digger wanted to be part of the action but their request was refused as they would be needed in case the mine detonation failed or was delayed. They protested that the galleries were sealed and nothing could be done by that time, but to no avail. As an enlisted soldier, even as an engineer, I was allowed in the line and wanted to make sure the infantry went at the right time. I was assigned to Captain McManus of the Camerons – who had once been a mining supervisor – he had been taken out of the line specifically for this action. As an officer, he could order the men in ways that I, as a non-commissioned officer, could not.

We agreed to start making some noise at 0415, building up the commotion gradually, with sounds of preparations and the clumsy movement of equipment, voices in unguarded calls. We would send over a couple of mortars and light up the terrain briefly. This was high risk, but I was sure this could be done and McManus had agreed, liking the idea of a punch on the nose for the enemy.

Unusually, the infantry were informed of a mine-led attack. This was done to help calm nerves, as they would then know it was less likely that machine gun fire would appear as they attacked. Also, a mine detonating so close can upset the attacker, who may also be surprised, and this needed to be avoided. The shock and surprise must be only to the enemy, not to us.

The infantry formed up into positions just before 0400. We had ensured all connections were sound and the explosive dry enough. Ammonal is made from TNT and ammonium nitrate, with a bit of aluminium added – it was quite soft when we got it and liable to water damage. The detonating charges had to be placed a little way down the tunnels. We hoped the detonating process was going to work – and not kill any of the detonating team.

The wait was always the worst part. We checked that the Germans were not preparing an attack themselves, nor sending over raiding parties, which would disturb our preparations or even ruin the surprise. There was a wire party out there from the enemy and we needed to let this party escape back to their trenches, to keep our intentions secret. We made sure they already knew who was on the other side of the trenches from them and left them in no doubt that something was going on, if not exactly what it was. This gave us an advantage because no one would attack with this little surprise waiting in the wings.

We all shook hands and made our traditional farewells – Paddy with his typically direct 'Fuck off then'. I took my place next to Captain McManus and retrieved my note from my tunic. It had the timings and plans, including a contingency. I had used a rudimentary code, which was essentially slang words and inferences, rather than exact detail. We did not expect any telephone communications and runners would be too slow and prone to being shot. We trusted to our plans and the skills of our mining team.

Towards 0500, we started to make more intense, coordinated and planned noises in the trench. Clattering bayonets and indiscreet calls of the type normally used to prepare for an attack could be heard along the mile line. The Germans initially appeared to be confused, from the observations we could make. This was good. The occasional head was seen above their lines and our snipers were instructed not to shoot this time. We wanted reports from the Germans to their officers when they popped their heads back down, to suggest an attack by us was imminent. That would ensure as many of their infantry in the line as possible. This part of Ypres had been mined before, but we wanted to make this look like anything but a mine going off.

At 0505, I knew that the detonating team were in position and ready via their traditional 'Course we're bloody ready, now bugger off and worry about your job'. I just hoped they would get the timings right and all get out safely. It was a dangerous process setting off ammonal – especially strings of smaller charges all at the same time.

At 0510, I took several deep breaths and made sure my kit was ready. Although going along as communications support for the infantry, I would be needed as a soldier in the line again, fighting alongside the fellows in the trenches. I loaded my rifle magazine. Ten rounds and ten spare. That would be enough, as fighting would be hand-to-hand in quick time. I took a standard army knife and another, modified to be shorter and narrower. I double checked my kit and my small number of bombs, checked my watch and looked up. Now I was ready as well.

At 0514 on my watch the detonations began. The trench in front erupted, followed by eruptions to the right and left, in rapid succession, in sequence. The trench line collapsed in dusty heaps and earth and bodies were flung into the air. The screams endured for a full fifteen seconds. It was as if a great burrowing animal was sliding along the trench, gnawing and biting as it went. The explosions continued, followed by explosions in the rear trenches where the support was located. The chain continued and it was clear that the Germans were in terrible order and in utter chaos. It must have been quite thin being an infantryman in the German trenches.

At once some of our men leapt up to go over but were pulled back. We needed to wait a few seconds, in case of an unexploded mine. After fifteen seconds, they have either blown or aren't going to. The tension was incredible. Fifteen seconds would still protect the surprise. Hold on everyone.

Then McManus shouted 'Go!' and everyone poured over. No whistles and no repeat of the order. It was an amazing sight, seeing all of the troops barrel over the ladders in ranks. We heard no return gunfire, but it was clear not everyone was dead. A couple of Germans had lived through the inferno, but it was only a couple. We reached the detonation site to see a complete mess of trench workings. Wire was gone, parapet and parados blown, with the ground sunken, but all in all, not too badly churned. It was at least territory you could fight over and defend. The infantry set up temporary gun emplacements, mortars and forward observation points from the new positions facing the enemy.

Within five minutes, the whole line was taken all along the mile stretch. At each flank, machine gun points were set up and we had chosen the end points carefully to be on rising ground with a view down on the untaken trenches, which were now to the side or slightly behind. We had taken the position and were defending it. Inside half an hour we had enough troops in the German line to hold and consolidate with no sign of a counter attack as the support trenches had also been levelled. We had taken only four casualties, none seriously wounded, and we had encountered only five Germans left alive.

The living enemy were horribly shocked. I asked that the two least wounded be taken back to our team for interrogation. I wanted to know what it felt like to be in the middle of that appalling mining attack.

When we returned to our unit with the prisoners, we celebrated with a little rum and a tot of Captain McManus' whisky from Islay. The two prisoners before us were in poor shape. They were members of a Guards division and were professional soldiers. We felt no anger or malice when we were face to face, but would not have hesitated to cleave them had we met them armed in the trenches. I still looked on them all now as gas canister openers, or killers of the Scots, so was less inclined to be with them.

But Fixer was on them as soon as they were sat down and looked at the first. He seemed dazed, so Fixer left him for now. The other seemed shocked, but stable.

'You speak English, mate?'

'Ja, Kamerad, I can speak a little English. Are you going to kill me?'

'Do you want to be treated like a soldier?'

'Ja sir, like a soldier.'

'Well you will be. No killing. Do you smoke?'

'Nein, I do not like the smell.'

'What is your name?'

'I am Thomas Moller. Guards Division. I am from Munich, but my family moved to Allerau when I was a boy.'

'Describe what happened to you in the trench.'

'My Gott, it was the horrible thing for me. We were in the line, waiting for you to attack. We thought you all er amateur soldier because of all the noise and shouting. We were loading our guns laughing because we were going to be able to pick off the boys against men, like a training time. You amateur English we all said. Then, my Gott, my Gott, the explosion was terrible.'

Moller put his head down, placed both palms on his face and slid them up and over his hair. He was young and clearly shocked.

'Go on Moller. The explosion.'

'Ja, the ground turned to, er, like water. It was a hell coughed up to the surface. Fire and hot air blasting upwards. Under my feet was like I was in the air with smoking and fire as the cloud. My Kamerad was torn to pieces and I saw his arm and head come away in the air. Oh Gott. We had bodies buried near to the line, waiting to be taken away and these were exploded also. Pieces of old body falling all around. My Gott, what did you do? I was trying to think what was up and what was down and you were up and over me. My whole body is hot, like I have been sat in an oven and left there to burn.'

Thomas was about twenty and slim. He looked like he was a good soldier. I could imagine him, side by side with us, joking and laughing. He was no different to us and I did not wish him to be hit in the face by my knee. He smelled strongly of burnt flesh, his hair was burnt and his scalp blackened.

The second soldier remained dazed and incoherent. Perhaps he was wounded with a blow to the head. He began to shake uncontrollably and to froth at the mouth. Fixer thought it was initially an act, perhaps to try to escape. Thomas told him that the soldier's name was Kroll and that he was a reliable and noble soldier, not prone to strange behaviour. The shaking got worse and we resolved to have him removed to the casualty station, where the orderlies were instructed to take care of him. Thomas was escorted to the prisoner area where Fixer went to him again but found out nothing further.

'Herr Cowling, you have not asked about my unit or our movement. Why is this?'

Fixer Cowling studied him before replying. 'Thomas, I care only about the mine. You have told me everything that I need. Here are two packets of cigarettes. Use them to trade for things that you want. I wish you well, you don't look like an enemy to me.' Fixer stood up.

'Right, get this soldier out of our trench.'

The reserves came up to reinforce the line and the position was officially declared as taken by communication to Brigade HQ at 0630. We had done it. Captain McManus in the following weeks was awarded a bar to his Military Cross for his actions that day. He knew his craft and he liked our ideas, executing them with a skill to admire. But there was more in my head still to do. We expected a counter attack to come, but it didn't. For three days, a high state of alert was maintained even after the relief company was put into the trench. Nothing happened. It was clear that the Germans, like our prisoners, were bloodied, shocked and bewildered by what had happened. Their positions were now overlooked and their ability to mount a counter attack was seriously disrupted because of that.

The survey of the trenches after the blast showed that our tactics were successful. If this type of blast could be scaled up, then there was every chance that a breakthrough could be possible. But I had more on my mind. We were still fighting soldiers in the field. How could they be prevented from being in the field in the first place? There must be a way of causing confusion earlier in their plans.

After the interrogation was over and the two prisoners had been moved off to the rear prisoner camp, I sat down with Fixer, the two of us still calming after the explosion. He from the technical excitement of success and I from the simple and enormous human tragedy we had invented. Fixer knew his business and I wanted to share with him some thoughts. We talked about how things worked on our side. The generals gave the orders to their subordinate generals and brigadiers and colonels, majors and captains until each unit had its orders. But what if confusion was created in that chain of command? What if information was wrong, corrupted, delayed and confused? Better still, information we already knew in the first place. Interrogating prisoners was at the wrong end of the process. They were at the arse-end of the line.

'So, in your mind, we attack the generals? We don't do that, it just isn't right.'

'I know, although not directly the generals,' I said, 'but mixed up planning might mean we may not be fighting an enemy who is prepared.'

'But that would mean getting behind their lines?' Fixer was thoughtful, shaking his head slowly. 'Look Will, seriously, if anyone gets stuck behind the lines, they stay quiet until a counter attack gets them back, or the bugger starves or dies, or gets captured and likely shot! You mean to say...' Fixer paused and scratched his nose, 'actually trying to get behind the Germans and operate as soldiers, not as spies?'

'Yes, I do. I mean exactly that. Take a force of soldiers, I don't know how many, and mine our way under the trenches and come out the other side. Then we can attack the enemy from behind.'

Fixer's mood lightened, 'Ha ha, no fucking chance, you fool, you're mad to consider this as a way of waging war. There are any number of problems in your plans.'

'Which you are going to tell me about, of course?'

'Yes.' Fixer was now making fun of my ideas by reeling off the various ways they were mad.

'For one, there is the dig. You know how hard that would be? You might get found or come up right under a fat German's arse. Another problem would be the numbers. Getting a meaningful force of several hundred men through a tunnel unheard and unseen would be crazy. Anyway, to get at a general would mean tunnelling miles or marching miles unseen. It can't be done.'

'Thank you for your assessment Fixer, but what about this.' I took a deep breath for effect and thought out exactly what I wanted to say. 'Instead of hundreds, we just send say, five boys over. A small force armed with bombs and rifles. No big guns, no other weapons, perhaps a trench knife. We travel by night, quietly, and if we need guns, we steal them. We eat off the land or pinch stores.'

'Why five? What can they do? Even more mad. If the Germans eat that well, I'd be surprised. Anyway, stores are guarded and there is no way fat-headed British fools can get away with it in France. Besides, what about the uniforms?'

'We won't be wearing uniform. We will be French citizens, or in clothing designed for us to live in the open, but definitely not British uniform.'

Fixer stopped talking and looked at me intently.

'Now look here Will, are you damned sure? Hmm, I see you are serious, aren't you?'

'Yes Fixer. I have lived in France and know the French. The Germans would not have the slightest notion of this and certainly would not expect to see this operation. No one does this, do they?'

'No. None of our bloody generals would see a hair on the head of an enemy general hurt. It's a bloody boys club and we're not invited. The reason why no one has tried it is because it's bloody stupid.'

'I was thinking of doing this without any official permission and certainly without orders, because I would never get them.'

Fixer began to smile at me, which was unnerving, 'I do like your idea Tommy Atkins, really I do, but you're only a fucking sergeant in the fucking Engineers and not even that, if truth be told. What are we anyway? A special force? Whatever we talk about here, isn't going to happen. You don't have the rank, or friends in high places. Although...'

'What?'

'Nothing. So, are we a special force? Secret doves in the carrier pigeon loft, eh?'

'I suppose, of a sort. I still think we can operate behind the lines and make a mess of their defences, especially if we know the terrain and the enemy positions with a high degree of accuracy.'

Admittedly, I didn't have any real status and no real authority and no real plan, except for some silly ideas. This wasn't going to put me off though. This had to happen. Question was, where and when. Fixer was unconvinced, but he did not actually ridicule my ideas and often came back to them, when in idle conversation, to ask more, which was encouraging. He would often say, 'By the way, William. Do you think a force of fifty would be better than five or would that make it too many to manage, especially on the quiet?' Or sometimes he would reveal his thinking, 'I'm not sure about the mining and digging bit. What about a boat landing and then crawling to the front from behind?'

For the next ten weeks, nothing much really happened for me and my unit. I was asked to write down some of the things I had learned from our operations. Doing this also helped me to clear some of my own thoughts. We could work behind the lines, destroying bunkers, or stores, or ammunition areas, perhaps even taking out the chain of command at the same time. Fixer and I would share a joke or two, but the mood was more sombre than happy, as the war dragged on and losses were continuing. The terrible gas was used more often now and the enemy became bolder with it.

It was at these times that Odile entered my thoughts the most. When I was busy, or scared, tired or terrified, I thought of her and the pictures would come in calming flashes. When we were quiet, there was time to let memories wash over me, which were warming and healing. Although I considered writing to her, the reported situation was that no communications were allowed or even possible to French villages in occupied areas. Besides, what messages would a Tommy send to a village in the middle of nowhere? But I resolved to write, just to keep myself together. I wrote a lot, never expecting anyone to read or care for the stuff of my dreams.

The weeks felt like an eternity and we were becoming bored of the waiting and inactivity. This is the way it goes sometimes in war. Then the day came when Fixer and Paddy were both asked to join the Mining Corps properly. Our lazy wanderings had perhaps been noticed by a zealous staff officer.

'Time's up for us, Will. I'm off to dig for Britain, eh? Send a couple of parcels over special delivery, ha ha. I've got some new boys to get ready for some action next year. Perhaps this will be the one!'

'Maybe Paddy, maybe. I don't know. The enemy want to stay here, that's for sure.'

'Anyway, my friend, you take good care of yourself and maybe, you never know, you might get to meet that pretty French girl again, eh? Wouldn't that be something to live for?'

He got into the lorry and it rolled off. Fixer came up behind me and put his hand on my arm,

'Will, this might be the last time we get to speak to one another. You have a lot to offer the army and the Engineers. Don't go doing any damn foolish thing and getting messed up in the trenches, just to rush at your girlfriend. Keep thinking, my friend and you never know what might happen.'

'Bugger off then Fixer. Good luck to you. Keep your head down!'

'You too, you dozy sapper. Off we go, driver!'

Fixer climbed into the front seat of the lorry. It wouldn't be comfortable, but it would be better than the benches at the back.

Fixer and Paddy went to form a proper mining company tasked with planning a massive offensive action in 1916, probably in the Ypres area, but no one really knew yet. They went, and with them went the ideas of close trench mining.

I spent my time dreaming of peace and a life with Odile, but it always seemed to fade that little bit ever further from my mind as my head became filled with horrors witnessed and terrible deeds undertaken just to survive. I had to kill to live. This was beyond anything my mind could ever have imagined, or would ever get used to. Every night, sleep came accompanied by that awful bald head popping up from the shell-hole, or the German backing up in the trench drawing a revolver on me and firing it wildly.

No one would understand this at home and no one here cared, because in their lives, every day was just the same as mine. No one was special. We all killed, that was why we were still alive. On the German side, their boys were terrified too, having no idea that somewhere on the British side, I was planning a way to kill them, to kill someone neither known nor understood. This time away from action can be the worst. At least at the front, things are clearer and the priorities are undeniable. Here, thoughts can turn too far away from the job at hand and rot a brain to angry dust.

Then suddenly, the fate of the last of our little operational group was revealed. Digger was wounded and sent home in October 1915. He was working with a trenching team repairing water-damaged parts of the line, when shrapnel from a shell hit him hard in the shoulder. Only one small ball got through, but his left arm was rendered useless to him. He was sent home to train miners for engineering operations. With a 'cheerio' and a 'good luck' farewell, he was waved off to England and out of the war. Envious, I resolved to push on to Odile and get the life I wanted for us, back again into reality.

November 1915

Again I was alone. The army could do this, with new soldiers coming and going and maybe the brass had forgotten me, as my unit was slightly unofficial and only a few of us were left. The word of mouth, fix-it-and-leave operations were not in line with military protocol. The mining companies were not for me, as they had orders to do things in conventional ways. My unconventional ways had been proven to work and needed further exploration, without the constraint of digging large ceremonial mines.

The secret areas in Poperinghe had been requisitioned by the infantry and converted into trench digging areas. My health was not great. I had seen trench warfare up close, over and again and was sickened by the routine brutality and the constant edge. There was little respite, every move could determine life and death and it only needed one wrong move, or one bit of bad luck and that was it over with. There was a better way and I was determined to find it, wondering all the time whether these ideas were even original at all. Perhaps they originated from an overheard conversation somewhere and I was simply copying the work of another, also toiling in secret.

Late in November 1915, I was officially reattached to the Royal Engineers, although they did not directly show any interest at all in me or my ideas. I was kept away from the front line for a few weeks, to allow my wounds to heal properly. This time was spent solving bridging problems over the canals and waterways of this part of Belgium.

Then I was ordered back to England for fifteen days, to supervise the shipment of some secret mine-listening equipment. As a wounded man, I could easily be spared and was given three days' home leave, somewhat unexpectedly, to visit my family. I planned to go to my old school and try and remember a normal life, without the guns and the bombs and the blood and to maybe stop some of the boys just signing up, without them having more understanding of what was really happening over here.

Other soldiers went to see their old schools and I had not been back for some time, having spent time in France before the war. However, my visit to the school did not work out well at all. My parents were kind and loving, but they were in a completely different time and place to me. My mind was in France with Odile or in the army trying to get to her. My life in England was not for me anymore and it saddened me being taken backwards, to a time already left behind. Perhaps it was the war affecting me in unpredictable ways. The bombs and the bullets had made me a different man and this had clearly upset my mother and father and it was a relief to leave. Maybe, once this damned war was over, when I could think of being a human again, with no thoughts of bangs, bullets and blood, it would be possible for me to return.

CHAPTER SEVEN - AN UNEXPECTED MEETING

Once again, I returned to Belgium, to rejoin the Engineers who were repairing dugout emplacements in newly captured trenches in the southern part of the Ypres sector. Sounds of more earnest digging-in from the enemy side filled us with sadness and dread. Operations in this weather, at this time of year, were difficult and many were cancelled. Winter was damned cold and the mud frozen, so some movement was possible, but it was still difficult to move at a speed that helped attacks or consolidation. We were still looking at mobile positions, whilst the Germans were digging in ever deeper, with concrete, metal and wooden furniture. Captured prisoners were surprised at the temporary feel of our trenches and the lack of reinforcement. We quickly moved them off and away to holding camps, as their words eroded the confidence of the younger lads.

At the end of January, the Germans launched a small offensive at our line in the south of Ypres. The line held, the fighting was sporadic and lacking in any decisive action. Still, the casualty rates on both sides were unbelievable. I could not see the importance of such actions and certainly none brought success. There would be hell to pay in the tiny villages of North Yorkshire this winter, as a whole lot of our lads just disappeared below the melting mud, all in one go. These unimaginative tactics would get us nowhere and leave us poorer for the effort.

February 1916

The fighting intensity increased in early February, as winter seemed at last to be moving away from us. The Germans launched a renewed offensive on our lines. At the same time, they attacked a town in northern France that none of us had even heard of. The French clearly had, since they reacted wildly to the news, yelling and screaming when they heard the Germans had attacked around the town of Verdun. I knew from some of the French in the line, that Verdun was heavily fortified and the soldiers were receiving supplies from Bar-le-Duc, but the Germans had launched an enormous offensive, almost everywhere and all at once. They attacked us here, presumably to cover their Verdun flank, or to draw out our own forces. What they had achieved so early in the year was impressive, but doomed the war to more deadlock.

For three days mid-month, we were bombarded, almost without any response from our own guns. The soldiers in the trenches were being worn down and nerves were visibly frayed. The explosive percussions forced the air from men's lungs in bursts, causing involuntary groans and grunts. Each explosion caused the whole body to convulse; you could not help it, because everything vibrated at every thud of a shell. Even though I was more mobile than others, getting around was still nearly impossible in this weather.

A couple of times, I was nearly hit – that shook me a bit. I was looking out for a wiring party, which was back late and that nearly did for me. They had been laying a new type of snagging wire, but the old reels did not pay out the wire very well. I had to look over the parapet unguarded for just a moment. There were no sniper loops to look through and no reinforced observation positions there. I popped up, took a very quick look and saw one of the boys was down, bleeding from the knee. His mate was crawling back to him. The wire was a bloody mess and they were trapped. As I looked up again, a pair of sniper bullets cracked off and landed with a ping behind me. One from each side, maybe the snipers were a hundred yards apart on their side, but there were two of them, fixed on me. I could not help those poor boys hanging in the wire.

Quite soon after, I was following an ammunition limber through Shell Alley, at Hellfire Corner along the Menin Road, on the back of a lorry. No one dawdled there; German artillery was zeroed in on the crossroads of the main road and railway works. They shell it at will and almost seem to lie in wait for slow-moving munitions. Canvas curtains give a false impression of safety. I wanted to make sure that the new tracks were properly installed in the line and had no choice but to pass through here away from Hooge. The limber in front just vanished, struck by a high explosive shell from the waiting enemy. The horses disappeared completely – I didn't even know that could happen. The Germans wanted to take this area and they were looking good to get it. I noticed that the incident was being recorded by a moving picture camera. The camera operator looked horrified and just crouched down in the road, breathing heavily and motionless. He was quickly shoved into the next lorry, as this was not a place to linger a second longer than necessary.

I met four young engineers on the same deadly path, all friends, who had joined together, from a village in Yorkshire called Catwick. They were new to the army and I was helping them understand the terrain and how to keep their heads down, whilst still being able to fight. I wanted to spend all day with them, but could not spare that much time. So, I gave them a bit of advice and helped them sort out their kit into those things that were important and those which were less so. More important was their rifle and having enough clean water to drink, keeping their feet dry if at all possible and knowing how to dress light wounds quickly to prevent problems later. Less important were books and paper and pen – you can get these elsewhere. Those poor boys, I hoped they'd all survive, because if they didn't, their village might never recover from the loss.

For some time now, I had wondered why I was living this nomadic army life, able to move freely about the line, unchallenged and unhindered. The army knew where I was and what I was doing, but never sought to control my movements and actions and no new orders had arrived for me. I had spent some time as a clay-kicker, planned a successful mine detonation and fought in the front line. Surely the army had some use for me? This inactivity puzzled and troubled me. It was certainly not getting me nearer to Odile.

Despite reporting frequently to the Corps of Engineers HQ in Ypres, to my growing frustration I never received any direct orders to report anywhere else. I had built bridges and trained soldiers to dig in and survive and it was now for me to dig in and survive as well. Each day I reported for orders, the response was to stay put and await further instructions. From where and from whom, was never revealed to me.

So, I decided to take a short period of rest in Poperinghe, having been offered the entitlement, if only to defuse some frustration. It was more a case of informing the unit than getting permission before leaving the rear trenches. Reeking terribly in my appalling uniform, such as it was, I took the lumbering motor transport and rode slowly and bumpily towards Poperinghe, ever further from the rumblings and the shells. In fact, we stopped so many times, it was easier to walk, so that is what I did for the last three miles.

In Poperinghe, I made for the town hall and the long square, which was the hub of the Allies' activity. This compact area was the beating heart of 'Pop' and was, I understood, the site for a divisional HQ or two. The cells in the town hall were clearly kept to hold army deserters and those with self-inflicted wounds that had been reported as cowardice in the face of the enemy. I moved quickly on and found a small smoking café, but it was currently reserved for officers. Desperate to sit down, before I had even got close, a hand landed on my shoulder. *This can't be right, I have not even sat down.*

'Don't turn around, keep walking. When you get to the corner, turn sharp left and then keep going. Walk past Toc H on your right but don't look in. At the tree at the far end you will stop. Now move.'

The voice was educated, calm and very Scottish. The hand lifted from my shoulder and I was tempted to run. However, I followed orders and upon turning the corner, I saw an army car near to the tree. It looked unfamiliar in design, unlike the ordinary staff vehicles. It was lightly armoured and had attachments for a Lewis gun, although one was not mounted at the time. By the door was a senior colonel. As usual, I saluted, almost automatically.

'Good afternoon Sergeant. Get in, as quickly as you can.'

I obeyed but my whole body convulsed with nerves. Behind me came the Scottish voice, a major in a Guards regiment. This was most unusual and felt closer to an arrest than a meeting. Sitting between two officers, reeking of the trench, I was in big trouble and knew it. But the senior officer had said, 'good afternoon', and that did not sound very arrest-like. It was almost friendly. The suspense was broken when he chose to speak.

'Sergeant, my name is Lieutenant-Colonel Arthur Cowling.' He let the name hang in the air for a few seconds.

'You do, of course, remember that name, hmm?'

I nodded my assent. This officer was clearly a relative of Fixer, but what the hell was he doing with me? Had I breached some bloody military protocol?

'I am cousin to the man you know as Fixer and I am the commander of, shall we say, an unusual unit now based in France. Your mining work at Hill 60 and your gas inventions did not go unnoticed by my unit. We have known about your ideas for some considerable time and I have taken a personal interest in your ideas for new offensive actions. My cousin of course kept me informed of your ideas on a very regular basis. He is a good judge of character and he has judged you favourably Mr William Collins.'

This left me feeling uncertain since I still did not understand what an unusual unit was. Here was a Colonel, possibly a field officer, in a strange-looking car, driving me somewhere I did not know. At least he had a friendly manner and a friendly name, I hoped.

'My cousin, because of my role, let me know about your ideas for unusual warfare tactics. As you know, he is now off with a mining posting on the Front, but he is coming back next month, all being well. He is now to lead some shallow mining work, for operations in the summer months. You, Collins, however, are being posted to me and my unit. We are currently called the 12 Field Operations Unit, but that isn't what we actually do, do you follow?'

'Yes sir. However, what does this mean for me?'

'We will come to that. But first, some formalities. You were released from your unit and have been able to roam the Front at liberty over the last few weeks and left entirely alone, without orders, so that I could observe how you might spend your time. You could easily have shirked off somewhere and hidden from view, or cleared off for some rest in Pop. But you didn't. You went back into the line of fire time and again and got moving on a number of ideas to save lives, quite without regard. Good.'

Colonel Cowling opened a file of notes and I recognised the recruiter's page, complete with marginal notes, was at the top of the pile. Cowling looked down and thumbed through a few pages. There seemed to be quite a lot for a simple engineer soldier.

'You don't appear to have completed a proper formal education in the ordinary course of events, but you have lived and worked in France for some time, I see. In fact, you have lived in an area of some interest to us. The Front in the sector around the Somme and Ancre Rivers is now, unfortunately, an excellent defensive position, which Fritz has carved for himself.'

Cowling looked up and out of the window. He spoke some words but the wind drowned out the sound. It looked like he said a prayer to himself. He turned back to me and continued.

'We may have to flush the buggers out, somewhere along the line where it is dry and relatively flat. We need some clever ideas to put Fritz off the job of defence. The Germans have been building a new front line and some second and third line works at the same time, curse them. Well, I think you can do a job for us, Collins. We are going to fight a secret war, not bombs and bombardments, but one of such cleverness, speed, surprise and ferocity that we will damned well ring the bells in Berlin. You follow?'

'Not yet sir, but I am very interested in the cleverness part.'

'Good. For starters your army training is a problem. You are good in the field, but this isn't enough. Hampson, are we clear of Pop yet?'

'Aye, we are sir.'

'Right, good.' The Colonel peeled away his staff moustache and removed his cap and with it came his short grey hair. Underneath he was years younger and his awful officer accent softened.

'As you can see we insist on secrecy and we need your sideways thinking. So much of what you are going to see is fake, false and deceptive. We are not here specifically to deceive, we are just here for secrecy. Remember, not fooling, but hiding. I don't mean periscopes shaped like tree stumps to fool the enemy, like the Aussie infantry does, I mean men behind enemy lines causing chaos, confusion and fear. Ferocity is important, we can't be seen and no word must get to anyone.'

Those words sent me cold. It seemed as though we were being

encouraged to operate behind the lines, in utter danger and if threatened we must act coldly and without mercy.

Did I hate the enemy enough to do this to them? I doubted it.

'Oh, by the way, you are no longer a sergeant. You will have to have a rank that gives you the authority to act and to command as you have been doing, seemingly without such authority and rank. You are now promoted in the field to major, understood? We will sort through the temporary rank paperwork on the quiet, it might cause an eyebrow or two to flutter. Right, you don't have to look like a major and you certainly don't need to go about acting like one. This is specifically to allow you to oil the wheels of planning and operation. I am really a colonel but Hampson there isn't really an officer. He isn't even in the military. He is a professor of engineering and one of the finest logistical planners, better than you, so don't bloody forget it.'

At that point he managed a thin smile, but there did not seem much humour to it. Private to corporal to sergeant to major. I liked the thought of it, if I was honest, but felt this was selling myself into something I could not afford. The conversation was, however, intriguing and I wanted to know more.

'Sir, can you please tell me more of what it is that, er, you do, in Field Operations?'

'First, there is, for you, no real prospect of going back to close mining work, or a mining or tunnelling company in Belgium.'

I felt a sharp pain in my back on hearing those words, but this seemed too great an opportunity to turn back now.

'The army, against the scale of France and Belgium, is stagnating and lacking in the true imagination needed to break out. What we need is incisive invention and revolution of the machines of war, if you see what I mean. The generals aren't at all stupid. Casualties are and will remain immense; there seems only inertia holding this all together. This will go on for years, until there is only one man left standing and it might well not be an Ally. Trench warfare fought like this is incredibly costly as you know, in every sense of the word. Kitchener's new million men will be ready in June and it is intended for us to attack in France, to relieve the French at Verdun. That bit is secret, by the way, although most seem to know it. This we intend to do. Haig is the commander and he has chosen the trench assault tactic, with massed formations. I've seen some of his planning. With him will likely be Rawlinson, or maybe even Plumer, if he can be prised away from Belgium. Bombardment, submission and occupation, that seems to be the mood. However, Rawlinson and Plumer don't like that so much and they have formed us to think up some better ways to achieve our goals. I have selected you to work up your ideas with the brains in the unit and come up with some options and alternatives, especially if it doesn't go too well at the start. You are a confirmed fighter, like it or not, and you have fought like the devil in the trenches. I suppose one has to, just to survive. Well, that will be helpful to you. I don't want lives wasted, but if they have to be spent, then let us see them as an investment.'

Cowling then glanced out of the window, drifting away for a moment. I wanted to know where.

'If you want that life in Albert, with your girl, then help send the bloody enemy back over the borders. I'm asking for someone who can think clearly, with a cool head. Someone who might have to kill the enemy, but certainly not do it unnecessarily. If you do have to engage, then it has to be quick, ferocious and decisive. No point getting caught behind the lines, they'll chop you to pieces and take you as a spy.'

I took a deep breath and considered this for a moment. Suddenly I was in the realm of senior staff, or something close to it, acting under indirect orders of the generals commanding what was likely to be the summer offensive action. So, the generals really do understand the work we do, but seem not to have the tools to work around the problem – and they think I do! Well, quickly to it old boy and come up with some ideas.

We arrived at a location some way behind our lines and at least the noise was less noticeable. I was taken to very nice quarters, conscious of the appalling order of my uniform and effects. I bathed and changed into a new, if ill-fitting uniform, of an elevated rank. It was like being reborn. The sergeant uniform was taken away and burned. Orders had already arrived from Division (how the bloody hell did that happen?) for me to take up a temporary field-promotion to major, effective midnight yesterday. The qualification and training expected for that rank had been waived, for now, because I was unlikely to survive very long, or so my own thinking went.

I was treated now like an officer. My quarters were already stocked with maps and materials for writing and taking notes. All of the paper was coloured dark brown and every single page had a number written on it for reasons that weren't entirely clear to me. The assumed rank made me uneasy and it made me wonder whether I would be able to pull off this particular deception.

Colonel Cowling called a meeting for 1800 hours in the officers' mess. His note was cryptic in the extreme:

1800 for a chat about pulling off the push

Despite being assigned a batman, I wasn't interested in being looked after. Corporal Neame was very attentive, but my needs were simple and Neame spent his time helping me to settle into this strange and complicated environment. If Neame was in on my story, he did not let on to me.

At about 1600, I took a short nap, just to help my thoughts to swim into focus and to consider my new situation and surroundings. In the last year, my amateur mechanical and engineering skills had been put to use.

I had spent time in the front line, living through horror and terror in equal measure, coupled with what seemed like weeks with nothing to do, which may or may not have been deliberate. Clearly, I was not an ordinary soldier, nor considered to be so. If I was going to get to Odile and her family, then my newly elevated rank would not harm my position. Here in comfortable quarters, nowhere near the awful fighting, no longer subject to rat bites, the cold and boredom, never mind the enemy shooting at me – what had brought me here? It must be the pioneering shallow mines, or maybe the way I got about the battlefield in good order, or maybe it would be because of my ideas. This reeled through my mind, over and over. My ideas were different, but could not be considered entirely original.

Never a military scholar by any means, I had heard of many great battles, but these had not featured in my thinking. My thoughts were simple. The structure of rank tapers sharply upwards, lieutenants are everywhere, then captains, majors, two ranks of colonel and then three ranks of whatsit-general to a single general proper, if you will. Removing a general itself does nothing, apart from demoralise some and embolden others. In any event, if the plan is clear, then others can take over and execute the plan. What was needed was either a complete decapitation of the plan, or disruption of its execution. Enough confusion in the enemy, a bit of chaos, and our soldiers may be spared being blown to tiny pieces, or ground into the earth, never to return. The trench sickened me enough to want to spare all others, if at all possible.

At 1800, partly reconciled to my new situation, I arrived in the mess, keen to know more. Professor Hampson sat at the head of the table and the colonel entered without ceremony. I was the only one to stand and felt foolish having done so. His calm smile and gesture indicated the informality of rank in this secretive service.

Around the room were assembled a number of non-military individuals, collectively in league with each other, as they all seemed to have an easy familiarity. However, the colonel put everyone in the picture with his first address.

'Good evening everyone. Here, I have assembled, at great cost to the war by the way, a team whose collective expertise will, if well deployed and supported, bring the end of hostilities nearer and to the advantage of the Allies. You may still be wondering how so few of you can bring about this seemingly miraculous event, so I am going to get us going and hope that we can all see how we can achieve this together. Does anyone have anything to say? No? Well look here, we question everything we do, all the time. We plan to the finest small detail and support each other, even when our ideas seem ludicrous. We must be at liberty to voice our uncertainties together. From now, we are one team, all working to the same ends and here we are.'

I glanced around the room at faces whose names were unfamiliar. As each was introduced to me, the calibre of mind that had been sought became ever clearer. There were experts on explosives, mining and fieldcraft, tactics and planning for different scenarios, mechanics and weapons, a tailor and costume designer (which seemed incredible) and a number of muscled junior ranks assembled to one side, all about twenty years old but looking every part the deadly Tommy Atkins.

'It appears that we are to attack the Germans this summer on a stretch of the line in France, on our extreme right. Some say that this is to help draw the sting of the Germans in Verdun, but I am not convinced. This attack is inevitable and unavoidable. To date, the planning has gone like this. We are to attack behind a considerable bombardment and then occupy the broken trench line. Seems fairly predictable. Within that role comes our work. We are going to operate outside of the trench assault plan, but the end will be to the benefit of soldiers fighting in the trenches. The exact plan and location of the offensive will become clearer at the end of April, so let us plan to be ready from sometime in May. Clear? Good. I want the team here to work on two stratagems. One, how do we operate in German-held French territory, without discovery and two, how do we poke the bastards in the eye so that they are unable to defend our assault when it comes? At the moment, I am thinking about placing a mining excavation under a stable section of trench and inserting a force of about a hundred soldiers to get them from behind. I am happy to be convinced otherwise. We shall meet back here in one week. Until then, I will give no order and expect no military routine to be observed. There are civilians here whose creativity would be stifled by army procrastination and the military staff will be so preoccupied on the routine that you will forget to be creative. Military personnel will continue to wear uniform, as you will need to work with the staff. Use your rank, gentlemen. We are doing some work here that the army will think wholly out of order. General Rawlinson knows of our existence, Plumer is interested, but everyone else is in the dark and I want it kept that way. Understood? Good evening gentlemen.' He stood, nodded and left.

We were dismissed and we looked at each other, unsure as to the next move. We had been given very little structure and we knew our fellow team members so little. I suggested that we dined together and then made a start on something after breakfast the next day, taking the evening to digest Cowling's words. He had given us little guidance, but this seemed to have been a deliberate move – don't set too narrow a goal and see what you get. I liked it and I liked him.

I woke at about first light, being accustomed to the outdoor rhythm, and quietly reflected on the evening before. No structure and routine, but a reliance on our own devices and an assumption that we would get on with it. In fact, we were very closely managed, we just did not know it at the time.

We quickly split into smaller groups, with much talking and discussing. The colonel was nowhere to be seen and Professor Hampson was right in the middle of us. If rank counted, I was the senior ranking officer, which made me smile.

I asked permission to write home to my family as it had been a while and it was encouraged to prevent questions being asked. The letter was brief, bland and to the point. All was fine, jolly well and all that and not to worry. No proper fighting for me. Please don't send anything, there's really no need. In fact, no mail or parcels would get to me anyway, because my unit didn't really exist and we were not on any army manifests or the postie's list.

We started with some discussion on what was called 'dropping in', in other words how we were to get behind the lines and if we did, with what and for what purpose? Traditionally, soldiers were often caught behind the lines after being overrun in an attack. Fast-moving soldiers get ahead of their comrades, and soldiers wander around disoriented and confused. Soldiers were told to hide out of sight, until a fresh attack relieved them. If they were caught, it might be prison as a belligerent, or it might be death as a spy. The concept of deliberately planning to be behind the lines was a new one and strangely exciting.

My knowledge of the north of France and my ability to speak with and be amongst the French was probably my reason for being there. I quickly learned to cease my self-doubt and self-questioning and take charge of the work. We decided quite quickly that the idea of a mine that tunnelled up to a mile behind the lines was impossible and ridiculous and we set aside that possibility. In fact, reluctantly, mining was dismissed as impractical. The army miners would be working to destroy trenches, we would get in the way, taking up valuable time and resource. We were not sure where we going to attack and a mine would only tie us down to a single spot weeks before we knew where action would actually be. Likely as not, the mine would be in the wrong place when the time came.

We agreed that our targets should be those that would disrupt the enemy on as large a scale as possible. Hand bombs in support trenches wasn't the solution. I wanted to task small groups to think about such small details. I intended to visit an aeroplane squadron to see if there was any possibility of using aeroplanes in helping us behind the lines. Some of our engineers had become involved in flying 'heavier than air' machines and some also operated balloons. Some of these chaps might have ideas – although they were not given any details.

The new staff car (the funny one) got some astonished looks from the squadron. They told me, whilst walking to the aerodrome mess, that aeroplanes had been used to insert spies into France late last year. It had been a total disaster but the idea in my view, was a good one. The pilot had crashed with the passenger, but no one said what happened to them. A further attempt was made in October of 1915 and this time the aeroplane landed, deposited the spy and took off again. The pilot was based now at HQ in St Omer, so he was sent for immediately (using my new rank). The squadron was due out on operations, and took me with them to observe the aeroplanes.

The aeroplanes were lined up at the side of a grass runway with mechanics sweating over them. The wood and fabric contraptions looked, and were, pretty lethal and the pilots were dressed for the snow. They took off in formation, three groups of four aeroplanes, all at once from the same strip of grass. Each one was equipped with some kind of weapon, but it all looked quite primitive and liable to fall to pieces at the slightest wind. Their commander was watching with keen interest the departure of his boys and he was a useful source.

'Major Hale, there are twelve aeroplanes going out, what will they be expected to do?'

'So, Major Collins, this is how it works. The squadrons take off together, then these boys will fly over the enemy trenches in formation. Then, four aeroplanes will split away to observe the artillery positions and take note of the coordinates for the gunners to target. Four others will watch for enemy aeroplanes and keep them away, using guns, where possible. The enemy use guns on the front to shoot at us, trying to kill the pilot or destroy the engine, they don't mind which. The third group of four is a reserve, filling holes, or taking on the enemy if there are more than four can deal with.'

'Do you expect them all to return?'

'No, we expect that four will fail to return. Sometimes they come down on our side and we get them back, often they land in enemy ground and others are killed outright.'

About three hours later, aeroplanes began to return again. Two appeared together and landed quite without incident and seemingly undamaged. The next one appeared about twenty minutes later, with fabric flapping and a broken wing (Hale informed me it was a strut). It seemed to lumber up and down and right to left, because of the damage. It approached the landing area almost sideways and then a small gust of wind caused it to roll around to the right and straight down. The machine crashed just short of the runway and the pilot was thrown about twenty feet into the air and landed in the long grass, almost certainly dead.

My trench pain returned at the sight, more death in a new and different way. The pilot was twenty-two and was originally a motor bicycle mechanic. Selfishly, I now longed to talk with him about my acquired Peugeot 1908 machine, still across the rolling fields in Bazentin. We waited expectantly another hour, but no other aeroplanes returned.

'Not such a good result today, Major. Quite bad really.'

'My apologies, Hale, I had not expected it to be like this.'

'It happens old chap. We may get back a few more boys if they landed on our side and we may get word of prisoners. Neither side treats fliers badly, all things considered.'

Now that I was intruding in collective grief, I decided to leave. On the drive back, reflecting on the operation, I still thought aeroplanes had merit and resolved to consider using aeroplanes in action against the enemy. The squadron would be invited to our very secret location early the next week. My confidence in aeroplanes had been badly shaken, with so few machines returning from the operation, but the other options were equally difficult. The cheerful stoicism of the commanders was admirable, but their losses were considered no worse than infantry in the line, or a naval commander losing a ship with all hands. Whatever happened, dropping in by aeroplane was the option that must be made to work.

My thoughts also now turned to the idea of decapitating the planning in the enemy camps. The Germans would know something was coming from the preparations on our side, building their defences where it seemed likely we would attack. What if they were able to see the preparations, but because of our work, could do nothing about it? They would go out to bat, but someone would have split their bat and set fire to their pads, ha ha.

Some of the team became uneasy about the liberties we were permitted. We were secret, but not secretive. We had no official status with the military, apart from our pretend name, although some of us had ranks and could work with the army staff. Some were questioning our formation and the difference we would or could make. I was convinced, I really was, that we could change the war. It was my duty, as a senior ranking commander, to keep the team focused and to channel this uneasiness to productive planning for offensive action.

The pilots described in detail the insertion of a spy into the Picardie area, in order to gather information about enemy units, strength and movement. The spy orders on day one were to keep out of sight, observe and to send back his pigeon with any findings. On the second day, he was to take detailed notes in code and hand them to a runner whose job it was to transport the messages to a boat near Ostend. The chain of runners was quite sophisticated and the tactics of avoiding immediate capture were of considerable interest. This use of runners was new to me as was the discovery that they did not wear uniform, which horrified me. The Germans would summarily execute them if they were captured. They knew this but they went anyway. Occasionally, some French citizens could be enlisted to run for the British. It was exciting and dangerous work.

For his part, the pilot would fly over enemy positions and show the tell-tale signs of crashing. This was enhanced by the use of a spherical flare, which made it look like the machine was about to explode. Soldiers usually pitied aeroplanes that were doomed and did not take pot shots. In this way, a low-level flight could be made over enemy lines and a 'crash landing' was possible near to the Front. After dropping off the passenger, the aeroplane simply took off into the wind and flew unsteadily over a different part of the trench, trying to avoid suspicion. Occasionally, a few shots would be fired to discourage a return flight. This hazard could not be avoided.

I asked about the maximum number of aeroplanes that could be used in an operation, over a limited area of ground, without arousing suspicion. We talked about carrying two passengers per aeroplane and what would happen if the plane did not have to return. That would make three per aeroplane. It was agreed that it could be done with fifteen aeroplanes safely, as the flights could be spread out over the trenches and then brought together behind the lines.

The tricky problem was that the deliberate loss of fifteen perfectly sound machines, all at once, would be noticed. Also, the rapid training of fifteen pilots, just to fly one mission, would be considered wasteful and would probably not be permitted. The fliers did not think it possible to get authority for that mission through the usual channels, let alone actually pull it off. If it were feasible, the mission would be easily exposed, should the cover story unravel. We would need at least fifteen aeroplanes, which did not need to be perfect, and in fact battle-damaged would be good for our cover story. The difficulty would be fifteen pilots, who would fly once and then turn into soldiers on the ground. It was hard enough getting pilots to fly in ordinary operations, let alone our special ones.

I continued working on the ground operation, considering that a series of smaller operations would be best – lightly armed and lightly equipped to move fast over open ground. My days of sleeping in the open and doing errands came back to me. The plan was coming to me slowly, helped by our team of brains and tailors. Based on our own side's structure and chain of command, it would be best if we interrupted strategic communications (that was the term being discussed in our groups). Just cutting front-line telephone wires wasn't enough. The overall defence plan would have been in place for some time and everyone would know their place. We had to attack, unseen, the brain of the plan – not specifically a senior commander, but the overall coordination. To attack properly over a decent area of front, we would need a dozen divisions, each one supported, or even led by, an HQ.

The time came for our next meeting with the colonel – again, an informal briefing, a cosy fireside chat. It felt odd but also reassuring that we had been given authority to behave in this way and that our experience won over military routine and discipline. It certainly meant that traditions and routine did not get in the way of our special operations team.

Our meeting went on long into the night. Each team described one element of the plan that they had been working on. We discussed some specific details, including insertion behind the lines. I described my meetings with the squadrons and it was agreed to add two aeroplane officers into the planning. We discussed what specific actions would be needed to make any infantry assault more effective. If the enemy infantry was not there in place, or could not communicate, well that was one thing – but if the enemy was hampered in new or different ways, that could be even better. I described how we could attack the enemy. When they grabbed their rifles to shoot back, they would discover that the barrel-locking nut was missing and their Gewehr rifle would fall to pieces in their hands, just when they needed it most. After the laughter had died down, I described in more detail my ideas, which had resulted from considerable thought since my time on the quayside at Folkestone.

CHAPTER EIGHT - AN UNUSUAL UNIT

A small force could be taken beyond enemy lines – how was not yet certain – to a location not yet determined, armed lightly with rifles and small bombs. It would be very mobile and would seek out targets not yet identified and destroy or disrupt them. These would-be targets would directly impact on any counter offensive that would be set off after our infantry had left our trenches. We wanted the enemy response to be ineffective, chaotic and to possibly give our infantry enough time to consolidate a new position, or perhaps break the line.

We spent many hours discussing potential targets. Perhaps we should simply shoot a general, blow up ammunition stores, or send divisions in the wrong direction with wrong orders. Maybe we were delusional in our wheezy ideas, but we needed to try something.

The next three weeks were spent working up ideas on assaulting the enemy with twenty soldiers and not eight-hundred. They would not be fighting attrition but using the idea of insertion. Being somewhere that we were not expected – I liked that.

All this time, Odile had occupied my mind constantly. The unfairness of separation played heavily on me and fuelled a growing resentment at the enemy occupying France. This, compounded by the ineffectiveness of our actions, drove my mind to keep working, if only selfishly to get my life back. I thought often of the hills and valleys of France. The careless days bicycling or riding precariously about the villages around Albert were given equal priority in my mind. I needed to do these things. I needed that awful bald head to fade from my mind and for Odile to replace that terrible image. My back ached and I rubbed it, threw my pen down, stood up and went to the window.

'Odile, I don't know if this is possible. Can my heart survive the pounding of the war hooves on my chest? The devil may come for me and he could take me, if you were not there to find me.' I wondered if there was an undiscovered ether to transmit my words, but shook the notion from my head. Reality had to win this game in my head.

Once the pilots had arrived and joined the group, our team of sixty was set. We had various nationalities in the team, chosen for our ability to speak German or French, or for proven ability in close mortal combat. We could not have men who could not readily kill and still think clearly about everything else. It paid to be ready for every eventuality and I had to be aware of that as well.

Training started without any of us really knowing exactly what we were training for, what the targets would be and how we were going to get back (if at all). We tried to keep fit and try out different ways to attack and to defend ourselves. We tried using a knife, trench tools (too noisy) and even some potential poisons. Combat skills would be most reliable, providing nerve did not fail at the crucial time.

By the time the weather improved in 1916, we had advanced our thinking and planning and now felt ready to make a difference. We aimed to identify and attack a target in northern France, probably somewhere in Picardie in late summer, maybe near the end of August. If we had any chance to prove our ideas, it would be a once only opportunity and the army would be watching closely. Still, whatever our idea, it would improve on the colossal slaughter of thousands by shrapnel, fragment and bullet.

Northern France was chosen as the British had a stable line there, with relatively little offensive movement from the enemy. Of course, the generals' plan was still cavalry when you can and jumping off from temporary trenches. But all in all, the terrain was generally drier than Belgium and less likely to change too rapidly, in terms of weather and ground conditions. Picardie seemed a good spot, notably because of some quite beautiful large towns, on the enemy side, that France wanted back, as well as terrain that could be defended if the tactics were right. The ground, wherever it was, was going to be relatively flat, with only modest hills and high ground and every scrap of height would be fought over, by both sides.

The French themselves were now suffering miserably in Verdun, with their soldiers being blown up and brutalised on the approaches to the town. The bulging front line meant that in some areas, the French were being shot at from the front and both sides at once, often from behind, to add to the mutual carnage. It was appalling slaughter and the tactics were predictable on both sides. The Germans had occasionally used gas and a new flame weapon to huge and terrifying success, but the French had some defensive forts built years ago and an enormous need to hold onto every inch of their homeland. At least they were defending their own – including Odile and her father. Every day my French lady was on my mind, but I was no nearer to getting back to her – although an operation in Picardie would offer some possibilities of getting through to her, once and for all.

At the end of March, we received news that might as well have been delivered attached to a bomb. We had known for some time that the British and Allies were going to have a go at the Germans, probably in France. Troop numbers in villages on our side were increasing enormously and everyone, including the enemy, knew something was up. But the news shocked me all the same. Colonel Cowling stepped out of his car with a very grim expression and walked rapidly into the mess room without acknowledging anyone. He removed his cap and flung it over a leather armchair, turned around slowly, looking at us with eyes now grey and determined.

'It is in strict and extreme secrecy, that I must meet with all officers and planners now, if you please.'

Inside two minutes, the team was assembled. The first time that a hint of military discipline encroached on our otherwise open sessions. Hampson was notably absent from the meeting. Cowling had one hand on the back of his chair and was looking grimly at the window.

'I have just been to HQ in Montreuil. I met with Generals Haig, Rawlinson and Robertson. The summer offensive looks on, possibly even as early as mid-June. It is going to be much bigger than thought originally.'

He paused and turned to us.

'Much too big for our little band to be of much bloody help. I'm told that we are to tool up with artillery and smash the Germans head-on until they submit. Haig is worried that the French might desert or capitulate, leaving us buggered on our right. We are going to field one-hundred-and-fifty-thousand men over a twenty-mile stretch of France – aiming at Bapaume. In all, with reinforcements, he wants to put over two-hundred-thousand out in three days of offensive action.'

Cowling looked around, searching. 'Bloody hell Willis, do we have any damned whisky?'

He looked down at his trembling clasped hands, 'We really won't be ready in time, so I have declared us formally out of this one chaps. There we are then, we will miss this show.'

We all looked at each other, unable to speak.

'We might be able to help out here and there, but the tactics are grandiose and bloody insane. We are to grind them down with a huge aerial bombardment, maybe a thousand or more big guns, with the enemy having full knowledge, of course. No subtlety in a howitzer. They plan to turn their trenches and dugouts to dust. We know that shallow trench mining works, if well executed, and we know fighting over massive craters is difficult, if not impossibly hard. It is planned, for the artillery, to mix up explosives so that we blow them up in their dugouts, cut the bloody wire and kill any living thing in the path of the shells. We know from our work that the Germans are well set and I am not sure we can pick these particular ticks off the dog's back, using just shells. In any event, it is likely that our lads will go over as the earth settles, fully kitted and only able to make slow progress, as they will weigh too damned much. It is possible, given the current trench layouts, that it could take twenty minutes to cross No Man's Land. Haig is convinced that artillery will have killed them all and leave us only to occupy empty positions, whilst presumably bloody whistling *Auld Lang Syne* as we bloody go.'

I had to say something. 'Sir, if I may? Are we to understand that at zero hour, whenever that is, we are to de-trench across No Man's Land? Are we then to make our way across the fields and ravines in close order to the sound of bugles, pipes and drums? Are we to carry full kit at the same time?'

His raised hand motioned my silence.

'Yes,' he said quietly and now calmly. 'In fact, it is the very aspect of walking pace that Haig emphasised so decisively. He is now convinced that our artillery, if properly deployed, will pulverise any and every German position – however deep and well set they might be. Sounds bloody mad to me, but there we have it. It seems to be done and the cards dealt as they are.'

Cowling rounded his chair and sat down slowly, sighing as he rested into the seat, before continuing.

'Well, we just have to keep going. We do at least have authority to carry on with the plan and obtain whatever resource we need. Whenever we are ready – we *will* be ready – ready to show our commanders how we can fight a bloody war, without risking all at any cost. Some sanity in this bloody mad game.'

I had asked permission to spend the early part of April planning ways to work behind the German lines. Up to now, if a soldier found himself behind the lines, the idea was to bunk down and keep quiet, until rescued through offensive action, or captured as a prisoner. Rarely would a soldier try and make it back unaided. He would usually have little equipment, and in the fury of a battle the lines become blurred and a friendly shell hole can just as easily be a well-defended, enemy machine-gun post the next hour or minute later. My ideas were quite different. We would be dropped in quite deliberately, in sufficient force and adequately, if lightly, equipped. Enough men to be able to attack and defend, whilst few enough not to be noticed by the enemy. We would not draw attention to ourselves, mixing it with the enemy where they felt safe. I had a mad notion of wearing false uniforms, made by our clever tailor, but this was quickly argued down, not least because no one could stomach wearing an enemy uniform, or carrying off the act entirely in German. Imagine being caught in an attack and being bayoneted by your own chums. I smiled and dismissed the idea. Our tailor gave us some thoughts on using extra pockets to carry bombs whilst still being able to move freely. The overcoat designed was light and comfortable, even if worn in the summer months.

I took our sixty or so out into the big field surrounding our main quarters and marked out some small scale dummy trench lines. We could come up behind the enemy and make a mess of their communications and command structure, assuming it was similar to our own. The Germans were not so different to us in their tactics and the ways they communicated. Providing we could decapitate the command in the field, then the strategy could fall apart. If we were on the offensive, then all the better and all the more surprise we could reckon on.

We planned out how an operation might progress. We could be deployed by aeroplane, with some bombardment for noise and cover. Most bombardments saw kites flying, as they were used for observation and gunnery ranging. I had not worked out how aeroplanes could deploy sixty men, but that could be tasked to our pilot friends. Once behind the lines, we could target the supply and reinforcement lines – maybe we could take enough bombs to set off the forward ammunition stores, to prevent rearming. We knew that the Germans liked keeping well-stocked ammunition dumps forward and they were well-protected. However, they were accessible to men and if we could figure out how to get in, we could cause some fun in the dark.

In terms of the command process, we dismissed an operation to go and kill a general, or something like that. A set-piece assassination would be possible, but would have far less of an effect, come the actual attack. Only if we got to the supreme commander, could this really be influential. That would not be possible for us. The death of a general would cause a degree of panic and fear in the enemy, but it would have limited effect in the longer term. No, if we were going after individuals, then it was the field commanders we needed. In our army, it would be the colonels and the majors and if we were lucky a brigadier. They had the local authority and local knowledge to react to our movements. Without them, they could be forced to retreat to think and that was enough for us.

The problem was, there were a lot of them. It would be better to confuse them and not kill them. In my childhood, I confused an army of ants on a pathway by dragging some into a circle. The others trailed after them, marching round in circles, piling up over each other, never realising that they could go left or right, because they obeyed instructions. Instructions that had become confused and destructive to their cause. The same might apply to our enemy.

During April, we were moved around quite a bit to ensure that we were never in one place too long, thus allowing others to question us too much. I was now very happy being out of the trenches, but so much of what had happened to me remained, governing and tugging my thoughts from this work. It was not easy to forget the trenches but I used my experience to spur me on, to try and end the war as quickly as possible. In my mind, I still saw the German cleaved in two, with heavy-booted soldiers pounding over his lifeless body. The poor Scot pinned to the trench by that bayonet. Increasingly, these memories surfaced and played out on either side of my vision during my daily work. Sometimes, when I thought of Odile, she was with these dead men, alive again in my dreams, tugging at her, beckoning her away from me. Their gaunt smiles reminded me to let her go. As she faded, their backs obscured my view of her. Perhaps this wobbly shock was creeping up on me now that there was time to think and I was no longer just acting on instinct to survive.

Redoubling our efforts, we looked to refine the aeroplane drops and worked out that with some modifications, we could use twenty aeroplanes carrying three men each. These aeroplanes would be sacrificed – flown in but not flown back – that was the only option. Twenty aeroplanes landing in close order would cause some commotion, but it was a managed risk and one we would have to deal with. Soldiers may see planes coming down, but their curiosity would soon evaporate, in the face of gunfire. Even so, landing together would be suicide. It would be the riskiest choice.

Towards the end of April, we felt ready to go, as and when we were given a final location. We knew that it would be in northern France, which excited me, naturally, hoping that it would be in the area I knew best of all. However, our soldiers were not advancing that far and the sectors in northern France seemed quiet. It would be good to get into the fight again, if only to feel I was still doing my best to free my beloved Odile – if only I could avoid the terrible trenches.

We had practised some take-off and landing drills, which terrified everyone. The problem with the aeroplanes we were using was that they were so flimsy and the weight made them wobble around and dip at the nose. Apart from being dangerous, it would give away the secret of the flight. We had some modified machines given to us which were better, but it was decided that once the technique was practised, we would not do any more training flights as it risked the lives of our men too early. The pilots took off a few times with sandbags in place of soldiers and there were a couple of near misses, which put the wind up all of us.

Once on the ground, we needed to know the terrain in order to move about. I hoped that the area chosen would be Albert or north of Amiens, even if it was occupied by unfamiliar enemy constructions. Northern France is quite flat, so, it wasn't going to be such a problem moving around quickly and quietly. One area to overcome was the need to carry a lot of equipment quietly and quickly. What equipment would we need? Our training in close combat and our study of historical battles told us that less was more, which seemed so completely at odds with our training to be well-equipped. Knives and daggers and maybe a revolver yes, but rifles, packs and straps, no. We practised different combinations of equipment and reached the conclusion that it was better to assign equipment to teams, rather than have everyone carry the same kit. That way, some could move faster, and others could perform very specific tasks. The tailor made us clothing to carry this equipment. We looked the part and our concealment would be as good as we could get it. One or two used boot polish, mixed with powder and butter, to conceal faces and hands. The slapping-up seemed to make a bit of a difference, but it was not for me. It smelled awful and I would smell bad enough as it was.

Communications was a real worry as it was clearly the weakest part of our plan and one we would have little control over. We would only be able to communicate by voice, only with the men around us and not across the other teams. Flares and telephones were out of the question and we would probably operate only at night. So whatever we did had to be simple, flexible and easily followed. All of this troubled our team, but we were determined that this small force – with the authority of a general – could be successful.

We read dispatches from Haig stating how he detested night attacks in general and sneaky attacks most of all. We had little surprise in trench warfare, mostly because of the huge preliminary bombardments and I thought any advantage should be embraced with both hands. However, I did notice an increase in the frequency and certainty of these messages from Haig and began to wonder if Cowling had anything to do with them. He denied it of course, but always in such a way that made me more certain. The plans were truly unfolding and this operation had become real. Cowling had excluded us from the opening day actions, but there was still hope that our plans would not unravel around us.

CHRIS CHERRY

CHAPTER NINE - A PLAN UNFOLDS
MAY 1916

May was the original target date for our operation to move, if we were to help the show in June. We were ready in many aspects but could do no more until we had a definite target for our operation – a constant cause of concern to us. Cowling had been to and from Staff HQ and moved from excitement to fury in equal measures. He grew tenser as the main offensive drew nearer and more inevitable, wherever it would be. The French were taking terrible losses in Verdun and we would be called upon to move sooner, rather than later. I spent less time with Cowling, as we prepared and rehearsed more and more, but knew when he strode over to me that fateful afternoon, it wasn't to hear a saucy tale.

'Major Collins, can we speak, in private?'

I nodded assent immediately to such a formal request, but said nothing, simply followed my commander into the gloomy outside office.

'William, we have had word on the main offensive – most secret still, even though every bloody Frenchman born seems to know about it. It is going to be along the Somme and Ancre valleys and we are now going after Bapaume.'

He lowered his voice and stared at me sternly and with the tiniest hint of shock still in his voice.

'The thing is, we had planned for maybe up to a hundred divisions. We can maybe assemble sixty if all the French that have been promised arrive. Chances are they won't as they have their hands full defending Verdun. Goodness knows why they hold on to that damnable salient with every sinew and ounce of strength, but they are trying like the devil. Looks like we are going to come up short on the numbers, so it makes our operation all the more important. We are back on, William. I was wrong to withdraw us. Rawlinson has insisted our preparatory work be a requirement for the offensive. You must come up with a plan for an attack, no date yet, in a place you already know very well. You should plan for an offensive action somewhere between Arras and the French left. I can't be more specific, but looking at the maps, we might be going somewhere north of Albert, left and right, attacking the new defensive lines, on those low hills. There is some higher ground and it looks like the enemy are building defensive lines further north nearer Bapaume. It is all wood and open country as you know and we will be around there when this all happens. You are going to give me the plan within ten days and then you are going off to align the plans for the attack with 4th Army. I want you to learn fast on your feet and solve the puzzles that are left in our plans. I will then have to brief General Rawlinson's HQ before we get approval. You understand?'

My legs became instantly heavy and I had to sit down. Cowling put a hand on my shoulder, held it there for a few seconds and then strode off without another word.

The problem was not knowing the details of what our infantry were planning to do and more importantly, where and when. Word was, it was to be the end of June that the offensive began, but it could easily be mid-July before anything actually happened.

After a few days of thinking this through, I went to speak with Cowling again. His office door was, unusually, closed so I knocked and entered. Inside, in his chair, he smoked his pipe quietly, as if miles away. He tilted his head only slightly to acknowledge my presence and beckoned me to sit with him.

'Let's hear it, old boy.'

'Thank you sir. My opinion is that we should fly in over the trenches from the extreme east of our target, aiming at dropping just south of Bapaume. Our troops should be there soon after we land. We will split into three teams and go after the communications, troop deployments and forward ammunition dumps. The infantry expect to be through the first and second lines on the first day, sometime in late June, and have rolled up the flanks as far as the south of the town in quick time. I see us being in enemy territory only for two days and once the infantry arrive, to be back here in Albert within one-hundred hours of departing. We will use bombs and knives to defend ourselves. Possibly a pistol, but not a British service revolver, as this might be suspicious if it is dropped by mistake, or left behind. We won't be able to communicate and we will rely on the timings of the infantry at the start. If the bombardment goes well, they will be on us in no time.'

'Good. The first day is a worry, William. I'm no soothsayer, but the enemy earthworks are damned good so we may not be in Bapaume so soon. What do you say to that?'

'Well, if we don't advance so quickly, we will be behind the lines a few days longer. We will do what we can and then make it back. It is always a risk and we won't all make it back. The men are trained to think for themselves and to live off the land. It is the most we can do.'

'It leaves much to chance old boy, too damned much, in all honesty. But, it is the only option we have here and now. The only option other than banging away with an infantry and artillery hammer.'

'Sir, what we are planning to do has never been done before. The fact that we can do it at all, must be a good thing and we can learn from any mistakes. We can adapt and move, improvise and solve. We have been doing that for over a year now.'

'Quite, yes, quite. I don't know that you will be able to walk about the enemy unseen, William. My mind's eye cannot quite see that.'

'Yes sir. But we are all willing to try.'

Upon briefing the team on the plan, we agreed it was full of potential, but with so many different variables, we would only be able to resolve the details when the place and time were settled. That might only be the day before we went.

I left to observe the infantry forming up slowly, but surely, in readiness for the attack, which would now certainly be somewhere between Arras and Albert. The original planning had us going over the top in August, but the French were suffering badly at Verdun so we were now going at the end of June. Already, there were lorries everywhere, with pasty-faced boys in uniform wandering about trying to be soldiers. They had the same training as me, but had not seen the horrors of the Front and I hoped that whatever death awaited them was clean and fast, not like some of the poor bastards who lined my departure from Folkestone in 1915. They all looked young, mostly quite fit and full of vigour and excitement. I wondered how many of them all came from the same towns and villages as pals, joining up together. Many of these would perform heroic deeds and gain medals and surprise even themselves at their courage and resolve. Others may well be dead seconds after jumping off, hardly getting out of the trenches. No one could predict and no one could truly know.

As it turned out, the number of divisions that could be employed was lower than planned and much lower than even the fifty divisions that were expected from Britain's Allies. Fewer of the promised French were appearing, which was perhaps understandable, and I felt for my comrades, cowering in the miserable trenches.

In Albert, I spent some time with the miners and tunnellers, who had predictably gathered in informal groups about the narrow streets. Movement was still quite unrestricted, so I got to know about fifteen or more mines that might be used on the first day. Cowling enabled my access to some of the detailed planning, if only to report to him on the progress of the offensive plans and the likely probability of gains on the first day.

The miners were the usual mix of civilian trades and military muscle. Happy and contented as usual – and not at all prone to setting off with the infantry.

With shock, I discovered that the new attack date at the end of June – which we had all kept so secret – was very precisely known to most soldiers, many of whom talked openly about the day. Cowling told me that the French had been writing home, telling of the British attack (although saying it would be in early July) and much of the coffee shop conversation was on the timing and size of our attack. New soldiers arriving on the troop trains and lorries knew the date and time. It was inevitable that such a massed movement of men would be known, but it still put the wind up me, that is for sure.

The price for my free reign was strict orders to report on infantry preparations and how that might influence our own operations. The new infantry soldiers had been trained specifically to move with full pack, at a reduced pace, perhaps even walking pace, in full certainty that the thousand guns ranged on the Germans would have the desired pulverising effect. Having seen the German dugout positions up close, I knew that it would need pretty high explosive to get through all of that, including the wire. That worried me, especially when the ammunition limbers were carrying large quantities of shrapnel shells and not the high explosive, bunker-shattering shells.

The troops were now billeted in fields all around the southern approaches to Albert and Arras, a few miles behind the proposed site of the battle. A field hospital chain had been set up and became increasingly larger and better equipped throughout May, especially at Contay. Plans for casualty-clearing stations were identified at key road points in both towns. Given that we had hundreds of thousands of soldiers in the field, the number of casualties would be staggeringly high, whatever our units could do.

Towards the end of May, the 4th Army pamphlet was circulated to all infantry. It made quite alarming reading to me – in particular the sections relating to the advance:

...battalions should advance in waves with two platoons per wave on a 400-yard front to leave 5 yards between each soldier. A battalion will advance in eight waves (two per company) plus additional waves for the battalion HQ and stretcher bearers. The advance would be carried out at a steady walking pace of 50 yards per minute. Soldiers in the leading waves to carry full equipment; rifle, bayonet, ammunition, two grenades, entrenching tool, empty sandbags, wire cutters, flares, etc. The later waves would also be burdened with the necessary paraphernalia for consolidating the captured trenches such as barbed wire & stakes.

It seemed to me that the level of tactical training required to do this was very small and that soldiers were not allowed to think independently. My blood ran cold as my mind went back to the trench attacks. Chances were, most of these soldiers would not get anywhere near a German trench in the first place, if these shells were not all dead on their targets. Walking at fifty yards per minute. My goodness, the Germans might have twenty minutes to prepare a defence. That could not be right – I sent a copy back to Cowling, with a brief note detailing my alarm.

In Albert, I felt very much at home, despite the town having been shelled heavily and almost unrecognisable with all the military equipment billeted in the streets. I had been here many times with Odile and her family and had arrived here by train on my first trip to France. I remembered the little café where that confident girl first planted herself next to me, those few years ago. I looked at the little square, but could not picture that moment. It was gone from here, torn away by the scream of a shell.

Most probably, I would be here for the battle when it started and observe the infantry that were clearly going to jump off from here or nearby, just to the north. Not being near the trenches seemed wrong, but I could not get involved in the fighting, at least not yet.

Soldiers were lining every corner of every street. Units that I did not even know existed were billeted nearby and around the town. Again, there were battalions of pals smiling and sitting together, as if it were a great foreign adventure. In fact, as I was to be reminded constantly, it was an opportunity for a whole community of men to be killed together and for their families to grieve together at a single shell burst, or sweep of the terrible machine gun.

I walked the streets, going north to the first support trenches of the front line, often being stopped by the sentries. The trenches began with a steepening barrier of sandbags leading to sturdy trench works. Nearer the front line, the trenches showed more shell damage and filth as the war progressed all around. Soldiers were filtering forwards and disappearing up the road, on the way to and from the lines. Supply wagons were rolling forwards, the tired drivers grumbling warnings to soldiers at risk of being flattened. Everyone rode, drove and marched slowly, with cheery resolution and total resignation, to the fight ahead. The road was reasonably sheltered here, less so further up the road to Bapaume. The soldiers could move in calm order, with cover only occasionally required. This was a quiet sector and the enemy were not yet expecting action.

Towards the middle of June, however, it became clear that battle was imminent. I made my report on the readiness of the infantry and it was clear the soldiers were not trained in being flexible and adaptable, but were all in good spirits and seemingly well-equipped. The tactics seemed clear, with little question of the likely success. Everyone had seen the guns ranging on the Germans and all were confident that high explosive would pulverise and mesmerise the enemy at the point of attack.

24 June 1916

The new guns that had been brought into the field began to fire upon the German positions, in a single lethal voice. The imminent battle had finally and unmistakably begun. And the rage that sought to send the enemy home again was unleashed.

Puffs of white smoke rose into the air over a wide strip of front. It seemed that the attack would be between Albert and Arras and the destination would be Bapaume or even Cambrai, if things went well. The objective of Bapaume seemed manageable at the time, covering a significant amount of relatively flat terrain in the dry. The terrain was also smooth and only lightly undulating, even with considerable shelling. Once out of the immediate battlefield, the ground was relatively untouched. My worry was for the sector that would form the major part of our attack. There were plenty of coppices and woods around the high ground that would mean splintered tree stumps as another barrier to our progress. Trees allowed defensive positions on the tops of low hills that would be hard to attack.

The sound of the guns now seemed to come from all around and all sides all at once. The barrage was fearful and sustained. Surely, this could not last for six or eight days? If it did, then I was more certain of our ability to mince the German Army to oblivion, right here and right now. It was emboldening at the same time that it was sickening. The guns coughed and boomed, unsettling everyone, even with the knowledge that it was our shells firing. There was some counter-shelling in return, some quite accurate, but not on the scale of our own guns. Soldiers coming back from the line after supplying the trenches reported a large number of duds and a high proportion of shrapnel shells – not the expected high explosive. I reported this finding repeatedly, but assumed that the shrapnel was for wire cutting and that the artillery knew what they were doing. Sapper shifts worked round the clock and soldiers practised wire cutting and close combat fighting in the rest areas. I pitied the sandbags, taking repeated energetic bayonet hits, but pitied more the boys with the bayonets. No enemy I ever saw stood there, taking bayonet thrusts passively. They usually had a wild look, every bit as keen to stay alive, with weapons aimed right back at you, just as lethal, just as well drilled.

28th June 1916

I moved up to the support trenches, just outside town, to estimate how far we could progress and where we might need to be when and if my own operation started. If Bapaume fell, well then there would be no need for us – all well and good.

The forward communication trench systems felt more packed now and quite chaotic, but the first waves had not even moved into the line yet. They would arrive three hours before zero hour. The numbers of soldiers in this attack felt enormous and were noticeable to everyone – including the enemy aeroplanes that occasionally flew over our heads. Everywhere, groups of soldiers chatted and smoked. Smoking would be stopped nearer to zero hour and so, as usual, soldiers were making the most of it. They all knew each other and had grown up on the same streets. A couple of the keener lads were cleaning their kit and so forth, but most were hanging around, writing letters, playing cards, or just idly gossiping, in the way army lads do. The weather held and they were just making the most of the last hours.

I pushed my way towards the very front line. It was still judged as relatively safe, the enemy were not visible in the trenches, but were likely tucked down in their bunkers. It took me about four hours to move the last hundred yards because of the sheer number of sweaty bodies, kit and equipment, all trying to remain hidden and out of range of any German snipers. Battalions were staking claims to their bits of trench and working out how they would finally make the move into the trench with so many other soldiers bimbling around. The sentries were directing troops into the right sections of trench; it was surprisingly well-organised, given the time left until jumping off and the new soldiers' general unfamiliarity with the trench systems.

The trenches were deep enough to walk without stooping and, with the din of the continuing bombardment, the Germans remained out of sight in their dugouts. The confidence of the new troops seemed to rise. They saw the flashes of shells and the puffs of smoke and could see the obliteration with some certainty that the German lines were totally destroyed. Even I began to think that we would break through, despite there being absolutely no surprise anymore. Perhaps our unusual operations would not be necessary. Walking amongst the ranks, I sensed excitement and fear in equal measure, and the patriotic pride to be serving together as soldiers of their home towns. Ringing in their ears were the cheers of their families and older townsfolk. Ringing in my ears were the sounds of shells going over to the German trench line. They seemed very high pitched for big heavy explosive shells and too many landed with a thump and without any explosion. From my previous trench experience and the quality of the German positions, this bombardment did not seem enough. My new-found confidence was jolted at this realisation and a wave of fear washed over me.

The new lads blustered and joked the evening away. Some were trying to lighten the mood and fill the space with jibes and jokes.

Others sat grim and tight-lipped, gripping their rifles closely. Fear can be expressed in many ways. It can consume a man completely, making him oblivious to his surroundings, so that he makes mistakes and does not notice what is around him. A soldier needs to fight and if he cannot truly appreciate that this is a fight, he is done for. Too few appreciated that there would be a man on the other side, who would kill him without a thought, for that was his training as well. Those sandbag stabs came back to my mind. There may be little opportunity to rationally discuss the situation, with hundreds of stinking bodies duelling for their very lives, along with hot lead and shards of metal seeking a billet. I wanted to tell them all, one by one, what they were in for, but time was a luxury for peacetime. Here, it was likely that these chaps would be dead by the end of the week – if they were lucky to survive that long.

Each man dealt with the prospect of going over the top in his own way. Some, I was sure, imagined invincibility, that some protector would be there, perhaps creating a shield. Others accepted the grim reality that they would be hit, with most wishing for a clean soldier's death and not the lingering, suppurating agony of infection, or amputation. Some talked of their legacy, sharing out possessions and messages to their mates. They were handing over watches and photographs, promising to tell each others' loved ones left behind that they fought well and died bravely. It helped them to believe that death might not be the true end of life. Cigarettes, a currency within soldiering, were being spent liberally. There seemed little point keeping them in the pocket.

Across my patch of trench descended the realisation that the comradeship of the training ground was giving way to the united fight for survival. Some looked to me for comfort, but there was none to offer. Empty of hope, I wanted only to get on with it, to do my little bit behind the lines, as these boys did in front of them. Not here through orders, but through choice, the inexorable draw of the trench was overpowering. I wanted them safe and wished them all luck, but in all likelihood this could be the last chapter of their lives – and they knew it.

'What do you think our chances of being hit really are, I mean really?'

'You've seen the shells, what do you bloody think?'

'Yeah, it's getting to me though. It makes my chest hurt – funny thing that – and this bloody shelling is wearing me down.'

'Tell me about it, but it's fucking raining death on Fritz, though, think on that. Begging your pardon sir, I did not see you there.'

The two of them were sat on an empty ration box, waiting for orders to move forward or back. I wanted to stop but there was not much time left to reach my rest area for the evening.

'That's quite alright. Where are you lads from?'

'Tottenham sir, me and Bob.'

'What do you think to all this then?'

'Dunno sir. Looks like the thing we've been training for, though. Bombardment and then over the top. You been over the top sir?'

'Yes, mostly in Belgium, in cold weather. Keep your bundle clean and check your equipment. Keep your wits about you. And keep moving, always keep moving. Anything that pops up in front of you is to be considered an enemy, especially if you see his bloody face. Keep your head down, got that?'

'Right, sir. It's big, isn't it?'

'Yes, this is really it, we have to make the best of it now.'

'I am prepared to die, sir but it's the being dead I am not so sure of. The wife and daughter sir, back in Tottenham, see. What will happen to them? Service maybe, or worse, if things don't go so well. Scares me more than the enemy, to think of them back home, struggling. It's on my mind see? It is the last days of it, I can feel it.'

'Bob, come on mate, it won't be that bad.'

I wanted to tell them both it would be fine and that they would be alright, but it was beyond me.

'Chance can play a funny game, lads. Anyway, the devil takes care of his own, so you two blokes will be fine, I am sure.'

'Ha, thank you sir. Good luck to you.'

'Good luck, the both of you, truly good luck. Remember, keep your heads down.'

Rations arrived and although not plentiful, were hot and not too terrible. The Germans, for their part, were not really returning fire and so movements continued as normally as possible. There was more wire and cabling in the trenches to ensure that communications were maintained. Gunner observers moved up and down the line, looking nervous, which wasn't a great sign. I sought out one of the forward sentries in our sector, who was looking through the trench periscope at the wire positions.

'Hmm, I am not so sure that the wire isn't continuous, over there on the right.'

'What is it supposed to be like, Corporal?' I had never observed wire through a periscope and was keen to find out.

'Take a look sir, here. Look straight at it, square on so the picture is clear.' I moved to the periscope and peered through, almost imagining that a sniper would get me, forgetting the two feet of earth wall above me.

'Right, cut wire should look like a dotted line, with different shades. You can find a loop and follow it until you see either a cut end or a clump, like a bush, where a shell has disrupted it. On the right, the line seems more even, all at the same height, no deviation. That's the bit on the map here, er, La Boysel is it?'

'La Boisselle. I see what you mean. Left of centre, on the little mound, I can see the wire is clumped and broken very clearly. Here, take another look and tell me what you think.'

'Yes, on the left and the centre, there are some cut areas. Of course, they might try and repair it at night, but in this bombardment it is nearly impossible. I wouldn't want to be moving about in that lot, trying to tie it up again. Look, on the right sir, uncut wire is clear. I would not want to be assaulting that area.'

'Hmm, yes Corporal. Thank you.'

'Very welcome sir. Have a look anytime.'

'By the way, have you seen any movement in their trenches?'

'Not a dickie bird sir. Empty, dead or in hiding.'

'Well, let us all hope they are not in hiding.'

We shared a humourless laugh and I left the post, which was taking some return fire from the occasional enemy gun.

As I crept away, the view through the periscope replayed in my mind. To me, it seemed that the wire placements were intact, but maybe it just looked that way from afar. My mind was filling in the blanks for me.

One or two of the younger soldiers setting up around me were writing last letters to loved ones. Some company runners were taking these notes back when they took messages. They were not supposed to, because there was a final post collection planned, but it was a time for favours and compassion, maybe the very last time.

The morning of the twenty-ninth was slightly cooler than the last two days. By now, the Germans had suffered almost five days of intense shelling, with continuous bursts up and down the Front. Some German artillery to our left was getting away the occasional shell, but nothing like their normal operation. At least that part of our bombardment was having the desired effect.

More and more soldiers poured into already overcrowded trenches in readiness for the action. The very front line was not too bad, but the support trenches became clogged with soldiers due to go over in the second, third and fourth waves, all preparing the positions, ready for jumping off. Again, the final troop numbers would be supplemented just before zero hour. With this movement, I began to appreciate the scale of numbers and to understand what nearly a quarter-of-a-million men looked and felt like. It seemed to me that numbers alone would be decisive in the upcoming battle and felt calmer knowing how many boys were going over. The enemy could not resist this push and I was less anxious that our little operation had not been ready to go for this first day of battle.

I spent the day making notes on the infantry, which was my job here after all, ordered by Cowling to learn the infantry way to help our longer-term planning. Most of my time was occupied on what might be happening in the German trenches. I had hoped that their ability to fight had been dealt a knockout blow and thought back to my description of the rifle that fell to pieces. Our chances would be so much better, if their counter attack disappeared down the drain. It would not be here that my plan could be attempted, but the chance might come soon.

There could be no doubt that a major British and Allied offensive was imminent. The amount of shellfire was incredible. A continuous line of explosions, all day and night, on the enemy positions told a very clear story. Tension in our trenches was now rising rapidly, because it seemed increasingly likely that the day for the attack to start had been put back – the bombardment was never supposed to be this long. Soldiers' nerves were clearly stretched and conversations once started, quickly died away. Humour was still visible in the conversations of the enlisted men, but much quieter and more cynical and the officers seemed grim.

Orders for the battle were now starting to come through and the plan was for a brisk walking pace, maintained at fifty yards per minute to coincide with a creeping barrage – one that started just in front of the German wire and moved over the enemy trenches just as our boys arrived. This would be spotted and coordinated by our observers with adjustments made according to progress. A number of mines were to go off at, or just before, zero hour to knock out important defensive positions and give our boys some cover from return fire. I thought back to Hill 60 and remembered that targeted shallow mines could work better than large mines, but the lessons had not been shared with the mining teams here. This disappointed me a bit, and so there would be enormous mines that would shatter the morning in waves of percussion and instant death. Having seen some of the mining entrances in La Boisselle, I knew that something very big was going to explode nearby.

On the evening of 30th June, the final battle orders for the officers arrived. The Allies were to leave the trenches at 0730 in the morning, 1st July. There had been a delay to the offensive. We were supposed to have gone on the twenty-ninth, but troops were still in transit and the choked up trenches had contributed to the delay. More worryingly, the delay was in part due to the reports of uncut wire and undamaged enemy positions, especially on the left of our line. I resolved myself now to fighting with the second wave, not just running uselessly behind them, armed with only a notebook and a grimace. It was essential to see how the assaults progressed on a wide attack front. Despite being keen to go over the top with our boys the urgent need to fight here on familiar soil was overpowering me. But by going over with the second wave, I could see how the troops deployed and how long it took to move off.

During the night, from about 0200, the first assault troops finally arrived and lined up in the front-line trench. Many of the lads around me were from Lincolnshire. Among them were a few Scots and this made for some edgy rivalry. Second and third wave troops formed up, just behind. This was it, the offensive was on for the morning and no more delays. The last of the letters and final wills were taken back from the front-line trenches. The very forward assembly trenches were packed full of men and equipment. Ammunition issues were being made to every soldier in every unit. Conversations were quiet and only between soldiers standing shoulder-to-shoulder. The men became grimly focused on their equipment, their mates and thoughts of home, perhaps. Soldiers were looking into the walls of the trenches, surely considering their fates. Still furiously writing, I noticed a young soldier peering at me from the next bay.

'Sir, beg pardon, I can see you are busy. Have you ever been over the top yourself? You know, have you had a go at Fritz like?'

'Yes I have,' I replied, not surprised that this question was asked of me so often. 'In Belgium. Some time ago, but I can still remember it well.'

Flashes of the gas cases and the bald head came back to my mind. Behind the ghastly head was Odile was trying to wave to me, but this awful, pallid image was always in the way, curse him to eternity.

'We got to the enemy that day and showed him what the British can do when we put our minds to it.'

'Jonesy lad, shut up and stop bothering this officer. Excuse me sir!' The corporal next to me placed his hand on the boy's shoulder and tried to gently turn him away from me.

'It's quite all right, Corporal.'

'Only, I saw your ribbons sir, if that's what they mean. What is it like to go over then, sir?'

In spite of my wanting to be inspiring and heroic, the words would not form for me.

'Well Jones, when the time comes, we all go up and over together. It helps when you go with your mates. It's noisy, as everyone shouts out together. Funny when the barrage stops, because you get so used to it, almost comforting with the regular bangs and crashes.'

'They are all dead though, aren't they? We are just going to take their trenches?'

'That is the plan Jones, that is the plan.' It didn't sound convincing, even to my own ears.

'Only, I said to my mother that we would all be fine and there is nothing to worry about.'

'Well you were right, I'm sure. Look, all you can do Jones, is your best. Keep going, whatever you see. Do the job that is asked of you, no one can ask more, and keep your head down – that is an order.'

Jones turned to his corporal, he looked uneasy and that is never a good thing in a front-line trench.

'But if I die, Corp, what if I die? I won't see my mother and sister again. My brother is in the Rifles, sir, he is here too. Whatever will my family do? What will become of them? My younger brother, he is a right dozy sort and he won't be good for much, love his heart.'

'That's enough, Jonesy. You won't die. I bloody won't let you.'

'I know, I know, it's just…'

'I know Jonesy, I know.'

'Fucking hell, Jones, shut up will you? You are putting the fucking wind up all of us.' The new voice came from further down the trench. A few grunts and humourless chuckles came over in our direction.

'Leave him alone, Charlie. This fucking waiting is what's getting to all of us. Fuck me, we are sitting here, all crammed in like bloody sardines, waiting to get it in the morning. What's more, I've got to look at your stupid fat shit-digger's face while we wait, see?'

'You will get it, you mean, you useless strip of piss. I've seen you shoot, ha ha. Could not hit a bleeding door even when you are holding the sodding handle.'

This time the laughs carried some humour.

'What do you know about bloody trench assaults? All you know is the arse-end of a turnip, you country bumpkin!'

'Oi, bugger off and shut up. I want some bloody sleep. Don't want to go over the top in my pyjamas, not looking me best for those Fritz lassies!'

So began a round of gentle humour, from a moment of tension, in the timeless way of soldiers across the whole front. The rhythm of fear, anxiety, eagerness to get going and thoughts of home ebbing and flowing.

The waiting really was the worst bit. Just get on with it and accept the inevitable. The constant Allied shelling was jolting, jarring and testing the nerve and resolve of even the old trench hands. Boys looked at each other with an emptiness, a void that could not be filled by words. Comrades could do nothing more to protect one another. Only if they made the objective, could they truly fight like soldiers. Until that point, their fates were not in their own hands. A random chance, governed by inches, seconds and an instantaneous decision to stand, duck or jump.

The front-line boys could hear the occasional shell from the Germans and they caught, through the din, the odd rifle crack, but the Germans were mainly pinned to their dugouts. The invisibility of the enemy should have been emboldening, but doubts crept in as nerves stretched and the reality of the attack took over minds.

One or two of the soldiers were quietly praying as well. Many were resigned to their fate and would accept whatever came their way. Few ate anything that evening, best to fight on an empty stomach in case you were hit. Perhaps appetite would not come to those in the front line anyway. The rum rations would be round early and most would take a tot, for courage.

The moon wasn't visible but it was quite warm and clear for the troops to move. A few German lights went up, but that was probably because of the wiring parties that had bravely carried on through the night bombardment, just as usual. Reports of the state of the wire along the line were conflicting and confused. Some reported the wire cut and others that it was not cut at all, just as I had seen earlier. The Germans had left channels for their own use and these would be defended by machine guns and bomb teams, for sure. No one was able to confirm whether the Germans were out repairing wire, but it seemed unlikely, and we could only assume the barrage had not been successful all the way along the front. That was devastating news to realise so late in the bombardment. Sometimes, it was best that news was not shared with the lads, just to spare them one more agony as there was nothing they could do about it. There was enough to worry about with the German defensive dugout positions. In Belgium, they were deep, well-built and intended to be held and there was no reason for them to be any different here. Our shallower temporary trenches were quite different. I hoped that our gunnery plans were based on their deep dugouts and not on our type of trench construction. If the shelling wasn't heavy enough, these dugouts could survive and the enemy would be waiting for us.

I could not rest, even though in far less peril than the other soldiers around me, who were in the first wave. At least I could avoid combat and just report the action. Small chatter and anxiety filled the air around me.

'Good luck Bob.'

'Good luck yourself, Johnny.'

'See you in Fritz's trench, you ugly bugger.'

'Not if I see you first, ha ha.'

'Keep yer head down!'

'It's bleeding big enough.'

I made my way to the observers again. These men would be awake and watching everything that was going on, they were the closest thing to news on this part of the front.

The forward artillery observers told me that from 0625 there would be an hour of the most intensive shelling ever mounted by the British Army. A wall of shells would hit the entire length of the German positions, so that in any square yard of earth, a shell would land once every few seconds. That time was approaching.

When the time finally came, the scene before me was hellish. Thousands and thousands of British soldiers were shoulder-to-shoulder, bumping along, in the very front-line trench. The assembly trenches too, were overflowing, with men and equipment and the contents of churning stomachs. Nerves were stretched. The noise of the British guns was incessant and deafening. The intensity of the bombardment was unimaginable and beyond all physical description. The bombardment was felt in the bones and in the core of your being.

Ahead, on the German side, the earth erupted in coughs and splutters and the debris fell back down over and over and over again, often in the same places. Occasionally, it hit a concrete emplacement and a chunk of casemate would be thrown up. Another would dislodge the trench wall and shower sandbags and wooden trench works. The most grisly were those shells that found a human target. Severed limbs and chunks of flesh would be thrown up, sometimes those already dead were flung back again into the air, like a ghastly cheer for the dead. The artillery were literally throwing everything at the German positions, you could see them almost picking up bathtubs and sinks and motor cars and bicycles and chucking the whole lot in a gigantic effort over the garden fence, at the enemy. Goodness knows what it must have been like in the German trenches, because it was no Sunday afternoon picnic for our boys either. My watch said 0705. The sun was up and the day looked set fair to be warm and, as the generals were hoping, a victorious one for the British Army, a day for history.

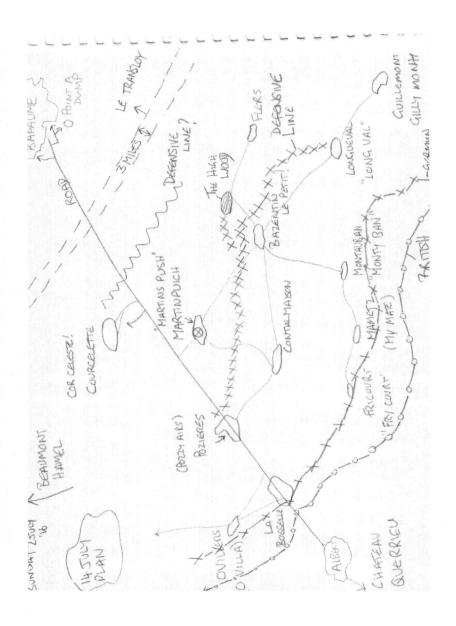

CHAPTER TEN - ZERO HOUR, LA BOISSELLE SECTOR, SOUTH-EAST LINE

We were huddled together in the assembly trench, just a few yards behind the front-line trenches. We had planned to go at 0800, or just as the first wave reached and attacked the German positions. The timings were different up and down the line, based on the distance across the trenches and the type of assault being made. The trench ladders were now firmly in place and the platoons were set at the foot of the ladders. The sight of ladders going up looked like the erecting of a scaffold, escorting the condemned to eternal silence. This was to be our lot. Death was really amongst us, seeking his grisly billet. At the trench wall, some of the boys were shaking and trembling as the nerves took hold of them. They would be brave when the time came, it was the damned intolerable waiting that was the worst, gnawing at you, filled with terrible imaginings of what was to happen; the real fear perhaps not of dying but of being dead, forgotten or not counting at all, in the balance of life.

As a major, I was able to move into the front-line trench very briefly to watch the soldiers forming up at the bottom of the ladders. Several, at this point, were openly vomiting, but since there was nowhere to move, it just poured over the poor chap in front, or to the side. The intensity of the shelling continued to its enormous crescendo, battering the living souls of the sons of Glasgow, Cardiff, Grimsby, Chatham, Newcastle and Belfast. With each series of bursts, the ground vibrated and rumbled, almost turning to liquid the dirt and dust on the ground. My mining experience told me that very soon the mines, wherever they were, were going to go off, adding to the collective misery.

I was alongside the Grimsby Chums, one of Kitchener's Battalions, who were going in the first wave. These soldiers were due to move forward to occupy the crater that would result from the enormous mine due to go off in front of us. They were excited at this, because it would be something different and, most likely, the enemy would be destroyed in front of them. The boys had seen some action already, although nothing that would compare to this day. They had been told to expect the mine and to be ready to rush the crater before the enemy could clear their heads and defend the position.

We were now finally located out on the right, along the old road from Albert to Bapaume. Some of the soldiers joked that we should just walk along to Bapaume for tea. I could not help thinking about being so close to Odile and so close to home. It felt almost unreal to be in this position, unable to just walk over the road – how dare the bloody Germans think they could do this and get away with it?

At 0715, I took a moment to think about Odile and her family, my mother and father, and England. I wanted to make peace with my thoughts, as this was sure to be a war-defining day. The scale and enormity was now clear to me – the first day of July in 1916 would be the day of glory, perhaps the day we broke through to the borders. But if this did not work, then it could well be the start of the end of the war for the Allies.

It made me recall the day I jumped out the bushes on my return to France, being doused in the water pump. The days riding around and the times in the little shed – oh, to look into her face again! The little touch of her finger on my hand, or the gentle grip on my arm. Even the punch with 'imbecile' would be welcomed now. I would swap all that was left of me, to be back with her, just a short distance from here.

The track that had been visible through the periscope, we had cycled many times. The field I would be moving across used to grow wheat for bread and was mown for hay. My mother came into my thoughts and shame flooded me for neglecting my parents through a sense of false maturity driving my need for independence. I told them all I was so very sorry for being here and taking lives in an effort to shorten this ghastly excess of suffering.

'Odile, my love, wherever you are, I love you always and forever. Whenever and wherever we meet again, find me your loving friend, ever hopeful to be your husband.'

I hoped the words could carry on the breeze, across the clouds of smoke and dust and not be cut down by the bombs and shells.

On a scrap of coded paper in my breast pocket, I wrote a short sentence or two, so that if I were hit, Odile would know my true feelings, always.

Mother, father, love to you eternally. I hope that I will have done my duty and made you proud. To my darling Odile. With love. My last and everlasting thought was of you. William

It was now 0720. To my left was the booming sound of an enormous eruption and explosion, which felt like thunder clapping over the distant hills. Although not directly visible, we all heard it and felt the vibrations. It was too early for our planned attack (we later learned it was the mine under the Hawthorn Redoubt, right in the middle of our attack line. This could allow the Germans time to recover – they knew we were coming and they would man their gun positions. Well, they would be dead, I supposed. Now was not the time to worry about that, it was all too late anyway.

As the clock ticked agonisingly towards 0730, other explosions went off as each mine detonated. At each blast, I thought about the mining team, their hard and unseen work and the fighting underground that happened all too often. And I also felt for the poor German bastards under the mines as they went off. An unimaginable, if quick death, and death was the best outcome – I had seen survivors of mines and they weren't the lucky ones.

At 0728, mines went off all around us, it really was time to jump off. In front of us, the most enormous explosion lifted huge amounts of earth into the air. The force was so strong, it rattled the bones in my chest and the vibration caused my throat to shout loudly. My eyes hurt from the pressure and we were all thrown backwards by the shock. It was a terrible and unnerving moment, and for the first time my courage seemed to fail me. The cloud of earth rose what seemed like thousands of feet into the air and started to rain debris onto our lines with lumps of unspeakable sludge – that a few seconds ago were living German soldiers – among the stones and earth clods falling on us. It was an awful moment that almost drained the will to move on, especially in those who had placed themselves nearer the enemy trenches, out in No Man's Land.

The next two minutes felt like an eternity and my breathing quickened sharply. All around, soldiers were vomiting and trying to control their breathing. Gripping rifles and tools close for comfort, laden with packs of unnecessary equipment, every soldier was trembling more or less – but to a man, they only wanted now to get up, over and away. The waiting in that two minutes seared an impression for always, of grim soldiering and fates in the lap of fortune. Small voices, trembling prayers, cries of anguish and questions of why were we here, huddled to die in this terrible place. The shouts grew louder and it took all the efforts of the NCOs to keep everyone calm and focused. It was agony and it had not even started.

On this beautiful morning, in full daylight, at exactly 0730, shouts from the company commanders signalled the first assault troops to leave the trenches and begin their slow march across No Man's Land. It was happening.

Bodies freed from the bonds of the trenches scrambled up the ladders and over the parapet accompanied by waves and shouts and swearing, loud guttural cries, releasing the tension in one lungful, as they climbed the ladder. To the left of me, a piper struck up a tune to steel the nerve and it seemed a wonderful and terrible moment, in equal measure. Some expressionless faces climbed the ladders and walked off, blindly following the directions of others. Others carefully picked their way ahead. The older hands were double checking equipment as they reached the top, urging others across, 'Quick lads, off the ladder, you are third lighters, and they know where you'll be' and, 'Better in the open moving about, come on.'

Those that reached the top composed themselves and trudged off over the disputed ground towards the enemy trench, determined to do their duty, however brief. From our positions, the lads cheered the first wave on and wished them all luck. This was really it and the British Allies, all of them, had played the ace card of their collective youth, here and now. There was no going back.

The Grimsby Chums and the Scottish lads poured up and over the parapet and out into No Man's Land, shouting and cursing as they went. The shouts of a thousand voices, every bit as loud as the shells. Flesh and blood was to be pitted against machine gun and bomb, by the tens of thousands. It would be a loud and tribal moment for all soldiers on the Somme.

They walked off. The artillery guns behind were dropping occasional shells on the German wire and it seemed that the barrage had been successful. The Grimsby lads were running though the smoke, dust and dirt to the crater and some of them made it across the gap in just a few minutes. There had been some random return fire, but for those who were posted close, it would not get them just yet.

Then, to the horror of all and to soul-splitting shouts of disbelief, anguish and pain, came the devastating realisation from our lines. The Germans were not all dead. We started to hear the murderous rattle of machine gun fire. Bullets came at us in dense patterns. We lived and now died, with the terrible knowledge that the German positions were not destroyed and could resist our soldiers' slow advance. I clasped my hand to my face, to stifle a shocked cry. My God, they were going to be slaughtered. Call them back, get them to duck, move faster, anything, but not this slow trudge across the deadly gap.

To the left, the soldiers were still walking towards the German positions along an area known as Sausage Valley. I saw them advance in their ranks and thought they were going well, when the guns opened up on them. The sight was utterly terrible. Several soldiers in line, crumpled and fell, as if they had suddenly lost their bones. Many were blown backwards as the bullets passed right through them. They fell onto their backs, with terrible injuries to their chests. One soldier to the left, hit by raking machine gunfire, had been cut cleanly into two pieces, the legs separated from the torso, which carried on forwards and then fell with a slap to the ground. Soldiers were being spun around, bullets, shrapnel and shell fragments bouncing off their helmets. Still, it seemed that some were advancing and getting on, none faltered unless and until they were hit, which was most of them. On all sides, the splatter marks of bullets on the ground made an impenetrable floor of lead. Within just a few moments, the German artillery was adding to the misery. The shells dropped in among the advancing troops, swallowing them in a pall of smoke and searingly hot metal. Chance was the only ally to the poor buggers left still moving over the ground. The close ordered five-yard ranks were now broken up and men were separated from their comrades and pals. The stretcher-bearers poured out from the support trench and set off to find the casualties, but there were simply too many of them. The bearers were as likely to be hit, but they went anyway. The padre, nearby, was shouting skywards a piercing, shrill cry that cut to the bone. He moved up the ladder and stumbled about trying to find a living soul to comfort. He found his first body, only about ten yards in front of the trench, not even having cleared our wire. The second wave saw this and it struck me that their bravery would have to be greater still, to go up and over, knowing that the fate of the first wave would be their fate too.

I knew now that the hospital provision, the small tent lines, would be stretched beyond all comprehension within an hour. The day seemed already to be a disaster. Perhaps some had made it to the German trench – we could now not see through the smoke and the confusion. The machine gun rattle was almost continuous. Who could possibly live through that, and then fight a battle on the other side?

The time came for the second wave to move off and I went with them. Around me were more lads from the battalion, who had witnessed the death of their school friends, workmates or the lads they met in training just a few months ago. Their anguish was visible – if you swept your hand in the air between them, it would be wet with the living pain of the moment, as if you had swept a hand through a pond. You had to be living though, to feel pain.

'Fucking hell, Joe, get that bloody webbing strapped up here. No, not like that, here let me check. There, you bloody fool. Leave the tools, no buggers are needed yet to reverse the trenches. Take more ammunition boys, load up with a few more bombs. Come on let's give our mates a hand.'

'Sarge, please, do we still go, even with all this shit here?'

'Yes, them's our orders and they haven't bleeding changed. Get ready lads. Good luck everyone.'

'Fucking hell, we are fucking going aren't we? Oh dear God, no, please don't make us go into this. We are going to die.'

'Shut it up, right fucking now. We are going. There's no one else, only us. We have to go. There's six other waves due after us. We have a chance and we have to take it. Get it now?'

'Fuck it, Sarge, let us bloody go then. I can't stand this any longer, please!'

'Sarge, there's bodies on our wire, we can't get through. What shall we do?'

'Oh fuck it. Look, you will have to cut them down first. Quick off to it, I will give you one minute to get them down. If they are alive, leave them be. If they are dead, just push them away, so we can get out. Their guns know there's a gap there, so don't fuck about.'

'Oh my eye, Sarge, please be alive lads, please.'

Then he was up and gone. He made it to the wire but was struck by a shell that sent him ten yards sideways, falling into a heap of hot flesh. At least he did not suffer, like the lads screaming on the wire, who saw everything. The shell burst, adding to their injuries and anguish.

It took all of our courage, having seen what had happened, to climb out of the trenches. The machine guns had found their range and were targeting the ladders. The first to go took deep breaths and let out the same soul-splitting cries as they emerged above the sandbags. We left the trench as quickly as possible and started out towards the German line, through our wire, through fresh shell-holes and the terrible moans of dying comrades, calling to us, God, their wives and mothers. We could do nothing to help them here.

Somewhere, off to my right and over the hill ahead, was my treasured French home. I was nearly there again, and had to make it onwards. Thoughts of Odile filled my whirling mind, to shut out the guns and noise and death all around me. But I could not let these thoughts last, and had to concentrate. As an officer, even one that was not assigned to this unit, I was at the front of the lines. We set off in good order, at least for a few steps. Some of the boys had seen the first wave cut down, but pressed on with clenched teeth and vice grips on their rifles, knuckles proud and chins up. Within just a few seconds, the heat and unseen mass of bullets whizzed past me on both sides. None of us could count on living through this. I expected nothing but searing agony or blackness at any moment. At least then I would know nothing of my own falling. Shells were landing right in amongst us, squarely aimed by some accursed enemy observer just like our own calling in the guns on us.

Two lads on my left simply disappeared in a red mist with not a trace of flesh on the ground, without warning and blessedly without them knowing anything. The wind from the shell took my breath away and when I did breathe in, the wetness of the explosion revolted and nauseated me. To my right, two soldiers embraced for support, as they were both hit at the same time. They encouraged each other to move on, out of this horror. As they fell to the floor, one was hit again in the stomach. The shrapnel slashed his abdomen, spilling his intestines, which fell to the floor, steaming, in an appalling splash of grisly stew. He looked down, amazed and terrified at the sight of his naked guts dropping to the floor. Mercifully, he died from this wound on that spot. The attending stretcher-bearer vomited on the corpse, was then shot cleanly through the helmet and fell forwards onto the growing pile of human remains. It was sheer murder and at this rate, no one was going to make it to the German trench, never mind fucking Bapaume.

I felt a new, but familiar, hot pain in my side and realised that I had been hit. *Damn, no, please not a wound that will leave me alive and motionless out here, unable to shelter.* But it was not too bad, and I could continue, even if at a stumble. At the rim of the enormous crater, a ghastly slaughterhouse revealed itself. It must have been two-hundred feet across, an almost perfect circle, and fifty feet deep. There were lumps of concrete and trench debris and human remains everywhere. Many of the bodies were completely naked as the blast had blown off their uniforms. This sight unnerved me most of all – probably because this was no way to die for a soldier, whatever country he came from. I did not know that this could happen. There were no survivors of this mine to interrogate. There was nothing left alive. Even the grass was burnt.

Inside the crater, the Grimsby Chums, some Irish lads and a number of tough-talking Geordie buggers were preparing a defensive position to hold the crater. They had gathered their courage and were looking to keep the ground already bitterly won. It seemed that the British guns were still firing on the crater, perhaps not knowing that it was, at least for now, in British hands. The smell of burning would have sickened me on any other day, but on this day, it was the least of the horrors confronting our men. The burnt explosive smell was comfortingly familiar and the mine blast had most certainly saved some lives, even in this brutal carnage. But the pile of smashed humanity below was a reminder that this was no place to hang about, and we had to press on.

The first and second waves were now totally mixed up, but those left were still grimly advancing towards the German positions. Within a few minutes, the smoke cleared enough to see that some of the soldiers were approaching the German wire – too few to take it, even with pulverised German defenders. It was also clear that the damage inflicted on the enemy front line was light. There were channels cut in the wire, but this only meant that machine gun fire could be aimed at the gaps where soldiers went to go through. It became a mad scramble for life. Many British uniforms were present right in front of the wire and trench wall. They survived the horror of No Man's Land only to die in the uncut wire of the enemy positions. They must have cursed the artillery, safer in the rear, and cursed the army for sending them out to prove this lie of intact wire.

Behind me and to my left now came the third wave. They were early – perhaps pressed into battle by worried officers as the day unfolded and the casualties mounted. At least this time, the men were advancing faster, as they were carrying less equipment and the barrage had long since lifted well over the German first line. In fact, the barrage was moving back and forth, but not ever troubling or defeating the rattle of the cursed machine guns. The third wave came up and around the crater and moved off towards Contalmaison, which was the major objective for this part of the line. Pressing on, with almost no prospect of reaching it today, if at all.

The lines were now in poor order. Many of the officers were dead or wounded and few were left to direct the remaining soldiers. The fourth and fifth waves were due out soon and this could and must not continue to be a ceaseless slaughter. I found two sergeants from the Grimsby and Tyneside waves. I knelt down to them, gripping my helmet onto my head as shells thumped around me. Some ghastly flesh-soaked soil was thrown up into my face and a clod of earth hit the back of my head. I shouted loudly at them, doubting they would hear me.

'Sergeant, get your men to that ridge on the right. See that shell hole? Get in there and set up some return fire, aim at the muzzles of the machine guns.'

'Sir, are we not going on at the trenches?'

'We can't here. Their firing is too much. Look at the casualties. The dead are lying on this line from the left, that gun is going to kill us all in this section. Get some control over their guns and we can have a go later. Quick, before we are blown to pieces.'

'Right sir. You three lads come on, up and away over there. Find the hole and get in. Where is the Lewis gun team?'

'Fucked Sarge. Copper and Ellis are alive, but they ain't going nowhere today and the gun is bent to fuck. I got two magazines here, look. Shall I bite on the bullets to fire at them, or just throw them at the bastards?'

I would try and get the Irish boys off and forwards towards the Germans, to pin them down and give the fresh waves a chance of getting through. Still, all around, the bodies continued to fall. Many cut down at the knees, because of the shape of the ridgeline. Not killed outright, but destined to bleed to death or linger in agony until thirst got them, surrounded by delirious images of their mothers here to rescue them and take them onward and out of pain.

Now I was moving right to the ridgeline shell hole, through a clump of tallish grass, still standing in defiance of the bombs and bullets, when I tripped over a poor Tynesider, who had been hit in the legs. He had lost both calves and feet and was bleeding to death. There was nothing to give him and my dressings could do nothing for him. I kept them on me, to use on someone who could at least be saved. It was an agonising decision. He had blood all over him. He had been wiping his hands on his legs, to see where they were. He was delirious and hopefully in a different place to here. Unfortunately, he was still in France, and he knew it.

'Am I to die, sir? Please tell me, is it bad?'

'Stay calm, Private. What is your name?'

'Thomas Albert Taylor, sir. From Cullercoats.'

'Well Thomas Taylor from Cullercoats. You just stay here and stay calm. Someone will come for you.'

'Will they sir, it doesn't look like much is getting up this far? It's cold here. I just ran at them, I did not know what else to do.'

'Well you did the right thing, Taylor, you did all that was asked of you. Your father and mother can be proud. You did your bit, now rest easy.'

A smile took over his face. He had done his duty alright, all that was asked of him. I left him and the clump of grass and made it to the shell hole.

'My God sir, are you alright? Here, let me dress that wound!'

'No, no it isn't my blood, it's one of your lads, a Thomas Taylor from Cullercoats.'

'Aye, Tinker! Dozy Geordie ran off straight at the enemy. Is he alive sir?'

'Yes, he is in that tall grass over there. It's bad though, so don't risk the stretchers this far I'm afraid.'

'No worries on that score sir, fuck all else getting this far. We're fucking dead, the fucking lot of us.'

We ducked for a shell that we knew to be coming close and we looked back over the shell hole to see it land. The clump of grass was gone.

The lines had now fully broken and we were fixed in, hopping from shell crater to shell crater, to get out of the continuous fire. We were pinned down on all sides and being fired upon from both directions. This was futile madness. Although given few orders for this operation, and not supposed to take part in the battle proper, I had been ordered to bloody well survive, to report back and amend the plans for our little operation. The information from today would be used to improve our tactics, ready for the next time. Maybe Cowling knew how much was committed to today, but I certainly hadn't appreciated the scale of this offensive. If we were going to make anything of our work, then it was to support this action today. It was bloody clear to me that the German positions were intact and although they had suffered, it was not nearly enough to prove decisive. Today was going to be a bloody disaster and all we were doing was counting their remaining guns with the lives of our poor pals.

The regimented rows of the fifth and sixth waves gave way to groups of three and four advancing through the smoke, all crouched down. Still taking incredible courage, they seemed to survive better and have more chance of advancing. Some of the first waves left alive had now made it into shell holes, just outside the German wire. They were only able to exist there unsupported, they could not advance and they were too few to launch an assault on the trench itself. Just ahead, the trench cut across the road from Albert to Contalmaison and that became the focus for my next movement. We had to get up and away, or risk being trapped and cut off. I had to get back to the start lines today. Around me landed a few of the fifth wave troops, seeming fresher and attuned to the sights of slaughter, grimly accepting their fate, whatever it was to be. They were ready to move forward in what was now a smoky and dusty landscape. We were all blood streaked, having been splashed by the dying all around us. Now was not the time to think about any of this, now was just for survival and moving onwards.

At the junction in the smashed up road we saw a natural break in the German wire and crawled for it. The earth continued to convulse as if wild animals were trying to escape from just below the surface. It was no time to stay here and wait to be blown to pieces. About fifteen of us moved sharply off towards the gap, keeping low and using the ground where possible. I felt another searing pain in my leg. A piece of burning hot shrapnel had lodged in my trousers, but with no damage to me. I would keep that piece of metal in my pocket as a souvenir.

Five of the boys ran into the gap and through towards the first German trench. The machine gunner was firing slightly to the right, but he had seen these troops and was frantically engaged in turning his gun around the fifty degrees or so needed to bring the gun to bear down on us. We saw for the first time, the faces of the German soldiers. They were not fully dressed, and looked dirty, tired and shocked. But they were alive and pointing machine guns at us.

The gun in front, guarding the approach to the trench, was aimed towards the left, along the main road. That meant we could sneak up and drop on top of them, which two of the Irish lads did. With cries of 'Hello Fritzy', they lobbed a bomb into the position and it exploded, destroying the position and killing the defenders. The two of them dropped into the trench, but were not seen anymore. They must have been killed and I hoped that they died quickly. These brave lads, as far as I could see, were the only boys to make it into the enemy trench so far in this part of the line.

The machine gun swinging round to us had completed its move and was now firing just above our heads. As a result, the shell hole was pinned down and ten soldiers would be unable to move unless the gun moved on, or was silenced. Only when some lads from the final two waves got to us, could we make an advance. These Scottish lads were fresh into France and it was their first action. They came into our holes and had the sense to bring bombs with them, rather than their equipment packs and trench tools. I ordered them out left and right. Perhaps they could draw the fire from the machine gun. The gun could not get to both groups at once, so perhaps we had a chance. One or other would be the target – it just had to be so. The group on the left climbed out first and was immediately subjected to machine gun and rifle fire, but it was not well aimed and they all got out alive, without wounds. The lads on the right crept out, on hands and knees, making it to the rim. The rest of us put our heads up and fired towards the trench, trying to pin down the enemy. Four of the lads made it to the brim of the gun position and dropped their bombs in, with little fuse time left. The Germans saw the bombs come in and they all piled up and over the rim in front of the trench as the bomb went off. The last two over were blasted up and over the position, dead, and the two in front were killed at the bayonet. It was an extraordinary act of bravery and later I made sure their officers were aware of the action in front of the enemy position. They moved up and over the rim and beckoned us into the trench. About six of them made it to the edge of the trench and down into the enemy positions, with much shouting and firing of rifles.

Just along the road, there was a small ridge in Sausage Valley, but to me, it was one of my old shortcuts. I was so close now to Odile, that I could almost see her. But I might as well have been in Australia for she was almost certainly no longer in Bazentin.

My group was relieved and overtaken by advancing soldiers from the last two waves. They reached the German trench and some further fighting took place. I know, from later reports of intercepted German messages, that some of them made it almost to Contalmaison, but I also know that none of them came back. None at all. My job today was not to lead a trench assault, but I did wait to see the 103rd Brigade go by. They advanced down the valley towards Contalmaison and it looked like some of them might make it as well. That cleared a path for me to return to the start lines, to get back and report.

My little wound, which was bleeding and open, would need to be dressed. It wasn't too bad though and certainly would not need a trip beyond a casualty-clearing station. I hopped back from shell hole to shell hole. Some occupied by the living, but many by our dead. As I made my way back to the start line, I was shocked again by the sheer number of dead bodies and dying men littering the ground very close to our lines. These poor buggers had been recruited, had left their home towns to cheers and tears, spent a year training, imagining glory and a victorious homecoming. They had been sent overseas on an adventure, only to die within a few seconds of going over the top for the first time. They suffered horrendous, undignified damage to their bodies that their families would never know. At least these bodies would have a burial. There are bodies here that have simply disappeared, without trace. Nothing. All over were pockets of dead and wounded, those still living moaning softly, calling out for dead comrades to come to them. Calling out for their mothers, their mind softening their suffering with images and visions of home to help them to their death. I certainly could not help them, the wounds to their bodies were just too great and in any case, stretcher-bearers were now mercifully moving between them, issuing morphine to anyone that could take it. Those with flesh wounds were encouraged to crawl back, where possible. Only those who could respond to their questions really stood any chance of help. Those with large open wounds that were bleeding were most likely to bleed to death. Many were left where they fell to die overnight. There was simply nothing else that could be done. Haunting screams, calls for help from the wounded, would echo around the battlefield only ceasing as each one succumbed to the indignities inflicted on their bodies.

We were still under heavy machine gun fire, but less was now directed at the start lines. Soldiers advancing drew the attention away from the opening positions. The barrage was now more concentrated, but still ineffective, still led with shrapnel which pinned down infantry, but did nothing to destroy the trench lines.

I reached the patch of ground just outside our wire where we had started and saw dead and dying soldiers draped over the entanglements, in full kit, with rifles in hand. Most had been hit by machine gun fire or shrapnel and some had been hit after death by shellfire as well, an extra and undeserved insult to their bodies. Soldiers were still jumping off and going through this grisly gate to move forwards. These were the last of the eight waves and many of them were either reserves or reinforcements, or communication teams, detailed to establish forward positions for messages, which would make grim reading.

At last, I carefully jumped down into our front-line trench and sought an update on the battle as a whole. The exasperated voice of an infantry captain came from the door of a small dugout.

'You say that *all* one-hundred-and-fifty are down? Are you quite sure? Look, let me say it again. I sent out one-hundred-and-fifty from the 101st Brigade over on the left of this, yes, that's right. I sent instructions for an update over two hours ago and all that comes back is a single runner telling me that they are all bloody dead. They can't all be dead?'

The poor lieutenant at the end of the statement bowed his head and solemnly replied,

'Yes, sir. They are all dead. The first wave was cut down completely, barely a dozen made it more than a hundred yards. The rest, in the second wave, were hit by artillery ranging on the first wave. There are none left alive, sir.'

The Captain, filthy and covered in a pink haze of blood, like the rest of us, had a shocked expression. He had already seen too much.

'Bloody hell, this is a damned disaster, a complete royal balls up of the first bloody magnitude. Any news from the Grimsby and Tyneside lads, Lieutenant?'

I was able to offer a reply.

'Captain, I was with the Grimsby lads. Many of them are dead, that's for sure, but some are defending the German side of the mine crater ahead. They are in there and putting up a show. They need more support, though. More bombs and some reinforcement. The Tynesiders are also advancing slowly along Sausage Valley, I don't know if they have reached the German lines yet, they were close, but not very many of them are there together. Some have taken out the machine gun positions, up there on the left.'

'Who the bloody hell are you? Ah a major, sir? What the devil is happening to my infantry operation – sir?'

'How many lads do you have left?'

'I'm taking a roll call. Information is scattered all about this place. What is clear is that I'm taking eighty per cent casualties – that's eighty per cent dead.'

'I'm sorry? Did you say eighty per cent?'

'Yes, sir. It's a bloody shambles.'

It was clear that the attacks along the valley, south of Contalmaison, were not at all successful. The Grimsby Chums taking on the mine crater had not broken through, despite unbelievable courage. The German defenders are fine soldiers and had done for our lads today. Reports from further south showed some success, but to the west and north our soldiers were cut down, too. My nerve slid away and I wanted tea, oddly, to stiffen my back again. Right from the start, I had promised Odile that I would not give up. Not that she heard, of course. Perhaps she was the only thing preventing me from becoming the poor bugger wobbling down the steps at Folkestone, being gently but firmly moved into a lorry, to goodness knows where.

Tea arrived and the roll call was taken, as planned, after the reinforcements were sent out. Of over four-hundred soldiers, in the waves near my action, only eleven were accounted for and a further fifteen were known to be alive, but still out in No Man's Land. The casualty rates were appalling. Troops were arriving for the evening garrison. Their orders were to move off from Contalmaison and consolidate the captured German front lines and convert them into British positions. I explained to their officers that the objectives set were not going to be achieved today, or any day soon. They would be better off attacking the forward trenches in support of the Geordies and the rush along Sausage Valley.

Back down in the trench, for the first time since coming to France in uniform, I gave in to the war and wept. It was unstoppable, an outpouring of emotion pent up over the last year, focused on the battle today. Wave after wave of tears came over me. Pink tears slipped off my chin, tasting of sweet blood and dirty salt water, stinging my parched lips.

I could still see the dead and dying in my head. I could still see the bloody bald head, the boy with his guts spilled and the Irish lads turned to dust in an instant. I could still see the frightened faces of the poor kids at zero hour moving up over the ladders, hardly looking like they knew what they were doing, with uniforms too big for them and rifles gripped with trembling hands, full of unfailing courage to do their bit. It was a pity that their bit today was to die on the parapet, barely yards from where they started. The poor buggers' faces came to me and I needed to let them go, or it would get me too. An hour of sleep, kept shallow by the constant flow of soldiers jumping off, left me without refreshment. I thought of Thomas Taylor from Cullercoats and the letters of sympathy his mother would receive. Well done, poor dead Taylor. Your idea for the battle, thought up in the field, was a damned sight better than the one the generals had thought up for this day, months in advance. Rest now, lad. Your duty was done. It was up to us now, to make your sacrifice worthwhile.

I made my way back through the support trenches, in a half-awake, half-dazed fog of Odile and the dead, entwined in a duel for my thoughts. Fresh troops passed me, coming up for the continuing attacks. It was clear the offensive was being pressed through with all vigour. They had to pass lines of wounded and dead to move up and goodness only knows what they were thinking as they passed the limping, grumbling, bandaged souls that were the living remains of the first waves.

The casualty-clearing stations were completely overwhelmed. A scene of total chaos made more appalling, as men were dying at the threshold of help. Stations set up to handle fifty casualties an hour had lines outside, stretching for hundreds of yards, perhaps upwards of five-hundred wounded soldiers awaiting attention at a station set up for fifty. Movements were confused and unplanned. The offensive had utterly unravelled and the failure to achieve any of the objectives would surely, over the next few days, mortally erode the morale of those troops left alive.

My authority got me on to a hospital transport, up front, so that I did not take the place of a seriously wounded soldier. As the lorry lurched towards an undamaged road, my wound was looked at. It was slight but needed tending, because an infection could be fatal. The lost blood had made me tired and weak, but hot tea worked wonders on my spirits and spurred me on to reach Cowling and report back. I had survived what would be named The Big Push or the first day of the Battle of the Somme. Later, I learned that over fifty-seven-thousand casualties were recorded on just that one day, with 19,000 dead. It was a casualty list that was impossible to comprehend, especially as the next day could be just the same. The next time I came back here, so close to Odile, it would be very, very different.

I was ordered back to the relative safety and calm of Albert, in the late evening of 1st July. The town was more subdued, still busy, but grim. The spirit had evaporated. The faces of the reinforcements and troops moving towards the Front, were grey and empty, no longer the cheery and smiling faces photographed on their way up. News had travelled fast. Some wounded had made it back this far and the tales, true and imagined, were beginning to trickle back from the battlefield. Staff officers heard with disbelief the lack of Allied penetration into German territory, especially in the area of north-west Albert, where I had been. The positive push further south and east and the French gains on the extreme right, were horribly overshadowed by the slaughter in the north and west. Nowhere had seen positive gains and the advance had been halted everywhere by the hellish gunfire and shelling of the intact German defences. It was planned to keep going with the offensive, come what may. If this was going to continue, I had to act now and get a plan put into action to get back at the enemy – this time, from behind.

A car arrived to collect me and inside was Cowling, looking stern and focused. With no introduction, he started talking without looking in my direction.

'My God Collins, look at you. Is this how it is for us fighting here? Dear Lord. Well, seeing you like that, I am resolved. We have to move fast. Today must have been terrible and I will read your reports with great interest. However, we must move now and with all haste, put an action into the field. Do you feel ready?'

'Yes, sir. Do you think we will be anywhere near the starting point we want? We were supposed to be advancing on Bapaume by now, but we are stuck and cut to pieces.'

My voice trailed away and there was resignation in my reply.

'Well, we have to create enough mayhem in the right place for long enough to give us a chance. If we push on, we will have La Boisselle by maybe the third or fourth and the goal is still to be Bapaume. Can you get in from somewhere east of the Albert–Bapaume road and work back towards Longueval? That's the enemy's second line of defences and they are not finished building yet.'

'We did discuss it, sir. But the infantry have hardly moved, it was truly appalling here today. So, how many will we have to operate – the full sixty?'

'That will soon be discussed. You need to meet someone first, in absolute secrecy. Stay in that wretched bloodstained uniform. It may serve as a little encouragement to act.'

We drove along roads now choked with reinforcements and the

wounded, both groups eyeing the other suspiciously and then with compassion and mutual sympathy. It seemed that every few yards was a makeshift dressing station. So this was what forty-thousand wounded looked like. And it would be the same tomorrow and the day after if nothing changed.

My hands were still dirty with the awful pink colour, mixed in with dirt and darker blood – probably from Thomas Albert Taylor from Cullercoats. He was no different to Thomas Moller, just in different uniform. My hands were trembling, as if I were standing in the freezing cold. Cowling noticed, but said nothing. My chest was still vibrating, as if I had sat on a lorry engine all day, at full speed. The sounds of the shells still reverberated in my head and down my spine. The sights of soldiers crumpling under fire and disappearing would not go away and haunted every moment my eyes were closed. When I breathed out, a low groan accompanied every breath as all the muscles in my chest were tensed at the same time. The war was weighing heavily on my shoulders and I had to survive and see Odile again in this life.

Behind the lines of returning wounded were more companies of fresh troops forming up for action over the next few days. They had the same expression I had at Folkestone. They looked shocked, but they would not falter, until cut down by bomb or bullet. These fellows were just the same as the ones out there on the battlefield – they just hadn't seen the shells of the Somme yet.

Cowling said no more, but looked out of the window and rubbed his neck thoughtfully. *Had he spoken with Rawlinson again? Were our plans serious?* I had a feeling that I was about to find out.

As we left Albert, we turned off to a smaller side road, off the route to Amiens, almost untouched by the war. In a small tent at the side of the Amiens road, stood two perfectly crisp unformed staff officers and a sentry in a blood-red military policeman's uniform. There was senior brass inside the tent. The door of the car was opened for me and I was almost thrown inside the tent. My uniform was dirty and no doubt smelled of the trench, but that was, after all, the result of being in the middle of this bloody war. Inside, there was a small map table and two lamps. The evening light was good, but they had been lit, lighting up the region of Picardie I called my home. An older figure of authority emerged from a curtained area to the right of the tent.

'Ah – Cowling? Good. You must be Collins, Major? Goodness, your kit is a state. I suppose you were in the action today. Things are moving quickly here, gentlemen.'

Bloody hell it was Rawlinson himself, having made a journey in secret to meet with us, right in the middle of his reading the first battle reports. He did not look to be in a good mood. Something had happened to him, or was about to.

'Good evening sir!' I snapped off a brisk salute and realised that it had been unnecessary, as Rawlinson was already preoccupied and not inclined for formality this evening.

'Collins, I have heard with interest your plans from Mr Cowling here over the last few weeks and months. I am not a great fan of underhanded practices. A dirty and cowardly way to fight a war – it was only twenty years ago we fought in red coats so that the enemy knew we feared them not. Oh, sit down by the way.'

Rawlinson gestured grumpily to a chair in the middle of the canvas room. This felt like an interrogation of my ideas and perhaps this might be followed by the necessary assent. I reflected on where my life in the army had taken me. From a lowly nobody in Folkestone, to a major in the field, in the presence of the commander of the 4th Army at the Battle of Albert, Arras or whatever it was to be called. It was a big thing, but I still had not comprehended how big or how much of an investment in risk the military had put into this effort.

'Cowling, this evening we have sought to review the positions on the left and right of the Bapaume road. Talk to me about the right. You proposed to me an action, operating from an intended base in German occupied territory behind their front line. This is untried, untested, damnable in the extreme and risky. You propose action in an area that we have no way of knowing will have been captured. If it does not succeed, it will be the death, by execution, of all who move into enemy territory. You know the Germans execute soldiers they find behind their lines? I'm giving you authority to put into place this action but I can give you only one day to finalise details. You know where we are now and where we are likely to be. Give me the final location for your assault and I will authorise your operation. Let me tell you, I want the second line taken quickly before they get a chance to finish building the defences.'

Cowling looked to me, nodded and then simply said, 'High Wood, that is the Bois de Foreaux, Longueval and Pozieres.'

That was it, I was going to return to Odile. My heart leapt.

'When do you think you could be ready to launch the attack?'

'The battle today has given us few clues as to the rate of progress. Our soldiers attack at every turn with bravery and zeal. We won't make Bapaume in a week, so let us aim to be at High Wood to launch in exactly two weeks. It is the highest point around their second line, it will soon be well defended, but we have some thoughts on how to take it.'

I looked at Cowling and then to Rawlinson.

'Sir,' I fixed on Rawlinson, 'if we want the French to help, then it needs to be worth it. Two weeks' time would be 14th July. That would stir the courage of any Frenchman, or woman.'

'Agreed.'

'One thing, Cowling. The Germans have evacuated the civilians from the whole area, north of Bapaume, possibly even Cambrai. How do you think the French can help?'

'I don't know, sir. But if it is possible to contact them, then something could be done, I'm sure.'

'Excellent news. General Gough is picking up the bill west and north of the road. I want this objective taken, make no mistake and be under no doubt of the gravity of this day.'

I left in higher spirits, if that is the right way to describe my feelings for we were moving slowly forward from La Boisselle. On our right at Fricourt and Mametz, the French and the Allies had moved over the ridge and taken the valley in front. We had taken Montauban and we were forming a circle on Mametz Wood.

Mametz Wood, I had spent so many afternoons there, with Odile, lazing in the breeze and taking in the sunshine. An occasional kiss and some occasional wine. How different it was now. Mametz, like all the other villages around this battlefield, was barely visible amongst the angry churn of war; the ground, so insulted and blighted that it would be hard to recognise. However, the date had been fixed and I had been given a day to finalise our plans. This required quick thinking about where we might get to and what we might be in a position to achieve.

On the journey back, my mind was full of this operation. My hands bore the blood of Thomas Taylor and my mind was filled with the dead, but there, at the back, in a ray of perfect light was Odile. Now a symbol of my struggle in these times and the reason for pushing myself back into the line. I must live to be there for her, she was worth this effort, this sacrifice of my soul. If only there would be enough left of me to love, come the end of the war. It was hard to know how the war would turn out – this had been the worst day of our lives. The war was a damnation of humanity and for the first time, I really considered that we might not win.

CHAPTER ELEVEN - TWO WEEKS TO M DAY

We returned to our temporary billets near Albert in desolate silence, my thoughts on the job to come and the day just completed. Some of my team, upon seeing me cast in a shroud of death, seemed visibly shaken. In time, they too, would be in my place. But for now, they had to quickly engage with the plan. The appalling opening day would be lived again soon enough. Our time had come swiftly and not as we had hoped, but such was the nature of our new business.

In the early hours of 2nd July, we set off for our training camp nearer to the 4th Army HQ at Chateau Querrieu, with fresh ideas and the general's order to put a plan together. We rocked over the bumps in the road and eventually Cowling leaned sleepily across to me.

'William, you know we aren't going to get to Bapaume, whatever we throw at the Germans. The futility of our attack, well it staggers me to the core. We have sent over wave after wave of our Allied youth and all we have managed to do is to capture a few yards of trench and put the wind up most of the rest of the 4th Army.'

He rubbed his nose silently for a second before continuing. I wondered if he was deciding whether to say anything further, or hold his tongue. He chose to speak.

'Do you think we are wasting our time on some folly behind the lines, or is this a serious proposition? I am wavering, William. Am I to commit less than a hundred men to a battle – expecting nothing but success – when we have left thousands dead in No Man's Land today? God, I can barely say it. Thousands, William, our own boys. We can't ever bring them back.'

'Colonel, I am certainly willing to give this a try. When the enemy picks up his gun to fire back at us, we will have made sure that it falls to pieces in his hands, or better still, blows up in his bloody face.'

'But sixty, Collins, sixty. That's not much of an army.'

'But see sir, that's the whole point. A small number of men will not be expected. We will be in amongst them and we can tear them up a bit, don't you think?'

'Hmm. Tell me more about Bazentin again. That's just south and west of their second line.' Cowling turned directly towards me on the seat. His face looked pale and tired.

'It is a simple farming village, sir. But it is surrounded by small copses and dense woodland. We can hide in the remaining trees and launch an attack from an area not yet destroyed by shelling – providing there is one. The ground isn't done for everywhere, and I know the roads well, if they are still there. We can move in the dark and if we get behind the German front-line sentries, we can mix it up a bit.'

'Can you be ready in two weeks?'

'Yes.'

'How do you know? Talk me through your preparations again, and in particular tell me about how you will operate in Bazentin.'

For the next hour, I talked about how we might deploy in the aeroplanes, overloaded and coming at the drop zones from different directions, with varying levels of apparent mechanical damage. I talked about the equipment and weaponry we would use and what our objectives might be. I talked about how we would move and how we might fight our little war in support of the front-line troops now due to attack. We discussed various options for launching the attack: early morning at stand-to; in the evening in the hour after dusk, not before. We even discussed my thoughts on a night attack, the major fighting occurring right before dawn. This offered us surprise, coupled with more opportunity to confuse the defending Germans. It was much riskier to us, whatever the Germans might do, as the soldiers could get lost and confused in the fighting and there was more chance of injury from wire in the darkness. Although the sun rose in the early hours in July, it would still mean an hour or so in the dark. That idea appealed to me best of all.

'In terms of actual targets, Colonel, I am in favour of blowing up their ammunition stores, the ones right on the Front. These are the ones feeding the machine guns and they take some transporting. When we shell them, we do see a difference. We just don't get enough of them – they are mobile, I suppose.'

'William, that all seems sound, but is it enough? How will the French be involved? How can we get to them to help? Are you just going to walk up to them and whisper in their ears that you need their help? We have no communication with the French north of the Front at all. The ones south are windy as hell. They think the enemy is going to break through at any point. Verdun has been a sickener for them, of course. It's nearly dropped them out of the show altogether, poor buggers.'

One complication that must be overcome was the likely position of our front-line troops on the fourteenth, which we could not know in advance, especially after the day's action. Having decided that Bapaume was unlikely to be reached and with an unproductive first day of battle, the potential rate of progress was hard to judge. The soldiers had pushed on, and no doubt over the next few days would push on further, but Bazentin was still a couple of miles from our current location. It would be a big gamble, to assume we would be near enough on a specific day. Cowling was a gambler, Rawlinson was not, but might have had his hand forced. Cowling had discussed all of this with Rawlinson and he agreed to consolidate at Mametz Wood, assuming we had made it through the wood by then. If we could get to the wood and hold it, then it would be an excellent place to jump off from, to take the villages over the ridge and on towards Bapaume. The second line was, after all, a target that would need a special effort to overcome.

A meeting was arranged for 1100 on 2nd July. In the hour before we gathered, I thought back over the four years to 1912 and walking in Mametz wood with Odile, the picnic we had with some stolen cider and that brilliant, if oily, motor bicycle. I wondered what the wood looked like right now. It was at once incredible and distressing to imagine that beautiful countryside, so torn by this war. It would not be the same place. The woods in Mametz would be blown to matchsticks – if they were not already – by the war creeping towards the villages. Would the village, the roads, and the fields be recognisable? It was doubtful and I found myself using the drawn map instead of the one imprinted in my head. Thousands of lives would depend on me, my knowledge, my nerve, fighting abilities and my experience. My proposal was to sneak out of the trenches and land in German territory to shorten this war at a single stroke.

Cowling had informed Rawlinson that we had selected the target and were ready to depart. The meeting opened solemnly enough with further reports of continued casualties on the morning of 2nd July. The general also confirmed the new command structure. Rawlinson himself would focus on the east. However, gains were being made at a terrible cost, in the south at Fricourt and on the assault through Montauban by the tough lads from Liverpool and Manchester. Trenches and shell holes were being occupied under terrible and murderous machine gunfire. The slopes meant that many soldiers were being cut at knee height, which can result in agonising death. Soldiers were being brought into hospitals with catastrophic amputations and with lumps of useless flesh hanging off them. I tried not to imagine that appalling suffering and to focus on the meeting.

'Gentlemen. We are in play and have to move quickly. The assault on the first line has not been successful and we are to plan and execute an assault on the second line from Pozieres to Longueval. Because of the losses, we are leaving immediately. We depart tomorrow at 0800 for a temporary billet south of Albert. The aeroplanes will then take us over the German lines at 1100 in groups flying a variety of routes over the lines to avoid suspicion. It will be daylight, but it would be less suspicious and would rouse less curiosity than a night flight. We will then land in German occupied territory, within striking distance of their regimental quarters around Bapaume. The aeroplanes will make distressed landings and scatter quickly. The Germans will expect a single occupant. We have to get into hiding quickly and avoid detection. The German units discovering each aeroplane will not be in communication with units on the other sites. It would look somewhat suspicious and coordinated to see every cockpit empty, with every flyer having been able to escape undetected and unharmed. It is a risk and we are going to take it. We may need to destroy the aeroplanes, by bombing the cockpits, to buy us more time to get away.'

The faces of the team remained expressionless. They had not passed their threshold of disbelief just yet, or were stoically professional, listening to their officer's ideas.

'Once we are down and away, we are to split into the three smaller teams detailed here in this note. The first team's objective will be to find and disrupt the munitions dump at the junction of the Albert road on the map marked with the blue letter A. It was there on the twenty-ninth and I have no reason to expect it to be either empty or to have been moved. When an attack comes on the second line, this dump will take on greater importance, to supply the guns and the small arms of the machine gun teams.'

Still, faces were unmoved and unchanged. No one yet appeared to have doubts, or they still elected to suppress them.

'The second squad will make their way directly to the Bapaume HQ buildings and discover how their communications operate, through observation of telephony and telegraph. We must be as disruptive as possible and cause total confusion. It will be the riskiest and least planned element of this operation. Look round and do what you can. We should have had more time to think this one out, but there we are. What was Professor Hampson's phrase? Adapt, improvise and solve!'

The first eyebrows twitched. This looked like trusting to luck and not knowing what we intended to do. This response was no surprise, but the team would work independently and pull off their objective with limited direction from me.

'The third squad will work back towards Martinpuich and follow the terrain closely, using every hollow and valley, to get to the German strong point from behind. This squad will be led by me, as I know this part of

France extremely well. We will then make our way via the old road, up the slope towards Bazentin Wood. We must hope that the army makes it to Mametz Wood by then, or we are all for it. The objectives will be to poison the preparations for the second line. To confuse, misdirect and handicap their ability to supply a battle they may not know is coming.'

Some appeared to be forming questions in their minds, but none were asked, at least not yet.

'Our objective will be to disrupt the enemy from behind. We haven't done this before and it's not absolutely certain what we can do here. We have authority from the commander of the 4th Army to try, so try we will, using all resources possible on the ground to disrupt front-line operations.'

'Sir, what is the timing for the days after landing in Bapaume?'

'Squad one will have three days to locate and destroy the munitions dump. We are targeting the rifle and machine gun ammunition dumps, as we feel this will cause the most problems at the front line. The artillery dumps are too well protected, if they are anything like ours, and we won't be able to get to the fuses anyway, so it would be a suicide mission. The rifle and bullet dumps will stop their damned machine guns when we go. You can set bombs with instant fuses, set the way we practised. If they get moved, then everything goes up. Squad two will remain until the assault on the fourteenth. They will try to prevent effective communications and disrupt the movement of orders if at all possible. I don't expect assassinations of officers – what I do expect is the extraordinary coincidence of pigeon release, mysterious fires in key buildings and orders going astray. We have worked out what works best on our own side and so these are the likely targets over there as well. Squad three will move under whatever cover we can get from Bapaume back to Martinpuich. We can seek to prevent the units receiving orders and maybe to estimate their defences and help the infantry in their assault of this new second line. Then, when we do attack, they may well not even know about it and certainly won't have sufficient forces in the lines for a decent defence. If we can help stop the damn thing being built, that might help as well.'

During this brief, casualty reports were coming in from other actions on 2nd July. The Grimsby Chums had found some ground to hold and the Tynesiders had consolidated, but still at a terrible cost to their ranks. Further waves had jumped off from the new forward positions and were beginning to make some slow progress. It was smaller, less grand with thankfully fewer losses to troops traversing No Man's Land. But in the north, it was again a disaster and no progress was being made anywhere there, with the German lines holding. This worried me enormously, especially when it was revealed that attacks would be more locally directed without an overall plan across the broad front. We saw this as being a recipe for high casualty rates.

But, a chance to get a local battle in play at last.

That afternoon, I spent more time with Cowling. This was likely to be the last time that we would be together before we went – possibly even the last time we would see each other. Cowling was going to try and anticipate our needs, once the operation started, as communication would be impossible from behind enemy positions. We could not carry pigeons, there was no possibility of telephone connections and nothing locally in France could be used to get messages across. We had objectives and lists and that was it.

'Colonel, tell me again how we are to ensure we are ready on the fourteenth. We might have overrun Bazentin Ridge by then and then all of our preparations go out to sea?'

'Collins, don't think for a minute that we will have made that amount of progress. If we do, then we will make sure the attacks are concentrated and planned to put us in an ideal position to attack on 14th July, and no further. Beyond the ridge is their damned second line and that will take an enormous effort to overcome, Longueval won't be easily taken.'

'Yes, very good sir.'

'Collins, this looks like it for us. We will need to get on with our respective plans, so best of luck old chap and for God's sake, stick to the bloody plan.'

'Yes sir!'

We parted at that point, quite formally and politely. Perhaps Cowling had it do it like that otherwise he may not have been able to do it at all. The troops were ready to embark on something never attempted before. Anyone learning of these plans would have laughed and called us bigger fools than we probably were.

But, we were truly ready. We at least now had an objective. July 14th 1916 would be the day of return to my real home in France, even if, as suspected, it was in total ruins and empty of Odile and her family.

CHAPTER TWELVE - MOVING THE PIECES

I knew that from the time our operation received approval, the clock would be ticking and timing would be everything. The infantry advances planned for 1st July had failed. The memory of men walking slowly – beating a pace that was shocking with hindsight – towards utter destruction sickened my torn soul. Having seen this appalling trench warfare up close, it took all my strength to hold on and keep going. My strength and my desperate desire to see Odile again. The loved one drawing me back to that beautiful little village would not be there, but I wanted to hold on to my future and not give it up on this battleground. Most likely the buildings and fields would be gone by then and the slopes would be a landscape from hell. My need was to feel closer to her and to be normal again. I had been lucky so far, moving in and out of the line pretty much at will, and with strange jobs to perform. Engineer, miner and now tactician and battle planner. The world was a whirling madness around me and I was being drawn ever nearer to the centre.

Cowling had left me a letter to read, but under no circumstances to take with me. In fact, he had detailed his batman to take it off me by the time night fell. The contents were strangely non-military and still etched on my mind.

Major William Collins RE
(Attachment 12 Field Ops.) 02 July 16

William,
You are about to undertake an operation in enemy held France that stretches to the limit all military credibility and credulity. A team of only 60 men of junior rank is to undertake operations to disrupt enemy activity to force an opportunity for a breakthrough to the high ground of the Pas-de-Calais region. Our hopes for rapid victory have evaporated and withered on the vine of the Picardie hills and valleys and now, we have been given a chance to redeem morale and press on for the work to be done. Do what you can, you are assured of free passage back through our lines, wherever they may be, at any time, for I do not know where this operation may end – STALKER –. I suspect we may not meet again, by that I mean if we are successful, we both may be assigned other duties. If we are unsuccessful, my heart will be torn from me, for I have invested every sinew of courage into seeing this operation have life. If you should be captured, then I can imagine only one fate for you and I must speak plainly on this matter. You propose operating in and out of uniform. I can state no official position on your decision. But I seek no awareness of your methods and actions. Remember, you are an honourable soldier of the line, I can say no more on this matter than that. For the operation I will ensure that the preliminary preparations and actions are undertaken to put us north of Mametz Wood and then hold there, short of what we believe to be the second line preparations. I think this is possible from where we now find ourselves. I think Longueval and Contalmaison are the best for our options. You know the ridge and the Bois de Foureaux behind it. Think about that and we will be there. It feels like a game of chess playing out on the field squares of France – seems like a mad game to me! Remember what we said about the 14th, the time for the attack and what we plan to do. I will try and have something special for you in the morning – a parade – you remember what that was?
We have done everything we can to ensure our success. I have some influence with HR, but he is his own man and we can't be sure it will be allowed to proceed. Plans may change if success is denied us until M Day.
I have just had word that the enemy has moved a Guard division into the line. I also understand that a senior general, possibly even Falkenhayn, has visited this sector today. We might field five divisions. Also, on the aeroplane landings, have arranged 10 escorts imagined to be bombing the railway lines in Cambrai as cover for your movements.
Do not forget to give this to Wilson to burn. He has orders to recover by all means.

Arthur Cowling Col. OC 12 Field Ops

Eleven days behind the lines, beyond No Man's Land and behind the German second positions. *Was Cowling's letter a warning written in a friendly note?*

I read the note over and over, sitting on the wall of the convent that we were using as our temporary base. The French had evacuated the occupants in 1914, as the Germans appeared over the horizon. Little was left from their occupation, but there was lots from us – trodden gardens and open spaces dug up or tented over. The war was here for the foreseeable future. But this would be my last night at the convent. It was my turn again to have a go at the enemy.

In the morning, we would move back to the aerodrome in order to take flight over the lines. The pilots had again assured us that this drop off would be entirely possible, even fun to do. We would be well covered with bombing runs off to the north and Cambrai, as well as spotting raids over Bapaume. Here though, the Germans liked taking potshots with their rifles. Normally, a pilot would expect one or two minor hits, but Bapaume was a hub for the German Army and lots of well-armed soldiers delighted in trying to take down aeroplanes for sport. We could not afford their interest in our operation.

The soldier pilots had completed their rudimentary training in flight. The soldiers could make their flying look functional and convincing – that's about all they could manage anyway – it was likely we would look every bit the distressed aeroplanes necessary for our cover. The Flying Corps was concerned at the planned loss of twenty fully serviceable aeroplanes. They had only around four-hundred in service anyway. We were going to commit about five to ten divisions to this attack, so we needed this machinery to give ourselves a chance.

Thinking back to the men in the line at La Boisselle, the memories washed over me again – inescapable now – the shouts over the top, the screams, the pain, the flesh, the smell and the visceral courage to go on and through, even after seeing the faltering attack. I could still feel the vibration of the big mine, in front of the village. It was appalling slaughter on a scale I had never ever imagined man devising. There would still be fresh young faces, peering around their mates, to see the front and get to the action. My God.

During the night, there were sporadic attacks with the rattle of guns and the crack of rifles. There were shouts, whistles and thuds of shells exploding – mostly shrapnel, for this was now men in the field, not wire to be cut and bunkers to be blown. None of us slept at all. The view north from Albert was tinged with red flashes, lights and the sounds of men fighting, if they made it out of the trenches in the first place. Ashamed at the thought, I wondered if the men cut down on the first day had been rescued, or whether they had all died in the field from their wounds.

Hopefully, their final thoughts were of home and their minds protected them from the true horror of the battlefield.

At 0400, the sky started to lighten and it was time to get on with the day. At this time of day, there was enough light to move about on the ground. Perhaps a night attack might be worth a try, after all.

The field kitchen was under orders to prepare something half decent, but we still got corned beef, which we called monkey meat, with almost solid potatoes, as no fuel was available to waste on cooking. Army corned beef wasn't too bad, but because it was all we had to eat, it got on our backs.

By 0630, we were ready to go. Our equipment seemed so light, how exposed we would be if spotted, or worse, captured and interrogated. If that happened, we would certainly be shot.

The men knew as little as possible of the details in my mind. They needed to know their own objectives and the timings, but I had not entirely thought through the full range of outcomes. Besides, if interrogated, they could tell all they knew and that might imperil the rest of the operations. Cowling and I had thought through the next two weeks and hoped that we could at least get some of the details right. He had hoped, and would be planning, to get the infantry in position for a five-division attack right on Bazentin Ridge, to the left and to the right.

It was hard to believe that this was exactly where the happiest time in my life had been. The little, almost insignificant slope, was where the enemy had chosen to make a stand. So be it. Cowling would try and bring up the right from Montauban and on the left, from Contalmaison. In the centre, Mametz Wood and Bazentin-le-Grand would be the target before and on the 14th July. These names and places were so familiar to me and every one could be walked in an afternoon, each with a loving and tender memory. Here, we would be committing five divisions in all likelihood.

It was impossible to take in the enormity of this action. Cowling seemed confident the preparatory actions would be successful. The hills and valleys were not really in our favour yet, but I trusted his word. His plans would mean that there would not be a single concerted attack all along the front, but smaller battles for limited objectives. We would see how effective these might be and Rawlinson, this time, happily agreed.

I had planned to go ahead in advance to the aerodrome and see the aeroplanes we would be using. We had been given some new machines, just out of the factory, that had been specially modified to take men as cargo. It was a short flight and there would be almost no fuel in the tanks, so that allowed for an extra passenger. They were also modified to look like they had been attacked. Some of the frames were knocked about a bit and some of the skin was deliberately torn in places that would not change the flying abilities, but look to an infantryman like the kite had been shot at, or hit by shellfire. They were called BE2 aeroplanes and normally carried a crew of two. They had two seats so both crew could fly the aeroplane. The pilot and second crew member were soldiers and the third would be in the mid-section, but crouched towards the front, to keep the aeroplane flying straight. We knew the machines could do it and they could fly like they had been hit, which was good for us.

The three occupants and all of the equipment could not weigh more than nine-hundred pounds. It would be a sitting target and any enemy fire would cause casualties, especially to the third non-flying crew. Any damage would likely bring the aeroplane down, as the pilots were barely able to fly – we just did not have the access to aeroplanes to make them better pilots. Still, our chances were better here than in the murderous trenches that were being attacked now daily in our sector. The aeroplanes normally had a machine gun, but we would not have any use for it in the air, or on the ground, so we gave the ones that came with the aeroplanes to the infantry. They liked the novelty mounting and took them off as souvenirs, with the guns being pressed into service.

The weather was not perfect, but it was calm enough to fly and it was decided to go in daylight as planned. Whilst it made us more of a target, we were hiding in plain sight as we had aeroplanes flying over constantly, especially on bombing and spotting raids. If it was dark, the landing would be impossible and with pilots so lightly trained, that would mean certain death.

We gathered on the grass near the aeroplanes, idly checking our equipment and eyeing the machines suspiciously. To avoid trouble, we would take off in groups of two aeroplanes and fly out in different directions, each looking as if it had no connection with the others, perhaps spotting for the infantry. We did not say much, but stood in quiet reflection. What we were doing was nearly impossible, mad and many of us would not see each other or home again. I sat on the grass and spoke with my Odile, quietly.

'Darling Odile. This is the day I have been waiting for, for such a long time now. My silly plans to get the enemy have come to life on this ground we call home. Wherever you are, whatever you are doing, I hope that just for a second, you can really feel me in your thoughts and dreams. You are always on my mind and you are the biggest part of my being. Please be safe until I can come to you and keep you safe always. Stay strong my love and if it is at all possible, think of me now, sitting here. I may not survive these next days.'

'Sir, sorry, sir. Better be getting off. It is time to go.'

'Thanks Watkins. Let's get at them.'

'Still feels odd though, sir, aiming to land in enemy ground.'

'It's not theirs, Horace, it belongs to France and we will give it back to them.'

We climbed onto the machines, which were already hot and smelling strongly of oil. The smell reminded me of that motor bicycle in Bazentin, which gave me a strange comfort – part of clinging on to anything that reminded me of normality. It was almost impossible to visualise this as being the same land. The aeroplane itself was awfully cramped, painful and there was nothing but a bit of metal, wood and canvas to separate us from a deadly drop to the ground.

In our planned groups, we took off towards an uncertain future. It was a tremendous sensation to move so fast and then lift up into the air. I was certain that we would crash at any time. My own aeroplane took me over the right of the lines, past Mametz and Fricourt and over the French lines at Combles. Others flew away and we would not see them again in this operation. The aerodrome was quite a long way back from the lines, but it did not take long to get to the front. It was an odd and superior feeling to fly above the lines and see just what a narrow strip of hell we had all created.

We carried on away towards the east but no further, as a British aeroplane over French lines would look suspicious to German observers and it would only take one suspicious call to jeopardise our operation. We were also on the lookout for German aeroplanes keen to send us back, or even down. My pilot, Henry Miles-Dunning, had shown me how this could be done. He at least knew how this machine worked. He wasn't a trench soldier like most of us, but he was good in the planning and had earned his right to come with us many times over.

My third companion, to ride with the pilot, was Horace Watkins. I had been told he was a tremendously brave soldier in the field. Watkins had been recruited directly for this mission. He was a hard, tough sergeant regular who had joined the army before the war. An 'Old Contemptible' he had been at Mons and the Marne. He apparently had not taken any leave since 1915, and had not returned to England at all since war was declared. He spoke good French, but his German was as poor as mine and we both hoped not to be captured. He was a ruthless soldier and this trait would be needed on this mission. With him, I was fighting with a capable and loyal soldier. I liked him immediately and selfishly made sure he was in my team.

We turned left and I peered through a little hole that had been cut into the skin as part of the preparations. The air coming in was icy cold and dried my eyes terribly, but I wanted to look. We flew towards Le Transloy, now in enemy territory and committed to this venture. There was no going back. Below was some war damage through shelling, but there was surprisingly little evidence of battle elsewhere, north or south. The war had not been this way for some time and the land was healing. Towards

Longueval, I could make out some fields, which could be the area we would attack on the fourteenth. Albert and the spire were visible in the far distance. Below and in the middle distance, was the grey and brown mess of the Somme battlefield in our sector. Bapaume looked so close, barely any marching distance. It should have been taken by now, but was as far away as ever. Hopefully, we would be going that way very soon.

As we started to descend, the ground below seemed green and fresh, almost untouched by the war. There were German units around and pockets of soldiers and machinery, but it seemed fairly quiet this far behind the front line. We chose a field that was deserted on a downslope to hide our landing. There were no other aeroplanes around, so none of our comrades had come this way. By starting to fly erratically, it looked like we had been repeatedly hit. We came in at a terrifying speed and touched the ground with an awful grinding noise. The skids caught the earth, dug in and we tumbled over. I was thrown probably five feet into the air and landed feet first onto the earth, which was soft. Unable to keep my feet, I rolled over a few times but at a slow speed and on thankfully soft ground. The pilot was unharmed, as he had been tied into his seat. Watkins was also fine, a bit shaken and upside down, also still tied in his seat – that had been a great tip from the spy missions. We quickly pulled all of our equipment out from under the aeroplane and ran for the cover of the hedge, which was slightly further downhill. No one came to investigate in the first fifteen minutes. That was good. We had been spotted, but had not caused any alarm. Aeroplanes had been flying over this area every day without being shot at, or setting off any alarm. The bombing runs north towards Cambrai had left the army on the ground bored of seeing overflying aeroplanes. At least this part had been successful.

We had to sabotage our aeroplane to make it look like a crash landing and one in which the pilot had already been thrown out and presumably killed somewhere else. We tore a few bits from the engine and although it was hot, my hands were comfortable being on an engine again. Quickly, we completed the task, and hid in the hedge again. Still no one came. This was going to be a good start to our action. The aeroplane now looked like it had crashed, without the aid of a living pilot, who had clearly fallen out before crashing, possibly miles away. With any luck, the enemy would take a curious look, shrug and move on unconcerned.

We would see nothing from the rest of our men, once we were in the field and the action had started. Each of us had objectives, contingencies and escape routes, so there was no real need to group together. However, we would meet up with just one other group and seek our nearby objectives together. Everyone else was now following the plan, using their own initiative and relying on their training.

Moving off from the hedge, slowly and with our heads down, we used the slight slope to cover our open ground movements. We were able to keep out of sight and move quickly. What we were not able to do was to see into the distance to work out if we had been spotted. Once out of the open field, we could move about more normally, as we could begin to blend in with the surroundings. A curious group of German soldiers idly wandered up to our aeroplane. They kicked it a couple of times and then left, hopefully satisfied that there was nothing else to see.

By now, we were now quite near to Bapaume itself where some of our team had been detailed to disrupt communications. Telephone wires would be cut in places that would be unexpected and hard to find. Several German divisions had their headquarters there and we would be able to disrupt the flow of orders to the front line. As time passed, our ability to know the movements of the Allies would diminish, as many of their actions could not be planned so far ahead. The movements of the Germans would be easier for us to see, but we could do nothing to help our troops with this information, such was our position now in this war. Some of our team could go on and create diversions in the town, especially where munitions were stored. We were not intending to go into Bapaume, although I really wanted to, just to see how it had changed.

What was immediately obvious, was the degree of general alarm that the Allied offensive seemed to have created. The Germans were sure of their defensive lines and the depth of their dugouts, but despite this, there was movement at pace, especially in the transport of ammunition for the artillery. They were moving more artillery shells nearer the line. When we spotted a transport, we would follow them, note the position of the dump and return to disrupt it under cover of darkness.

We moved quickly to the south-east of the town, in a quieter area away from the open roads, which were full of German carts and limbers taking machinery and weapons to the front line a few miles to the south. I was able to make out some of the orders being given. The horses were due to go out towards Mametz and the wood nearby, which the Germans were planning to occupy and defend as this was in front of their new second line. I thought about the lads from the 15th Corps who were there the last time. Some of them were looking forward to breaking through, but the defenders here looked strong in number, with plenty of equipment. I was planning to make my way south and east towards Martinpuich or across to Bazentin-le-Petit, where the terrain would help me. The strength of the defensive positions was an unknown, but that would be something to deal with upon arrival – no sense worrying about it here. This was a familiar area where I would be able to operate easily, even at night. Getting there required the use of two sunken roads, well known to the British and used by the Germans to move troops and machinery. The whole ground from

Bapaume down to Albert was generally flat, but there were undulations that we could at least use under cover of night.

We approached our meeting point, near an intersection of two very small roads. My pilot, who was now a soldier like me, seemed more ill at ease than I had hoped. Watkins seemed calmer and although quiet, worked efficiently. We waited until nightfall, as agreed, for our three companions to come to meet us. They had planned to land much further away from us to the north and so had further to traverse to get to us. Despite waiting until three o'clock in the morning, they did not appear and we had to move off, for fear of capture, abandoning them to their fate. They had been trained to survive in this place, and if they could at all, they would. Reluctantly, we moved off to a small farmhouse on the track leading away to the east. First, we had to check whether it was occupied. If it had been in the British lines, it would be home to a small company, who would have used the opportunity to improve their lot. Here, with so many better billets and better food, it was empty and unoccupied. Although it could be a target for shelling, it was unlikely as the guns were too far away for accuracy and shelling here would be a wasted effort. This looked a good prospect to consider our options now that we were alone.

Our plan was to obtain food and supplies as we went and the equipment was light and horribly inadequate. I tried to summon up some thoughts on our position. We had successfully landed in enemy territory, albeit in French farmland which was, to me, like being at home. However, we had failed to meet up with our comrades and there were only three of us in our venture. We were not expected to meet up with any of the others, who all had their independent tasks to perform. They would be in similar positions to us. My small notebook contained their names in a crude code, as well as some coded reminders on the hoped-for timings from Cowling, and I read through them. The night was waited out in anxious half sleep, leaving me tired, with the weight of the operation pressing on me. Perhaps too much had been left to chance – where the front line might be, what we would be able to achieve, how we would supply ourselves. Now we were here, it was hard to think but it was essential to remain calm and constantly alert, otherwise none of my little party would get out of this game alive.

In the morning, the light came in just after 0400 and once visibility improved we had to move on. There were plenty of wooded areas, not badly shelled, if at all, but there were long open spaces between them, so we were always exposed outside of the town. We were dressed convincingly enough in our costumes with secret compartments, but our movements, I was sure, always appeared to be furtive and suspicious.

At around 0600 on 4th July, we saw the first glimpse of the terrain we were going to attack on 14th July. I was still not sure that Cowling could get the infantry and artillery to move in such a coordinated way, with smaller battles, rather than the original big-push tactic. I could see puffs of smoke from the larger shells, but we were too far away to really hear and see the action at the Front away to the south. The terrain on the enemy side was lightly shelled and quite a bit of it was from the earlier battles in 1914. Had the front really moved so little in all of this time?

It was up to us to move back towards Martinpuich and the ridge over towards Longueval. We were now really only going to be able to disrupt communications and munitions on a small scale, to harry the enemy from behind. By now convinced that I would be dead in a few days, I wanted to press on to see if my ideas would actually be achievable. Maybe not for us, but for future operations.

By the evening of 4th July, after a day hampered by heavy rain and wind, we had arrived north of our objective of reaching the current front line and put ourselves back into the mix. We stalked close to the ground, which was quite untouched around here by the devastation of war. There were some areas shelled from the battles of movement earlier in the war, but no soldier had fought here for some time and much of the debris had been cleared to allow more effective transports to the Front. The ground was wide open and gently undulating. We would be seen for miles around if someone took the trouble to try and observe us, but we thought perhaps they wouldn't and gambled on that all day.

From the top of a ridge, we saw German preparations for what would be their second line, or possibly their third. This ran through the Bois de Foureaux, where I had spent many peaceful afternoons with Odile, sometimes on the motor bicycle and sometimes just cycling or walking up along the slopes from Bazentin-le-Petit. It was hard to imagine the terror that would take place here in a few short days. We had to move on, dwelling on a lost past would not help.

From memory, I knew that on the approach to the Bois de Foureaux, the ground sloped at first gently and then steeply, towards Bazentin-le-Petit and then down into the valleys. It was here that the battle would be fought, if only we could get this far. Cowling had to come through and our troops had to dig deep and push on.

Once we had moved towards the current trench line, we had to be very careful. We were at the limits of open movement, our presence here would be immediately noticed and we would be summarily shot as trespassers, spies or for any other reason the enemy desired. German movements were along specific paths and channels. The ground undulations meant that we could at least not be spotted and shot by our own snipers, looking for careless enemy movements at very long range. A little further along the ridge could put us in range of a sniper's rifle. We moved with extreme caution, always looking at the lines of possible fire, which changed almost at every step. German trench construction was moving ahead apace. Some bundles of wicker twigs were visible on the approach to the first sunken trench. We would not be able to move ahead of this line, except at night.

From experience, I could move about a trench quietly and hoped that luck would be on our side, especially as this was not a front-line trench guarded at every turning point. We split up temporarily and covered ourselves in turf and soil to break up our silhouettes then waited for darkness. Little did I know then, that this spot that would later be attacked over and again by the Allies. But for now all was quiet.

I began now to think of Bazentin and the villages there. It seemed that there was not too much damage to the village on this side, with it being just behind the battle lines and protected by the sloping terrain. Perhaps we could make use of the ground, to cause the Germans some difficulty in defending their new lines. I was unable to make out Odile's house, but tried nevertheless to see if it stood, or if it had been shelled.

We were able to move westwards using the slopes I knew well to our advantage. Some scarring of the earth from earlier battles could be seen, but the ground had been cleared as this was now behind the German front line. There were the remains of two cemeteries, now abandoned, with mixed up German and French graves marked. Here and there were buildings that had fallen down from the effects of shelling, but many stood and the ground bloomed with crops that had not been tended and harvested. Most food had been removed and used by the soldiers, but some areas remained untouched.

That evening, we were upon the outer flat fields near to Martinpuich and very close to the German second line, which seemed to be lightly occupied and still under construction. It was dangerous to linger here as the surrounding locality was heavily occupied by Germans. There was fighting at the front line to the south in this area and the trenches in the distance were bathed in smoke and noise. From the lines of shells, it was clear that the British had made little progress still and that was disappointing. On the road behind, were some smaller buildings and the wall that Odile and I would sit beside out of the wind – how different it was now. We had to keep out of sight on the western side of the wall, which would be in shade if the sun ever came out again, and it would be good for digging a shelter. As we rounded the corner post, we saw five German soldiers playing cards in the middle of the yard. Worst of all – they had seen us.

They were seated in a rough circle, three with their backs to us and two others facing us. They slowly rose without a word, just staring. My two companions drew long and startled breaths. The other three Germans turned around lazily, presumably taking us for idiot peasants who hadn't listened to the orders to get out. It would be unusual to see three young men together since they had generally been put to work. But thankfully, they were too drunk or stupid to realise that quickly enough. The tallest stepped over, waving his arms about in what seemed like a gesture of welcome and the German group laughed loudly. Their weapons were stacked some distance away and they would not be able to get them if we got close enough quickly. By speaking to them in poor German, with a heavy French accent, I hoped they would not become suspicious. I had fought Germans up close, but these men looked like a guards regiment, and although worse for drink, the best in the German Army. Not daring to turn to my companions, I gestured to alert them to my plan. I held my palm upwards to the German approaching me and then pretended to look round and gestured palm down to each of the other four. I would take the one facing me and my comrades would take two each of the others. There was no choice, this was what we had all agreed beforehand. Take a life to save a life.

Once certain that I was understood by my team, from under my cloak, I quickly took out my general purpose knife, super sharpened by the Engineers. I lunged at the startled soldier who fixed a stare on me as the knife plunged into his neck, and I pulled hard until his throat was cut cleanly. My two companions did likewise at their targets. The Germans on the left had their backs to us still and both died of stabs into their necks, almost without a sound. On the right, my pilot had stumbled and fumbled with his knife and the two Germans he was detailed to attack were able to punch him twice into the ground. The knife remained in his hand and he managed to slice into one of them who fell, covering Henry completely and bleeding all over him. The other turned on me and I hit him with the back of the handle of the knife straight into his face. He collapsed in agony, defenceless and unable to move, but this was a violent war. To survive, we had to be ruthless and think fast. But while I was thinking about plunging the knife into his chest, the task was completed for me by Watkins.

'I know, sir. Come on Major, we have to move now!'

We had made some sound, but not enough to raise an alarm as there was plenty of noise around us as the British Allies hammered at the German lines.

Miles-Dunning had received a severe blow to his face and his jaw was both dislocated and broken. He could not carry on with this mission and needed medical treatment now. We moved the German bodies into a rotting cart and covered them with an equally rotten canvas sheet. The bodies were covered, but they would not remain undetected for long. The soldiers would be missed and they might have companions meeting them. They would realise that someone had placed the bodies in the cart, but they would hopefully be confused as to who had done it and why. This was not the front line and there would not be quiet for long. Perhaps the Germans might suspect a murderer on the loose, not their enemy stalking them.

We moved quickly and concluded that our injured pilot friend would have to pretend to have been freshly shot down. This was not going to be so easy. However, as a pilot, he would be convincing, except for his lack of proper uniform, and he would be able to give enough detail of aeroplanes to pull it off. His flying log might deflect the Germans without giving anything away. As he would not be able to speak for weeks anyway, there was a small chance of him getting out of this alive as long as he was far away from the cart full of dead Germans. What he did not have was the aeroplane, but we had to risk it, or he was dead anyway. Some pilots get thrown out or burned out and it was a chance. So, we moved him away from the dead Germans and into a wider alleyway. We tried to leave few footprints and made him crawl a few yards to look like he had come from somewhere else. Then we left him on top of a wall on part of a crumbled roof. However, he was covered in blood and the broken jaw was not likely to be the cause of that much gore. So we removed the worst-affected clothing and threw it into the rotting cart. Overall, we were now in a poor way. Our mission was over before we had even started.

The plan for my team of three had been to get to the German forward positions and destroy the small ammunition dumps around the second line using their own equipment against them. We would then wait in a forward area, out of sight, until the advance overran us. Then we would be able to pop up and get back to our lines. This depended on our boys being there on time as we had no means of communication and were desperately exposed in the German forward areas. We were also liable to be shelled by our own side, or shot by a sniper, although Cowling had assured me that the artillery bombardment may be a little different here, less of a hammer blow, more of a hurricane storm.

I had no idea at all how the other groups were proceeding. This was one area that we had to leave to fortune and trust to our training. We were not able to find ways to communicate with each other and the only way we would know if we had been successful, would be through intercepted German signals and from the reports of any surviving and returning soldiers. It would just have to wait until we were back in British trenches. Hopefully, the others were doing better than us, which would not have been difficult. We were supposed to be six, we never found three and now we were only two and neither of us gave us a chance in ten.

We decided together to scout this patch and move east towards Longueval, when the weather and time allowed. Because the ground is so open, full of long sweeping, shallow valleys, we were able to move, but always with the fear of observation arousing suspicion. I was certain we had been spotted many times, but with this number of men moving, we had not raised suspicion to the point of investigation. It is strange to think that on these roads and valleys, so little movement used to take place in this sleepy farmland outlook.

As we moved out of the village area of Martinpuich, Watkins and I took a deliberate detour to the shed that Odile and I used to use as it would be a great place to hide and take stock of our position. A few shells had landed in this area, but the walls and roof were still standing and there was enough debris to cover our movement. We unpacked the last of our bread and ate while we discussed our bleak position.

'Are you quite alright sir? Were you wounded by the Germans back there?'

'No, no I am fine, just wasn't looking forward to killing an unarmed German.'

'See it like this sir, his tongue is a weapon. If you had left him alive, they would be after us and we would be dead by now. I had to do it. This is not a war of polite virtues. It is bloody murder and we didn't bloody start it.'

I wanted to deflect the conversation to the practical. This was not a safe place to be at this time.

'It seems to me that our original plan is no longer at all possible. We should have been south of Bapaume with six men aiming for the Frankfurt bunkers and the dumps there. We can get there with just the two of us. My hope is that the others can make it and destroy it. We should now try and disrupt the second line construction if we can.'

'Sir, there is an ammunition dump on the hills near the Foureaux track, it was on the map. We could give it a go – we can get there.'

'The High Wood? Hmm, it might be a little diversion, but it isn't going to change the damn war!'

'Sir, we are in a terrible mess. It is the only thing we can do, given our position.'

'Yes, yes, of course.' I held out my hand towards Watkins and noticed it trembling slightly. We were not in good order at all.

'Watkins, find us some more to eat will you? Your fettling skills are significantly better than mine. There has been enemy here in the last day or so, we might be lucky.'

With a smile and a nod he was gone. I wanted some time here to settle my nerves and deal with the mixed feelings of war, death, killing and sitting here in one of my most treasured places, the space I had shared with Odile.

Watkins came back in hurriedly.

'There are four fucking Germans in the fucking lane. I'll wait for them to pass, if they haven't spotted us. Shit!'

The little party of Germans shuffled past without a glance towards us. They carried on smoking and telling their tall soldier stories.

Feeling relieved, but tired of these moments of total terror and alarm, I rubbed my hand on my forehead, scraped off a layer of brown blood and dirt and turned my gaze to the small window, still checking for immediate death.

'You know Watkins, I spent many hours in this little tool shed with my French girl. It's hard to imagine this being the same place. It is now so different outside and with the war... Sorry, I am not making any sense. My life here was perfect with the perfect girl. I may never get that back. It is lost to me and now just feels so distant.'

Watkins just bowed his head. He too had thoughts of his own family home and the life that had been destroyed.

'You know Watkins, Odile and I used to drop secret notes to each other here. Things we were too afraid to say directly to one another, just here on this ledge. Fuck me.'

'What is it sir?'

'There is a note hidden here, one that I haven't seen before.'

'What? How is that possible? It must be an old one sir.'

'No, no we took the notes and kept them – my notes from Odile are back in England. I can't believe it to be possible. She has been evacuated, or worse, surely?'

'Best keep it to yourself for now, sir. Fritz is just outside. Let's keep low and quiet.'

I said nothing, nodded and crouched lower, excited because this must be a letter placed by her after I left for England. Maybe she thought one day we would be back here and I was to read it then?

Watkins and I had to stay in that shed all night, as there was still German activity close by the village that we would not be able to keep away from. There would be no light until the early hours of the morning. It would get light from around 0400, and I intended to read my letter then, if we were still undiscovered. We shared the duty of keeping watch, but we did not expect the Germans to come looking in a shed, as they were totally unaware of any presence and the tool shed was meaningless to them. And we were far enough away from the dead card players for their discovery to mean danger for us.

As light filtered slowly through the cracks in the door of the shed, the unmistakable sounds of birds singing softly in the distance also crept through. I heard a woodpecker, recognising the sound from my time here, even though it was perhaps a little late in the year for such a clear sound of industry. I smiled at his bravery and tenacity, carrying on in the face of war.

Finally, it got light enough to read. Watkins was still sleeping quietly and not due to wake for an hour or so. I opened the envelope slowly and took an excited deep breath. It was from Odile and dated August 1915, she opened with *Mon William adoré* and my heart began racing as I translated while reading.

My ability to read French was not as good as my ability to speak it.

Odile had always used simple phrases to help me whenever she wrote to me but this seemed completely different. It was hard to make out much of what she had written, the words were mostly unfamiliar and my head spun. It was possible to make out some phrases clearly and these stuck in my mind, with the sickening glue of realisation.

I read the words *Germans in our village... escape to Albert* was it? *Father beaten?* Oh God no! *Meeting a beautiful girl? German boy? My heart has hurt for you and now I must say goodbye?* Did this mean that she had given up on me and been forced, or perhaps had even chosen, to be with a German boy? I shook my head so that this would go away and be right again, but it would not.

For almost an hour, I sat in silence before waking Watkins. My world had ended, I cared no more for anything. *Odile, my darling from over the sea. I have gone through this only to be with you again, to survive this awful war, and to kill if necessary.* Now it was all meaningless and my chest felt empty and cold. *You have given in to the enemy and are now somewhere with a soldier, perhaps a brother of one of the five in the cart.*

'What time do you think it is sir? Is it about an hour to sunrise proper?'

I said nothing, heard nothing, felt numb. I did not want the sun to rise at all at that moment.

'Sir, are you alright? What is it? The letter? Is your girl dead?'

'No Watkins, it feels worse. She has taken up with the fucking Boche and left me here alone.'

'Ah, sir, what would you have done in the same situation? Your home and family kicked out and all your world turned upside down. Do you fight it and die, for you have no weapon? Or do you hope to live to see the day break again? I know what I would have done in these poor buggers' situation.'

'I don't know Watkins, I don't fucking know anymore. The death and the mutilation, the instant dealing of cards to survive or die, was just about bearable. But now, there is nothing left but a soul burnt from the inside by this bloody war. I want to get out of this place. Let's go.'

'Very good Major.'

If captured now, we were done for anyway, so I decided to keep the letter and read it again, in case I was mistaken. Odile must have had to go through quite a bit to get it to me, but why? To shatter my world? I could not be at all sure of anything anymore. Only Watkins was a constant for me now, everything else was out of my control. I wasn't thinking straight and my unpreparedness would cost us both. It was essential to shake this devastation from my head and live the war again, if only to get Watkins through and the job done.

Now caught in the middle of a major troop movement south towards La Boisselle and Contalmaison, I wondered if we had tried again to take these objectives. But it was quiet now. The paths were well-trodden and lightly shelled and all seemed quiet. The awful news from Odile was put out of my mind in order to carry on with the mission. Watkins was very much alive and we depended on each other for our mutual safety.

We moved slowly eastwards to find the track to move off towards the rear slope of the Bois de Foureaux. The only chance to help our effort now would be to disrupt the construction of the new defensive line or to destroy some small arms dumps in the area. Although we had tried to cover ourselves with other plans, with only two of us, we were out of options.

The battles at the front sounded clearer from here on the lower ridge line. The routine and rapid bang, bang, bang, bang of shells. The thud and pop of an artillery gun firing. Straight on ahead from the line to Bazentin was the village of Longueval, in the dip between the ridges. The British had attacked south of here on 1st July and had not made the progress needed, but even so, still took some of the objectives at a terrible cost. From here, we could see why. Line after line of German guns dominated the ridge. The infantry seemed fresh, and less alarmed than a couple of days ago. The country was wide open and the second line was being constructed with heavy materials and I did not like our chances of easily taking it.

Making our way around the path towards Contalmaison, we were almost back to the edge of the German support trenches. Here, the ground was more exposed and too close to the line to move about without being in a trench, so we traversed further along the ridge towards Bazentin village under cover of buildings and terrain. The sunken road led to the north of the village, and the view up towards the wood and down towards Mametz and Montauban was good. It was possibly overlooked by the British, but there was less likelihood of being spotted by the Germans. The village was lightly manned and we could therefore stay here for the night. I knew every single building and every cellar from my delivery boy days and the memory made me wonder what had happened to the old.

At that very moment, there was a burst of British shelling close by, perhaps the guns were finding a range in preparation for an attack on the rear positions of the Germans. But it seemed to me that the British were giving away their intentions too early or at least letting the Germans know they were there. We took cover, beyond the reach of the guns, in the churchyard at the top of the village rise. The steps of the church were still undamaged and these were the ones that I had dreamt of standing on with Odile on our wedding day. That was now not going to happen and I growled to myself about some damned German bastard who had his hands on my love. My anger rose, but now was not the time or it would corrode me from the inside out.

The Germans patrolled the village lightly as it was a distance behind the front lines. Trenches had been dug near the road at the foot of the slope and there were emplacements for observation in the roadway, but otherwise it seemed the war had not fully taken over this village.

Bazentin-le-Grand must already be in British hands, as the shelling could not have made it over here unless we were on the slopes of the sister village. It was impossible to know for sure, as we could not see over the slope. The shells were high explosive and some shrapnel and it was not clear what the British were intending to do from this position.

That evening, the patrol moved through the village and down into the roadway on a regular fifteen-minute cycle. We were on the reverse slope under cover of the trees and the steep slope in the north. Occasionally, a German would stop for a cigarette, we could have killed them, but did not as this would raise the wrong sort of alarm. We just had to watch what they were doing and find other ways to disrupt them, not least because we needed to get past them when the British attacked for certain.

The cellars were often used to store food rations and some ammunition and the Germans used the local resources well. We were becoming more and more isolated as the numbers of troops increased, so we decided to stay in cellars and use the stored rations to keep us going. It wasn't much and it wasn't fresh. Trying to make adequate latrine provision was also a challenge. But we could not give our position away for any reason, so we improvised behind walls and kept clean enough not to fall ill.

My resolution was to make our stand in Bazentin village, whatever happened, and then try to get back to our lines when the battle started. Unfortunately, troops poured in rapidly over the coming hours. The guns were definitely closer and the British seemed to be on top of us, ready for the assault. It was clear that the British were attacking over and again in the area of Contalmaison, a mile or so away. There seemed a lot of Germans here and I doubted that the assault in Contalmaison could succeed if we did not attack from Longueval at the same time.

In the evening, there were British voices, perhaps Welsh, but it was hard to be sure.

'Where do you think they are taking us Robbie?'

'Not too sure. Where is this place anyway?'

'I think we are going north is it?'

'Maybe. Do you think we got to the village by now?'

'Don't think so, these Germans are hard to shift and they keep on coming don't they?'

'Well, we are going over that second line. If we take Contalmaison, we are nearly there. Still, looks like we are out for now.'

'What will happen for us? Do you think they will shoot us?'

'No, prisoners of war, us. Likely take us to a camp or something.'

These soldiers were prisoners of war being moved north. They seemed cheery enough, perhaps happy to be out of the battle. They were close enough to hit with my cap. I wished they could have helped us in our tasks, but they were out of the game now, moving north east. There were also some small German mobile ambulance trains moving back with casualties from the battle. The Germans were suffering as well.

We moved between cellars easily at night as I knew this area so well. Watkins was a great companion, nimble, quiet and without fear when he decided it was safe to move. Often, we wondered how the rest of the team were managing. Most were likely dead or captured. Had I not known this area so well, we would most likely be dead as well, having achieved absolutely nothing.

In the village for three full nights, we moved between the newly constructed and freshly stocked small arms dumps. These were usually unguarded as there was no expectation of any form of enemy attack. In reality, soldiers did not want to be here for fear of a shell landing amongst the munitions and setting them off. We were able to defuse some of the grenades that had been prepared and to remove many of the fuses from the small bombs. Some we were able to set on instantaneous detonation, with fuses set to go off if the bomb was moved, these we placed in the middle of the stacks. When the piles were emptied, the pin would be drawn out and with an instantaneous fuse, causing it to explode, and with luck for us, setting off all of the others in a single fireball. It was quick and easy and we could make them look as if nothing was amiss. Some we moved to another store that only we knew so that we could use them to destroy other dumps nearer to the fourteenth, again using the booby trap method. It was piecemeal and small revenge, but rather the whole lot kill one German than the individual bombs kill and damage hundreds of our comrades.

We also moved bullets and a couple of cases of small charges for use later as booby traps for moving soldiers. These trench tricks were learned from the Germans, who often abandoned positions with innocent looking temptations like pistols and helmets. But, if these were moved, they set off bombs to kill the invading troops. Since we were now doing the same, we were all just playing the same terrible game. We also moved and hid some cases of wooden handles for the grenades so that they could not be used to mount on the bombs. We were able to come and go from different directions completely undetected, repeating this task all along the new line.

With increasing frequency, shells landed in the village, but they became more targeted than the previous broad flattening of everything above ground level. Guns were being moved up by the Germans to shell the British positions in return. We were not able to do anything for these, as there were just so many Germans around. It was clear then that the British were making progress, with help from our Allies and it was possible that an attack to break the line might now be feasible.

As time passed, though, it became increasingly difficult to move about unhindered. There were just too many eyes and line-of-sight angles that could give us away. We were being shelled and troops were more numerous. The Germans were building a strong line in the Bois de Foureaux north of us and the British were shaping up for battle. On the left and the right, the front line was coming closer. It looked like the fourteenth was really going to happen. What Cowling had cooked up would soon be unleashed on the enemy digging in right here. He had managed to pull off the battles of alignment to be ready for the assault.

It was now time for us to act, or be captured. We could do no more damage just the two of us, and hoped that the others had been more successful before death or capture. We achieved some success since there were occasional loud crashes, followed by alarmed commotion. Either a shell had hit the ammunition dump, or our booby trap had been sprung early. Either way, there would be fewer bombs and bullets aimed at our advancing comrades.

It was likely that the British had taken Mametz and the wood nearby. We had become more exposed as Bazentin-le-Petit filled up with enemy soldiers in the buildings and barns. So, we spent the day of the thirteenth in the cellar of Odile's house. It was deep and had a lower level that was not immediately obvious from the steps. And it still had a tool shed, which hopefully meant extra equipment. The Germans had not touched the cellar, but even if they had, they would not have discovered the lower levels. The outbuilding that had been my former home was now used as an observation point for the road down to Contalmaison, by the wretched enemy, and I felt violated yet again.

'Major, we will need to find a route down the hill, perhaps over to the left where the old cemetery meets the footpath'

'Yes, Horace. But for now, we are pinned here in this cellar. The blasted enemy are crawling all over me, in my home, in my life and with Odile. It makes me want to blow them back to the bloody sea.'

'Yes sir. We should move around 2200, as it will be dark by then.'

'Agreed. Keep a look out for the patrols. We must not now be seen and we can't eliminate them either.'

'Understood.'

When it was almost totally dark, it was time to make our most dangerous move. It would be live or die tonight, simple as that. We picked up a couple of spanners and some rope, just in case it would come in handy. Near the top of the steps was a young German at the wall of Odile's bedroom just above us, now open to the elements after being hit by a shell burst. This angered me more than anything in this war so far, the vision of the enemy at the bedroom window of my love – perhaps because it represented an important part of my life being finally and truly destroyed.

Stupidly, without thinking clearly and against my order to Watkins, I grabbed the German round the throat and pulled him back down the steps, punching him in the face in a frenzy until his blood splashed onto the walls and floor. Only when the German was dead and Watkins grabbed my arm, did I stop hitting the man with all my might.

'That's for destroying my life you fucking bastard. Curse you, you wretched pig!'

'Sir, please!' Watkins placed a hand gently but firmly on my wrist. 'He is dead, sir. Crushed to a pulp. No one will ever recognise him.'

My sweat dripped onto his ripped and broken features and I burst into tears. Watkins pushed me roughly down the steps back into the cellar. Revenge had risked us both.

'Sir, for fuck's sake, get it together!'

He grabbed my lapel hard and snapped my face to his.

'You can't do this, you have to keep it together or we are both dead. We can get back to our own lines, but only if we keep thinking. This is death on a silver plate, if we don't get moving.'

He was right and I nodded. We pulled the remains to the bottom of the stairs. No one would believe the man just fell, but in a few hours it wouldn't matter anyway. Looking at the dead man's unrecognisable face, Cowling's letter came back to me. Absurd though it was, considering all the death and defilement around me, shame washed over me. Take a life to save a life. This was different. A change had come over me and I did not like what I had become.

Watkins took over our escape from the village. We moved as close as possible to the front line and looked to see if there was any movement on the British side. In the distance, there were occasional glints of metal and bursts of German shells on the edge of the road. The British had made the ridge as planned and were ready for the assault – at least on the Longueval side. It was not possible to see towards Contalmaison as the ground swept slightly upward. But behind it was a track leading down to where we had jumped off on the first day of July, two weeks ago.

Just before we sat in for the attack out of sight on the far slope, we were surprised by two enemy soldiers appearing. We were now clearly in the front line as the British had moved up in the last two days whilst we were hiding. Watkins moved fast to kill the Germans, who were carrying rations to the forward areas. He managed to kill them easily as they were laden down with a barrel of soup. He stabbed one in the back and when his comrade turned around, Watkins smashed the other in the face with a spanner. This soldier wasn't killed outright, but his jaw was crushed and he choked to death on his own blood. These are terrible things to write down but that is exactly what happened. We could not let ourselves be captured here and we were at war. My moral core had eroded in this war to the point where I did not care, because there was no energy to spare. I cared no more for the soldier in front of me and I cared less that they were taking my Odile further away from me, forever. At that point in my life, hate had won and the war had taken me finally.

As night fell, we got into position under the church walls. The night of the thirteenth was like any other in the world, except here in this little patch of France, hell itself would open and swallow us all – British and German.

We had orders to return to British lines if possible, or to wait until the British took the position, which was always risky for any number of reasons. The Germans had built a formidable position in the village that was still incomplete in some areas. Behind us, was the Bois de Foureaux and it seemed quiet to us, with the Germans working on the strong defensive position, deep in the wood.

There are many high and steep ridges here, ideal for concealment and stealth. We had been able to make a mess of some ammunition stores as the Germans would find out, but perhaps I had overestimated my ability to influence the outcome of the war, it was all just too big, consuming us entirely. I thought of Cowling and all the effort he had put into this single day and wondered what he was doing at this moment. I thought of Odile and what had happened to her and her family – thinking of her made my stomach drop in anguish. I thought of home in England and of my family and all the other families worrying for the soldiers forming up to attack here. Now I was pleased we were finally attacking, and liberating this village. Until now, I had not hated the Germans, but my character was beyond recovery – another casualty of this war. My body was a machine, no different to a gun, a bullet, a shell, or my old motor bicycle. Point me at the enemy and see me transformed from a dreaming fool, into a solidified, cold mass of twisted hatred. Odile was lost to me and the dream that brought me through the trenches of damage to wretched humanity was shattered. The eggshell protecting me was broken now and the war could come and take me. It could pour in like a sea of enemy soldiers with balding heads and grinning faces, and limbless shapes of twisted flesh. I was changed from a young man with hopes and dreams to a blunt killing machine that I would never, ever otherwise have been. Doing these unspeakable things, driven by fear for survival, to protect my comrades, and to keep alive the flickering candle of hope for the future. Damn them, curse them, for forcing me into this position.

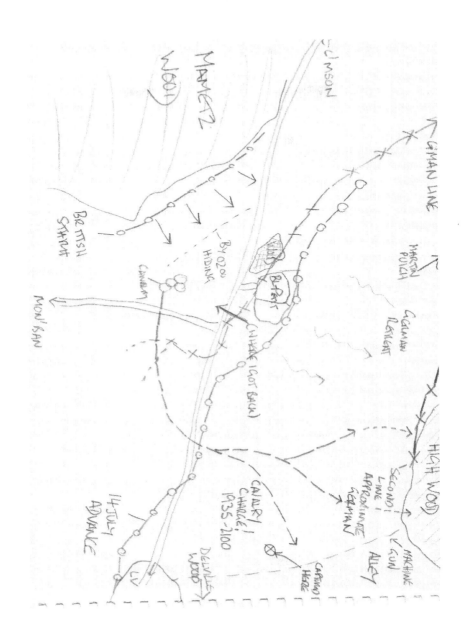

CHRIS CHERRY

CHAPTER THIRTEEN - COWLING'S REPORT

SECRET
Lt. Gen. Sir Henry Rawlinson KCB
4th Army and Task HQ Albert
13 July 1916 191607131845

Sir,

I write this report to you by way of recording the actions in preparation of our operation of 14 July to come. Gen. Congreve and I have examined the terrain south of the enemy Second Defensive Line (Sq 16/17 Pozieres–Longueval) and put in place such action as to secure the best advantage to the troops in front of the ridge south and south east of the new lines. I have endeavoured at every point to give our forces an advantage over the enemy in ways that cannot be anticipated by the German Army. We have attempted to make best use of the terrain and adopt warfare tactics not employed in the field to my knowledge to date by any force on the Western Front. Upon your release of the Front to the north of La Boisselle to General Gough, you tasked me with the preparations for an operation to the south from Contalmaison to Longueval, making use of the ridge crested at Bazentin-le-Petit. I am also mindful of the intention to assault to the north towards Le Bois de Foureaux (High Wood map refers).

It is my pleasure to submit my report of the operations to this date and the final preparations for the assault of 14 July. On our right in Ginchy and Guillemont villages, the enemy has constructed a strong second defensive position, including bunkers and obstacles to infantry. I made such arrangements for the advance from Montauban to take the woods at Trones and Bernafay. You will have already received the reports from Brigade and Division relating to the intensity of the operation to secure the area around Longueval on 3/4 July.

In the centre, we required the seizure from the enemy of Mametz Wood and Contalmaison village. These required repeated and intensive attacks from primarily the Welsh in the 38th Div. The line was secured only on 10 July to the satisfaction of the Divisional Commanders tasked with the assault to be renewed on 14 July.

It is with regret that I report that significant casualties were taken across the whole line. It is estimated that divisional strength has been reduced by 20,000 in the sector from La Boisselle north to Longueval south. Requests have been made for reinforcements and relief in those areas central to the planned operation.

I met this morning again with Gen. Congreve to finalise the plans for the assault, with emphasis on the taking of Longueval and Delville Wood and to brief him on our preparatory operations in the German lines to the west of this action on the slope of Bazentin-le-Petit. I submit my report of that meeting and the preparations herewith.

I tasked a force of sixty (60) officers and men led by Major William Collins to penetrate enemy territory beyond the German lines in a deliberate planned action via aeroplane on the morning of 3 July past. As you are of course aware, Maj. Collins has an excellent knowledge of the terrain and familiarity with the French language invaluable to this operation, forming the premise upon which action was launched. The planned dispersal took place in order to disrupt communications and the availability of weaponry to the enemy and to maintain secrecy on the nature of this assault. In the ten days since this operation began we have become aware of certain changes in the enemy preparations indicative of some success in this endeavour. We have had no communication directly with any of the men or Maj. Collins himself. However, intercepted communications show some encouraging activity. In particular, the movement of enemy to the Second Defensive Line is reduced in our estimates, due to unexpected and unexplained equipment shortage. Also, it has been reported that several fires have been suffered at either brigade or divisional headquarters, with some loss of senior personnel on the part of the enemy.

On 4 July, we understand that the primary ammunition dump in Bapaume suffered repeated explosions and detonation with complete destruction of weaponry. A divisional HQ (we believe this to include the Guards) was set ablaze with the deaths of four senior-ranking German officers, identity currently unknown. Dispatch motor bicycles were also destroyed in circumstances the enemy describe as unknown. It appears that our assaults in preparation for 14 July have been interpreted as the main assault and the enemy is unaware of any offensive operation planned for High Wood and the Bazentin Ridge line. They are anticipating an attack on either Longueval or further east. I have tasked artillery shelling to remain light and avoid the main ridge and High Wood in preparation for the cavalry assault on the morning of 14 July. With Contalmaison secure, there is an opportunity to move cavalry in the valley from Montauban to the Contalmaison-Longueval road now in our possession. We are moving the assault troops into the area this evening and we believe and trust the enemy is unaware of our movements, intentions or divisional strength.

The movement of German soldiers has been thus restricted, we believe because orders at their battalion level are confused and arriving too late for effective execution of the orders. *We cannot assume success from our operation, but the outcome in preparation is at least positive.*

We have received intelligence reports today from forward listening posts and from the observation aeroplanes in the sector of Bazentin itself. German soldiers in the lines are reporting a shortage of small arms and ammunition to defend the second and possibly new third positions at the present moment. Delays have been experienced in the supply of munitions to the very front line and infantry have been arriving late, despite departing in a timely manner. The artillery bombardment commenced on 11 July has been deliberately light, but highly focused on specific supply lines and ammunition areas forward of Bapaume, as indicated by the fires reported elsewhere.

I am acutely aware of the public opinion of General Haig on the matter of our assault in this manner and am ever grateful for your opinion and support for this operation. For the final preparations, I have actioned your requirement for a preliminary bombardment, but have arranged its timing and intensity in keeping with the nature of this assault. The bombardment will avoid the shelling of the ridge directly, given our intention to exploit gains with the use of cavalry. I anticipate the cavalry will be able to exploit the advantages from the morning assault, but I reserve the request to deploy mounted troops until such time as the area in front of High Wood is consolidated.

I do not expect to make contact again with the force deployed in enemy territory. However, they have been instructed, where possible, to make contact with our lines no later than 0100 hours on 14 July in order to achieve safe transit back into our lines. Battalions have been briefed to expect and to challenge the return of raiding parties. If any are identified to have returned, they will be debriefed and a report submitted to you for the evening report of 14 July.

I also acknowledge with deep appreciation your confirmation of my elevation to Brigadier-General. I have informed the appropriate divisional commanders as requested.

Brigadier-General HAE Cowling
4th Army
12 Field Op. HQ Task Group, Albert

CHAPTER FOURTEEN - M DAY

I crawled along the wall, knowing that there were two adjoining cellars below in case we needed to use them. We were being very lightly shelled and very little was falling on the village or on the surrounding slopes. If I could make it to the church, the steps would provide a chance to see to the left and the road off to Martinpuich. Here, though was a lot of German activity. Soldiers were being moved forwards towards Contalmaison, down the hill from the track, out of sight of the guns ranged on the village.

It was now dark, so our movements would no longer attract attention from a distance, as long as we moved like soldiers. The road down from the church to the main road was quite steep. Not as steep as Folkestone, but still a reasonable slope if you had to carry full kit, so soldiers moving down were rattling and grumbling as all soldiers do. On the left of the church was the schoolhouse. It was open to the elements as the roof was missing. Although hit by a shell, like most other buildings, it still provided some good cover from prying eyes. The front of the church had a sheltered alcove which still stood tall enough to cover our movement. The time was probably around 2300, we had to move quickly if we were to make it back at all. Neither of us was really sure how we were going to do it, although we did not expect a continuous trench line here as the slopes were tricky and the line was not straight along the high ground.

'Watkins, it's going to be a problem, getting over the road. The enemy are everywhere at once.'

'I know sir, we will have to time our movements carefully, we—'

'Hang on, there's a sound. What was that clicking?'

'Could be anything sir, maybe it's boots on the ground. Twitchy sir?'

'Yes, I am very bloody twitchy, this being where I bloody live.'

'Right sir. But nearly there.'

'Right Watkins, let's move. I've had enough of skulking around like a bloody thief.'

We crawled out over the road, which was only occasionally busy. It was dark, but not pitch black. This meant we could move, but there was a slim possibility we would be seen, so we moved fast and quietly. We were not going to be able to pick off any Germans who spotted us now, and would be dead in seconds if we were spotted – there were too many around. Capture as a prisoner of war was unlikely, as neither of us were wearing uniform, but we were too close to the front to pass as French civilians – whatever my knowledge of the village. I passed by a lovely old house on my way down. It had a large cellar that I had been in before. We ducked into the doorway and down the steps, which were open to the outside. At the bottom of the hill was the German front line, or at least the line intended as the defence of the village. A continuous trench was impossible just there as the slope rose sharply on both sides of the road. If it were me defending the position, I would site sentries on both sides and a machine gun right down the road. And there it was – positioned as the road started to flatten out. If we were not seen here, we might make it back alive. To the left of the main road was the track leading to the village cemetery. I had been down that road many times and it led to a rocky hole created by ancient quarrying. This track had been the site of sheltered German billets, but these were gone now as this was the new front line. The British on the other side could not aim sniper fire as this position was above the trenches and there was no clear line of sight. I decided to take Watkins down this side, as it was out of view and range of the machine gun. As we neared the bottom, crawling on all fours, we discovered to our disappointment an enemy listening post and sentry. The soldier in it was wide awake and actively listening to his equipment. We dared not kill him, as he would be immediately missed. Instead, we skirted around him using the rapidly flattening ground to obscure our movement. However, we fell into a partly dug trench, where wire and jagged bits of junk metal had been thrown. Watkins let out a stifled yell. The sentry looked out but did nothing. It might, just might, have sounded like a bird or something other than an enemy soldier falling into a trench. No shell bursts covered our movements, so we had to be very quiet indeed.

'Damn it sir, I've cut my hand a bit, shit on it!'

'Try and keep quiet, the bugger is looking this way. Is it bleeding?'

'Yes sir. Should be fine, if I can tie it up with this bit of shirt. Bugger it.'

'Right, he has gone back to his job. Ready to go? We might have to kill him after all, be ready.'

'Yes, let's go.'

We could not remain so near a listening post, or in range of shelling this close to the line, so we climbed out and crawled back around to the right in full view of the second support trench. We were now in harm's way and the devil could have us at any moment.

Moving towards the main road again, we got to the very edge of the first main German trench. I was not certain whether this was the front line or not. It was well- covered with loose wire and some sandbags, but not enough to make it impossible to traverse if we were quick, or lucky. The trench did not cross the road and we were able to move over the top in a single leap without being seen. There were only a few soldiers in the forward area as most were moving down from Martinpuich to join their comrades. It did not look as if they were expecting a large scale assault, but if they did, it wasn't going to be immediately. This was encouraging.

Once over the trench, at the junction in the road we could turn left towards Longueval – about a mile away. The German line swept right and down the hill. We would have to traverse the ridge and get through what was now likely to be the very front-line trench. To the right and Contalmaison, just over a mile away, we would traverse the trench along the road and then cross the stronger front-line trench towards Mametz Wood. Our best chance would be to go straight down the hill, otherwise we would have to cross the same trench twice as it turned back towards the Montauban road.

Stealthily, we dropped down off the roadway into a slippery copse, the leafy dampness muffling our movement. My heart raced and my mind blazed with thoughts on how to make the final leap across the trench and what would happen if we made a mess of it. Our only real hope would be the sloping terrain and surprise. When we dropped down, we disturbed a few broken branches and snapped twigs, but nothing that the surrounding noise did not adequately cover. We carried on straight at the hill and crossed over a narrow unoccupied German communication trench, perhaps an abandoned position. It was possible to leap it in one move as it had a very narrow planking track above. Now moving ever closer to what we had called the Flatiron Trench, we realised crossing this would be difficult. There were many soldiers here as the line was stronger and subject to Allied attacks. The Germans did not want to give up the ridge lightly, and they wouldn't. Their defence started here.

As we dropped into what had been Bazentin-le-Grand wood, Watkins and I had still said very little to each other and we just focused on moving forward and keeping ahead of the enemy. In the wood, there would be a short drop and then a raised bank, sloping both ways. We would be hidden, but most likely trapped, especially if the attack came now. Still, it was really our only option, having come this far from the village.

Watkins jumped down, quickly followed by me. I was navigating entirely by memory now since this area was so familiar. In the trees, there were no trenches dug, as the wood was dense and formed a good barricade of naturally occurring ridges and tree debris. We soon came upon what was clearly the German front line, just visible through undamaged trees. In front, we clearly saw the massed wire placements ahead. Intact in the main, there were several gullies cut to allow the Germans to move forward to repair wire and raid if they wanted to. We waited to see if any patrols went out, which we thought they would, given the time of night and the likely expectation of troop movements. Because we could see down and into the trench, this position was ideal for observing the British ahead and I fully expected to see an observer come up alongside us at any moment.

We followed the edge of the trench a little further, our heavy breathing masked by the metallic clatter in the trench. Inside, there were Germans, but they were quiet. Watkins looked at me and I thought that we could get over the top unseen – perhaps by jumping – then negotiate the wire through a clearly visible gully and crawl towards what looked like British lines. The German positions here were quite fresh, so I hoped we would only be a matter of yards away. The gully was protected, but the sentries were not active and movement in the trench was limited to card playing and the odd cigarette game.

'Watkins, what say to us making a jump for it over the top of the trench, just here where it narrows? The turn covers us left and the pile of bags gives us a little shelter over on the right there.'

'Possibly sir. I don't like it. We will have to crawl through the wire gully that they have prepared. They will be watching.'

'Bomb in the trench? Throw one in as we go?'

'I don't like it sir. Too much can go wrong. First thing the others will do is look out for where it came from.'

'Fine, what about we wait and see what their routine is? See if we can catch them at cards or something like that. They don't seem to be on alert just yet.'

For an hour we waited, watching movements and sentry positions rotate and change. We had trained for this. From previous assaults, we knew that the Germans tended to post smaller numbers of sentries than the British and the main soldier numbers were out of the trench in dugouts. There were more movements here as time went by, perhaps the Germans now suspected an attack; the sentries were not yet watching ahead, but focused on the right towards Mametz wood. Clearly, they felt the wood was the likely objective. That was good for our purposes.

We stepped up to the parados behind the trench, signalling with hand movements, without words. Constructed from wicker and sandbag, it had been hit by a small calibre shell, perhaps shrapnel, and was lower than it would otherwise have been. A sleeping German was present in the small section that turned away left and right so we were quite well hidden and in a dip. We had to chance it. The trench cut away and our single movement might be unseen if we were quick and lucky. But it was wider than hoped, and once on top of it, it became clear that it would not be possible to simply leap over it.

So we dropped into the trench through the lowered section – mercifully without awakening the sleeping enemy. Watkins wanted to kill him, but a mistake could alert the sentries, and do for us. Now was not the time for plain revenge but if he had moved in the slightest, neither of us would have hesitated. There were no dugouts just here, but there was one a few yards to the right, as the trench changed direction. We had no intention of starting a fight here so we crept forwards. The front of the trench had a small fire step and we were up onto it in a flash – no time to waste. I was able to scramble up the side without making a noise but Watkins caught his sleeve on a wooden peg and it snapped loudly. He froze, totally exposed and unable to defend himself. But the sleeping soldier did not make any move at all and Watkins was quickly out of the trench and free of the parapet, without rousing any other soldiers. All that would be left of our visit was a small pile of earth on the floor of the trench and a snapped plank. Neither would cause any suspicion at all and we were away from the lines in no time.

We found the gully cut in the German wire for their soldiers to pass out. There was a machine gun ranged on the gully, but it was unmanned and unloaded. If we were spotted it could take up to fifteen seconds to load and by that time we could be away. The gully was not cut in a straight line, but was a sweeping curve. It was only about three feet wide, enough to pass with a pack on the back and with rifle shouldered. We were crawling slowly but unseen, knowing we could be shot, but trusting to luck as there was no other choice.

The ground in front of the German lines was solid and not too badly shelled. Most probably, we were just about on the track to Mametz wood, but the track would not be visible to us in this battlefield. Fortunately, there was a half-familiar fork in the track after about a hundred feet. At that point, we could stand up, although there was danger from both sides now – since neither the British nor the Germans knew we were, we would be treated as enemy on both sides of the line.

We kept following the depression, hoping it was the track. This ran south and west, so eventually it had to lead to the British lines, where it would certainly have a Lewis gun trained down it and the British sentry would be awake. It was almost certain that we were not heading back to German lines since the trench would not be so steeply turned away down the hill, making it hard to attack and defend.

After a few more paces south, just to make sure, a voice froze us in our tracks.

'Oi, who the fuck are you, pissing about in the fucking dark? Ah, you two fucking idiots were supposed to be here ten minutes ago you thick bastards. Where's your bundles you stupid fools?'

I replied instinctively. 'Sorry, we were lost coming out of the wood.' I thought that would seem reasonable.

'Where are we now?'

'Hang on, wait a minute. Who the bloody hell are you?'

'Major William Collins, 12 Field Ops. I am returning to British lines. Where are we? This isn't a trench.'

'The trenches are behind us about a hundred-and-fifty yards. But you aren't fucking going anywhere, even if you're bloody Haig.'

Seeing the sergeant stripes, I gave him more verbal identification as neither of us had any paperwork or written material to prove who we were.

'We have been working in front of the German wire and are now returning to our own lines.'

'Fuck off you are. Look at you. What the hell are you wearing? Soldier? My hairy fat arse you are.'

His tone thickened. It wasn't uncommon for misdirected soldiers from either side to appear at the wrong trench. We were not in anyone's plans and no one here would know us.

'Look Sergeant. Get us back to our lines and I will explain. We have been working unusually in the German positions.'

'Right, well I don't believe your cock and bull story. Unusually? What the bloody hell is that? I'm sending you two back as prisoners and the Captain can sort you out. Miles, Ball? Escort these two fine fellows back to the Cap and get them the fuck out of our position.'

'Yes Sergeant!' said Ball. 'This way you two. Out of it, it's our position ha ha.'

We were escorted in the crouch position back to British lines. We gave the line code word – *STALKER* – through Ball and we jumped down into a British trench. The position was bristling with soldiers and equipment. They seemed ready to go. One or two gave us quizzical looks, but most carried on with their grim preparations, very much as I had two weeks ago.

'Captain, my name is Major William Collins, Royal Engineers and this is Sergeant Watkins, Infantry.'

'Well you certainly don't look it. Here come inside and let me get a proper look at you.'

We went inside to a dimly lit room, constructed from sandbags and with a canvas roof. On the table was a small military map of the ridge and the woods beyond.

'My name is Captain Henry Jones of the Queen's. We are part of the 21st Division. Your names appeared in a communication received on the eleventh from a Brigadier Cowling. I have a list of some sixty names of Allied soldiers who might come at us from Fritz's side of the water. Bloody odd. What say you?'

I took in the news that Cowling was now a brigadier. This plan was being taken very seriously indeed.

'Captain, firstly, I'm relieved you know who we are. We have been operating in the village for the last few days. You should know that the Germans have placed some very effective troops in the village and on the slopes in front and behind. I know your operation and what your objectives are from working on the planning for this operation with Colonel – sorry, Brigadier – Cowling. Is he here?'

'Yes. I was also given a very specific briefing note on him too. He is currently in Montauban with officers from 15 Corps. We will escort you back and get you looking like an officer again, er, sir!'

'Thank you. Captain, if I may, I would like to come back here and attack with you later on. Would that be acceptable?'

'Yes Major, the briefing note also mentioned that you may wish to turn and fight the action tonight. I will assign you a suitable position. After all, you are my superior officer.'

'Thank you Captain. Until later then?'

'Yes, Major.'

He chuckled and nodded and we went off with two junior officers towards Montauban. The road was shelled but we were able to move by mule under cover of the steeper slopes and the darkness. We got to the village within about thirty minutes, against the flow of soldiery. The time must have been around 0100 on the fourteenth. It was clever to put the troops out just short of the wire, rather than have them cross the entirety of No Man's Land here. They would be upon the Germans almost instantly.

I saw Cowling's profile immediately and was glad to see him. He held out his hand to shake it, I wasn't in uniform and did not offer a salute.

'My God, William it is you. What ho Watkins? Good to see you too, fellow.'

Watkins smiled back and fell to his knees in exhaustion.

'Look, let us get some tea and you can tell me what happened. You know, we have had some great successes from this operation already.'

This was cheering.

'We did? Well we had a disastrous time sir. Sorry, congratulations on your promotion. Captain Jones informed me in the trench.'

'We have destroyed quite a bit of Fritz's kit William, and have confused them enough to put them off the scent in this action. We may not have got it all right and you may not have achieved what you wanted, but the operation you were part of is about to bear real fruit. Will you accompany me back to Albert?'

'No, sir. I want to take part in the action, with your permission of course.'

'If you insist. Will you be any use to them?'

'Sir, Captain Jones has agreed to me being there. Watkins, go and get some rest.'

'Major,' said Watkins, 'I'm with you for all of it. We trained for this together.'

But I raised my hand, 'This is personal my friend, I cannot ask more of you. Sir, look at this letter.'

Then, I handed Odile's letter to Cowling. He read some of the French.

'This was in a secret place known only to the two of us. I have lost her to the Germans sir. The bloody enemy has wormed his bloody fingers over her and my life. The bastards have forced her hand.'

'You think your girl did this willingly? Seems to me she had to be friendly to Fritz to survive. Looks like her father wasn't up for German rule old boy.'

His words made me feel better inside for a time.

'Look William, if you have the red mist for the Germans, that will be bad for your men. It might make you take the wrong path and make poor decisions. Heaven knows we need to make some good ones.'

'Sir, I am fine, really. Look Watkins, come if you really want to,'

'Yes, sir.'

Cowling smiled. 'Right, fine, I expected as much. Let's get you some uniform. It might not be entirely right, but the whole team's kit is stored towards Albert. It might take an hour to get it to you. It is not too badly shot at and the sappers have built a decent track back. Might even be good enough for cavalry, eh?'

The kit arrived at 0245. By that time the whole road was a hive of grimly determined activity – quiet, purposeful movements to get to the front line, carefully planned so that no one was able to get lost. We would be going in the dark, but light was not far behind. Despite being bone-tired, the nervous tension drove me ever forward. My anger at the enemy had subsided slightly, but I still cursed every boot print in my beloved France.

At just after 0300, Captain Jones told me that he had sent much of his force over the top to close the gap on the German positions, some hundred or so yards from their front line – exactly where we were intercepted earlier. We were to attack in three sections, left, centre and right 13 Corps would attack at Longueval and Delville Wood on the right and we were in the centre and left attacking Bazentin-le-Petit with 15 Corps. What artillery had been used was very focused on destroying the German guns.

Planning had made a big difference in not giving away our intentions. Our troops were already out in No Man's Land in ground not too damaged by shells. We were to attack right between Longueval and Contalmaison and we were at the centre of that section of trenches.

Jones had reported that everything seemed to have gone well. Except that the ridge was so steep relative to the British positions, that some of the British shelling from the rear was catching the top of the trench positions on the way over. If we were to take the ridge, it could get worse. The guns needed to be closer and to shoot higher or we needed to move forward and avoid it. Apart from that, all seemed ready. Four divisions were in the line or in front of it. The barrage was to begin at exactly 0320 and last for only five minutes. To make it effective, some nine-hundred-and-fifty guns were ranged on the six-thousand-yard stretch of the ridge, just as planned. Cowling had done it. The night march to the forward positions had gone well and not many troops had got lost, which had been a big uncertainty in our planning and one of the Commander-in-Chief's biggest concerns. Keeping several thousand men quiet and not giving us all away was the major risk this night.

Although I hadn't expected being here and my world had been turned upside down, I felt much calmer and in control of my thoughts now. Perhaps Cowling had read my letter correctly, with him not being bound by a personal connection to the author. But for now, I was back in this madness again and there would be no going back. My thoughts strayed back to Odile and my stomach dropped. It was still not possible to accept what she had said. Even if Cowling was right, another had still been let into her heart, an enemy at that.

Enough William, you are now fighting for your comrades, no more a lost dream of another age. This is the last stand of your plan. I would be cast to the earth and there was nothing to do about it. Although I cared no more for myself, no harm would come to my comrades if I had anything to do with it. Any bloody enemy popping up from a shell hole now would get both knees and a bloody bayonet to follow. And I would look the buggers in the bloody eye whilst doing it.

The men were getting to their starting positions and most were out there in No Man's Land already, on the slopes and ready to move. While the village was defended, the Germans were not ready for this, a massive surprise attack – right here in the middle of the night. With hope making me jubilant, I felt that revenge was maybe not so bad after all. This was *my* village and *my* home just as much as if it were Blighty. Fritz had been here quite long enough and it was time to pull this particular tick from the dog's back.

One of the biggest differences from the initial operations discussed with Cowling, Rawlinson and the Corps commanders was the element of complete surprise at night. Pounding artillery for days on end, with too small a calibre as it turned out, alerted the enemy, signalling a matter of when, and not if, an attack would be pressed. When we attacked from the front, the very front line might be taken by surprise but everyone behind would be alerted, giving them hours to get ready. Instead, we should follow Roman tactics and charge on through, leaving those behind to take out the front line. Like the waves from a boat in its wake, meaning that the enemy is either always meeting fresh troops, or the speed of advance is rapid and not bogged down with actions that only hinder progress. I liked this idea. It was an idea I had written down on the quay at Folkestone.

Now 0320 approached. Jones had asked me to lead an assault that would mop up the front-line trench, quite near where we had crossed. He welcomed the extra pair of hands, if not the inherent confusion of rank. But I was more than happy to get my hands dirty since this was my home village and I would be able to help.

His forward troops were carrying bombs only, some even chose not to take a rifle in order to carry more bombs. Cowling had really thought all of this through. The army had named the two main trench lines Aston and Villa trenches. How the army loved their humour, if not their football!

At 0320 the barrage began, with a single gun followed by the others opening up all at once, aiming directly at the very front line and first support area. The noise was unbelievable, my chest was vibrating and the air was sucked out of my lungs in a single stroke. Nearly a thousand guns opened up on a line that stretched only around three miles. Crash after crash after crash – without a single pause – this would last only five minutes and then we would set upon them. The sky was lit with constant bursts. It was, without any doubt, the most intense bombing that the world had ever seen. Some five shells for every square yard of trench, by my calculation. I would have pitied the poor bastards on the receiving end, except here and now, they bloody deserved it. They bloody did.

The five minutes took what seemed like hours. Troops in our forward areas were looking skywards, shaking and screaming at the top of their voices from the shelling. This would be a test of nerve and courage all right. Holding on, even for five minutes in that screaming was almost impossible, even knowing it was our shelling. The hurricane was unleashed and the enemy were going to get a terrible reckoning.

Some of our troops in the Queen's had not seen action before and none of us, even the regulars, had seen shelling like this. My chest was visibly vibrating and it became harder and harder to breathe. Even my deep breaths were empty and airless. The percussion shook every bone in a terrible tune and I was unable to control the sounds in my head. Left and right were the soldiers of the Queen's that I had been asked to lead and to fight with. We had lots of nods and smiles to keep our nerve, but there were many more in agony, yelling at the sky and willing this to stop. It did not matter that this was our shelling. The officers needed to stay calm and professional so I turned to these men to help keep their soldiers calm.

Next to me were three privates, new to the army, looking upwards and swearing loudly.

'Can we live through this? Dear Lord, we will all be dead. The shelling is too much. Sir, is it always like this?'

I lied to keep him calm.

'Yes, shelling is always like this. Imagine the buggers being shelled, eh?' I hoped it sounded convincing.

'Is it always like this, really, is it always like this? It can't be, we will all be dead. It's too much, the world is dead and we will all be dead.'

I put my hand on his shoulder to help him calm down and he went back to grimly gripping his weapon for comfort and unholy solace. God had forsaken us all on that slope and France was ruined for me now, so I hoped our guns would bomb them flat.

Then the bombardment stopped as suddenly as it started, final crashes and sounds of screaming agony replaced the vibration in the air. The silence broke as deafened ears tuned to the sounds of dying again. The air returning and the vibration subsiding offered no comfort to the soldiers prone on the ridge. My body continued tingling for several seconds and my ears were numbed, albeit temporarily.

The troops in No Man's Land began to move forward in one line and we had to catch them up. So, we jumped up and over the top into the darkness, charging headlong uphill for the German positions. We approached the Contalmaison road, carried on forward and came upon the German wire, now smashed and cut to pieces. This was going to be better than 1st July, for sure. The troops in the first wave had already topped the trench and were bombing the support trenches. The screams and yells from the dugouts made it sound like hell itself had opened up. The troops were ordered not to touch any equipment in the trenches, which might be booby-trapped, and they were not to stop, not for anything. The reserve trenches were receiving a smaller bombardment for a further two minutes. When this stopped, the screaming could be heard again and became almost unendurable. Watkins was by my side at every step. He carried bombs and a pair of Webley revolvers, looking forward to bombing dugouts in the front-line trench. He had suffered enough of this war as well.

Some Germans had made it out of bunkers and were returning sporadic rifle fire and some of our troops fell in a familiar slumping fashion, weighed down by kit. But most had much less equipment and it became harder to target them as they moved around more with the Germans less able to pick them off. There was very little sweeping machine gun fire, which was a good thing. The front line was shocked and overrun in this area. Our troops moved right and under the village while others headed up and over the road towards the church at the top of the ridge. The machine gun on the road was silent, presumably hit, but rifle fire could be heard occasionally. Less death from the terrible machine gun, which made me thankful.

The first wave of forward troops were now well and truly mixed up in the reserve trenches, dropping bombs into the temporary dugouts and shooting any enemy soldiers that emerged alive, which wasn't many. Our men were in amongst the troops moving into the line and were able to inflict terrible casualties on the enemy from above. Puff after puff of smoke followed the muffled explosions. Swearing and cursing at every step as the troops moved forwards. There were some Germans that made it out alive. They were usually met with the butt of a rifle across the face, in the fashion drilled into soldiers when they were recruited. Give them the round in the chamber. When that has gone, bayonet in the shoulders or stomach – not the chest in the dark unless you wanted to get stuck. If he parries your thrust then get the rifle into the jaw, hard. If you are running at full pelt, the effect would be the same as a hammer in the face. Deadly, but that was the nature of our brutal war. We could not accommodate prisoners on this slope and were not going to take any, not yet. Turn and run. Run all the way back to Germany at the bloody double.

Watkins and I arrived upon the front-line trench, here again in the horror and the thick of it. Some Germans were out in the trench. They looked in poor order, bewildered but still with weapons around them. Those of us with revolvers were able to shoot them directly they emerged. I dropped into the trench somewhere around the Flatiron Copse, armed with a knife and some bombs. My own revolver was holstered for use if we captured the position and moved further forwards. Around me, the 21st Division attacked in two further waves over and again, leaping into trenches and taking over positions. Where we were, the attack was very successful and as the dawn broke to daylight, we were occupiers of the trench line near the Contalmaison road. While I had not used my bombs and had not yet had to engage any Germans directly, I had a terrible feeling that this would soon change.

The trench system was quite complex because of the British advances and the slopes, but if we pressed on north we would be through it all in maybe three hours. The Germans were in quite poor order and much of their kit was missing – having had severe delays in rearming and in being reinforced. I told some of the officers that we must press on into the village and up the slope towards the church, where the ground was higher and gave a good view up to the main second line. At around 0530, we crossed the road where I had come over with Watkins just a few hours ago. I positioned myself at the base of the road leading up to the church and then on to Martinpuich.

The Germans had evacuated Villa Trench and the line through the wood, but had taken up positions within the village to return fire. The trenches were not dug through the village and for a time, it became a war of surface fighting, hand-to-hand and with hand-thrown bombs. Where it was possible to fire directly at enemy soldiers, the infantry took up firing positions. With the Germans going backwards, it was easier to attack than if it were a series of trench positions.

I ran up the road straight at a German gun position, which had been hastily assembled using some damaged sandbags. The Germans had not set up a machine gun yet, but it was clear this was to be a stronghold and we could not allow it. Watkins went ahead with four bombs and threw them at the position. The first bounced off the front wall and exploded, causing the men behind the bags to duck. As they put their heads up a second time to take a look and try to return some fire, the second bomb exploded in amongst them, killing them all instantly, but causing a terrible bloody mess. As Watkins carried on up the road, he was shot in the arm and fell, but he caught the bomb he was about to throw and tucked it underneath him. He was surrounded by some fifteen troops of the Queen's going to rescue him when there was a dull thump and the bomb exploded, showering his would-be rescuers in blood and clothing. Watkins was not killed immediately and was lying face down on the approach to the village. When I got to him, he was beyond help. I looked into his eyes as the life left them and they glassed over.

'Don't die Horace, please you can make it, please hold on to life. Here, let me tell you a joke. What about the day...'

It was no good, Watkins was already dead. Pain shot through my whole body as if a lance had pierced me from head to foot.

'Horace old boy, it has been an adventure. Rest now, my friend. Rest now without care or worry.'

I fell forwards onto his back and felt the warm blood pooling on his shoulder cool until it was cold. A private from the Queen's pulled me back gently.

'Better be going on sir, it's not safe here.'

Watkins, my flying companion, had died as the infantryman he was. I detailed two young privates to carry him back to Cowling, no arguments, with all care. They did so, but all three were never seen again and the two soldiers were listed as missing, never to be found.

By now, the third and fourth wave had entered the village from the road in a wide sweep towards Longueval. We fought up the slope towards the church and I wanted to be the one first to Odile's house in open order, free to move about the surface. Perhaps planning to take this village was a personal mission and perhaps this was not such a strategic goal, but the wood up the slope was, so we would not be staying around here for very long.

When I got back to the steps of the church, it was strange to think that only last night, just a few hours ago, I was here, with Watkins alive and well and looking out for my back. Some shelling had destroyed parts of the village since then, but it was not so smashed up as to be impossible to move into or recognise.

Up the slope to the road to Martinpuich, the Germans had set up a temporary redoubt across the road. Moving from house to house, and cellar to cellar, we cleared any remaining troops and set up sentries. We did not want a swift counter attack destroying our plans, having made these gains. The Queen's in particular were shooting from the shoulder and taking good aim at the retreating soldiers. The first of our Lewis guns appeared and it gave us respite from the possibility of a counter attack. We had to be careful as bombs thrown were impossible to hear and therefore avoid.

I wanted to be less involved in killing Germans in this village. Still shocked and reeling from Odile's letter, here I was standing in the smashed village where I had spent so many happy days with her, covered in the blood of my dead comrade and the memory of a lost love. My memories should not be ones of killing any more enemy soldiers or taking revenge for their damned invasion – that poor bugger on the steps of Odile's home was quite enough. After the war, if I survived, I didn't want to think of some poor boy from Bavaria who was in the wrong place at the wrong time.

We moved up past the Church and around where the road sweeps to the right to get a better view of the German position, which was at the top of a rise, in plain view. I could see the steps and the splashes of blood from the German I had killed. My hand started to ache at that point. Now I had a hand *and* a knee to remind me of my war.

We moved around house by house to within bombing range. The machine gun that had been set up began to rattle amongst the brickwork sending lethal stone chips in all directions. We had several bombing parties already in place near the road and hoped that one of them could throw a bomb far enough. By around 0700, the party had managed to silence the machine gun and the northern approaches to the village were secure. I detailed parties to take away our dead and wounded and to clear the German bodies out of the village and into the captured trench. Selfishly, I did not want to see them in this village. It was their fault we had to be here in this situation.

On the left, the retreating Germans were taking many casualties, but the fighting was all at close quarters. Many of our soldiers were being shot at close range, some machine gun fire was accounting for some of them, but most were dying entwined with their enemy. Some local shelling started up from the enemy positions as well, enemy gunners clearly unsure whether their troops were in the village. All was confusion and miscommunication for the enemy and some of this was hopefully down to my little band.

Hopefully a lot of this chaos was down to them as they had sacrificed so very much.

On the right of us, the church cemetery road and the slope we hid behind were proving more difficult to break down. The windmill ridge provided some higher ground for the enemy to observe and they had seen us coming. There, the wire had not been so well cut and casualties for the Allies were high. But the Germans had not reckoned on being attacked from their own side and we were upon them within an hour of our securing the northern approach to the village. By placing soldiers with rifles, machine guns and ammunition on the top of the ridge, we hoped to protect it until sappers could make some better defensive positions. Then, we descended upon them and took many prisoners.

At 1100, with the approaches and limits of the village in our hands, I retired from the village which was now secure – liberated, even. How I wanted to tell Odile! Perhaps this might change her outlook and she would drop the damned German in a heartbeat, when she knew what we had done.

Back on the road, I learned that the assault from Montauban towards Bazentin-le-Grand on the hill had not gone at all well. The village had needed a second burst of shelling and was in ruins, if not obliterated. We needed this cleared if we were to launch our cavalry. On 13th July, Cowling had called for cavalry and some good horse troops were in the Albert area, but they were not here yet. It was nearly the middle of the day and I wondered when they would come. We were all tired and in need of a definite breakthrough to push us ever onwards.

The Germans had by now been well and truly alerted and the later barrage had not been so precisely placed. Trones wood was in British hands and I could only hope that the assault would be successful as the next phase had to be launched before the inevitable counter attack. More than anything, I wanted the High Wood. The Germans were retreating towards their second defensive positions. We had to keep pushing them back to prevent this line from becoming a strong position. This meant moving forwards, and quickly.

From the village summit, we could see the shallow valley towards High Wood and the path was clear for us to assault. The Germans were running about in disarray and the victory long hoped for might yet be ours. We did not have enough troops to assault the slopes yet, we needed time to form up after the early morning attack. Tiredness and fatigue would overtake the courage of even the hardest fighter. The fresh reinforcements were needed now and some of them began to arrive. Cowling had anticipated more casualties and had instructed the waves to stop at the end of the village road and wait for the reserves to move past them. Whilst this was sensible, as it turned out we had a big advantage that we could exploit if we pressed on. Perhaps caution had crept back into the planning.

I sent a runner to Cowling with urgent instructions to advance the cavalry as soon as the other village was taken. They could move into the valley between the villages and form up on the road in the shelter of the ridge. We all called this point Crucifix Corner as the roadside crucifix was still standing, complete with some war damage and shrapnel embedded in the ironwork. A defiant France and bloody good for it.

In front of the village, our soldiers were now resting and smoking in the cover of the downslope, having successfully secured the entire village. It was as much a reaction to the brutality and the intensity as anything else. At the top of the ridge, the fields of grain were waving in the July light and the ground was dry. We needed to push on now to prevent any counter attacks. New troops were needed and they needed to be there. None arrived.

But, at long last the 7th Division appeared on the eastern side of our positions. They had done it. Their reserve brigade behind looked good to press on towards the High Wood and secure it ready for the cavalry charge, which was Cowling's centrepiece and a compromise to get the Commander-in-Chief to agree to a night attack.

I wanted to drop back and see what was happening. There was little else for me to do here – our little party had completed our job brutally and efficiently. Mostly, I wanted to think of Watkins and his family – I had spent almost every moment of peril for the last two weeks with him and now he was gone in an instant. Another comrade lost. But I could give him no thought at that moment. It took me an hour to reach Cowling and he was in telephone discussion with Rawlinson himself. When the conversation ended, Cowling put the phone down and simply said, 'Damn.'

He wanted us to press on and take the High Wood. However, the divisional commanders were unsure and wanted to commit cavalry that wasn't yet here. Congreve was pinned down in Longueval and the ridge was exposed to enemy fire from the side.

'Hello Collins, I am pleased you are here and made it through this morning. Right, I requested the cavalry at 0740 this morning. They are in the wrong bloody place, too far south, not even in bloody Albert. They have to make it up and around Albert then on through either Fricourt or through Montauban. Not the smoothest going after the last two weeks of pitching.'

'Can't we request 7th Division to go? By my thoughts, they would get an easy time through to the High Wood.'

'Yes, agreed. I asked for it and Rawlinson looks likely is going to agree it. There is some concern that we haven't taken Longueval and this might mean we get shot at from both directions at once. Our attack might falter at the first bloody step, just like the first day.'

'There's still time, sir?'

'Yes, but let's keep thinking Collins old boy, let's keep thinking. By the way, you look damnable, where have you been?'

'With the assault wave sir, into the village. I can't tell you how strange it felt walking such familiar streets.'

Cowling said nothing at first. He ran his hand along his chin and cheeks and very slightly slid his cap back on his head for a moment.

'We have to put the cavalry into the fight. Haig expects it and Rawlinson did a deal on it to get this show through. I want the Bois de Foureaux Collins. Would you be good enough to take it for me?'

'I will try sir, but will we have more infantry to support us? The men will be rather exhausted, whatever is left of them.'

'I will request the reserve.'

He consulted his notes for a short time.

'In for the duration – so we might as well. Let me see, ah the 33rd lot are set up at Fricourt, lucky buggers. Let's get them here and support the 21st.'

'Thank you sir.'

'Anything else old boy?'

'Yes, sir?'

'What is it?'

'Watkins is dead sir. I intend to submit a citation for an award. Perhaps you would be kind enough to submit a request for a Victoria Cross?'

'Entirely in order, William. Also, you know you were promoted quite unusually to temporary major because of your record, skills and unique knowledge of this part of France? I applied for the temporary promotion to be made permanent. Well, it has been rejected.'

'Sir? What have I done wrong?'

'Nothing, they are making you a bloody half-colonel – on one condition.'

'What would that be sir?'

'It has been insisted that you go and get bloody trained to be an officer, you over-promoted trench rat!'

We both laughed and that helped the aching loss of Watkins. Soldiers can do this – deal with terrible news with a sharp word, or a joke, usually at someone else's expense.

Cowling was evidently lining me up to return to England to train as an instructor. What with all the odd things that I have done, that did not seem unreasonable. Perhaps he was protecting me and reassuring me that this would be all right? I wasn't sure. So far, I just about managed to get by through focusing on reaching Odile. Now, without her, it was just sheer bloody murder. I did not have her now and the war was washing over the bows and dragging me down. It was obvious now in my words and in my deeds. By nature, I was not cruel and was rather a curious and friendly character. But here, I had turned to shade and lived the life of dirty, dusty, damp survival in the earth itself. The threat of instant death was around and about all the time, watching me, stalking me. At any moment, death would strike and carry me away. William Collins had drifted away on the wind, crumbling to dust, leaving an empty shell of bitterness and revenge in his place.

The division was ready to go in relief of the morning attackers and was intent on taking the wood from the enemy. However, the ground was not entirely cleared on the right, with Longueval still posing an obstacle to Congreve and his men. Cowling was to go out himself to provide concrete evidence that the ridge from the village to the High Wood was feasible for cavalry. And 7th and 3rd Division generals were to accompany this incredible walk right up to the very edge of the woods.

So it was, that three generals and two other officers made an incredible scouting trip through the fields that early afternoon to see for themselves the undamaged grounds, the waving corn and the empty German positions. The cavalry had been called again earlier in the day and was agonisingly distant and only slowly on its way. No one knew exactly when they would arrive, but they could not arrive too soon, with their glittering sabres and sturdy horses – probably a sight not seen on this Western Front for many months.

When the scouting party returned with a favourable report, Cowling tried again to get 7th Division to rapidly advance on the woods to exploit our morning gains. General Watts, the commanding officer, initially agreed. At just after 1200 we were at last to move on the empty woods. However, it soon became clear that the advance at Longueval had again faltered on the wire and the Germans still had a clear line of sight to shoot across the ridge onto the approaches to the wood. At that time, the initiative seemed to be slipping from our fingers – perhaps not everyone was in the same theatre – and the advance was desperately cancelled. The risk was seen to be just too much and the time elapsed had cost the advantage. Approaches to the woods had been undefended to the point that generals could walk openly in the fields, but no infantry were permitted to advance. It was an extraordinary scene, watching Cowling implore the commanders to see it his way, but the risk to the right might let the enemy off the hook this day and would certainly cost thousands of dead another time if the enemy got back into position. The infantry recommended the cavalry to go and so the cavalry were seen as the last throw at the ridge from their point of view. Cowling had apparently thumped the table and kicked the stool in frustration, in a shift from his usual self-control.

Cowling and I had conceived a plan that was working, but the 4th Army were juggling with the pieces and letting them fall to the floor. Perhaps through a lack of confidence, experience or nerve, the initiative was being wrested from us and given back to the enemy through inaction and indecision. The ideas I had thought through on the boats at Folkestone and refined in my days of tunnelling were to wither on the slopes of the very place I truly called home. A swift night attack, an enemy weakened from behind and a lightning raid on their positions had gained us so much, but the infantry and cavalry tactics that followed had learned little from our early success.

However, Cowling knew his business and was not out of it yet. He asked for the reserves to be brought up from Fricourt and the divisional commander agreed. At least the cavalry had not gone that way and word was that they were sighted south-east of Montauban – agonisingly close and yet still not in the battle. The fresh troops would be moved forwards and through the 21st to settle on the High Wood when the cavalry attacked. This elegant move would surely keep the Germans guessing and keep their shock levels high enough to get us into the wood. It would also ensure that infantry took and held the wood, allowing the cavalry to retire and regroup.

After all of this trench war, I wanted to see the cavalry charge for myself. Once Cowling and I had discussed the plan for the afternoon, I made my way to the designated jumping off point. By this time, the approach to the ridge was firmly in British hands. But this success had come at an enormous price. There were bodies everywhere, having been picked up from the lower slopes to make way for the horses, but those slopes were now ours. The ridge was taken and the wood ahead was empty. The 33rd Division was coming from the right – Longueval would be ours, I was sure, and the High Wood was unguarded. Nothing could stop us now, if we kept our collective nerve.

It was near to Crucifix Corner that the message came regarding the return of our special troops from behind the lines, as the deadline for their return had now long passed. Of the sixty that were in the original team, we knew that fifteen had been captured – all but one of them being shot. Eight had been killed on landing or immediately after landing as the enemy surrounded the aeroplanes and twelve had made it back to British lines. The rest were still missing, although missing was not quite an accurate term. Many of them most likely wanted to appear to be missing and maybe this action might yet have allowed some to make it back alive. Not exactly the perfect operation, but who knows how many lives were spared that morning as a result. Perhaps we will never know.

Time passed on and there was no sign of the cavalry. They had been called so long ago, at about 0730, yet they were still not there. They had to pass through the battlefields from 1st July onwards and it had been very slow going. The 33rd Infantry was arriving at their jumping off point and they would be passing through towards the High Wood in just a few hours. We might yet make this, although we might yet lose everything. Although I had lost almost everything in this war, I had enough energy left for one more hope.

CHAPTER FIFTEEN - A PLAN UNRAVELS

In the late afternoon of 14th July, the troops from the morning assault on the village were resting and recuperating. The village was now firmly held and the Germans were not to be seen in the surrounding fields. Their front line troops were dead, wounded or captured. It had been a very successful action, although it was not yet over. The High Wood was not yet ours to command.

It was almost surreal waiting for the cavalry to appear and I wandered up from the waiting area to the road at Bazentin, recalling, with every step, a little of my life here before the war. Odile's letter sprang to mind, unbidden, finally I was becoming more reconciled to its contents as I read it over and again. The French was difficult for me to read, but when Cowling had read it to me in French it was possible to make out more of what Odile was saying, and perhaps even what she was saying between those difficult lines.

Now that we were finally able to move about in the open, I walked to Odile's family home and sat on the porch floor. Not for the first time since being back in France, I felt tears quietly appear. The physical exhaustion of the last two weeks had caught up with me and I was not able to hold back.

But, I needed to get back to see the cavalry and at 1700, word came through that they had been seen near Montauban. At 1800, they appeared from around the hill and what an amazing sight they were with their lances. There were Hussars, who were quite familiar, but the Indian horsemen from the Deccan Horse were an amazing and emboldening sight. Their uniforms were quite different to the Hussars and they wore an array of hats and caps, including a few tin hats. They did not take long to form up and were ready to leave at 1900. The horses were large and solid-looking. The mounted cavalry looked intimidating, easily lethal enough to make any enemy scatter in disarray, if they could get close enough.

Cavalry charges on this French and Belgian front were now almost non-existent. The machine gun and accurate shelling had put an end to that old way of fighting. By this time, though, the High Wood had been left alone for some six hours and the initiative may have been wrested from our grasp. Yet, these horsemen! Some had bombs around their shoulders and looked like nothing could stop them, some had revolvers and the rest had lances. But it was by no means certain at that time whether they would actually have the chance to use them. All now looked grimly towards the slope and rise where they would soon be charging, right and left.

I went from the assembly area near Crucifix Corner to the top of the village under cover of the slope and the sunken part of the Contalmaison road, whilst the cavalry was still lining up for the charge. They were going up the slope straight on and to the right, to the very base of High Wood. Once the cavalry had emerged from the Contalmaison road, the ground was quite flat and level, with a gentle rolling slope up to the edge of the wooded area. It was dry enough to take the churning of the horses' hooves, perhaps some hope remained then, even for a break in the second line. There did not seem to be many of them though – to me no more than maybe two-hundred horses, but there might have been more horses further back, it was hard to see.

The cavalry formed its lines and began to arrow across the ridge back. Their speed seemed incredible even at this distance and they looked unstoppable. The roar of hooves built gradually as they ascended the short rise, muffled in places where the ground was softer, or where bodies were still strewn across the field. I saw them first and the sound came later, just like shell bursts in the distance. Even though the horses always tried to miss landing on a body, with so many horses, occasionally a dead human body was flung from the back of the pack. The rumbling grew in intensity as they built up some speed – not flat out – but certainly at a decent gallop. The artillery laid a few shells ahead of them into the wood, but not too many as it would possibly cause the horses to misbehave. They were certainly brave horses. Some of the leading riders broke into the clear and open ground, wheeling right between the wood and Longueval. Perhaps they were detailed to help capture Longueval. My dream of a true breakthrough was laid out before me here on these slopes, seemingly nearer and now a real possibility. The quayside daydreams galloped on unhindered.

They had moved quite a way across when I heard the first artillery shells being launched from the German side in dull thumps. A shattering sound, they had obviously managed to regroup and range some guns into the open. Then, a sound that I dreaded above all others. The unmistakable death rattle of the machine gun. The rounds landed very short at first, the bullets kicking up mud and dirt in smooth cloudy lines of overlapping fire.

At least two were in the wood itself, which worried me the most, but perhaps that was all they had. The firing rose slightly and began to land in amongst the horses' legs and necks, with telltale puffs of dust on the ground. Horses began to drop in small groups as the guns swept left and then right, a couple of degrees at a time. The riders tumbled forwards, and some did not get up. The fire rose again slightly and was now at the height of a rider. As men fell, the horses lost their formation and carried on, right at the German positions, some still wheeling right, putting them in range of fire from Longueval itself and the rear of Delville Wood. But some riders reached the edge of the High Wood, and one or two were able to leap in amongst the trunks and branches of those trees undisturbed by shelling. One of the riders was hit in his chest and exploded instantly, in two or three bursts as his bombs went off on impact. The horse behind was immediately shocked and tried to spin around. Its rider was unseated and was flung into the remains of the destroyed horse and rider. He did not seem to get up from the fall and in any case a shell landed next to him a second or two later and did for him.

Despite the machine gun fire, horses streamed over the border of the wood, especially on the side nearest to us on the ridge. This heartened the watching infantry, who were wary now of any advance as the Germans now knew we were attacking again, this time up to the wood itself. Infantry had been creeping forwards left and right of the wood, on the right under fire from in front and behind from Longueval, but had been pinned down by fire from seemingly everywhere. Some horses were emerging from the wood, all without riders. Then, some of the riders emerged with other moving figures – perhaps prisoners. It was quite a long way off, but it looked like some of the wood had been cleared. Some of our infantry were now advancing to the edge of the wood, but most at that point were still being pinned down.

I went to move forwards slowly, with a couple of the Queen's who were watching the charge with me, feeling both cheerful at the spectacle and saddened by the lateness of this action and the harm to the horses. As we moved off, carrying bombs and revolvers as before, we noticed the second wave of the charge catching up and entering the wood. It seemed that the third and fourth waves were perhaps being recalled, but it was not clear to me, not being trained in cavalry warfare. We got almost to the edge of the wood and were about to enter when we heard and saw the unmistakable thumps of machine gun bullets on the ground, coming right at us. We were now pinned down. Again, anger that some bloody German was firing at me wanted to take me over, but it subsided and I tried to keep going through the extreme fatigue and constant threat. From the front, came well-aimed machine gunfire, which meant the crew was operating normally and was not just engaged in random shooting. To the rear over my right shoulder was coming sporadic and less well-aimed machine gun fire maybe from the direction of Longueval, but I could not be sure. It was from a long way off, at the limit of effective range, but a bullet is a bullet. Here was not a good place to stay and be minced up, but we could not move. This was likely to be the worst mix I had been in yet, being fired upon from two sides at close range and we were all catching stray fire from Longueval – maybe even from our own gunners.

We would be safe if we got down and dug in, once again reverting to trench war. There were enough of us to scrape a widened shell hole to stay in. In the open, we were in danger of a shell burst, or from a gas attack, but it was better than just being face down in the field. We had not seen gas here today and I did not recall seeing any gas dumps on the other side of the lines.

It was possible that another division would be attacking as the cavalry had clearly entered the wood and there had been some success in holding the very edge. We waited until that deadly machine gun had been moved or silenced. At night, any firing would attract mortar fire or artillery shells from our positions firing at the flashes. So we crawled dead flat towards another nearby shell hole, trying to get a bit closer. There were plenty of them around and we dropped into a double one. Some German artillery was firing from well into the rear, aiming at the junction of the Contalmaison and Montauban roads at Crucifix Corner. It was clear now that was it for the horses and no further cavalry attack would be made today. They had gone from the ridge and that was that. Some must have been holding on, but very few so late in the day. The fear and alarm seemed gone from the enemy and they were damned well shooting back at us.

We were not in a good position, with some of the younger lads from the Queen's out in front of the wood. I was puzzled that the Germans had not launched any form of counter attack anywhere along this stretch of line. This was odd because they should have done by now. Maybe some of the team had been successful behind the lines, after all. Knowing nothing and with no communications possible, we had just feared the worst. Anyway it seemed that at least now until nightfall, we were safe. I hoped that they had not just decided to sit behind their new second line, because that would mean it was finished and ready. That would be a disaster for us all.

On the right of us, Longueval was still under assault from our infantry pressing on and forward. The poor buggers must be done in by now and fed up of the attrition against the strong line. There were still sporadic cries and shouts of an attack coupled with the gunfire in response. It did seem that less and less resistance was being fielded and perhaps we might prevail, at least to some extent, in order to free up this side of the approach to the wood. It was now nearly 2100 and the wood seemed quiet, except for some small pockets of exposed fighting. Some other infantry were approaching and entering the wood under heavy fire and it seemed that we should follow. Some German prisoners were being taken back to our lines, lucky buggers. The cavalry were clearly holding some or even all of the wood, it was hard to be sure at that time since the field was a confusion of movement and material.

Under cover of our helmets, we waited for dusk to fall. It took until nearly 2200 for it to be sufficiently dark to move without alarm. We were more exposed than most.

'Right, lads, looks like we need to get out of here.'

'Yes, sir. Are we off into the trees, or what's left of them, or away back to the village?'

'We need to go into the wood. If we can take a part of it tonight, it might keep this field clear for the morning – if it ever comes for us. It might be a long night.'

'Will they attack us sir?'

'Almost certainly, but we can't stay here. We will be chopped into tiny pieces. We can't go back, and having got this far, we might yet be shot in the back.'

'Onward, it is, sir. We are right there. We got enough ammunition there you boys?'

'Plenty enough to scare them, but it ain't much! Not enough to take a bloody wood, ha ha.'

Smiling at the tenacity and bravery, I gave the order to move forward, having checked we really did have enough ammunition and bombs to make a show. We had about forty bombs between us and ten rifles. Enough to irritate for a bit. I left two boys behind as communication sentries. Any soldiers coming in as relief or to support our attack would have pass to through here and we could at least avoid being shot from behind. We moved off.

Gradually, we made our way into the edge of the wood. There was a track running parallel to the edge that had been bombed and shelled but was just deep enough to cover a crawl. We were able to move inside the remaining tree line and saw some of the cavalry, without their horses, huddled in the wood with revolvers and bombs still at the ready. Some of the trees had been felled and some stumps rose at shattered angles. Other trees were damaged and liable to fall or drop large branches. We held the southern tip, a positive for us, and located where the gunfire was coming from. There was a pair of machine guns on a small rise about one-hundred yards into the wood. We crept up on the Deccan boys and whispered a greeting.

'Oi, you buggers. It's the 21st.'

'Who are you boys?'

I almost chuckled at the broad accent, which was an unmistakably Indian accent. The post was being held by eight men of the Deccan Horse. These lads were from India. They had set off for the right wheel to Longueval, but artillery had forced them left and up to the wood. They thought it safest to go in and shelter as they could not, like us, easily return. There was a muffled laugh from the back of our group.

'I said the fucking 21st! Blimey, you lot are brave or stupid for sticking around here. Anyway, we might help you a bit, with all our piles of ammunition, eh?'

'Come over here, then.'

This was whispered by another steady Indian voice over the general noise.

'It is quite safe. The machine gunners are cleaning the gun. It has jammed you know. We were about to try to blow it up, you see?'

I wanted to establish our strength and our options.

'Well done you boys for taking the wood. How many of us are alive? What do you think the German strength is?'

It was the best I could do, trying to move away from what would have been a damned fool suicide attack on two machine guns. Chances were, they weren't both jammed at the same time.

'There are fifteen of us here, that we can see. There may be more. The enemy has one trench line to the north with maybe two-hundred in it. They are not really firing at us and not really looking to attack us. They are just sitting there.'

The musical tones in the voice of the cavalryman delighted me. He had certainly come a long way to get mixed up in this bloody war. I placed a hand on his shoulder, although he was much older than me, wanting him to know we were here and that there might be more coming.

'Fine, then we must hold our position here. We are not enough in number to attack further. We may see the 33rd come through tonight.' Hopefully, I sounded clear enough.

But I was wrong. A few minutes after arriving, four of the cavalry – now infantry – took off in a rush at the machine gun which was too quiet for my liking. My order had not got through yet and they had already decided to move off. Two stood upright and nimbly moved towards the machine gun from the right and two were walking slowly from the left. Walking slowly? What was going on? The gunners caught sight of the two ambling soldiers and quickly got the gun set to fire. They loaded and ranged the weapon, but it did not fire. It was not possible to see the look on their faces, but trained crews were used to this and they would solve the problem fast. They did. It took another ten seconds to sort out what had happened and clean the jam. They opened fire and both walking soldiers ducked in time. The two on the right were on top of the position in a few more seconds, using the smashed trees as cover. They threw in a bomb, but it failed to detonate. I nearly shouted. One of the gun crew drew a pistol and shot one of our two in the head. He fell dead. The other was still moving to the gun position, he fell on them all, and using the barrel of his revolver, he slashed wildly. Whilst the gun crew was distracted, our other two moved up and shot the gunners. All three then moved quickly back, the two from the left carrying their dead comrade back. They threw in another bomb to destroy the gun. It didn't go off either. I gave them one of my bombs and that did the position in, sure enough. It was an unbelievably brave and stupid act, although it certainly would save the lives of some of the 33rd coming up later.

The second position was slightly obscured by fallen trees, but the three went off and did exactly the same thing again. The gun opened fire and then there was an enormous explosion as gun, crew and ammunition exploded at once.

This might have greatly improved our chances of survival, but it didn't. The noise unnerved the trench garrison, who began concerted rifle firing towards us. It seemed less well aimed than usual, so perhaps they did not know exactly where we were located. Some of the Deccan troops returned aimed fire and we took some casualties. We could not stay here now, because quite soon we would be subject to short-range bombing and this gunfire was not going to stop.

I intended to recommend the Deccan troops for an award. It was an incredibly selfless act, repeated a second time, and I would speak with Cowling about it, if we got out alive. After managing to get the troops' names, and guessing at some of their spellings, I made a very short note and put it into my pocket. Perhaps some good could yet come from this day, if we kept thinking our way out.

It was now fully dark, which ended the possibility of repeating these little raids further. I had already decided to dig in a little and wait for the infantry. The Germans, however, had other ideas. They had obviously moved out many of their front-line troops and the defenders were light in number compared to Cowling's expectations. Even so, there were plenty around and it seemed that during the very early morning, more troops came back into the trench line. We were subjected to two small counter attacks, both of which went through our position without even noticing us. Behind us, the 33rd had likely arrived and it was with them that the Germans seemed to engage. While there may have been other cavalry in the wood as well as us, their numbers were unknown to me. There was fighting for sure, but our little group was isolated and we needed to wait for our chance to attack, or to make good our escape.

At around 0200, still fighting off tiredness, I had to fight off a small

German patrol, clearly sent to assess how far into the woods we had penetrated. The patrol consisted of four troops well-armed with bombs.

The cavalry team saw them come across the wood, and it was just possible to distinguish their shapes from the background and the blasted wood. The cavalry boys carried a short cloth rope with a knot in it, as well as small and large knives, which they used expertly. Without a shot being fired, they took down the patrol, each soldier killed swiftly. The small rope with the knot was shockingly impressive and worth adding to the training course – if I got out of the wood alive.

'What on earth kills a man so swiftly in silence?' I enquired of one of the Indians.

The Indian trooper looked at me and smiled.

'Thuggee sir, thuggee. This is a rumal. I tie a knot around a coin here, see, half-crown. Edge on the neck, jolly deadly sir!'

From the papers carried by the dead soldiers, I could see that these were good quality lads from the 3rd Guards Division. Another killed to our left was from another regiment, so it was possible that a relief had been planned or was underway. That was always a good time to launch a surprise attack as the Germans were concentrating on other things and not our movements. Happily for us, more of our infantry troops entered the wood and asked for the commanding officer. That was presumably me, but there was no way of knowing. So, I told the soldiers who came behind us that I was in command and helped them adjust to this position.

To my relief, they were from the 33rd, who had arrived at about the time the cavalry began to charge. They had waited on the ridge as a reserve but had now been tasked with occupying the wood. They understood that the whole wood was taken, but sadly, I had to inform them differently. They had begun to openly dig in to the south but had been fired on constantly and they had been partially withdrawn. The sentries I had posted were both dead, having been hit by a whizz-bang. There were pockets of cavalry occupying areas of the wood, but unless they were going to press on with the attack, we would be stuck here until a proper assault could be arranged, which we could not do alone, with everyone so mixed up.

With terrible realisation, I saw that our advantage was finally slipping away. We had won a swift and decisive advantage using a night attack without bombardment. We had cleared my beloved village and liberated Odile's home. We could and should have been able to press on to Bapaume, but our troops had been stopped, held back or wrongly positioned at the critical moment. Unless we quickly reassembled, this was going the way of other battles. I suggested to that the troops were better off digging in just out of range of the wood on the ridge and waiting for the division to move up and launch an attack on the whole wood at first light. The Germans were now clearly back in the wood and willing to hold on to it.

We quietly withdrew from the wood, knowing the 33rd were there to watch our backs and provide a stop to a German counter attack. I held back my anger that the advantage was ultimately lost, having so carefully constructed and executed this plan. My concerns now, were the cavalrymen and the Queen's boys that held this little section of the wood – and my own fatigue, which was consuming my ability to think clearly and stay calm.

Retreating back to the new line, I met with one of the 33rd officers, who looked me up and down suspiciously.

'That's not the uniform of anyone in a division in this bloody battle. What brings you here?'

'I'm with the Queen's and we were consolidating the wood with the cavalry this evening, as you know.'

'Well, it has turned around into a right bloody fuck-up. We watched the cavalry into the wood, picked off, one by bloody one by machine guns and shells. What stupid fool sent them off into a wood which is being so well defended? Now we get here and are told the wood is cleared, which it isn't, and we are here to occupy and consolidate. Guess what? Fifty of my lads are hanging on the bloody wire, because the bloody wood isn't clear. Then you lot trip us up from right in the wood, half a dozen cavalry, without, by the way, any bloody horses.'

'It would appear Lieutenant, that things are not unfolding according to plan. There was caution at the point we needed boldness. However, we are here on the ridge and we really need to take the wood tonight. Can you get your men ready to continue the attack just before first light?'

My uniform was a mess and my rank impossible to determine. I decided not to engage at all in a scrap with this officer.

'We have orders to consolidate the wood, not capture it. We are equipped to dig and prepare, not to fight an opening assault. I'm sorry, my orders come from my brigadier. Besides, the horses are withdrawing from over in Longueval under cover of the mists. Looks like they will be away before it's fully light.'

I didn't know the Deccan were retreating from Longueval. That really sealed the day for me. It calmed me slightly and I accepted that it wasn't their fault.

'Understood. Dig in well, they are in their defensive line and are probably bringing up machine guns and mortars as we stand here.'

'We will know later in the morning. Goodbye and good luck.'

Then he was gone. I made my way back slowly to the edge of the village, which was now again within range of the enemy, having had the Germans fleeing north back towards Flers or even north-west to Bapaume.

The attack was still to be pressed, but thousands would have to die to get back to what we had earlier achieved.

I spent the rest of the night on the doorstep of a house in the village that offered cover and some protection, shelter and safety. With me were fresh troops from the division and included some South African and Welsh troops. Cowling would be back with Rawlinson, perhaps proposing a new resurgence of effort on the wood. After all, without it, the gains here would be impossible to hold onto as the top of the ridge and the wood were at different heights and we needed higher ground to fight.

As day dawned, it became clear that the wood was now occupied again by the Germans and getting back to where we were yesterday could turn out to be impossible or hugely costly. This hurt me inside and made me resent every senior officer away from the Front for their lack of confidence and decisiveness when it really, really mattered.

At six in the morning, in full daylight, but with a pall of mist covering the whole ridge, the boys from the 33rd Division moved into a wide formation out of sight of the enemy. From our dip, we could see that they were clearly looking west at Martinpuich and not at the wood. Surely, they must attack the wood?

'Quick, over here with a runner.'

'Sir?'

'Run like the very devil to find this officer, here on this note. No other, you understand?'

'Yes, sir of course.'

'Go to division if you have to, but make sure they attack the wood first and not sidestep it, be very clear about that. There are guns in there and bloody dangerous ones. Here, it's on this note, but make sure it gets only to the officer, here – right? Brigadier Cowling, remember, only him.'

'Very good sir.'

'Good, now quickly to it.'

I moved forward to the new position and tried to find their officers, first coming upon a soft-spoken captain of the 16th in front of the wood. They were not being fired upon and they were not taking casualties. A makeshift latrine was being dug in the slope and we spoke in front of it, as it was a flat and clear space, well dug in.

'Captain, I know you have orders to advance to the west, but the wood is not in our hands, despite what the divisional commanders think. You can't go that way, you will be cut down in enfilading fire from the side, even if the mists linger. You must speak again with division.'

'Major, sir, I have spoken with division. They tell me that there are Dragoons and some Indian cavalry in there and some men of the Queen's. I'm sure it will be in line to attack as planned.'

'No Captain, I was in there last night with the Deccan and Hussars who charged the wood. It has been filling all night with enemy and what cavalry survived were limited to pockets of soldiers being fired on from the new defensive position. We do not hold the wood at all, it is very much in enemy hands. If this were yesterday, I would say yes go ahead and attack. You would have likely been successful. But today, you will be cut to pieces in short time.'

He raised his palms to me and told me again that division had received the concerns, but were still content that the wood had been taken. The 33rd had confirmation last night and cavalry were in the wood. No fire had been seen across the ridge. However, he did let me take a company of his to clear the wood. He did not want the Germans to have time to build a new defensive position on the ridge line towards Martinpuich and Pozieres. This was some insurance to cover their forward movement.

So, a company of the 16th was assigned to me. These were the Church Lads Brigade Pals. They were keen and understood their task. But there were no more than two-hundred of them and I now knew the wood really needed more, maybe even a division, to capture and hold.

I instructed their officers and told them about the positions of the guns and trench lines. I hesitated to give the number of enemy, because it would be a thousand or more after what had happened yesterday. They went off and set about their task. It looked likely that they and the 100th would go before 0900.

Just before 0900, the Pals went off into the wood. Quietly at first. The gunfire started after a minute or two and the first casualties emerged about ten minutes after the initial move forward. They pushed on into the woody depths, up and down, following the terrain.

At 0900, the main wave emerged and made towards Martinpuich. The Pals had clearly come up against a superior force in the wood as it seemed now that there was not less enemy shooting, but more. It was clear that enemy guns and troops had been successfully moved into the trench during the night. Unlike the first attack, when there was uncertainty, confusion and alarm, here they were ready for an attack. So few into the wood and so many exposed to fire from the front and the side. A deadly combination. Here we went again.

I was not close to the attack but could see the figures falling in the fashion common to battles here. Instead of rapid flexible movement with bombs, the soldiers were walking again, albeit in small groups, into the enemy positions. They did not stand a chance and the attack within a few minutes was the deadly disaster it was always going to be. I was sorry to see this sight, but had resigned myself to the familiar expectation of slaughter.

It transpired that the Deccan squadrons had secured a new line from High Wood towards Longueval. At last, some good news that we had now a decent line over the ridge and could begin looking down on some of the enemy, even though they held the woods on both sides. This also meant that the sunken road from Montauban was now almost completely out of view of the enemy so we could now move more troops forward.

I resolved to get back to find Cowling to see if there was anything else I could do, perhaps even take some rest. There were some aeroplanes in the distance, launched as the mists cleared and it made me wonder again how our operation might have gone if we had had some better luck.

But it was done now and the cards had been played.

CHAPTER SIXTEEN - NO RECOVERY

I got back to our little outpost on the road to Montauban on the afternoon of the fifteenth. So much fighting had been taking place around the ridge it was difficult to judge what was going on clearly. I needed to clean up a bit and find Cowling.

Outside, sitting at the field kitchen table, I assessed my situation. Anyone looking at me would have thought me a remnant of a man run over by a lorry and then pulled backwards through a trench. There was no opportunity to get my kit clean and tidy as it was beyond all repair. There were two clean slashes in my trousers, where shrapnel or bullets had come close by. There were a few singe marks on my sleeve, so I had got a lucky break somewhere. I would see if some new uniform could be brought up for me when it was less dangerous and not such a low priority for the supply trains. But now, sleep was essential and I tried to get some. Sleep would not come, but a fitful rest was better than the alternative.

I took out Odile's letter again and read it once more as far as I could. It still made me angry that she could, it seemed, forget me so easily and take up with the bloody enemy. How she was able to drop our life together so easily, how she was able to let go of the special bond of love we had grown together. The seeds of hope planted in the garden of Bazentin, blasted to dust by the shells and bullets of the bloody enemy and there she was, gambolling in the sun, whereas I was drowning in blood and shit.

While shaking my head quite vigorously trying to get the thought out of my head, I felt a tap on my shoulder.

'You alright mate?'

It was a soldier from the 33rd who was in reserve for the looming disaster in front of High Wood.

'Er, yes?'

'Only, you looked a bit windy just then. Where are you supposed to be? Who is your lot?'

'That's complicated, er, Corporal. I need to sit here and think for a minute.'

'Well you can't fucking do that, mate, there's a bloody attack on you know! Get up and get on with it you idle bastard'

'Look, Corporal, I don't want to appear rude, but as a major just returned from the bloody attack, trying to get some rest and trying to think, would you mind clearing off and leaving me alone?'

'Oh, terribly sorry sir, I can't see your uniform clearly. Is there anything I can do?'

'Can you whistle up hot tea?'

'Actually I can sir! That at least is something that is working today.'

'Good, well thank you, I'm a bit distracted.'

The tea, when it came, was brutally strong, but good for the soul. The supply lines were operating well and this at least allowed us to pursue the attack with force, if not direction. But I needed to find Cowling as soon as possible. He was supposed to be here.

Finally, I located his small party on the sheltered hill going back to Montauban. He was in the process of moving up to the village of Bazentin-le-Petit itself.

'Hello sir. Can I join in the fun?'

'So glad you are fit and alive Collins. Have you been able to find out what has been happening?'

'I think so sir.'

'No, I don't think so sir.' His frosty tone meant only one thing. 'The infantry were held back, we wasted time on the Cavalry and now we are off to take Martinpuich and that bloody church as some bloody symbol of victory. I'm pulling us out of High Wood this evening if we haven't managed to break through. It is costing us terribly. General Rawlinson wants us to press on with the attack on Longueval and Delville Wood – that's being attacked now.'

'Do you want me to help?'

'No, William.'

Cowling's tone softened considerably. 'You've lived the travelling life at this Front long enough. I am going to suspend the unusual Field Operations team until we are better able to manage the communications. This attack is novel and clever, but it will fail because we could not fit all the pieces together at once.'

'We could have taken the wood, sir. I know we could have done. Would the casualties have been higher if we were not in operation?'

'Look, William, we have put into play around eight full divisions of soldiers willing to take this bloody ridge and we have lost nine-thousand casualties. We have had cavalry, night assaults in front of the wire, bomb teams, tactics to weaken enemy supply and create confusion and we have lost brave men we won't get back. We have not secured the woods and chances are, it will now be weeks before we do, the defences are so much stronger there.'

'Does this mean we are ending our operation?'

'Yes, William. I have just left Rawlinson and he is still keen on the idea, sees its merit and thinks we have saved lives. But the army can't put the ideas into operation yet. There are just too many uncertainties. As of 1700 tonight, the operation is suspended and you are to return to England to take up your training as an instructor in field operations, for a time when we are able to do this better. You have done so much in the front lines, it is time not to push your luck too far, you see?'

'Yes, sir.' This didn't sound convincing, as I did not want to quit the field yet. I decided to seek permission to go and help with the attack on Longueval. Martinpuich was going to be a disaster and the attacks on the High Wood were more or less over. The only place fighting hard was on the approach to Delville Wood and Longueval village.

'Brigadier Cowling, sir. May I beg your leave to set out for Longueval and offer whatever assistance I can until this evening? I can be here again at 2000. Would that be acceptable?'

Cowling just smiled and nodded. I wonder if he knew what I was thinking.

'Good luck, William. I will arrange with the commander of the 9th Division that you are to offer tactical assistance for twenty-four hours as you are an expert in the topography of the region. Is that enough for you? Keep out of the bloody way though, and that is an order.'

'Thank you sir.'

I immediately stepped away. Had I stayed longer, it would have been impossible to leave at all. Cowling had been so kind but I still wanted to get the Germans out of my village and out of my home.

It took me some time to get to the 9th Division at Longueval. The road from Contalmaison was now secure, but it was in range from the High Wood and unless keeping just off the road, it was possible to be shot at directly from the positions in the wood and also from stray gunfire in Delville Wood. The ridge under Caterpillar Valley to my right was now filling with reserve troops about to go into the attack on Longueval. As I walked through the track ways the grain was ripening in the fields, still relatively undamaged by the shelling, which had at least been focused. I was sure that enemy soldiers were still hiding out in the fields waiting for any attack and readying themselves for a counter attack, hidden not by sandbags and trench works, but by gently waving corn.

I got to the forward HQ at about 1900, just as the 9th had begun consolidating a success to the south-west of the village. This area was raised ground and a track led directly towards High Wood. Here, they had sited a Lewis gun team and defended the position with bombs in case the enemy crept along the road, which they had been doing all afternoon. The Deccan Horse had also secured a new trench line and the infantry had eventually followed up behind them and dug in. Even further to the right, the sweep around to Delville Wood was sharper as the British had been unable to break into the wood. Troops had been assaulting the wood for some time and had met with terrible opposition. The element of surprise here was less then over in Bazentin-le-Petit and the enemy had been able to hold out more easily. Further right still was the extreme left of the French line. Until the villages along that line could be taken, especially Guillemont and Ginchy, a breakthrough would not only be impossible, but a German counter attack could easily break our own lines in a bigger disaster.

At Longueval, the officers were looking over a map of the area. Two of them were tough fighting Scots who had been in the army long before this war. The major to whom I had been told to report was from the Highlands but had a soft well-educated accent. He welcomed me in, offered me his hand and sat me down at a small table that had been put up just off the roadway. The evening was cool and fighting was close by. We were occasionally shelled by the enemy and the intensity was increasing.

'Major Collins, it was an unusual request from Brigadier Cowling, but a welcome one. He asks that I accommodate you in my division and afford you a cordial welcome as you know this terrain very well. And he tells me that you have been into High Wood and were part of the assault on the ridge yesterday. Here, things are a wee bit different. The Germans are well dug in and they are proving difficult to shift. We have sent over many patrols to assess their positions and they are defending a strong line. The cavalry came over last evening, tough and brave but hours late for our liking. It would be helpful if you would assault along the track here that leads from the windmill up over this small rise to flank the village about here.'

We both considered the map before us.

'Yes Major. How many men can you spare me?'

'You have the brigade, Major. We don't have many officers left unwounded. We have taken casualties in the junior officer ranks and in the men. Look after them, they are brave Scots and deserve good leadership. I understand you are a talented and aggressive soldier. Good. Best of luck. I will lend you some clothing to replace what you are wearing. We pride ourselves on keeping our kit in good order. Fight hard and bring my men back Mr Collins.'

I was led to a small tent that had been put up a few moments before. In it were two captains and a young second-lieutenant. They had already been given their orders and now I was to lead them into battle. I felt that feeling again. Again and again, fending off every ball. They only had to get through once and it was all over. Out of the corner of my eye I could see Odile being held back by a bald-headed German. Both were smiling at me.

We had a brief chance to have some rations – some monkey meat and dry bread. The ration parties had been shelled and not much was getting through. At about 2200, we were to move forward and attack the Germans by trying to roll them right away from Delville Wood and Longueval.

I was taken to the newly dug communication trench and met some of the remaining officers. There were not many. The brigade strength was about one-hundred-and-forty men, little more than a company, but that was all the troops available. There were already casualty listings coming back with dead and wounded, with most unaccounted for. The Deccan Horse had taken over fifty casualties and some seventy horses had been killed in the charge yesterday. There was no reason to doubt that any Deccan and Dragoons getting into High Wood suffered the same or worse.

There were nearly two-hundred reinforcements coming from the reserve brigades and they should arrive in time to go over. All of the troops had been in the line already and were now at least used to this way of fighting a war. I spent the time prior to the attack familiarising myself with the soldiers. It seemed that fighting in different units was the way I was going to spend this war. I was not allowed to mention being in enemy territory for the last two weeks as this was still a strict secret. However, I was able to tell them that while the enemy were not as well supplied as they might otherwise have been, they were good quality well-trained troops.

'Good to meet you Major. Have you been in the line long at all?'

'Since early 1915. I have seen much of our lines from Belgium to here. Mostly mining, but some trench operations. Where are you from?'

'I come from Kingussie, maybe more height than here sir! I joined in 1914 and arrived here just four months ago. I had not expected that we would make such slow progress.'

'I can walk from edge to edge of this battlefield in an hour, we have hardly moved at all in two years.'

'Aye sir, but this is the push. We will keep on going surely until we break them?'

'Break them? Unlikely here. It would need a point three-o-three miracle to get out anytime soon.'

'Aye, right enough. These Fritzies are good wee soldiers. I don't much fancy our chances. Do they use gas here?'

'I have not seen any myself. We might be alright.'

'They are tough to fight. They shoot straight and they don't give in easily.'

'I rather think we are not so easy to beat either. I wonder what they say about us over there. I think we should go and find out don't you?'

'Aye, I do.'

The attack was designed to be swift, decisive and in true Scottish tradition, aggressive and fearless. The troops moved out of their positions just on the hour and moved through the remaining untouched fields towards the enemy. There were pockets of Germans out in the fields, some popped up to shoot and were cut down and some surrendered with the familiar shouts of *Kamerad*. Some were taken prisoner but some were overrun and killed with bombs as the soldiers did not know they were trying to surrender.

It was time for me to move forwards. I had been in this very field with Odile not two years ago. It dipped down on the right and then up onto the farm track, so I crossed the road and jumped into a small ditch. Three Germans crept forwards with rifles and bayonets in front, they had not seen me. They looked terrified, no different to us. One of the Scots appeared from the grain and shot the first one, killing him. His impact took him into the next one and knocked the rifle from his hand. But the third used his rifle to slash the Scot across his face, which knocked him to the ground. Compelled to help, I stood up and stepped forwards. At that point, a huge explosion right beside us, knocked me into the air and backwards into the grain. I could not move. The world went silent and the night darkened. Managing to muster some clarity, I realised that I had been hit, badly this time and was helpless, unless found by a stretcher bearer. Because I was just one of hundreds, unless I could show signs of life, I was likely to die in this very field, hidden amongst the grains. The day had now completely turned to black night and I was alone.

CHAPTER SEVENTEEN - ENEMY TERRITORY AGAIN

I woke up, unexpectedly, but was unable to open my eyes. They felt like lead weights and had been covered by a bandage to stop me from opening them. Although I could just move my hands and arms, my legs were unable to move. My face felt like an anvil was sitting on it and my head felt like it was going to explode.

Somehow, I sensed a bed and sheets and that was good. Perhaps a casualty-clearing station had sent me on to a hospital in Albert or maybe further back than that. I had missed the battle and now was likely to be out of the war. Back to England and no chance to find Odile again, even if she was now lost to me.

In any case, someone would have searched me and the letter in French would have now been confiscated, stolen, thrown away or would be part of an investigation into me and my whereabouts. Perhaps orderlies were laughing at me or wondering what on earth a French girl was doing writing to me about a German. Perhaps I was to be considered a spy? My uniform was certainly not one from any units in the line that day. Tired again, I drifted into a half-sleep, one that was interrupted by strong German voices, which would not go away. With horror, I realised that Germans must have picked me up and this was a hospital behind the German lines. Not that I was in a position to care or to do anything about it.

After what seemed like days to me, someone came to me and there was warm medicinal breath on me. A soft and light German voice whispered to me but it was not possible to understand what she was saying. The bandage was removed and blazing bright light blinded me, causing my whole body to convulse in pain. Quickly, the bandage was replaced and darkness returned. Then, the bandage was removed again, but this time the room was darker. Perhaps curtains had been closed. Now, it was possible to make out blurry shapes all around me, and one of them was white and moving. A hand came to my brow and the shape was a woman, now unmistakably German.

'Be still English. Do not try to move. You have wounds, not too bad I think. You are in Cambrai and the war might be over for you too.'

My situation was confusing and it puzzled me for a while. But almost certainly, I was in enemy territory in Cambrai – a wounded prisoner of war, if I survived. I was able to move my head and look down at my body. My legs were burnt at the front, but nothing else seemed to be wrong with them. They had been bound and that was why they would not move. My chest and stomach were also burnt and scratched but nothing too bad. In a few days they would send me away to a prisoner of war camp.

There was no news from the front. The nurses either did not say or did not know. The German soldiers around were either very friendly and waved, or snarled and would not speak. In any case, any information would most likely be tainted with patriotism and so it was pointless asking about anything to do with the battle on the ridge, or elsewhere for that matter.

'Ensheuder, er zie, er sorry. What is the date today?'

'Be still, English. It is 19 July.'

I had been in hospital for four days. The morphine they had given me took away the time.

'Today is only rest. We think in tomorrow, you can go to a house to recover.'

'And then what?'

'I think you will be kept in a house to recover and not be allowed to leave.'

I imagined being allowed to recuperate prior to being sent to an internment camp for captured British officers. It would be somewhere near to the Belgian border at first, most probably. And perhaps then on to Germany and to the heart of the enemy.

Whenever I tried to move my legs, apart from the pain from the burns, my legs would move with effort. In all likelihood, I had been hit by the shock wave of a shell that landed close by in the fields between Longueval and the Contalmaison road. I had been lucky.

Finally, I was allowed to sit up and was given something to read, to help my eyes recover and focus, but they were fine once the bandages were kept off. The book was a dreadful novel written years before and it only served to annoy me and make me even more determined to get away as soon as possible. My mind started ticking over with ways to get away from here. If my location was known to me, I would be able to get out of sight and make good an escape. I felt obliged to try.

However, I was given something that took away all of my strength again and forced me to lie flat. Any thoughts of escape would have to wait until another day. On waking again, I was in a different room. This one was much less like a hospital and much more like a barrack block. I was alone in a room set up for four, at least there were three other beds, but they were unoccupied. The nurses were all men and looked like they were German Army orderlies and not civilian nurses. They must have moved me into a garrison. The orderly attending me did not speak, or at least he did not speak English. Although he did not smile at me, he was not unduly harsh and did not treat me badly. My burns had been tended and moving my joints was bearable, even if my legs would not bend fully.

The orderly gestured me to stand and I tried to oblige. Although the headache had now gone, I still felt dizzy. Perhaps days spent on my back had taken their toll. Finally, I stood and was able to take my weight. The strength returned slowly and I realised that fortune had been on my side since the shell must have come very close.

Next, I was moved to a chair and the bed was changed and my dressings reduced to a simple bandage. It was clear they wanted me away as soon as possible. It was still not clear whether I was in a prison camp or a military hospital. The view from the window was no help as it looked out over another building. The view at the end was green, perhaps a garden. It was a glimpse, but no more.

In the late afternoon, a German officer came to see me. He spoke in a kindly voice, and on first glance, he may have been a doctor.

'Major William Collins, yes?'

'Yes, may I ask who you are?'

'Ja, I am a doctor in the German Army, your enemy ha!'

He broke into a smile and I half imagined that he was going to buy me a beer to celebrate.

'You are in Cambrai. Officers of our German Army brought you here, they think you were alive and should be saved. There is a camp here that contains some British soldier officers, some French civilians and a small garrison made up with reserve troops and some other troops from the Empire. You are a prisoner of war yes, but you are also a gentleman so you will behave with honour. Ja? We help your wounds to be better and then you can be moved from here.'

'Doctor, I am a British officer and will behave like a soldier if treated like a soldier.'

The doctor stood up, laughed again and slapped his knee.

'Good, good, so we have an agreement then. You do not need any more medicines from me, you can have another bandage, but your burns are not so bad. Then, you will be able to walk normally, if a little slowly, so you can move to the blocks. There are two other British officers there. Do you like a visit with them?'

'Yes please. Thank you Herr Doctor.'

Then I was gently escorted to another room where an old tattered wheelchair awaited me. I was wheeled down to the basement and out the door into the sunshine. It was a large run-down country house and it was only lightly guarded. They perhaps did not expect anyone to try and escape. Perhaps they wondered why any soldier would?

'Good afternoon, Major Collins.'

The voice came from a well groomed man in a smart gown and overall set.

'Good afternoon. Sorry, but you have me at a disadvantage.'

'My apologies, Colonel Matthew Smith of the Seaforths – English but joined a Scottish Regiment in 1910. I know you because we were told who you were. From Longueval, I understand.'

'Thank you sir, yes. Why are we here?'

'They are assessing us for injuries and then we are to be moved to a camp in Germany. Thought they might have interrogated me, but nothing in the two days since arriving here. I was injured in the taking of Longueval a few days ago. All that happened was a knock on the head, but my position was overrun in a counter attack.'

'So, we were defeated at Longueval?'

'Oh no, we took Longueval on the eighteenth. We have moved on to attacking Delville Wood. It's only a few yards further on, but it is a gain to say one has liberated a village.'

'Did we have many casualties?'

'Ninth Division took it hard but took Longueval. They have moved right towards the wood. Units are forming up on High Wood as well.'

'Good, good. If you are with the 9th Division, did I not meet with you when I arrived on the fifteenth?'

'I arrived at the Front on the eighteenth and was hit almost immediately. Came as part of a reserve brigade and put straight onto the assault, with almost no preparation.'

We talked for about fifteen minutes and I discovered that we had taken Longueval at terrible cost and had now been able to attack Delville and High Wood together – not easy battles by anyone's judgment. The other officer was in a chair but his face was almost fully bandaged. Although he was unable to speak, he could wave when we nodded in his direction. He was an officer with a Welsh unit, but it was impossible to get any more out of the Germans.

That evening, we got word that the two of us were to be moved again. Our Welsh friend was returning to hospital. Any escape plan had to be now and I reconsidered my situation. If it were possible to get out of the grounds here, I could get into hiding and assess my chances of getting back to the British lines. It was worth the risk. To be able to make my escape, I needed to know where the weak points were in the German arrangements here. It was not a prison camp, but it was still a military building and a garrison was not going to allow a British officer to escape – least of all one that had come to them as a wounded prisoner from the battlefield. My anger at the Germans had softened. They had treated me well and were no different to us – just scared boys doing unspeakable deeds at someone else's behest. It was just a matter of who had started the confrontation and why we were engaged in the fighting that separated us.

It was necessary to know how many German soldiers there were and what they were doing. By adopting a casual air, it was possible to make my way along the perimeter fencing, waving cheerfully at any German soldier visible on the way. They usually did not wave back, but none seemed suspicious of my recuperative stroll, with an obvious limp. There were two other entrances apart from the main reception entrance. The gate at the side had been a service entrance for local suppliers to bring in their wares for the occupants. At the back of the building was a smaller entrance, like an old escape route, possibly dating back to revolutionary times, but it was hard to be certain. In the passageway underneath was what appeared to be a civilian working party moving supplies into the motor lorries that were parked on the road. A couple of men were looking into the engine compartment as the engine was not sounding particularly healthy. One of the men was poking a spanner into the chest of the German driver and pointing at the tyres whilst shouting loudly about the poor driving skills of the Germans in a heavy French accent. The other was diligently tightening some pipework.

Curious, I walked further round to get a better view and, to my utter astonishment, looked straight into the eyes of Odile's father. Just in time, I stopped myself from stupidly waving and calling out to him, and just stood there instead. If he looked my way, he would see me and would know exactly who it was looking back at him. But he kept his head down until, at last, for the briefest moment he looked straight at me. He looked only for a second or two, smiled just a little and then carried on with what he was doing. Had he recognised me? I had changed in the last couple of years, so perhaps not. He had clearly suffered much and any recollections of me must surely have faded over time. Then, I thought that he had recognised me, but because of Odile's position with a German, he was trying to discourage me. It was confusing and thoughts of Odile flooded over me once more. Now, I could not escape without trying to find out if she was near. At the same time, I could not stay much longer without escaping. It was difficult to know what do to. Perhaps it would be possible to create a delay in my transfer by pretending to be more injured than I really was. A hobble and a pained expression might buy me a day more here to consider my options.

I walked back up the slope to my room, trying to catch his eye again, but it was clear he neither had the opportunity nor inclination to look up at me. But I felt newly energised, especially considering my acceptance of Odile's decision to let me go from her life. Would she be with him now – her German? Her letter seemed to indicate that she was. Maybe she had been moved to another labour camp away from the grind because she had taken up with the enemy. I needed to think clearly, but clear thought eluded me that day. My world was in a spin and I wanted now to see her more than anything else in the world.

The rest of the day was spent sitting in the garden in a light drizzle until it got dark, pondering my situation. I had spent over a year in those damned trenches on and off, and had been exceptionally lucky to have been plucked from the ranks to lead some unusual operations. Now, I found myself a survivor in this horror, at least up to now.

Although I had got to know a few men well, it had never been well enough – apart from Cowling and Fixer. Perhaps it was for the best since it was always harder to lose someone you knew well. In some of the units, no one tried to get to know the reinforcements that well, especially the Kitchener recruits, since there was just no point. The war gnawed at me as the rats gnawed at the flesh rotting at the bottom of trenches.

Now, however, it was over for me. The remnants of civility, beaten out by the pounding of the guns, might have surfaced as shell-shock as with the poor unsteady bastards on the docks. For me, it surfaced as a drive and passion to find my love in Bazentin. Somehow, I had made it there, only to have the rose plucked from my hand, the thorns dragged through my palms, cutting them to ribbons. Thoughts of Odile had provided an initial shield into which the war did not really penetrate, keeping it matter of fact and all in a day's work. Once that went, the foul-stinking awful realisation of men being broken and smashed and disappearing in front of me over and again was taking its toll. No longer could I resist by using my shield of love, held out in front of me, for lost Odile. The war soaked in to my body with the rain, and tiredness wrapped the wetness tighter until I felt myself immersed. The magic spell of love was broken, snuffed out by the never-ending shells and this damned rain.

At around 2200, when it was dark, they called me in. My eyes were red and my face damp and cold. The nurse orderly was concerned at my slight turn for the worse and would not allow me to be moved. He had stated quite plainly to the military that I was not fit to be transferred today or tomorrow. That night, I slept fitfully and thoughts of Odile and her father and my life in Bazentin overflowed my ability to be calm and concentrate on my options. I was used to working and living on my feet, but it was not possible to think clearly in order to conclude my business here.

The early morning was misty and the dampness in the air and the gentle warmth of the morning combined to shroud the area in low cover. Perhaps now was a good time to move? Perhaps not, since I had not properly thought about how to make good an escape. After breakfast, my nearly healed wounds were tended to. They really were not that bad now but the scar on my side felt worse. During breakfast came the welcome news that a French volunteer party had been allowed in to meet the troops and to offer local delicacies.

Colonel Smith was still here. Since my transfer had been postponed, they kept him here to avoid an extra trip. He told me that we were usually off limits for a visit, it was only for the Germans – probably assuming the French might try to pass us information along with the local fruit and vegetables. However, we were allowed to attend the ceremony today. In the absence of anything else to do, I would also go along, perhaps spotting a way out in the process. Odile's father might make an appearance, although there was no real reason he might attend, it was just an idle hope. Perhaps it would give him the chance to punch a German on his bloody nose, something he would most certainly want to do. It would have been so good to tell him that although his village was not very recognisable now, it had been liberated by our troops. His house and cellar stood – just – and he would be able to return again. I wondered whether he knew his village had been a devastated battlefield, but I supposed he did.

It transpired that there was to be an evacuation of the French civilians further back in order to continue their labours and forced collaboration at bayonet point. The Allied advance had clearly worried the Germans and it seemed July might be a time of movement, after all. Most civilians had already been moved further north out of the field of battle. Although Bapaume was now a faint hope for our offensive, it was only a few miles away from here and Cambrai would soon be within range of our long guns.

Once the Germans had assembled, the French were escorted in with their baskets and packages. Many of the German military present were recuperating soldiers and others were on garrison duty, but most were very, very young. There was some limited giggling with a couple of the girls, but mostly it was quite quiet and not all the French seemed to be here voluntarily.

One of the French girls appeared quite shy and sullen. She merely tossed apples in the direction of soldiers without much ceremony and certainly no words. With her back to me most of the time, she spoke in German to one of the officers – perhaps she knew him. It was impossible to recognise the voice, as the vague-sounding German words ruined the tones for me.

The girl was allowed to approach us and she passed an apple to Smith, which he took with a grateful thanks. He immediately bit into it and sat back to watch the rest of the show. She took an apple from her basket but this time she chose to look up.

It was, unmistakably, the face of my darling. The one whose face had comforted me in the trenches, conducted my dreams, drove me on and allowed me to live. My love, Odile. Her face hit me like a hammer blow and I tried hard not to shout out, to fling my arms around her and to ask her what her letter meant and why she was mixed up with the bloody enemy. How clever she had been to hide it there and how devastated I had been by its content. She did not give me a smile of recognition and did not give away any familiarity, but the apple she gave to me was not tossed, but handed over gently with just a hint of contact of her hand on mine. She slid one finger gently over the back of my hand and then away. That was it! I remembered that touch, a special touch of her love for me. Without a word, Odile moved on to the next soldier and that was that, until she was escorted out. For those two minutes after seeing her face, she did not look again at me but my gaze did not leave her for an instant. Smith had seen this.

'Not seen such a fine young woman for a long time, eh Collins? You clearly have taken a shine to her. She seemed a bit sullen though, not a friendly type. Perhaps the guards might allow you to try out a couple of French words on her, to cheer her up a bit, or give her something to laugh at, what do you think?'

'I'm not very good with women, you know, a bit shy.'

'Ha, I bet you are old chap. Still, not a bad looking young lady. Pity she seems tight with the Germans though. Never mind, never mind.'

With that, he sat back and did not speak again for some time. Perhaps he too had been transported back to a safer place and safer times. For me, Odile had told me all that I could have wanted. Perhaps I was reading into it something that simply wasn't there. She could not have known that I had received her letter. I played over that second of tenderness over and again. It was a better thought than the ones of shells and bayonets and entrenching tools and damned German faces that constantly whirled around my head, with my lovely Odile looking on.

I had lost Odile's letter, or it had been taken from me. Since no one made any reference to it, it may have blown off my body when the shell burst, or it could have been stolen by one of the enemy soldiers as a damned field souvenir. Odile, though, had returned to my life. Was she trying to make contact without alerting the Germans? Was she just trying to reassure me that it was all fine? Was she saying goodbye? I did not know and could not think straight in my mind at all. But I needed to make contact again somehow, to know finally and to tell her how I still felt.

All that afternoon I prowled the perimeter, looking for a glimpse again. At around 1700, I stopped cold when I saw her again. Odile stood in the narrow alley, away from the gaze of most people, and just looked at me.

She did not smile but her face was not hardened and she softened when I waved to her – making it look like it was only a wave of politeness. She did not wave back. We looked at each other for perhaps two minutes before she turned and left the alley. That stiffened my resolve to escape that evening, after dark. I now had access to clothing, if not uniform, and just enough food to get me on my way.

The evening could not pass quickly enough for me. We three officers ate bread and some broth that was edible if not full of flavour. It seemed to me that this was a larger meal than normal, meaning we were going to be moved during the night or early in the morning. So, it was now, or not at all.

Once the doctor had made his last visit, I looked for an opportunity. He barely visited me now but still made a round of those on the wounded list – British and German. He came to me and sat at my bed for the last time. Once he had made his customary jokes, he left. We were going to be moved away very soon.

As I got up to move to the door, it opened again. Three German soldiers, armed and carrying papers in their right hands, came to each of us one by one. They gestured for us to dress as we were to leave in ten minutes. That gave me no time to act. I was trapped and about to formally become a prisoner of war. These soldiers handled me more roughly and they seemed to resent having to escort British soldiers, especially ones who had been part of the costly offensives on the Somme.

Quickly, and without any ceremonies of rank, I was moved into a waiting lorry. The rear was open, but the presence of two guards meant it would be impossible to vault over the side and make an escape, which realistically would have been out of the question in any case. So, I was loaded on and seated in the centre of the floor, not on one of the benches along the side. My hands were loosely but firmly bound at first and I was only just able to see above the sides of the lorry. As it moved away, from the right, a figure ran down the low hill to the road. It was Odile, who had certainly been watching the entrances for my departure and was probably caught out by the swiftness of this arrangement. She ran at top speed to intercept the lorry and got to the road in time to see it pass. Although she held out her hands and shouted something, I could not hear what it was. The German guards looked at her and laughed, pointed their fingers towards her and exchanged a joke in German. She ran behind the lorry for some time, but then tripped and fell to the ground. I held her gaze for the few seconds left before I was too far ahead to see her face clearly. As her form receded into the distance, she was helped up by two German soldiers and I wondered how she explained her actions to them. Now, I knew for certain that she still loved me and that her time with the Germans was for a purpose – to live in peace, to prevent her father being beaten, to feed her family and dream of a time when this bastard war would be over.

I thought that the lorry would only take us a short distance to the station in Cambrai that the Allies liked to bomb. And that we would then be transported by train, possibly into Germany, as prisoners of war. My rank allowed me to travel in slightly more comfort, but the number of guards would mean no possibility of escape once the train departed. Smith could not act with me, as he was not recovered enough to survive an escape attempt, and perhaps did not want to escape. The war was over for him after all and there was no dishonour in being taken prisoner. You had to be in the war to be taken out of it.

We were moving slowly through the medieval streets of Cambrai and the streets were busy with military and equipment, especially horses and transport limbers. The men appeared weary and most seemed very young for military service. Even so, I would not survive an attempt to escape here. My heart began to sink. It seemed that finally, I was to be out of the war as a prisoner and that would be it. It would no longer be possible to help Cowling, to become an instructor in order to save men in the field. And Odile would be beyond reach for many years to come.

From the front came a series of jolts, followed by curses in German and then in French, followed by laughter from the drivers. The road was nearly blocked and so a route was being cleared along a side road, which was very narrow. My bindings were firm, but not impossible to remove. I tried to ease my hands out and had made some progress when we hit a much bigger bump in the road. It tipped me forwards, making me bang my head hard, as I could not reach out to balance. I made angry gestures to the Germans with my head, arms and eyes to indicate that the bindings should be taken off. With a couple of shrugs, the bindings were loosened, but not before my arms had almost been pulled off my shoulders. The lorry was stopped and was now completely stuck in a narrow side street. It was temporarily quiet – a half chance – it had to be quick and it had to be now.

The two guards in the back of the lorry were working on Smith's bindings, grumbling and roughly bumping him around. Both had their backs to me. Smith looked at me briefly and then looked away and started yelling at the Germans that his hands were tied too tightly, causing an excellent commotion. I considered jumping out there and then but realised my only chance would be to disable the guards completely. Neither of these two had been in a trench before and had no experience of hand-to-hand fighting when it was personal. They were crouched side-by-side and so I had to strike hard and fast. Both had rifles but they were slung over their shoulders, giving me an opportunity to try a trench trick.

The one on the left had his rifle shouldered on the right. I grabbed the strap and pulled hard upwards. This overbalanced the soldier and turned him towards me. Then, I hit him with the flat of my palm right onto his nose as hard and as fast as possible. Even though I was eager to get away and angry, the force I managed to use actually shocked me. The crunch of bone made me recoil and lose the element of surprise with the second soldier. However, he was distracted seeing his companion drop back instantly dead, his face smashed. He glanced at me and then down to his friend and then back to me. By the time he turned his gaze to me, I had turned the rifle in my hand and raised the butt hard under his chin. His jaw shattered and his teeth went out of his mouth and up into his brain. He was not killed outright, but fell back in agony. The blood from his wound was falling back into his mouth and he was spitting and gargling. I had to kill him to spare him further agony. When I turned towards him, he leapt at me and grabbed my throat, but he was dying. I had seen this before but could not step sideways or backwards. He fell on me and he fumbled for the bayonet that had snapped off one of the rifles. Blood was still pouring from him and it was only a matter of time before he was dead anyway. He brought the bayonet into the air, aimed and to tried to stab me, but he was trembling with shock. I grabbed his wrist and slowed the movement of the blade but it still pressed into my ribs and I felt unable to resist it with the full weight of his dying body behind it. I held and held with all my might, the pain increasing as the blade moved onto my bare skin, slowly cutting through my clothing. My skin had broken but I did not know how far the blade was sliding into my body. I willed the soldier to die and finally felt his strength ebbing away. His warm blood was all over me and as we writhed, we slipped and slithered in his blood. Then I felt a huge hammer blow hit the German on the back of the head and realised that Smith had freed his hands and smashed the rifle into the skull of the German. Both guards were now dead. Smith had also killed the driver whilst he was distracted, by bayonet. His fighting ferocity was equal to anyone I had imagined, especially for someone so apparently cultured.

So there we were in a lorry in the street. Smith was covered in blood but in all honesty could not make an escape, his wounds were not healed. But if he were captured now, he would be shot – whatever he had to say. There was just too much death and blood around him to be easily explained. He pushed me out of the lorry and into the window of a building inches away.

'Major Collins, it has been a pleasure to go into battle with you. Now away, you have to go now!'

'Sir. Thank you!'

I held his hand briefly and turned to leave. Smith sat back with a smile on his face. He took out a packet of cigarettes and matches from the pocket of the German guard he had killed. He began whistling the tune of *The Dark Island*. For a moment, he was back in Scotland with his men. I turned away and ran.

There was only minutes to clean off the blood. It was unlikely that many people knew the sum total of cargo in the lorry. Smith would tell them nothing, probably just laugh at them until he was shot. There was some time to make an escape if I could get the blood off my body. My clothes were soaked through and all I could find in the house were old shirts and trousers, dusty, worn and far too small for me – they would look ridiculous and give me away in a moment. I had to get out of this house because the second the Germans discovered the bloody scene, they would be in this house – not least because there was blood all over the curtains of the window I had been pushed through.

I risked moving. The buildings were not destroyed, most stood undamaged and I climbed out of another window, not daring to use the door, and crept along a very narrow passage. After passing four or five houses and then in through another window, I discovered untouched drawers of clothing. In them, I found some larger trousers that would help me to pass if no one paid too much attention. The legs were too short, but I could use socks to cover my bare legs. There were civilians moving here under supervision and there were non-uniformed men moving about, which would help. I had to look slightly disabled to explain why I was not working, at least to cover me long enough to escape.

At night, I could move out of the town and along the road back towards the front line. I had nothing on me as identification. If captured, I would be killed on the spot.

I took some food and water from the store dump that the Germans had set up in a sheltered copse near to the main road out of Cambrai. Although it was only a week since I had been behind, it felt like a lifetime ago and here I went again! Staying off the road in open country was best as long as I found shelter regularly. I remembered a small series of houses and a small farm with an outbuilding. The artillery bombardments had not reached here and any artillery fire was aimed for Bapaume, not Cambrai. Aeroplanes flew over my head, but they were aiming for the railway lines. Besides, I would rather die in an escape attempt than stay amongst this enemy.

Slowly, I made my way south and only dared to move at night. This terrain was less familiar to me, having only been this way infrequently. My intention was to aim for the edge of the defended line using the wide ridges on the other side of the Bapaume road. I would keep around Bapaume using the slope to cover my movement. The north-east of Bapaume had not been too terribly shelled. The British had made less progress on this side and it was easier to work out where the lines were. To come down the Cambrai road would be certain death, it would be better to aim for the village of Courcelette.

After four nights of creeping through the countryside, hunger was my constant companion and I did not try to disrupt enemy operations. My wounds still ached and exhaustion had set in – along with a resurgent desire to see Odile.

After a few near misses, I reached the village without capture – thankfully the countryside was vast and well known to me with many areas to hide – even in the open. In Courcelette, I found a small farmhouse that had not been badly shelled. Normally, these buildings would have been occupied by soldiers, but the infantry were moving out to defend the line near to Pozieres. According to my rough calculations, it would be a couple more days before soldiers came looking for better billets near the front line. Fortunately, I managed to get some stores together to last me a short while whilst planning my next move. The farm had a small outbuilding that kept my stores cool. To avoid moving about and being spotted, I stayed in the cellar and moved only at night. The jars of food in my store were rough, coarse and tasted of raw vegetables. Not pleasant to eat, they also upset my stomach, which did not help me in trying to remain well hidden.

The cellar was damp. Numerous bags of well-rotted stores made the smell almost unbearable, but provided cover for my unwashed and ill state. There was a little fresh water in the well-sump and some fresh rainwater gave me a supply for a couple of days. For the latrine, I just had to make the best of it, which was deeply unpleasant. Again, I thought about Odile and moved between optimism and despair in equal measure. The darkness always brought on the worst feelings and brought terrible dreams about the war. The shelling in the near distance was British and seemed to be building up to another push. I was careful to sleep only a little and constantly tried to wake myself from sleep. My mind was full of blood, smashed bodies, bombs, lunging cavalrymen and the bald German head – every single bloody moment. Increasingly, these dreams included the soldiers in the lorry, but now they turned round and got to me first. I was stabbed to death often in that dream. There was not enough left that wasn't war to keep away the nightmare of this life.

On the third or fourth day, my wounds began to worry me. Whilst in hospital they had been dressed and did not appear to be too bad, here they looked very red and sore. This concerned me as I was living in dirty surroundings, which may have made my wounds fester. It was manageable though, and there was nothing to be done in any case. Under cover of darkness, I fetched water and had to watch my food supply. For the time being I was trapped. The British advance was not rapid and there was little movement on the Front – at least not enough for my purpose.

After what seemed like a week, the noises from the Front grew ever closer. The house was now in range of the British artillery. I had to watch out. The evenings began to get a little cooler and damper at dusk. My wounds were stable if not healing particularly well – it was impossible to keep them dry enough to heal or clean enough to repair. To make matters worse, it had become clear that German occupation of the farm was underway. Carts and horses were clattering and a substantial amount of equipment was being moved in – including ammunition and ration supplies. It seemed that a mobile kitchen was being set up. This meant that hundreds of soldiers would be around the farm all of the time. Movement would now be nearly impossible and discovery was almost certain. There was no good reason for me to be here and this would get me shot. With movement being impossible, I would starve to death inches away from food. This would be akin to torture – however well deserved.

By day, I hid myself in a large storage chest, leaving the nights to get out for food, drink and a latrine trip. Night after night was spent creeping about, taking scraps thrown into buckets that were usually fed to the horses. The soup was watery with very little vegetable matter in it, but the bread was passable – when it was available. Quite often, I failed or felt it was just too risky to fetch any. Smelling the cooking and seeing soldiers eating sapped my strength more than anything – more than my throbbing sores or my parched mouth.

This went on and my physical condition was suffering and I felt weaker and weaker. My weight had dropped considerably as it was easy to fit into the storage chest and now it was even possible for me to turn over inside it. For shaving, I simply tore at my face with a stone – to keep a beard was tempting infestation. It was only slightly effective, and agony. My clothes were rotting on me and there was no way to get at any fresh clothing. The soldiers' discarded clothes were every bit as filthy as mine. Besides, they would be missed. I was totally alone, in hiding, afraid for my life if discovered, hungry and in weakening health.

Days passed without me realising and I feared at every minute that my little box would be discovered. Soldiers came here for one day at a time and in that time they had little opportunity or inclination to explore too widely and that was good for me. They left food scraps everywhere, but were more careful with water and it would often be two days between drinks. This made me weaker, more tired and tested my resolve to get back to British lines. On one occasion, a small pile of bombs was left unguarded so I took the opportunity, if only to pass the time, of setting a fuse to detonate instantaneously. I don't know where or when it was used, but if it was used, then the soldier would have suffered either a quick death, or an agonising death. By this time I did not much care.

By now, I was utterly trapped, the German supply troops were well and truly dug in. This position was clearly now very close to the Front, protected by a ridge and the walls of the farm were sturdy and would put up a fight against artillery. Some artillery was moved in to the adjoining copse and began firing regularly in the direction of Pozieres. Perhaps the

British were coming closer, it was my only hope, because I was not going to last much longer in my little shit-hole. I remembered a discussion about the second position going up and through the High Wood. This was the other end. I had hoped to get around it, but had clearly not gone far enough west. This could mean a grim end for my little war. There was no way to cross the lines again now.

It was vital to keep my mind together, but I veered between despair and hope. Every thought of Odile focused on that little brush of her finger and the letter that now existed only in my head. It seemed that she was still in love with me – and yet she had forsaken me for a German bastard. Maybe she was only saying goodbye after all.

Every day, every little sound in my box seemed like death was coming for me. I had cut a couple of larger holes to see through but had no weapons at all and would be helpless if discovered. However, I was now so haggard, they might think me not in control of my senses and therefore an object of pity. A lost civilian, woefully and illegally out of place. My clothes were as thin as paper, threadbare and in appalling order. My skin was crawling and the smell was terrible. My body reacted badly. Everything externally was sore or itching, and internally, it was little better.

Possibly, I had been in this hole for at least three weeks or even a month. The fact of my survival pleased me but left me desolate that this was to be my lot in the war – after everything that had happened since leaving Folkestone. Now, I envied the wounded on the quayside and wondered how those poor fellows were getting on. Maybe it was better for them than for me. It was impossible to know, but I had some idea of the mental torture inflicted and the human brain's ability to be resilient. But we all had limits and by this point, mine had been surpassed.

The shelling intensified over the next few days and soldiers stopped coming to the farm so much. Late one evening, the whole kitchen set up was taken down and moved out in a hurry. In its place came two large field howitzers. The war was getting close again. There was now nothing to eat and only poor quality water to drink. I was desperate, missing sunlight and fresh air and wanted just to get it over with.

Then the shells began bursting in the farmyard itself. Perhaps the attack could be this far left, after all. During the day, shells fell all around and one hit the farmhouse, chipping off the roof and landing rather too close for my liking. I could do nothing but scream as the shells came close and duck if I could. The Allies were aiming for the howitzers. They got one in the early evening and it caused some terrible screaming, causing a huge vibration, but I did not see it hit. Now unable to move at all, hungry and thirsty all of the time, I occasionally managed a few drops of water but there was nothing to eat. I had to stay there, in that shitty box, listening to shell after shell hit the surroundings. I expected nothing but death, but hearing each blast meant it had missed me. The one that got me at Longueval had come without a murmur as I was out before the sound was heard by my ears.

Infantry constantly passed through the farm, stopping only for a brief rest. They left behind some water and scraps of food which I devoured willingly, grateful for the chewed and discarded scraps.

Then early one morning, there was a battering of boots all over the farmyard and all kinds of noise as equipment and rubble seemed to be thrown around the yard.

'Hey, you fucking idiot, don't touch anything in case it's bleeding booby trapped. Just search for the enemy and keep your bloody eyes open.'

'Sorry Corp.'

'No buggers here, they must have scarpered when they saw them ruddy tanks, ha! Fuckers, eh?'

'Blood happy they are on our side, Corp. Scared the bloody shit out of me – fucking rumbling – and nothing bloody stops them.'

There was a crack of a rifle and an immediate scream of agony.

'Corp? Shit, Corp? Are you alright, was that on you?'

'Fuck it, bloody fuck it. My shoulder's gone.'

The shot brought more soldiers into the yard and a quick burst of rapid rifle fire silenced the sniper.

'Weren't you watching what you were doing Corporal Peak?'

'Shit, sir. Get me out of here!'

'STRETCHER BEARERS! Lance-Sergeant Burley, over here if you please!'

The officer's voice was clearly Scottish. I felt able to call out.

'British soldiers, don't shoot. I am a British officer. In the cellar of the outhouse. Please come and get me. I have been trapped behind the lines. Can you see me?'

'What, where was that, who goes there?'

'Major William Collins of the, er, 12 Field Operations and Royal Engineers.'

'Guardsman, go and get that officer of Engineers.'

Profoundly weak and blinded by the daylight, I was barely able to stand and was terribly conscious of my dreadful stench.

'Thank you. Who am I addressing?'

'Captain Marsh-Holmes of the 2nd Grenadiers. What the bloody hell has happened to you? You look terrible. You fellows weren't in this action?'

'Captain, what is going on?'

'We've taken Courcelette. We took High Wood earlier.'

'High Wood? Do you know of a Brigadier Cowling?'

'No, was he your commanding officer?'

'Yes, but he may have been moved out now.'

'Right. Goodness sir, you are in a bad way. Let me get you back to our lines and we can make sure you are who you say you are, beg pardon sir.'

'Burley, get this officer back on a stretcher. Treat him like a Major for now. We need to confirm his identity. Get a message back to a Brigadier Cowling, informing him that a Major Collins has appeared in our position, north of Courcelette village. Quick man, he looks in a bad way. Cigarette sir?'

'No thank you. Water would be good if you have any.'

'Burley can find you some sweet tea, I am sure. You must be cold. Sorry, we have no rum and my whisky is gone.'

I was placed on a stretcher next to the unfortunate corporal. His shoulder was shot through. He would live, but would never use that arm again. He had a definite Blighty one and he was lucky to be out of it.

The bearers carried us unintentionally roughly through sporadic shelling towards the village centre, such as it was. It was now in British hands and this made me glad. The news of the capture of the High Wood pleased me too, but it had taken such a long time. It must have cost thousands of lives. I wondered again what might have been long ago on the fourteenth and had to ask.

'Can you give me the date today?'

'It's 21st September sir.'

'September? Shit. I have been trapped for two months.'

No wonder no one remembered Cowling. He could have been long gone by now, for all I knew.

'Just rest there, sir. The Guards will get you back alive.'

I laid back and wondered if I was yet to live through this.

CHAPTER EIGHTEEN - BACK HOME

I was taken to a casualty clearing station where my identity was investigated. After a night spent in a curtained area away from the other soldiers, the morning brought two unfriendly military policemen. They asked me my story and I told them everything since leaving for Longueval in July. At first they did not believe anyone could survive in No Man's Land or behind the lines for months. They started to mock my story, questioning my injuries even though the physical evidence seemed to fit. They had not heard of Cowling either, so remained suspicious. And when I told them to contact 4th Army HQ and Rawlinson directly, they laughed out loud. However, they did check and when the reply came back, their demeanour instantly changed.

'Colonel Collins? We had some trouble sorting you out, given you told us you were a major, sir. We are to escort you to Albert and then on to Chateau Querrieu to meet with General Rawlinson's adjutant. If I may suggest a bath sir, while we get you some fresh uniform, begging your pardon sir. Your wounds also look as though they could do with some attention.'

I had to laugh loudly in return. Once again, my fortunes had turned. Two months in a stinking hell-box and now spending the night in a chateau.

The uniform offered was without any marking or insignia. The battle of Flers-Courcelette was drawing to a close and the army had advanced through with tanks. I would have loved to see that. Cowling would have a wry smile too, well, he probably knew all about this. Perhaps this was the surprise he had wanted at Bazentin Ridge, if the tanks had been ready. The cost was predictably large and it was disappointing to note that the advance had been waves of infantry and prolonged bombardment. Upon hearing that, I knew Cowling was not in this show.

I was shaved by the adjutant's batman and my uniform was improved significantly. The uniform requisition was for that of a colonel – it reminded me of my promotion – so the paperwork must have come through in my absence. But I still felt a fraud for having such a rank, which seemed entirely down to my experiences and not at all on merit – my fitness for the rank was doubtful.

While being measured for the new uniform, I noticed that my measurements had lessened by six inches in the trouser waist and four inches in the shirt. Although my weight loss and weakness were well known to me, this was still quite a shock, nevertheless. But it was even more of a shock when they issued a stepping-cane to aid me when walking. How old was I?

The adjutant came in and immediately smiled, which was a good sign. He recognised me, but it probably took some time for the memory and the reality to match.

'Lieutenant-Colonel Collins, it is a genuine pleasure to see you again. In all honesty, I remember you fitter, but your exploits have reached the very highest levels. Over the next two days, we need to debrief you on your movements and actions over the last couple of months. But you are also due some care and attention in reward for your, well, interesting and successful service.'

He turned to his left and picked up a sheaf of papers.

'Colonel, you have been awarded the Military Cross and it appears that you have subsequently received a bar as well. Are you aware of this?'

'No, I am not. May I please ask about my mission in July? Who came back?'

'Well let's see. Ah yes, here it is. Grim reading in one sense and incredible in the other. The team of sixty was landed in aeroplanes near to Bapaume on or after 3rd July 1916, you know that.'

He was skim reading the detailed report I recognised as Cowling's.

'Hmmm, yes, hmm right, fifteen troops we know had been captured and were shot, unfortunately. Ah, except for a Corporal Robert J Burrows esquire. He was caught in the cockpit of an aeroplane and was treated as a prisoner of war. He is in Germany and apparently quite alive and well. Eight died in the aeroplanes, never having engaged the enemy. Twelve returned on or before 14th July. Quite a tale to tell it seems. The rest remain missing, with no word on any of them. Did you know what they all did?'

'Not all of them, do you have any information on the outcome?'

'It appears from German transmissions and captured prisoners that they suffered a string of ah, unfortunate coincidences, over a very short space of time. The 3rd Guards HQ caught fire, casualties, dead officers and all that and required complete evacuation, ha ha. That did cheer us all.

Several documents it seems were either stolen or destroyed. Over fifty ammunition stores were also mysteriously destroyed, with an unusual pattern of faulty stick-bombs and defective ammunition fuses. How unlucky they were, what?'

'Yes.' This made me smile since I had not heard this before.

'It appears that some elements of battalions or entire units were in the wrong place when we attacked on 14th July and some orders were confused, contradictory and, in some cases, downright suicidal. I don't suppose you know anything about all of this?'

I smiled again, 'Please go on.'

'Hmm, well it seems the Germans were considerably unprepared for the battle on Bazentin Ridge and were most surprised at the scale and ferocity of the engagement. Pity we didn't press on to High Wood, but we have it now.'

'What happens to me next?'

'Well, after we've had a chat about the last three months, got word of your return to Brigadier Cowling and fed you up a bit, you are off to England to instruct on unusual field operations. Your temporary rank of lieutenant- colonel is to be made permanent immediately upon your return. I have strict instructions to make sure you comply. Last time you were let off the leash, you trotted off to Longueval and became a missing man.'

'May I ask about Horace Watkins?'

'Ah, yes, sorry. I was saving that. He was awarded the Victoria Cross, posthumously of course. His citation is here. Do you want to read it?'

'Please.' I eagerly grabbed the sheaf of yellow paper and read the citation.

On 14 July 1916 at Bazentin-le-Petit, when one company and part of another was held up in the attack by British troops on slopes to the village, by a hostile machine-gun that was causing heavy casualties, Sergeant Watkins, with utter contempt for danger, and in spite of being wounded in the arm and shoulder, advanced alone over open ground under fire, in front of the gun and bombed the gun team from their position. Subsequently, a grenade was dropped, posing imminent danger to his comrades around him, Sergeant Watkins, with utter disregard for his own safety, threw himself upon the ground, thus bearing the force of the explosion, knowing it would likely cause his own death. This act not only saved many casualties, but materially helped the operation of clearing the enemy out of the village.

'Thank you.' I passed the citation back.

'No, please keep it.'

I placed the paper neatly in my new uniform pocket.

'I have also submitted citations for awards for riders from the Deccan Horse. Do you happen to know what happened to those?'

'Cavalry? Yes I have seen them. Are you quite sure they lured the machine gunners like you say? The general was most impressed by their bravery if they did, but he isn't at all sure it happened that way. However, before you range on me, Brigadier Cowling told us all, that if you said it happened just like that, then that's all that can be said on the matter. I like those Indian fighters, tough buggers. The use of a garotte was an especially grisly touch.'

'Thuggees, they're called, I think. So, what was the result?'

'Oh they got their VCs all well and good, all four of them. Problem is, none of them survived to get them. You got the names of two, we got the rest later. By the time we were told, they had unfortunately been killed by shelling as they retired from High Wood.'

'I am sorry to hear that, they were incredibly brave and had some tricks we could learn from.'

We talked for four more hours. Recalling the events clearly made me truly appreciate my luck and my fortunate in serving with such brave troops – including Colonel Smith, who I knew to be dead, circumstances unknown. By now, I had seen enough of the trenches and the blood and the concussion and the guts and the splintered bone and the grey uniforms and bald heads coming to kill me. Now, I just wanted to go home to England and I would think about Odile when the time came.

My stomach was still quite raw and could only cope with a little bread and soup. After my meal, I was offered a comfortable bed. Sleep came more easily now because I had been able to tell it all. In the morning, I rose at sunrise and dressed in my new colonel's uniform, still feeling a fraud. I had joined only two or so years ago and was now a colonel, if you please.

The tea at headquarters was more refined than in the trenches. I wondered how many of the staff here had served in the trenches. It wouldn't be many but there were some who knew the awfulness of the attrition. The morning was cool and misty, a typical late September morning. I was due to drive back to the railhead at Amiens and then on to the coast, likely Boulogne. I was reconciled to going home, having seen enough of this bloody war. Now, I needed to recover. I was safe in my knowledge that Odile was still mine and I would find her again. But the eager drive to crash through at any turn was gone. My almost tribal craze to get at the enemy had faded. I first needed to survive the war and my health was not good enough to slog it in the trenches, or even to staff the battles from HQ.

The car was a little late, but it drew up right outside the chateau. I opened the door for myself and got in. To my surprise, there was already an occupant in the other seat. I knew who it was immediately.

'Good morning Brigadier, for some reason I knew it would be you.'

'Hello Lieutenant-Colonel William Collins with a medal or two to boot.

I wanted to give you a send-off to England, partly to make sure you bloody well go and also to tell you some things that you may not already know. Our little operation in Bazentin-le-Petit has caused quite the stir. Our boys have come in for some rare praise. The battle on the ridge was a tactical victory and everyone knows that if the infantry had been given a fair chance and the cavalry had arrived a few hours earlier, it may well have proved decisive – might even have brought the war to a close. That much has not been forgotten. We haven't been able to follow up and so we are back in trench war again, but our time will come. Did you see the tanks at all?'

'No, but they sound very promising for the future.'

'Yes, that is what you are to go to England to do. I want you to think how infantry and tanks can break through properly. Good creeping barrages, timed movements, all of it. You are to get every possible resource to do it. The ridge showed the possibility, but the time wasn't right.'

'Very good sir. What about you?'

'I'm here until the offensive succeeds or winter takes over. I have some ideas of my own you know.'

We both laughed and I enjoyed the ride taking me away from the trenches for the last time.

At Amiens, I was greeted with a chaotic scene of lorries, cars, motor-bicycles (much improved on my little 1908 Peugeot), troops and horses. It was clear that more troops were going into the trenches to keep up the push on the German lines. The railhead was full of young, fresh troops eager to get a taste of the trenches. I remember that being me not so very long ago, a single stripe on my arm. Now I was the old hand with the scrambled egg and pips, looking to crack jokes at the young greenhorns. I wanted to tell them everything at once on how to survive, but I knew that nearly half of these troops would not be returning to England alive. Although barely older than any of them, I wished I could extract my experience and give it to them in exchange for better memories.

The train journey took nearly three days to complete. The tracks were often shelled and troop trains going to the front had a priority over us going back. Most of the passengers on my train were on home leave and others were wounded, including the usual crop of eye-bandages, arm-slings and crutches. There were no wobbly troops on this train, but I now had a deeper understanding of how the shelling caused this damage to a soldier's moral fibre. I had probably tipped over the edge more than once and was lucky to come back. That was purely down to Odile holding me together and I wanted her to know it.

Having arrived in Boulogne, it took a day more to arrange a passage across the Channel. So many more troops were here and many were now due to go off to Belgium and I was pleased not to be amongst them. When

I was finally able to cross the Channel, it was in familiar and comforting poor weather, which meant less danger of being torpedoed at any time. Otherwise, the danger was as acute as ever. In all my crossings, I never once saw a destroyer anywhere nearby protecting us.

On arrival at Folkestone, I was due to take a troop train to London and then on to Salisbury for arrival in Warminster, but I was diverted to Victoria Station and met by one of Cowling's junior officers. He took me by motor car to Salisbury, which was pleasant if long and tedious, especially given the lack of conversation. On arrival at the mess I was given some replacement equipment and then had to spend an interminable evening recounting stories to young officers yet to depart for the Front. I remember telling them almost nothing of interest, except where keeping my head down saved my life in the hope that it would save theirs. The same dull lecture of my school visit.

The winter of 1916 was one of the coldest in my living memory. At least I was not in the trenches but billeted in a very comfortable quarters on the camp. I had received training at the staff college in Camberley in order to undertake the permanent rank of lieutenant-colonel and I was able to write home, if not to make a visit. My role was deemed secret and so I was not able to leave the camp without an escort. My work involved planning for offensives in 1917 and these would properly include troops, tanks, artillery and aeroplanes, mines and cavalry in concerted attacks – with some subtle disruption to the enemy beforehand. I was putting another team together of experts in new warfare techniques. We were focused on several areas, including Paddy's shallow mining, deep mining and operating deliberately in enemy territory on their side of the lines. In addition, we were working on perfecting the creeping barrage, which provided a moving wall of covering shellfire. If we could work on using tanks and aeroplanes better, then we could make a real difference in the war.

On three occasions, senior staff officers visited me, including a couple of the general staff. There was still interest in our work and Cowling's reputation afforded me courtesy and interest. In fact, Cowling was still making much of unusual field operations and our success in France assured us equipment and time to perfect our techniques. The Australians and New Zealanders also visited us regularly. They were actively tunnelling under Arras for an action planned for the spring of 1917. They were planning the jump off right in front of the German trenches from massive secret underground bunkers, or *carrières* as the French called them. That seemed like the kind of idea that might work or else be disastrous – twenty-five-thousand men pouring out of a few exits and up some steps in full kit. Whoever was planning that action needed to know their business well. The Kiwis were tough and they would dig to the centre of the earth if they were asked to.

I could not imagine scaling the flights of steps underground, leading to the surface, whilst hearing the booming and flashing of war and the screams of the dead and wounded above through the small exits. Perhaps soldiers hit would come tumbling down the steps before their very eyes, sapping soldiers' morale in an instant.

It became increasingly clear that the British were planning an offensive action in Ypres in 1917. Nowadays, I had become wary of grand actions, having seen the Somme at close quarters. However, we had learned many things from that battle and the commanders wanted those bitter lessons learned to be put into operation. It seemed though, that this was going to be an enormous mining operation. The planning for this operation would not involve me, as my role was to train the tunnelling companies and advise on tactics once the mines had blown. This was going to be a big operation and I still had a part to play, even if it was only a small one, I had to give it all I had left.

CHRIS CHERRY

CHAPTER NINETEEN - WIPERS BOUND

In February 1917, I received orders to move to Belgium again in order to train the troops in mine occupation and in the use of mechanised troop advance tactics. My orders explicitly stated that, being unfit for front-line service, under no circumstances was a front-line combatant role to be assigned to me. Indeed, I was not even to be permitted to undertake one voluntarily.

I tried to remember the first day of the Somme offensive – watching the charge to the Lochnagar crater occupation in La Boisselle. Some four-thousand Germans had been blown up or buried there and the division took terrible casualties. This time, the infantry should be better prepared for this type of attack and however I could help, I would.

Boarded on a troop ship for the continent, once again I was going to be in the fight – even if just a little bit. I did not want the trenches any more, but wanted to protect our troops and offer them some chance of success, just to shorten the war a little bit. Cowling had not been in touch for some time and I began to wonder where he was in the planning of all of this. After arriving back in Boulogne, I immediately boarded a train bound for the familiar Belgian border. For two days, we rolled slowly through the flatlands of northern France and the border with Belgium. It wasn't far, but the rail journey was interminable. We stopped often to drop troops or equipment but eventually I found my billet near to Poperinghe. Once more in Pop, I was given an instruction to meet Cowling the next evening in Talbot House – or Toc H as it was generally called. Until then, I was to settle my small team and set them up for the mission coming to them. It was disappointing to discover that the front line was almost exactly where it was when I had first made this journey two years previously.

At 1800, I waited at Toc H for Cowling to appear. I had not seen him for some months and was keen to find out what exactly my role here would be. Cowling arrived a little late and appeared somewhat distracted.

There was a second figure hovering behind him. When Cowling moved aside to allow this figure to enter, I looked straight into the eyes of my old friend, Fixer.

'My goodness, Fixer Cowling as I live and breathe!'

The old railwayman looked at me and laughed.

'Still skinny as a pole then you old bugger. Let's see, a colonel now, if you please.'

'Thanks to your meddling cousin. It's sir, by the way, you slovenly clay-kicker.'

'Yes, Arthur, what have you done to this over-promoted corporal?'

Fixer slapped his cousin in the back and punched his arm. He was now a captain in the Royal Engineers and in Toc H, a captain hitting a brigadier raised few eyebrows, especially between family members.

'Well Fixer, young William here now knows his business. Unfortunately, so do you, so I have brought you both together to help plan our next operation. Believe it or not, we are going to mine a whole bloody strip of German trench on the high ground south of Ypres and you are going to help me, the Australians and a bunch of miners to pull it off. From approximately Hill 60 to approximately the village of Messines, we are going to decapitate the enemy positions. This time, we are going to get it right.'

At first, I was dumbstruck. Cowling was suggesting a string of large mines to be blown along a length of trench, stretching for miles, in the horrors of Ypres. He talked us through it using a map of the suggested front from the artificial summit of Hill 60 to the long rise of the ridge at Messines. It looked nearly impossible.

'In the morning, we are going to see General Plumer and talk through the plans in more detail. He has maintained an interest in our work since Bazentin Ridge, although he has only really been up here in Belgium. Both of you will work on how to get the mines completed quietly, get the spoil out on a light railway and place the detonations to inflict the greatest possible damage on the enemy. We have been working on this and digging preparatory galleries for over six months. What I want is some sophisticated advice on getting them positioned exactly.'

Fixer and I spent the remainder of the evening catching up. He had been involved in counter mining and listening for enemy mining activity. As it turned out, the British were far more active miners than the Germans had been. He was convinced that a string of mines could make the difference to the stalemate in Ypres.

'You know William, I am convinced that big mine blasts shock everyone, our own boys included. Startled troops don't think and move fast. A series of mines, placed well, shocks them to the core. We have to make sure we have enough advantage, so that when our boys recover their senses, the enemy are not pointing bloody machine guns at our chests.'

'Agreed, Fixer. It seems that there are plans for fifteen or more mines here. That is a lot. You working with the Aussie boys from 1915?'

'Yes, a few of the Kiwi boys are about Arras in the carrière operation and some of the Yorkshire pit ponies are in on this too. The ground is still wet and flooding is still a problem. Also, the enemy can hear us more easily as the spoil is claggy.'

'Let's sleep on this one and see if we can find some way to pull this off.'

'Yes, but you are buying my boy. Mine's a treble.'

In the morning, we travelled the short distance to 2nd Army HQ. The buildings occupied some exceptional countryside, sheltered from the salient by a low, wide ridge. In such a flat area, there is hardly any high ground, so what little height the land offers is vitally important.

The tunnels were being dug by a whole range of Commonwealth troops from Australia, New Zealand, and the British Isles with help from non-military geologists and cartographers. This was going to be another major operation. We worked hard on improving maps, planning how the artillery could be targeted very accurately, and how to use infantry wisely and with caution. In addition, we sited the exact locations of the detonations to allow occupation of the craters without creating an impassable terrain for the assaulting troops, especially if it was raining.

We worked on using aeroplanes to spot and to provide up to date positions on advances and captures. This time, there would be no mistakes and the plan would be meticulously planned with everyone in the military at the same table, with no compromise cavalry operations in the planning.

When I arrived, the preparatory tunnels were already complete and the sappers were about to dig the drift galleries to the final positions of the mines themselves. Plans were in place for up to twenty mines and we agreed that the priority be the ridge through Messines and the ridge through Wijtschate. Tanks had been ordered for the attack and these had been delivered early, then cleverly hidden from the all-seeing eyes of the Germans. We had planned for counter-artillery, counter-mining and had even constructed scale models in intricate detail to train the troops on what was to be expected when the mines went off. Looking back at stories of the Hawthorn crater and on my own experience of Lochnagar, I did not want our troops to be so startled by the size of an explosion that they failed to capitalise on the element of surprise. Objectives for advance were set daily and held, with the next wave leap-frogging over the last. This was going be a clever battle, no more slow march to death, but a stealthy, aggressive, intelligent push for the high ground.

At the end of May, after some time spent with the models and with the commanders of the brigades fully briefed, we planned to visit the forward positions, although it was against Cowling's orders. Fixer and I wanted to make sure the large mines would explode and were ready for the action. We visited a mine on the Wijtschate ridge and were taken into the neutral gallery before turning left into the drift gallery specifically for this large mine. Huge amounts of ammonal were about to be placed inside. The cans and bags were disguised, but there they were. It was nearly complete and the cavern gallery that had been dug seemed huge. The Australian and Canadian miners seemed pleased with its siting. Fixer thought it was shallow enough to break the line and deep enough to give a wide damage field, which was what we wanted. We talked through the plans for detonation and making sure they were all timed together. All of us, old hands and new boys, were still in awe of the scale of this offensive mine field.

The tunnel walls had been greatly strengthened with wood taken from nearby copses and forests that had been blown by shelling. The timber was good quality but a couple of mine collapses had been seen up and down the front. In some cases, this had led to the abandonment of the mine or had alerted the enemy to our mining operations. This led to counter mining and the terrible sight of hand-to-hand fighting underground. As we left, I made sure that the wall looked secure enough.

Our little party had moved quietly into the mine, but its floor had been weakened by a German gallery that had been dug in parallel and below.

'Sir, best keep three yards apart. We are building back because we think the enemy has dug below. No signs of enemy at the moment, all seems quiet, so we can go a little further. The enemy has only spotted about fifteen yards of this tunnel, so in a few seconds, we're back on firm ground again.'

'Thanks, Lieutenant. Are we sure this is unoccupied?'

'Yes sir, been listening all day. They were last here, last night about 2200. No real activity, just a sapper inspecting the tunnel, I suppose—'

From behind came the unmistakable crack of timbers and the earth fell from beneath us. We fell for what seemed like ten seconds, but it could not have been that far, it was just false sensation. I hit the floor hard on my back and the old pain in my side and legs come flooding over me again, just as if a tap had been turned back on. Looking around, I tried to keep alert and conscious. Bits of timber fell around me and one pole landed on my chest, knocking the breath from me with an involuntary groan.

There were no enemy in their gallery, which was a blessing for our survival, but the walls had caved in and we were now trapped underneath our own mine gallery – pinned against the walls of a German position. There were as many as a hundred of us now trapped. Above my head, there was a loud crack, a flash of bright light, a blast of heat and more white-hot pain in my back. The world turned from cloudy to pitch black and then to silence. For some reason, it occurred to me that if I got out of this, Cowling would be the one to kill me, or at least strip me back to corporal.

CHRIS CHERRY

CHAPTER TWENTY - THE ENDGAME

The silence seemed to go on forever. In my pain, I imagined German soldiers pouring over my head in waves, and kilted Scots soldiers meeting them headlong in a scrum of metal and death to the tune of *The Dark Island*. In my dreams came the sight of Odile in a white dress, with her finger to her lips, seeking silence from the raging anger everywhere. Her eyes fixed on me as I looked down at my broken body. This was a dream, but seemed as real to me then as any real memory does now.

Occasionally, there were quiet and calm voices, some in English, some in French and some in an accent from America or Canada – it was hard to tell. The voices used words I had not heard before, which was strange, because there was nothing in a mineshaft that I would not know about. And while rescue would be difficult, it was not impossible. It was hard to work out why this was taking so long. We were only in the gallery about one-hundred feet and we had rehearsed mine collapses and rescues before. I tried to call out, but only a muffled whisper came out of my mouth, however hard I shouted.

Sometimes, something pressed on my back, then lifted, followed by pain. Was I being tortured? Who was with me in the gallery? *Think William, work this out!* But I could not. My mind was focused on my body, which was telling me to be still, but I had to dig my way back to the gallery entrance.

Occasionally, a searing light registered in my brain and then went dark again. This happened more and more and my dreams became less and less real. I dreamt of mules in the gallery pulling me out and taking me into this bright light. This was impossible, but there it was in front of me. I wondered why I was not awake and planning the mining attack, but Cowling came to me often, holding his hand in front of my face.

The lights grew less bright, but more persistent. I became aware of lying down in a sleeping position. My mouth and throat were parched and sore and I could not raise even the slightest cough to relieve them.

Somehow, my arms felt pinned down, but it seemed to be a good time to get out of here, so the first thing to do would be to open my eyes.

At first, there was nothing real in my view. Everything was blurred and full of shadows, but I kept going and blinked to clear my eyes. As time passed, the picture cleared a little and it became apparent that I was again in hospital, only this time, it seemed to be more serious. I was pinned down with dressings and bandages. My back seemed numb but I could still move my hands and feet, which was a relief.

Wondering what must have happened to me, I tried to see whether the hospital was British or German. In my dream there were memories of the English language, but it might have been only a dream. It was difficult to separate the dream from the reality in this state. My old wounds hurt – along with some new ones.

For some time, I lay there trying to position my brain into the same place as my body. The door to my room opened and a nurse with a red cross on her tunic leaned over me.

'At last, Colonel Collins, how are you feeling?'

'Where am I please, Nurse? I cannot speak properly, my mouth is so dry.'

She bustled to the table and brought me a glass of warm water.

'You are in hospital, of course.'

'Yes, but where? France? Belgium?'

'No Colonel, don't be silly. You are in England.'

'Why is that silly? How long have I been here?'

'About three months.'

'Three months? That means I have missed the action?'

'Whatever action you were in must have long ago been over. You must rest.'

Three months. My goodness, this was really bad. How did I get from a mine shaft in Wipers to a hospital bed in England? Someone must have taken me out of the collapsed gallery and fetched me all the way to England. Another boat journey and one more stretcher case in Folkestone or Southampton. I remembered none of this at all. My mind was snapped back to the present by a sharp, but kind voice.

'Colonel Collins, I am very pleased to see you awake. What can you tell me of your injuries?'

I hesitated. Was this a German ruse? Were these doctors and nurses really spies? Was this actually England? Had it really been three months? It seemed less than plausible but it really did not matter anymore. The enemy knew the mine I was in, if not all of the other twenty or so.

'Good morning Doctor, is it morning? I was, er, visiting a mine in Belgium and it collapsed and trapped me. I don't remember anything at all. Possibly German soldiers and maybe some British? It isn't very clear to me.'

'You have had an incredible journey and a very lucky escape judging from your injuries – not your first either by the looks of you! Your back and your legs are scarred and internally, some of your organs are in a bad way. Shrapnel wound here, bayonet or bullet scrape here, puncture wound here and what looks like a bullet entry here, perhaps – or possibly a puncture from barbed wire.'

'It was wire Doctor, from the brambles and bushes tangled in the High Wood. I was there in July 1916.'

'July? So not when it was taken then? I read about that cavalry push and attacking at night. Bloody clever, but ultimately not clever enough.'

I smiled and turned my face to the window. *No, not clever enough, were we Horace.*

'Well, at least you can remember something, so that is good, very pleasing. Your back injury will take time to heal, but it may not be the same as before. You won't be returning to the Front again. You will not be fit or well enough to fight, or for anything else in the army.'

I was to remain there for some weeks still. There were no messages and no one visited. That was curious as at least one message must have been sent to me by someone. I needed to know how it turned out, and to know how my friends came through. Still, orders were orders and I was being told nothing.

'Nurse Henry. May I ask you a direct question?'

'Yes of course, Colonel.'

'Are you allowed to call me William?'

'Not a very direct question, but yes, if that is what you prefer.'

'Sorry, yes of course but I have another question.'

'Yes?'

'Why have I not been given any messages? I know that at least one would have been sent to me soon after my injuries, so where are they?'

'You have quite a few William, but the doctor will not allow it at all, until you are much, much better.'

'Will you get them for me? Straight away?'

'The doctor must have his reasons, but I will ask.'

Nurse Henry left without another word. The doctor's face soon appeared at the observation window in the door, his expression a mixture of sadness and concern. He pushed the door slightly ajar and then it closed again. When it was opened a second time, Nurse Henry was carrying a pile of white and brown papers and envelopes.

'The doctor does not think you should have these yet, but he knows he cannot keep them from you. You must read them in the order here. He insists.'

'Has he read them?'

'Yes, he had to. It is for your own health, you understand.'

'Yes, I understand.'

She placed a hand on my arm, squeezed gently and then left, locking the door behind her, perhaps to keep others out. Whatever was in here, was not going to be good news. Her tone of concern worried me and the doctor's instructions seemed oddly harsh and specific. What exactly was in this pile of papers?

There were two envelopes and two sheets of paper. The top one contained orders from Cowling that were to accompany me wherever I was transferred.

To whom it may be of concern:

Regarding Acting Colonel William Collins MM/Bar (R.E.12FO)

This is to ensure that Colonel William Collins is afforded every care and attention, without preference, commensurate with his rank, without prejudice or hindrance and at all times in possession of such effects as are to be found about his person. It is requested and required of all in possession and with entitlement to read this order that William Collins is treated in such a way as to aid his recovery to full health and encourages his convalescence, not the convenience or expedition of the War or in the specific interest of the army. It is to be understood unequivocally that the primary concern is to be his survival, recovery and convalescence and this should be borne in mind when assessing his fitness for transfer or service assessment.

Major-General Arthur Cowling.
(Undisclosed)

Cowling was protecting me and had concluded that my war was over. It probably was anyway, judging by these injuries.

The second sheet of paper was a notification to my parents that I was alive but wounded and had been brought to England. No other details were provided and they were not told anything further about how, where or when they might see me again.

Next, came an order for uniform and other effects for when I was able to return to wearing a uniform again. The rank was to be set as full colonel. Why, I was not sure.

The final envelope was marked with a lot of red stamps and had clearly moved from place to place through the hands of many censors. Trembling, I opened it. It was from Cowling and it was brief and purposeful.

To inform Colonel William Collins. Fixer, NP same place. AC/OC 12FO

Fixer had died when the mine collapsed, the message stated NP. Nah-Poo. Perhaps he was crushed by the falling walls or struck by the timbers. I was devastated and desperate. This had been kept from me, for obvious reasons. It was hard to read on, but there was one more sentence.

Action successful, business learned.

My friend Fixer was gone. Those I had known slipped through my fingers as sand on a beach. No one able to stay long enough, always called on and away. Yet here I was. In the battle time and over again, wounded, cared for and thrown again into the row. Why was I alive, in this war of the dead? A small tear slid down my cheek and away. It tasted salty and bitter on my lip. Curse this war, this damned conflagration of doomed souls. In my mind, I saw the bald-headed German take Fixer away by the arm, he went willingly, with a thumbs up on his way, lighting a fag.

The attack on the high ground in Ypres had been successful. I knew nothing of the detail and asked nothing. All I knew was that many mines were blown and the infantry moved forwards under better cover than ever before. Perhaps the lessons of the Ridge had not been forgotten after all.

Very few people knew of the existence of Odile in my life or why I had moved from corporal to colonel in two years. Only Cowling now knew of my knowledge of France, French and the geography of Picardie. Here, everyone had a family, a sweetheart, a missed soul, and everyone had experienced death in the trenches. Once again, I allowed Odile into my memory and allowed myself the hope of finding her. My hand still felt her touch and I knew now that it had not been an accidental touch. That knowledge sustained me in hospital, knowing that we could be together again. Almost certainly, any alliance with the enemy was to save her family from starving to death.

Eventually, I was moved to a convalescent home in the south-west of England and remained there until New Year 1918. I had very little military contact and saw nothing of Cowling. Perhaps he was busy or perhaps he had moved on from our acquaintance. Both thoughts made me feel sad.

No longer did I dream of actions and plans to take or save lives. My silly ideas on the quayside no longer burned into my brain, forcing me headlong at the enemy. No longer did I wish this uniform to be around my shoulders. The fire of anger had faded to bitter embers and all I wanted now was peace and to return to Odile – albeit a broken man, perhaps less of a man, torn to matchwood by this war.

I sat on the cold porch looking east towards France and the battlefields, although they were really too far away. From here, I could sense nothing of war, except the stream of newly wounded young men moving through this place. Now, I felt like an old man, aged by the war, wearied by its consumption of me and spurred on only by the hope of finding my sweetheart again. In the end, the war had taken the better part of me and buried it in the earth. Home was too much to face and meant little to me – the people there with their kind faces, shared features and love. I couldn't give it and I couldn't receive it. What a mess this war had made of my soul. Tears came again, wave after wave for Fixer, Watkins, Smith, the boys on the ridge, Hill 60, the miners, the sappers, the infantry from Martinique, even the bloody German with the bald head. It was all there and it flooded out.

I had no idea how many enemy I had killed, and dared not try to remember. Tears flowed for their families, and for the wives widowed by the Western Front. For soldiers returning home with no soul or body left. The tears kept coming and I let them.

As darkness fell, my view over the water receded and my tears washed away the sin of my generation just enough to let me sleep. A sleep that was still filled with dreams of whizz-bangs, bombs, mortars, bayonets and trench tools used to cleave men into two. Body after nameless body now came to me in my sleep. The cavalryman turned to dust from the bomb around his neck, the Deccan riders, the gun nest, and Smith's sacrifice of himself for me. Some forgave, some condemned, but none offered the chance of rest my wounds craved. There was still plenty of potential for me to go out of my mind.

The winter was harsh and my hold on my thoughts slipped quietly away. Only the daily routine kept me ticking over – breakfast, dressing in agony, sitting with my decaying thoughts on the porch, tea, dinner, bed and the chance to dream again of Horace and the bomb. Perhaps spring would bring some happiness and the chance of peace.

The porch was a good place to watch the ships on the sea, carrying food and equipment to the Front in an endless stream, day after dreary day.

The Front was still largely unmoving but it appeared that the Germans were throwing one more iron into the fire. Bazentin had again fallen into the hands of the enemy, the High Wood had passed quickly back into German control and the sacrifices at the gates of France had been easily given up. There was no end in sight and the casualties were more terrible than ever.

Early in June 1918, I received my first visitor despite giving up hope of ever receiving any. There had been whispered words as to why I had been left alone, abandoned even, by the nurses and orderlies, doctors and administrators. All were whispering the same sort of thing, *Who is this*

Collins? Why does no one ever visit? There were so few people who could have visited me anyway.

I saw the uniform first and recognised it as a major-general. Cowling looked thin and weary, the sparkle gone from his eyes. He closed the door slowly and deliberately, looked at me, sat and then began to weep, unable to hold back. A while later, he grasped my hand and we sat in silence for many minutes before he chose to speak.

'William, I am quite tired of this damnable war. It has taken from me my brother, cousin Fixer and dozens of comrades and thousands of men that I never knew but was required to send to certain death. This weighs heavily on a soul, however dispassionate one becomes. I have come to seek your forgiveness for ever encouraging you to risk yourself time and again for me and this madness. Do you forgive me, William?'

No words came to me and I just kept hold of his hand, perhaps a little tighter.

'The Germans are through us you know, but they are fading fast. We have tanks and men pouring in from every part of the world. This may finally be the year we could say with certainty that the war will be done by Christmas. It gives me some comfort.'

I stared ahead, wishing to be resolute for my commander and my friend. He broke the stare by snapping his head towards me, brightening as he did so.

'If I may say William, you don't look too well. You are stick thin and yellow as sulphur. How are you?'

Looking Cowling square in the face, I took courage.

'Beaten, sir. The war has taken from me my life in quick time. Imagine it as having a bottle of life, brim full when you are born, and it drains away slowly as the years go by.

Well, the war has knocked my bottle over a few times and it has splashed my life over the fields of France and Belgium – there is little left to live with now.'

Cowling's eyes glazed. I wondered if he felt the same. His soul had also let go in a hurry.

'William, you will be sent home as soon as possible and your family can visit you now. The secrecy of our work is gone anyway – we could not make it work and we have lost too many men in the operations.'

'Sir, what's the final story on the sixty who went over in July '16?'

'In the end, we only ever got back the original twelve and one prisoner – Roberts I think it was. They made a fine mess of the enemy on the way. Caused mayhem apparently. We found out so much more from a captured German colonel in December last year. Ammunition dumps mysteriously exploding when they were emptied, rifles falling apart, lots of small stuff that added up. Communications going astray, officers turning up dead and any number of stories of stray shells landing in strange places. Not bad all in all, showed it was a runner, but only when we can fix the problems.'

'One more question sir. How did I get here from the mine in Ypres?'

Cowling took a long deep breath and sat back. He ran his hand through his thinning hair. Evidently, he knew this was coming but the telling did not seem easy for him.

'The mine, well the gallery at least, was discovered by the German listening post and they set a few small bombs to blow it. You and Fixer were down there, creating the commotion that made them set it off. That blew the floor out and you both fell into the German mineshaft, only about ten feet in height, but it put you in the German tunnel. The enemy came after you, you were unconscious and Fixer tried to hold them off for a bit. A couple of men dug through to you in a few minutes, but they had been told to bomb the hole. Luckily, they didn't do it straight away. They held off the Germans with pistol rounds, I think two were killed side by side blocking the tunnel, but you were behind them. Fixer dragged one off and started to pull you though, with the help of a couple of Scots sappers. Once you were back in the hole, the boys threw some bombs down the German mine and that closed it up. Our gallery was re-sited and the mine went up as planned on the day. Fixer took a bullet in his chest though and in the end it did for him. I suppose you are even on that score now, my friend?'

Fixer died saving me, as I had nearly died saving him – certainly more than once apiece. My friend and comrade. I had to live now, he had given me life, like Watkins had done and it was not to be led by despair.

We sat for more time in silence, reflecting on those we had lost. The war was not over, but it was for me and I suspected from what Cowling was saying, that it would soon be over for him too.

'Where will you go next General?'

'Please William, here and now, call me Arthur.'

'Yes sir, what does the war mean for you now?'

'I'm posted to Palestine, leaving at the end of August. Quieter and they need some clever thinking. I had hoped, of course, that you might talk me through some ideas when you were well and in your training post. I don't think that's the plan now, is it old boy?'

'No sir. The war is over for me, either way. I have not walked a step on my own for nearly four months.'

'Well, looks like you will get a discharge. Do you have a plan Colonel Collins?'

'I do now sir. The day after peace, I will return to France and find my life again.'

Cowling smiled, stood, brushed my forehead gently, patted my shoulder and left without another word.

EPILOGUE

The Armistice could not have come at a better time for the British. We were pushing the Germans back and the Americans had joined us on the Western Front, but we were still taking terrible casualties in the open countryside. Trench warfare had given way to open country fighting again but the machine gun was still in play, and without the trenches, every side took desperate casualties. For me, the Armistice was signed the day after I was to be discharged from the army, but required to act as an adviser in the deployment of engineering solutions for the use of tanks. I had also been visited by the Intelligence Service with a view to planning an unusual operation in May 1919. But finally, the war was officially over and my engineering skills might be better employed in the peace to come.

I was able to walk now, still a little stiff, a little damaged, but able to move myself around slowly. It was possible to think clearly, but every time I thought of Odile, my mind turned to gun cotton and exploded in memory and sadness. I had not heard again from Odile, of course and I feared the moment in the alley would be my last memory of her.

In early 1919, it was agreed that the Engineers would be part of the operation to clean up the battlefield. I was asked, not ordered, to help with some of the planning. Should the fields be ploughed over, everything left where it was, bodies where they fell? Should they be dug up and the bodies recovered? Should they be covered up for evermore in darkness and silence? Some areas were excavated and soldiers buried and identified where possible. In other areas, such as in the High Wood, Courcelette, the ridge at Messines, Lochnagar, there were too many bodies, too badly mutilated to recover. They were left where they lay, already buried or covered over by the terrible grinding of the war. The remains of many of the men who had fallen were churned over and again by shelling and the pounding of boots. I knew many of these and remembered their faces. Right there too were the faces of the enemy I had fought against. Them or me – it was a simple calculation for a simple soldier.

I volunteered to help as long as I could return to Picardie. My offer was gratefully accepted because I knew the terrain so well and would be able to help select the best option to recover equipment. Again, I found myself crossing the Channel, but this time with no danger of being sunk by the enemy. By this time, I was able to walk quite normally with a stick and hoped to dispense with that before too long. The train journey to Albert was much faster, and I arrived on a pleasant if very cold morning just as it was getting light. I quickly scanned around to see what was different. The German occupation of the countryside had left its mark in signs and graffiti, but it was not so different from when I had last stood here in 1916, two years previously. French folk were openly moving around, many desperate and homeless, almost nomadic.

A car was waiting and took me to the Contalmaison road. Still visible were the mine craters, especially the one named the Lochnagar crater. On the edge of the ruined village was where I had first seen deep mining in action, as distinct from my shallower wide mining around Hill 60. I stood on the small temporary road leading off towards Becourt, which was in the middle of No Man's Land for the start of the Somme battle. Around me were temporary graves with wooden stakes for markers. Burial officers from a whole number of regiments darted here and there, busying themselves in bringing order to this horror. Fragments of uniform, letters and tags were all used to identify the identifiable. However, so many were listed as missing, it almost struck belief from the world. I was not encouraged to stay here as I was needed on the second line from Pozieres to Longueval through the High Wood. Finally, I would be going back to Bazentin.

The road north of Albert slides over and around and under the slopes of the ridge. In the war, it had provided cover and safety. Happy Valley on the right and the sunken road in the distance were two locations of particular note. I had been here many times and had used them to move quickly to and fro when Cowling and I were planning here. I passed Crucifix Corner and the site of the cavalry charge. On the right was a cemetery being dug and populated by soldiers killed in the taking of Longueval and High Wood. Caterpillar Valley was anything but. Little more than a dip in the rolling fields, it at least provided a nice spot to hold for evermore the ridge. I turned up towards High Wood and saw the devastation of the taking of the wood. It was a hellish and macabre sight – still full of bits of body and torn clothing. There were large numbers of unexploded shells and many areas were totally inaccessible. It was hard to walk on the ground without ducking for this was the battlefield in my nightmares still. Behind me was the sweeping ridge with the death of the cavalry, the glittering Deccan Horse and the admirable plunge of the

Hussars. I grimaced at the decision to hold back the infantry, a gut reaction to the indecision that had condemned the soldiers now being buried in the cemetery here.

The terrain was still very uneven along the cleared track down into the north-east of the village. I glanced to my right towards Martinpuich and thought of the poor buggers who were sent that way with the wood still full of Germans. Now it seemed a dream, but then it was a horrific reality. In this corner of the wood, photographs were taken of one of the most terrible and awful sights of the war. Bodies of soldiers were recovered, mostly naked, from the torn branches of the trees. Some were stuck between branches, others impaled. Shells had blown them out of their uniforms and up into the trees. They appeared as grisly and almost religious symbols of the terrors of war and of the damage possible to the human body. I shivered and moved on into the village where I had hidden and watched the withdrawal of the Germans at close hand.

Finally, I reached the site of Odile's parents' house, to find a sign on the gate:

Lefebvre: Pierre, Marie-Louise Armandine, Odile. M213433.

The numbers meant nothing to me, but the sign had been placed by the French Army for the first villagers to return. My heart jumped for a moment, but there was no sign of Odile and her family. It was merely a sign to mark their plot. Little now remained but the cellars and outline of the buildings. A voice snapped me from my dream.

'Ah, good morning Colonel Collins. Good journey? Welcome to hell.'

'At least no one is shooting at us. You have me at a disadvantage?'

'Colonel Herbert Mason-Brown'

'Ah, the Engineer who blew up the Messines Ridge? Yes of course, very sorry.'

'Yes, and now defusing all this stuff and trying to make sense of the patch from Pozieres to Longueval. I understand you even lived in this village? Quite a celebrity apparently.'

'Yes, I did and I know most of the people here.'

'Do you want to meet some again? There are a few stubborn old devils here that want to get back to their homes. I want to let them once the ground is cleared. You know, bodies in cellars and bombs on the ground, awful stuff and not very sanitary, safe or pleasant. Here, we are spraying some of the ground now and marking out squares. Starting with the village itself and then moving up to the open ground. You remember the battle here?'

I stopped abruptly, my stomach dropped to the floor and Watkins' face appeared clearly in front of me.

'Yes. I do.'

'Monumental bust I hear?'

'In some respects, yes. Colonel, you mentioned some villagers?'

'Yes, of course, this way. This may have been the Mairie up here by the church, but I am not so sure. The maps are not that specific and the photographs are not here yet. Found nothing locally, perhaps you can help?'

'Yes, it is the Mairie, the church steps here are still in the right place. Along here was the old schoolhouse and the farms went off from that wall towards— Oh, is that a cemetery being dug?'

'Yes, being labelled the Bazentin-le-Petit Military. We've also used a bit of the Communal Catholic cemetery down the hill. Quite a lot of unbanged shells down there as well, so if you go, take care and watch for the red flags.'

'There weren't any flags there last time I was here, I think I can manage.'

'Ha, well, look let's talk more later?'

Before I went into the temporary building, I stepped down the hill to the spot where Watkins died. I knelt and scooped up some of the dirt exactly where he fell. I rolled it through my fingers as it fell back to the floor.

'Well. Horace old boy, I'm still bloody here, thanks to you. I promise to be worthy of your sacrifice old chum. I know not where you are, but wherever you are on the ridge, you hold it still.'

I let the rest of the dirt fall to the floor, then stepped back up the hill and entered the temporary building. Large sheets protected a screened area where some of the villagers had returned. They had left the holding camp and travelled here by whatever means they could to their village, perhaps little realising what was here, or rather, what wasn't. Most were devastated and openly weeping at the awful mess of their land. Some had been here for over two weeks and still had not changed clothes, nor stopped their weeping for a life destroyed.

Some seemed to recognise my face, but could not place me. The uniform and the years had aged me and placed me outside of the village. When I told them, they hugged me as a son and my face was tenderly patted by everyone. Some asked after Odile and I could only tell them that she had been evacuated to Bapaume and Cambrai, but nothing more than that. We had occupied both towns and she was not there. I suppose the attack in 1917 forced the Germans to move civilians even further north, perhaps into Germany itself.

Our job here, was to clear the mechanical remains of the war and to gather and catalogue the dead as far as we possibly could. For every soldier we identified by uniform and unit, there were perhaps fifty listed as missing and who would remain so. There were very few graves in the two cemeteries, when compared to the soldiers listed as casualties. By now, we knew the missing were dead, so we carried on about our grim task. My job was to oversee the clearance of ordnance and equipment quickly, safely and in such a way as to disentangle our equipment from that of the enemy. Salvage what we could and scrap what we could not. I had to prevent looting for souvenirs as this was dangerous but I was not altogether successful.

As April turned to May, I worried for Odile. No word and no family here. Perhaps she was with her German after all, reconciled with her father to a new life.

By the end of May, we had made great progress in clearing our sector from Longueval village and Delville Wood to Pozieres and south to Montauban. The bodies – such as could be identified – were separated from their German comrades in death. The German burial teams were under strict rules to treat enemy remains with the utmost care as they went about their task. More than once, we found bodies and skeletons entwined in a deathly embrace with bayonets and trench spades thrust at each other. Some were more intact but most were smashed to pieces. It was grim and not what I wanted to see after witnessing bodies like these as living and breathing souls.

My time assessing equipment that could be salvaged was less grim in comparison. Large guns, rifles and bombs were quickly assessed, and most would be melted down and reused in other ways. Wire could be salvaged, crushed and melted into cutlery. I didn't want to know of such things, but efforts were made to salvage scrap. The French authorities worked hard with us to try and keep everything in France that belonged to France and whatever German spoils were found were kept as reparation for the devastation.

I made a temporary billet for myself in the village as it still provided a great lookout. The corn was again ripening, some surviving the churn of war. No one was to harvest this year, the ground was still too poisoned – quite apart from the dead human remains that could find themselves in fresh crops. The ground still smelled strongly of sulphurous fumes, sweet aromas of decay and the stench of dead bodies all together. The smell of burning was ever present whilst the villagers worked on building their properties again and clearing their gardens. The local officials were still hated as they tried to manage the process, but the French wanted their homes back. They did not ask for war, they did not ask for this to happen to them and it was only a misfortune of the German advance that meant the battles were even here.

The burial officers were diligently completing their task. There were thousands of bodies under the surface, but it was decided that since they were so badly decomposed and damaged, mixed up and churned, any effort to excavate and identify would be too costly, distressing and contrary to the practice of burial where fallen. Many poets had written of the conflict and verse was often read over graves, holes and bunkers. It offered some small comfort. A padre moved amongst the soldiers to help soothe their distress as the awfulness of identification and burial penetrated the gruff exteriors of these old soldiers. Since religion and I had long since agreed to go our separate ways, I nodded politely at the padre but took no part in his services.

We were also gathering names for the missing as plans were in place for a monument somewhere on the Somme, probably on the high ground at Thiepval where the British attacked on 1st July 1916. There were some officers around taking names and matching them to army records. They had a huge amount of detailed information and I began to see the scale of the attacks. I had not realised that some eighty-thousand soldiers were involved in the attacks on Bazentin Ridge and High Wood. The scale of the numbers would have been unimaginable had I not seen the stinking trenches and grumbling Tommys at first hand.

Now back in the village, I yearned for Odile, but there was still no word. I tried to find out where her family may have been taken. Other villagers who were here had made it to Cambrai from Bapaume and some had been moved to Germany. One or two had been transported there because they would not submit to German rule and I supposed Odile was one of them. I considered taking leave to go and find her, but without the German records, I would be touring France and Germany looking for a single person in all of the chaos left by the German retreat. Reluctantly, I resolved to stay and wait for her to come home. If she didn't, her father would – if he was still alive. Then I would know for certain.

At the end of May, out in the fields, the villagers began the process of ploughing in and over the shell holes and craters, supervised by shell clearance teams. Horses were used to flatten the areas between the shell holes and spoil was dropped into them to bring them up to the same level. At first, it was almost impossible to plough, but over the course of three months, the land began to give up its scars and return to chalky farmland, albeit with a dreadful and malignant secret contained underneath.

Summer came, many of the villagers had arrived home and money became slowly available to allow a rebuild. Most villagers were given temporary shelters whilst homes were rebuilt and funds were agreed to provide food and clothing for what was described as emergency use. The British soldiers were becoming fewer in number and the French military became more of a presence on the Somme and they were welcomed to their land again. I was pleased the day the village was officially handed back to the French authorities. A simple ceremony with a flag. The village had appetite for little else.

As the summer reached its height in August, I was ordered to make final arrangements for the Engineers to leave. Wire, shells and bombs had been removed as far as reasonably possible, and trenches obliterated. For the last time, I saw the spot where Watkins and I had jumped over the enemy trench.

Bullets were too small to search for so they were left. They would become inert through water damage and pose less danger over time. Piles of bombs that had been discovered were blown up far away from the fields. As conscientiously as we could, we had located and buried the Allies dead and helped locate the enemy fallen – or at least those whose bodies were largely intact, which wasn't many. I went to cemeteries at Delville Wood, Trones Wood, Bernafay Wood, Longueval Road, and the temporary cemetery between High Wood and Longueval. Roads had been laid and villages were again properly linked. Traffic was now more local than military and whilst it might never be the same again, it was in French hands at least. Some locals had flags to fly and did so proudly. Whilst 14th July was a sombre day, full of remembrance and sadness, the August sunshine offered an optimism not seen in France since my delivery boy days in 1912.

I moved my billet to the foundations of Odile's house on the corner of the Martinpuich road. It was a bivouac and tent but it was home. Outside, I sat reading the first copy of the newspaper printed in Albert since the end of the war. There and then, I made up my mind to visit Bapaume and seek the paperwork for Odile's evacuation. My work here was done and if I returned it would be as a citizen villager to rebuild a life.

In the sun, sleep came easily. The sudden jolt of a mine or bomb would not disturb me, the images of dead Germans and comrades were now as companions in my life and I accommodated them as old friends, albeit uneasily. The images of bayonet and bomb darted here and there and they came and went as part of the demonic daily dance in my head. One was allowed to pass with no threat to me or my soul. Perhaps it was possible to heal after all.

I felt the soft touch of a hand on my arm and the quiet whisper of a voice I knew and loved. In my dream I heard my name over and over and it made me smile, if only in this now pleasant dream. The hand was warm on my arm and the heat coursed through my whole body, calming my soul and refreshing me. Although sleep started falling away from me, the touch persisted and I opened my eyes with a jump. I was looking at the face of my beloved Odile. This time I was awake.

She was smiling and saying my name over and over quietly. I looked at her and blinked in the light. I put my hand out onto her shoulder and yes, it was Odile! She was real, but so much thinner than the day she had given me an apple. Today, she looked tired and weary and yet it was unmistakably the girl who helped me survive the Great War.

'My God! Odile. It is you. Where? How? It doesn't matter. You are here, my love, my life you have returned to me.'

'Mon chéri. How I have wanted to tell that which happened to me. I wrote you a letter William, but it has maybe gone and so I cannot show it to you.'

'Beautiful Odile, I got that letter. I found my way to our shed and took it to read. I did not believe you were with a German boy. It hurt me to my core.'

'Non, imbecile. It was, say for, to help my father not be taken to Allemagne.'

'Darling Odile, in my life so much has happened. I need to tell you what has happened to me, but not now. For now, let us just sit here together and heal.'

'William, every day, every single day, I dreamed to find you again. I did not know if you were in France, in the army, in England or even if you lived. There were opportunities to be with the German boy because that meant food and better rooms to sleep. My father cursed them all the time and was beaten for his words. He is a patriot and would die for the flag.'

'Odile, I have lived through this war with the hope of finding you. The devastation of this village and the letter took me away from you. I am here again and wanted you here too. I still cannot believe you are here and you are real.'

'I am, mon chéri, I am. The war has spared us both for more, I think.'

I held her and did not let go for the whole afternoon. We both succumbed to uncontrollable weeping as all of the emotions of four years of war poured out. The evening was spent in the village and I had to know what had happened to her.

'Tell me then, what happened here?'

'Ah, William, so much since you left, I think. First, I was evacuated to Bapaume, then Cambrai. My father, ha, enraged the Germans with his insults and offences. He would pour petrol on the army bread, and shove rags into the petrol tanks for the motor cars. So we were always moved around and he was forced to work to earn bread for us to eat, which he often did not.

I had to laugh a little at this little rebellion. *Good for him!*

'Oh Odile, it must have been terrifying for you all.'

'Yes, I thought we may have all starved, so I had to get the Germans on our side. There was a young soldier, who seemed sensible. He often spoke to me kindly, so I was able to get bread from him. To do this, I had to step out with him and be seen to love him. He wanted this and talked much of love and a life after the war. For me, it was for the war, William, only for the war. You know this.'

'I know that now. Oh, how you sustained me Odile and how you devastated me with thoughts of your loss.'

'It was survival, William, my father was skin and bone and mother was always unwell. If I had not acted, we would all be dead and gone, I am sure of it. He was deported to Germany and is still there, I think, now at least free and working to repair French equipment on the Belgian border. He is to come home at the end of August for good.'

'Tell me of you and your war. So, you had this boy around you, your father gone. What of your life?'

'I was taken to Germany, my life was to be the wife of a German officer. I did not know how to resist this, without us all being killed. I had to go along with it and I did. He was planning to propose a marriage and he was seeking permission to marry me. I was in a foreign country, alone and with no means to travel. He had behaved well to me and had looked out for my father and I owed him a courtesy at least. Perhaps I ought to have loved him, I was so unsure and you were so very far away from me William.'

The tears returned as she told her story. My heart ached and I too, was consumed. Her red eyes and soaked handkerchief belied the steely heart beneath.

'In Germany, things changed. He wanted marriage quickly and had already secured a job for me in service for a large aristocratic family. But I could not do this. This was not the life that I wanted and certainly not in Germany. When I told him as much, he was very angry. He confined me to a room and visited less frequently. Any sympathy for him turned to rage and embarrassment.'

I squeezed her hand and brushed her hair from her face. Damp tears streamed downwards and reached her chin, where they gathered and dripped at every movement of her head.

'Keeping me locked up was his way of controlling me and bending me to his will. I hated him for that. He had protected my family but sought a revenge on me for the privilege. I thought I would die in that place.'

She leaned towards me and clasped my arm tightly, her fingers digging into my flesh.

'I needed to escape. He went away for army training. He did not say farewell, and left me in the care of his sister. But she was kind and allowed me to share her clothes and her home as a sister would. She would leave the house with no idea that I would be intent on escape. I simply left, taking her papers with me and took transport to the borders on the pretext of family visits. It was easy to get into Belgium by pretending to be a war widow, desperate to see the battlefield. Tears and a smile, with a kind word, can work a spell of magic on the border guards. On the Belgian side, I simply fell upon the authorities for help. Five days it took to make it to the border and safety.'

Her passage had been eased as there had been a regular train from Bruges to Paris in order to transport military personnel and equipment to the borders for reinforcement. At Paris, Odile had asked politely for passage north and found her way to the Amiens railhead and from there, military transports were easy for a polite and beautiful French girl to secure. At Albert, she walked some of the way back and took carts for the rest. She did not expect to find much and certainly not me. One of the villagers let her know the secret when she walked up the hill to the cemetery.

'I had hoped that one day you would return to me, not for me to return to you! What a surprise to see you in Bazentin, my love.'

In return, I told her that all my life in the army was in search of her liberty and her love. I told her a little of my life in the army – the return to France, the escape through the village and the attack on the ridge. We were saddened that fate had chosen her quiet, peaceful village for a violent and bloody struggle and the High Wood could never feel the same again. No longer could it be walked or rambled over. It would always be a scarred, violent and terrible place to be and I had seen it at first hand.

We sat by the roadside, such as it was, and just looked to find each other again, to heal the sores of the war in each other's care. I did not want to feel that the time apart had diminished our love or eroded our feelings. The war would not take everything from me. I was scarred, bruised, disabled and my nerves felt stretched to breaking point. But I hoped that underneath that, there was still a core that was forever William, one that belonged to Odile. A core that had been exposed when the layers had been torn away, but one that had healed intact. I only hoped that the same was true for Odile.

Materials to build were becoming more readily available and I had a faint hope that we could rebuild the village quickly with little to remind us all of the war, except perhaps the cemetery, which was growing out now with grass and flowers. Graves were still being added and bodies were still being brought in from the ridge. The burial officers were still working hard to make sure the paperwork was in order. It at least provided a fitting place for soldiers to rest. I knew some of them in this cemetery and some in the Caterpillar Valley cemetery and took Odile to visit. I talked of the Cowlings, both of them, and the heroic Watkins, who gave his life on the road to the village. She always gripped my arm a little tighter whenever I talked of my dead comrades – not many soldiers find themselves living willingly in the battlefield they fought in. It was a strange occurrence in a strange period in the history of my world.

The village was rebuilt from the very foundations, the roadway had been relaid and the verges restored. The gardens were initially ploughed and then levelled by hand, everyone working with each other as one big team. The blocks and wood sections took weeks to arrive, but eventually it was possible to begin building more substantial walls and to repair those that still stood. Farming was returning slowly but it seemed there might be more suffering to endure and it was possible that many villagers might starve if the winter was harsh. The ground was not able to be farmed fully yet and it would be some years before the ground was trusted enough to grow food for the region again.

For a little while, I was moved temporarily to Arras to help complete the clearance of the battlefields and to ensure that the network of carrières beneath the city were safe and closed up, where necessary. It was decided that in the section marked Wellington, some would be kept open for the townsfolk to view. After all, these caves were originally part of the town planning and the caverns and tunnels had sheltered some twenty-five-thousand troops on the eve of the battle for Arras. When I returned, there was word that my parents were able to make the trip over to France and that Odile's father was finally to return. Odile's mother had been moved to hospital as she had been ill. She was going to be moved home by ambulance in early September, so all was going to be well. I tried to ensure that the transport was in place and was happy to use my rank for that duty.

It was now that I realised that I had to complete my journey from boy to man. Perhaps the journey had been a strange one, but it felt right that we make the effort to be normal and I was expected to make this one last step. Odile's father was due shortly and so I resolved myself to ask him as soon as he was settled.

Monsieur Lefebvre arrived just after midnight on 8th September 1919. He had been away from his village since late in 1914. Five years away had left its mark on him. A strong man, he fell to his knees and was inconsolable when he saw the devastation. Even after months of peace, the war felt very close. I had only just managed to convince myself that a German would not pop out from behind a wall at any moment. Still, I was prone to ducking and throwing myself to the floor at the slightest disturbance. Some of the French men who had fought in the east of France, Verdun and the borderlands, did the same and we all tried to make light of it. From the village families that I knew, eight sons had been lost from the total of eleven that went to fight. There were no doubt others I did not know. The three that came back had all been terribly worn by the fighting. One had fought on the Mort Homme battlefield and two had been sent overseas to protect French colonies in Africa. None said much but went about the task of rebuilding their farms.

It took several days for Odile's father to come to terms with the situation in his home. He took charge once more and was clearly grateful for my care. Once Odile had described my role in the battle, he seemed to feel that I had been responsible for the liberation of the village on the night of 14th July 1916. I felt no such personal account, but was oddly comforted that I had managed to be here when the village was taken from the enemy. After a few more days of village meetings and plans for the future, it was time for me to take my chance.

'Monsieur Lefebvre, I would like to ask something of you. Would you perhaps—'

He interrupted me and turned to me with a grim look on his face. When he raised his hand to silence me, I feared this would not be the joyous conversation hoped for.

'William, I know what you wish to ask. There are many reasons certainly, why I should refuse your request. But there are two others that I must speak of, before you say the words you wish to say. Let me say this to you. First of all, Odile spent every minute of every day thinking of you English boy, how her life would be, here with you, if the Germans were beaten. She realised that it might not be possible for the French and the British, with the other soldiers from over the sea, to win the war and send the enemy home. She thought first of her family and for that, I can only love her the more. Her heart is with you William, whatever happened to us in the war. So when you ask, ask with a heart that knows her love for you is pure and untainted. I hope you know what I am saying, young man. For the second I can only say this. I could only ever have wished Odile to marry a strong and brave man, one who would love her as do her mother and father. I had expected her to marry one from this village or the next, perhaps a farmer. In you, I thought at first you might be a poor option, with your English roots and your lack of education, even though you are so good with machines. But when I saw you in the gown of a wounded soldier prisoner, my heart leapt. Odile had indeed found a brave man. I see now your uniform of a colonel and know that you are every bit the man I could ever have wanted. So when you ask me, ask boldly, boy, ask the question you wish.'

'I ask your consent for Odile to be my wife.'

Odile's father smiled and nodded slowly. He looked me up and down and said, 'Oui, Monsieur Collins, certainement.'

I rushed over to Odile and, having thought this moment through many times, just asked her straight out.

'Darling Odile, my beautiful girl from over the sea. Will you complete my life and agree to marry me here in this village?'

She did not look at all surprised. Perhaps she had been expecting this moment. There was no way to manage a romantic proposal amidst all this ploughing and burial and sadness.

'Oui, William, certainement.'

Odile's father asked the army padre to officiate at the wedding, when he came to visit the burial sites. Although Monsieur Lefebvre was catholic, he understood that a catholic ceremony would not be possible in the village at this time as the priest was still away and religious service had not been at the top of village priorities. Services had taken place but were often shared with other villages. For his part, the padre agreed that a catholic army priest could be found to be part of the wedding service.

The wedding would take place on the steps of the church and he would make arrangements to ensure the wedding was legal in France and in England and we were not to worry about any of that. It seemed it was all going to happen and my life could begin again. Perhaps the village needed something joyous to celebrate, to help the sores to heal a little more.

Meantime, I busied myself in helping to rebuild the village wherever possible. We started with a shelter for every family that was still there and then moved on to starting farming life again. The land here had not been stripped as it was elsewhere due to it being in the middle of the battlefield for much of the war. Instead, the land had been smashed to powder and soaked with the blood of thousands of soldiers from both sides. The villagers themselves had seen death. Several families had lost sons in the war fighting with the French, with many more being incarcerated or evacuated to labour camps. The wounds were wide and deep and would take as long to heal as the memories would last. French folk have long memories. It took time for heads to lift upwards and look to the future.

I was able to write to my parents, and used the army postal service to speed up delivery of my invitation to be present for my wedding. Their affirmative reply arrived on the same day that Odile's mother arrived back in the village. Madame Lefebvre had already been told of the arrangements for the wedding – she seemed pleased and smiled at me often. Perhaps healing could happen here and the ridge would see happiness again.

We tried to fix the date for the middle of September but it depended on my parents being able to travel. There were some special arrangements for British families to come to France, but this was more because a bereaved family may wish to visit. However, as a colonel, I was able to persuade a passage for them, taking care to make sure it was a spare berth. It was exciting, and for a time the memories of this war faded a little from the front of my mind, just enough to allow some joy to enter. The day of my parents' arrival could not come too soon. It was strange that I could not and would not go and see them in the war, but yet was able to see them here in France. Somehow, I needed to reconcile my life and my experiences before seeing my family again. Even after all this time, I felt a penetrating shame when recounting the things I did to survive. I had to look my father and mother in the eye and tell them that I was a decent man. I had to survive for this moment and for my life to come. I had to be a good man for Watkins and Fixer and the family of the bald-headed German.

Odile and I loved our time alone once again. We would walk the roads to Contalmaison and Longueval, but this time an overwhelming sadness permeated every step of the walk. Fresh tracks were being laid to carry away the machinery of war and the quiet lands were not quite quiet again. Delville Wood cemetery and Caterpillar Valley cemetery were very close together, and on the road to the right was the Longueval Road cemetery. Suddenly, this area became surrounded by memories of the horrors of war, to be retained here as part of every citizen's life for evermore. The road up to the High Wood, once so grisly and deadly, was eerily silent and any soldiers that now walked the tracks seemed to be silent for no conscious reason. The cemeteries for the London lads and the Scottish boys were under construction. It was dreadful how few graves there really were, given the numbers known to be dead. I supposed these were the few we were ever to get back. Odile and I agreed that we would visit these cemeteries every week for the rest of our lives, until our health failed.

Word came that my mother and father were to arrive in Amiens on 10th October. They were not able to get to France sooner, but at least they were able to get here. By the time they were due, a wooden house was built for Odile's parents. We were in the process of building one for the two of us at the edge of the village – on the very spot from where I watched the Germans retreat in July 1916.

It was time to visit La Boisselle again and I took Odile on the motor bicycle. There was a puncture mark in the oil tank, but it had survived the war hidden in the lower cellar and deserved its place again in our family. Another survivor hidden in cellars – I felt a stronger bond than ever with this joyous machine.

I rode through to Martinpuich as the road had been rebuilt and was now quite good. Then, I turned left onto the Albert to Bapaume road – the road along which we were to advance three years ago. At the village, I turned left and followed the road south. To the left was the corner of the village I was trying to reach when we jumped off on that July morning. The temporary road towards Becourt cut through No Man's Land and I took Odile to the spot where the Tynesiders and the Grimsby Chums marched from our right to our left in good order before they were cut down at the knees.

Odile placed her arm around my neck and rested her head on my back. Her warmth was comforting and it felt good to tell her what we had been doing that morning but I told her nothing of the scale of death, although she would guess anyway. She was not some remote relative who would never see this place. Odile was a girl born of this land in France and she lived every day seeing the enormous crater of Lochnagar. The ground was being ploughed and at the corners of the fields were piles of equipment. I saw rifle parts and fragments of uniforms, webbing, leather belts and some shells. Too many of them were light shrapnel shells and upon seeing the amount of wire around, the memory of that morning washed over me.

Suddenly gripped with a twisting feeling pressing down on me, I stopped abruptly, ducked down and clasped my hands to my ears. I could hear the mine going off, thundering over me in a wave of sound and rattling my chest until my ribs vibrated. I remembered the sound that was forced out of my chest and the storm of foul debris falling all around us. I heard the whistle, the roar and the rattle of machine guns. I felt myself roll onto the floor and scrape myself into the ground, fearing the fate of thousands of comrades. I crawled in agony to the side of the road and curled into a ball, fearing a shell at any moment. The war had waited in hiding to now leap out and take me, on this spot. I felt myself screaming loudly, my whole body convulsed and shuddered, trying to get the images out of my head.

Odile was on top of me, screaming and holding me down. I had lashed out wildly at the advancing enemy, coming towards her from behind. I tried to push her behind me for safety. I looked for my rifle and bombs, but there were none. I felt her shaking hands cup my face and saw her red weeping eyes. The wave passed and her face came into focus again, the war faded just a little away from her. Her dress was torn and I had swept mud onto her face and hair. I pulled her to me and would not let go. I would need all of her love to help me. I needed to leave this place behind. The war was still here, alive in my head and I could not let it now take me from the verge of safety.

We walked back in silence to La Boisselle, leaving the motor bicycle for the time being and sat outside a house that had been mostly rebuilt. The owner gave me some water and we stayed until it was nearly dark. I don't remember saying anything in particular to Odile and she was still quite shocked even as we set out to retrieve the motor bicycle. She looked at me, stroked my head gently, squeezed my hand and sat with me, even though it was quite cold and damp was in the air.

The next day, I was silent and avoided conversation with anyone. My wedding day was almost here and I needed to focus on Odile and deal with my inner agony. It was important to determine whether I was strong enough to take on this responsibility for the war had profoundly changed my world – and not for the better. Now, I had grown to be a man, an officer in the army and a husband-to-be to a beautiful French wife. I had to get up and get on and promised myself that this was going to be the last time the war got the better of me. Because I had lived when thousands had not, I owed a debt to them and wasn't about to let them down. For them, I would be a good man and would do all I could to take care of their memory, even if it took all of my strength to do it.

The morning dawned a little later as there were dark clouds and the threat of a storm. I walked to the road, to accept a lift on the cart going to Albert for the markets that had started again. Sitting amongst the vegetables, I could not help thinking that they had grown through the blood and bodies of soldiers. I picked up a potato and studied it closely. With a shudder, I threw it back down and sat back in the drizzle. At Albert, I thanked my driver and walked to the station to pick up the route to Amiens. The journey took over an hour as there were some problems with the weather and I was late for my parents. When I saw them I ran up and hugged them deeply, breathing in the smell of England on their clothes. My father looked thinner and gaunt in his face. He was happy to see me and after politely shaking my hand, pulled me to him and sobbed gently over my shoulder.

'Father, I am so sorry I could not come to see you in England. The war has changed me in ways I cannot understand.'

'William, you are alive and well. In Gower Road nine boys went to war and none of them have come home. Whatever your reasons, we understand. You have survived the war, and as a colonel if you please. We are very proud of you and delighted that you and Pierre's daughter have finally seen the light.'

'Thank you. Mother, I am so very pleased to see you too.'

My mother looked pale and tired, perhaps from the travelling. She looked at me and wiped the tear from my eye, placed her hand behind my neck and pulled my head onto her shoulder. My forehead fitted exactly still into her neck and she held me for what felt like hours. She was warm and her breathing and mine fell into time.

'My little boy is a man and alive after this horrible nightmare. It was hard to endure at home, living from day to day and dreading the awful news all the time. There was never a minute of peace. My, a man you are now and soon to be a husband. Come on, take me to your bride.'

I had arranged an old French service car to take us back home. My army pay was enough to afford a good life, if there was anything to spend it on, but even that could not buy this type of transport. I relied on my army contacts to help plan our wedding. This car would stay with us until after the ceremony. Once we started down the hill into the village, I began to describe some of the things that happened here. I didn't offer any detail but my parents were understandably interested in what had happened to me.

My father warmly embraced Odile's father as an old friend and he quickly introduced my mother. In an instant, my two mothers fussed over the wedding in a whirl of hand gestures and smiles. My mother thought Odile delightful, every bit the strong woman I would need to see my life fulfilled. She helped to finish Odile's dress and sorted out some of the other arrangements for the ceremony in the village.

The night before the wedding, my father and Odile's father took me to our nearly finished wooden hut and we discussed my future after leaving the army. I was not able to serve as a regular, despite the offer of an Unusual Unit training role in England. My health was not perfect and I was not able to serve a posting overseas and there would be none in central France. At the end of December, my post-war service commission would expire and I would be required to go back to England to be discharged from service. I would receive payment for my service, which would entitle me to some allowances and pension in years to come, but from now the future was less certain. Odile's father suggested that I start a commercial business helping to rebuild homes and farms, machinery and roads in the Somme region. I wanted to go back to Belgium as well and see what I could do to help. Both fathers gave me some money to start and there and then I had a business to go to when my army life ended. A colonel's pay was good and I had saved a significant amount, so we would never be short of money, even if my health deteriorated, which it would.

When I reported back to Odile, she smiled and knew that a family was going to be possible after all.

'William, we can have the life we always wanted. My war hero, hero to this village, I could not be happier.'

The army padre came to collect me at about eleven on the day of my wedding. The villagers had gathered on the steps of the church in the grim autumn gloom. A little patch of happiness in amongst the ruins of the village – a phoenix from the ashes of the war. The ceremony was to be a joint affair between the catholic priest and the army padre. We all wondered how that one would turn out, as it was highly unusual.

I waited in the cold for some time, expecting Odile to simply appear and that would be that. In fact, she first appeared in the distance coming up the hill in a beautifully painted, pristine farm cart, gleaming in white and gold, being drawn by two of the most athletic horses I had ever seen. Someone, somewhere had spent a great deal of time on this project. In front, was an immaculate gun limber being drawn by two perfectly groomed army horses and I recognised the gunners immediately.

'Good morning sir and good luck!' They saluted smartly and rode on by and off back to Albert.

As the cart rounded the right turn towards the church, I saw Odile properly for the first time. A touch of make-up and the most incredible dress I had ever seen. Goodness knows where she got the material – clearly, it had been secretly brought into the village.

My future wife smiled at me and her father helped her down onto a path that had been swept and covered by new sacking to keep it clean and dry. On the steps, we joined hands and I was never to let go again.

'William, mon chéri, I have loved you from the first day. When you came back to me, I knew that you felt the same. The time I had to wash you under the pump, was the time I knew that we would always be together. It might sound foolish, but it is true. I have kept myself true to you, English boy and today I am your wife.'

'Odile, I came to you never knowing if you cared for me, but wanted to come all the same. The war, oh the war. I kept it all away from me through thoughts of you, your love and the hope we could be here and now, in front of the village with your family and mine. I could never have known how this village and I would be ever entwined, but here we are.'

Our wedding took place on the steps of the church, in the road amongst the still shattered ruins of the village. A small return to normality in a cruel world gone mad. I saw the rows of bullet holes on those walls that had survived and even knew when they were first made – that terrible morning of 14th July.

As the ministers concluded the ceremony, I turned to Odile and kissed her in a deep embrace. We both sobbed and held on to each other to steady us with the village looking on, also in tears. When I finally let go of my Odile and turned around, I saw the faces of my comrades again. Watkins, Fixer, Paddy, the boys from the trenches, Thomas Taylor from Cullercoats, healthy and well, the Tynesiders and the Grimsby Chums, the Welsh and the Guards all there lined up in shining uniforms with Colonel Smith. My imagination had given me the most perfect present of an honour guard but there was one face that did not fade away when I focused on the memory. One uniform was pristine and clean amongst the dirt of the road, the face familiar and smiling. Unmistakably it was General Cowling.

'Congratulations, Colonel Collins.' He turned to Odile and tugged his cap towards her, 'Mrs Collins, enchanté.'

'General Cowling, I am so pleased to you have come here to see William. I know what a big part of his life you are and will be for always. Please, come and join with us to celebrate.'

'A pleasure, Mrs Collins. I must say, your English is possibly better than mine. Perhaps William will understand you better than he ever did me. He might even listen to you and do as he is damned well told!'

We three laughed and Cowling shook my hand warmly. He took off his cap and embraced me as a brother.

'William, we have lived when others did not. Let us not waste this opportunity. Let us enjoy and celebrate each breath, each dawn and each sunset. Fixer would be proud of you, I know that he would.'

'I know sir. I have seen him.' The general stood for a second, but said nothing.

We spent the evening drinking wine and dancing to some local music with instruments from goodness knows where. General Cowling was due to retire from the army and he intended to start his own mining company in South Africa, in tribute to cousin Fixer. He had arranged to stay in the village and we planned to meet in the morning for a walk in our field.

The evening wore on into the night. Odile and I managed a dance of sorts but then the time came for all to say goodnight. Families and friends drifted home, with a little bit of normality restored and feeling somewhat healed.

I took Odile in my arms at the doorstep of our home. Our place of safety, at last, carved from the suffering of the war, protected by the souls of dead comrades watching over us. I placed my hand softly on her cheek, which was hot and flushed from the dancing and singing. She leaned onto my hand and held her face there, looking into my eyes.

This was the face that sustained me through the Great War. This girl, from the very first day in Albert, all those years ago, has occupied my every day. She is my sunrise and sunset, my sustenance through the horrors. Her eyes and her hair, her lips and her smile are forever etched in my heart. I had survived because my love for Odile offered sanctuary to my soul, keeping the war in soft focus at the times of my greatest need. Here she was in front of me, at last, we had found each other again. Finally, the yearning of separation, and the worry for our love was over. We were together and I was not going to let go.

I drew Odile closer, breathing her in to me, her head in my neck so I could feel her pulse and her breath on my skin. We did not speak, for words would not come. I knew the suffering she had endured to return here and she knew some of mine. Now, I lifted her chin to find her lips. The sweetest kiss, earned from a thousand days of suffering, took away our pain, cleansed our bodies and freed our imagination to turn to the future.

'My darling Odile.'

'Yes mon chéri?'

'The guns have stopped.'

She said nothing, but her hand moved to my chest and she rested it on my heart. She breathed in and out in time with me and we stood at the doorway until the cold and damp was as rain on our clothes.

'I think it is time we went to bed.'

Odile slipped her hand in mine and pulled me gently to our little bedroom and closed the door.

Cowling and I spent the next day walking the whole ridge and following the route of the cavalry. At Longueval, a car drew up to collect the general to take him back to England.

'William, go and spend your time with your beautiful wife and leave this army behind. Remember them, but do not forget to live. God bless you William and take my very best wishes for the future. I intend to go to Africa and remain there, so it is entirely possible that we will never meet again. This moment, alive here and now, I will treasure always, my boy.'

'Thank you sir. It was an honour to serve with you. That seems so little to say, after all of this. General, God protect you.'

He smiled, nodded once and then tapped the driver to leave. His car bumped and bobbed away. I was never to see him alive again as he died some years later, as mysteriously as he had lived. He left me a sum of money and a little gold, as well as a plot of land that was mine, if we ever visited Africa.

With Odile busying herself about our new home, I decided to spend the next month making the most of our new billet. We were given some bits of furniture and some cooking utensils. More importantly, we had each other and we had fought so hard to be right here, surviving some of the worst horrors that anyone could ever have endured.

It was then, that Odile began to feel unwell. At first she was sick, but later that week, she could barely rise from her bed at all. Deeply worried, I tried to arrange for a doctor to call with all urgency, but now I was no longer in the army, I had fewer favours to call in. Instead, Madame Lefebvre was brought to visit her daughter. She went in looking worried at the symptoms I had described.

Finally, Odile's mother emerged some fifteen minutes later, this time with a broad smile and shaking her head.

'William, I am afraid that I know just what the problem is.'

'Dear God, Madame, tell me please.' My legs buckled from under me.

'Your wife is expecting a child. Truly a good catholic girl I think, ha ha.' She chuckled and embraced me by way of congratulation.

I remember ending up on the floor as my legs finally gave way. When I managed to recover my senses, I went in and kissed Odile quickly then ran out, down the street, causing such a commotion that everyone was outside demanding to know if the Germans were coming again.

Odile's father was overcome with joy. Ours would be the first new baby in the village after the war and for us all, it was the greatest gift anyone could have given us.

As the summer came over Picardie, the ground was again healed further, with a newly ripening harvest. Here and there, signs were being put up and more and more people visited the battlefield, from all nations. I was outside enjoying the warm sunshine and some terrible French tea when the telegraph officer from Contalmaison came to me with an envelope. In it was a sheaf of perfectly crisp paper. I unfolded it, puzzled and worried in equal measure.

My Kamerad William Collins,

Hallo. I wish to give you all God's blessing. I am sorry that I did not able to write this before. You are a hard soldier to find. You do not remember me, but I found you in a field not breathing or eyes open. But I saw you and I knew you were living and so had you taken away to hospital. I tried to find you but your unit and uniform were not understood by our officers and so I did not return to you, that which I took from you. I took from you to give you back, you understand. Soldier to soldier. Friend to friend. I only know from this month that you are alive and the army here took a year to find you through your field operations unit. Look, it is no matter. I have your address and I was worried as it was wrong as it was for Bazentin. No, no I said, that is where he was found, not his house. But it is your house and you are English? So, I send to you that which I took for safe keeping.

I wish you a long life my friend.

Walter Rolf Weisner
Ulm, Germany

I was numbed. This was completely unexpected. It was the answer to my questions of who had found me and how I had got away from the battlefield. It was so shocking that I did not realise the true meaning of the letter at first. After a second reading, I realised there must be something else and looked again inside the envelope. There was a folded scrap of dirty, torn and rotting paper at the bottom. I took it out, not daring to guess what it was. Odile's letter had found its way back to me. I read it again and this time, I smiled at the return of this unexpected treasure. But I dared not tell my wife. Not yet.

Odile presented me with twins on 11th November 1920. We had one boy and one girl and I could not have been happier. The boy I named Arthur Horace Patrick and Odile named our baby girl Armandine, after her beloved grandmother.

When they were first asleep, I took one in each arm and sat with my beautiful wife. I nodded down to the scrap of paper and she instantly recognised it.

'Mon Dieu! William? My letter to you?'

'Yes, my love. The kindest man in the world has returned it to us. Without him, we would not be a family and I would be dead. It must have been he that showed mercy that day. I lay unconscious and he stopped to tend to me. In all that had happened that day, fortune sent an angel to look after me, and he now has a name. Walter Weisner. An enemy, who chose to become my friend. He must have known the letter was important, as I had carried it into battle. I cannot believe it found its way back to me.'

'Let me read it again.'

'Read it aloud my love and then I will put it back where I found it.'

'I will.'

'Read it the way you wanted it to be read.'

Through a tear and a smile, Odile read to me the story of her war. I looked down at our two tiny babies as her words floated into my head. A bald-headed German stepped up, hands on hips, gazing at my babies, smiling. He came to me, held out his arms and embraced me gently. 'Hallo,' he said.

Then, he turned, waved and left, walking north. I looked up and watched him go. Then, I looked down again at my future. I would dedicate my life to these little ones and hoped that they would be able to live in a world free of war and that neither of them would have to live through the kind of horror we had witnessed on the slopes of the Bazentin Ridge.

If you enjoyed *The Mad Game*, please go to your Amazon page and leave a review for the Author.

We look forward to presenting the next titles in the Love and War Series in 2014

The Mad Game - Christmas Present 1913 (Kindle Short Story)
The Mad Game – Odile's War
The Mad Game – The Third Light

CHRIS CHERRY

THE LETTER FROM ODILE – TRANSLATED FOR WILLIAM BY 12 FIELD OPERATIONS

My Darling William,

I do not know if you will ever read this letter, or indeed if you will even know to look here for it. I have written to you many times and never had the courage to send them. I fear that letters are read by people that I would not wish to have knowledge of my private feelings and my daydreams, of how we used to live our lives.

I had many hopes for a life in France with you my beloved William, with us riding on your terrible motor bicycle and what seemed like endless hours together trying to make it work. That life seems so very distant now, as if it had happened to another and not to me.

My dear William I do not know how to say the things that I must, that have happened to my family, and me in the last year. The terrible war so close to us and the awful sight of the Germans in our villages, with guns and swords and bombs.

When they first came in 1914, we found ourselves the base for the French defence of the town of Albert. The French Army fought so bravely and the sounds of battle were most horrible. We had to escape at night and first we were to go to Albert itself, but it was not safe from the guns of the Germans. The terrible soldiers occupied our villages and our beloved lanes to Contalmaison and Longueval.

There was nothing anyone could do to stop them.

The Germans told us that we were to be moved North of Bapaume or even Cambrai, until the fighting was over. They thought that France would surrender and that we would again live in peace.

Dear William, you must know how terrible it was to be here. Everywhere there was the sound of marching and boots, horses and carts and the terrible menace of the German voices. The soldiers did not seem to wish us harm, but we did not want them in our villages. They took our food and took everything from the fields and we ate so very little in the early days.

Father was made to work repairing things that had been damaged in the battles. He works on the large guns and repairing carts and motor lorries. He detests utterly this work and wishes only harm on the soldiers. Because of this, they beat him and we do not receive any food. I too wish we could be rid of them, but we must make the very best of what we can.

Oh William, my love, my love from over the sea. I could not live my life with so little food and my mother and father suffering so in the hands of the soldiers. I wish nothing but peace and to be rid of the Germans, but I do not see the war ending soon. We were moved to an awful place, little more than a camp in a field, near Cambrai. We were with other families, but it felt like a prison. We could come and go but we were always watched, our every move was recorded, or so it seemed to me.

Some of the girls seemed not to care of the war at all and frolicked openly with the Germans. They seemed to be able to get more food for their families and were given new clothing, they almost looked like German farm girls. We were always hungry, father came home often beaten and bleeding and I could stand this no more. So I decided that I too must behave this way to get more food for our family.

William, do believe me when I say that I wish you were here with me now as I write this. Before I was able to become friends with the Germans in the camp, I met in the camp a young German boy, who was the same age as me. He was in the army but had softness in his voice that set him apart from the awful brutes that marched through our villages in 1914. He spoke to me in French and he told me how nice it was to meet a beautiful girl in the middle of this awful war. He gave me food for my family, he did not know my father, but it did not matter because he was kind and we could eat. I did not have to go and dig mouldy vegetables that other families threw away anymore. He gave me a new dress and we were able to leave the camp if he was there with us, which we would often do in the evenings. William, I just wanted to feel normal again. I do hope you could understand.

Life is so much easier now for us. We are able to live a life and we are not hungry and beaten. My father thinks the food is because he has promised not to shout and curse the Germans anymore. Now his family is happy, he does not need to anymore.

For three days I have left the camp to come to our place to write this letter. The war has not destroyed everything here yet and these villages are still away from the awful battle. They are empty and yet so full of the war. In the two barns here in the yard are piles of bullets and small hand bombs, it makes me want to cry that they might be used on you and your friends. Most of the buildings are used to store this terrible cargo.

The English are in Albert, I do wonder if you ever joined the army and if you are still alive? I do not know.

I have to live the life I have and not the life I may have had before the war. It has changed so much. I have to go back to the camp now, otherwise I will be missed.

My Dear William, my heart has hurt for you so much in the last years, but it is time to let you go as it is taking away my spirit knowing you are so very far away. I write this letter more in comfort to me I suppose as I do not think you will ever be here to read it. I can see no reason why you would.

Good luck dear friend and love

Odile, August 1915

ABOUT THE AUTHOR

As well as time spent as a military historian, Chris leads an education consultancy, inspecting schools and colleges and helping to improve the outcomes for young people in the UK. He has also spent much of the last twenty-five years researching the effects of the Great War on the lives of ordinary people, innocent of the blame for its cause.

Chris is also an active member of the Manchester 500 Advanced Motorcyclists Group, offering support as an observer for the Institute of Advanced Motorists/Motorcyclists.

In his spare time, he is a volunteer with the North West Blood Bikes Manchester. The charity transports blood and blood products, donated human breast milk samples and urgent controlled medications for local hospitals and hospices.

Chris loves nothing more than getting on his motorbike and riding off to the battlefields of Europe, seeking authenticity for his stories and adding a human interest to the calamity that was the Great War.

Chris is also a member of the Royal British Legion, the Royal British Legion Rider's Branch and The Western Front Association.

Printed in Great Britain
by Amazon.co.uk, Ltd.,
Marston Gate.